Anonymous

Rubina

Anonymous

Rubina

ISBN/EAN: 9783337218386

Printed in Europe, USA, Canada, Australia, Japan

Cover: Foto ©Andreas Hilbeck / pixelio.de

More available books at **www.hansebooks.com**

RUBINA.

NEW YORK:
JAMES G. GREGORY, 46, WALKER STREET.
M.DCCC.LXIV.

I DEDICATE this book to my sister. In memory of a love beyond the parental, a friendliness beyond friendship, brightening the darkness of our mutual lives, and exalting joy into the holier lustre of happiness.

RUBINA.

CHAPTER I.

It was still raining. I stood by the window, gazing idly out on the darkening landscape. This was the extreme of dreariness. No charm shone for me in the heavens, where stretched one vast robe of low hanging cloud; still less charm lay in the battered, dingy piles, called by courtesy dwellings, opposite. The street was narrow. The wet, slippery pavement was destitute of passengers. A tiny pool of water had collected in a hollow of the outside window-sill, which, with the usual fertility of infant imaginations, I was converting into a boundless sea, picturing thereon tiny, fanciful craft of marvellous shapes, and bearing extravagant names—how or whence suggested I know not.

Borne out on such airy pinions of fancy, the present—sharp, hateful, with its humble surroundings and its sad prospective —vanished in content. Insensibly, this fancy broadened, deepened. Earth contained it no longer. Now, it was a fairy bark, careering on aërial seas, with mortal life dropped far in the distance; then, *all* life receded, and color alone steeped my senses in gorgeous bewilderment. Swift courser, ever changing, is Fancy. What wondrous regions I visited; what crude shapes flitted through my brain, fretting it with vain attempts at analysis! What bright impossibilities dawned on me realities.

These, though not unusual, were my happiest moments ; a
rest when weary, a solace after punishment, a genial playmate
in hours of loneliness.

Mine was no happy childhood. I state this fact, without
regret or reproaches, from my present stand-point. It is
easily sighted.   Looking back to that childish drama of wild,
half-suppressed wonderings at more mature actors ; having
vague perceptions of truths they sought to smother from their
own consciousness ; revelling in interdicted puzzles over the
seeming uselessness of Life, and the dread certainty of Death,
I shrink back appalled at the intensity of the thoughts which
I dared not express. My mother repeatedly assured me, in
language severe, and with uplifted finger, that ingratitude for
the blessing of existence was sure to be visited with Divine
displeasure ; that " the hope set before us in the Gospel" was
all one ought to desire ; and that if we succeeded in glorifying
Christ—no matter whether we were saved or lost at last—we
should be supremely happy : a confusion of ideas, a conflict
of theory and practice, I did not pretend to understand, but
which left an unpleasant doubt to torture me.

Constitutions differ. It is essentially right that all should
not be happy. Pleasure cultivates some human soils, but
Pain is by far the more efficient agent. Heaven teaches us
this fact, and into some lives pours all its rains. It is as
though the dry, baked soil needed frequent drenchings to
soften it to fertilizing influences—a continual inundation of
sorrows, defeats, losses, and great, crushing disappointments,
to plough the unproductive stubble and prepare the furrows
for the heavenly seed. The earthly pilgrimage is made, with
grief for a haunting fellow-passenger ; and the couch of thorns
exchanged only for the oblivious one of the grave. A presentiment that such was to be my needed discipline hovered

around my thoughts that night—cheating the pictures held
there of half their brightness. Then they suddenly doffed
control, and swept far and wide over my backward horizon.

I remembered a home far different from this, where every
appointment was elegant. I recalled the lofty rooms, the
vivid lines in the soft carpets, the furniture—too sacred for
my baby fingers to touch—and the handsome woman ruling
over it. This latter picture I approach in awe. Pride speaks
from the polished brow. Will compresses the richly-tinted
lips. Energetic perseverance glows in the large gray eyes:
when angry they expand and brighten, as though the vindictive flame, lurking and warming the depths below, could no
longer brook delay; and they send forth sparks of warning to
keep away, as far away as may be. In vain, as I scan these
features, do I seek for a sign; some tender ray—a pitiful caress—to show me unsealed the door to her heart The cool
reserve of her manner is impenetrable. Conventional re-
straints warp diffidence into dignity ofttimes. So I am willing to believe that fond emotions existed there, if destined to
remain in their cave, unvisited, unseen. I used at times to
long—as passionately as an infantile nature can long—to be
lifted on that silken lap, to be pressed to the velvet bosom,
and thus quiet the insatiable craving for my mother's love;
but I never dared claim the privilege. When she was in
trouble I divined it, and would sometimes totter up to her, in
childish fashion essaying consolation. She never wept in
those days. When sad, a mortal paleness overspread her
face, and deep lines seamed the brow. I knew these tokens
well. Often I stood quietly by her chair saying nothing,
doing nothing, yet quivering over with sympathy; with an
intense desire to allay the pang. Sometimes I gently stroked
her hands; or leaned my face against her shoulder. Then

1*

she would look sharply around, and order me away in a cold,
implacable tone; not unfrequently accompanying the man-
date with a push, the sooner to enforce obedience.   If I fell,
she looked on grimly, deigning no help to replace me in a
walking posture.   If I cried, either in pain or anger, one
whispered utterance, "Hush!" compelled its instant cessation.

For this reason, of her unsympathetic indifference, I loved
my father better.   I have been told often enough since, that
he was not as good as I supposed him; but I remember many
a kindly kiss and comforting word which, an hungered as I
went daily for a little affection, sank deep in my heart, sowing the seeds of immortal love for him, which beyond this
life, if fate denies it here, will yield him a plentiful harvest.
I smiled incredulously when my mother spoke of his wickedness.   For me, these early wayside shrines, crowned with
forget-me-nots of an otherwise too dreary infancy, stood out
in freshened bloom, and memory at them knelt lovingly.

Children are keen observers.   The incidents of early years
surpass those of later life in vividness.   Waking suddenly,—
who ever notes the transition?—from semi-idiotic infancy to
intelligent childhood; from immature dreams -floating confusedly over the camera; the mental plate, freshly polished by
the great artist Nature, slides therein, receiving on its pure,
yielding surface the first presenting object.   Not all the
washings of after years can wholly efface the sharp outlines.
I caught and fixed indelibly the spectacle of two dissimilar
natures, indissolubly bound in one daily life—to each, in dif
ferent ways, uncongenial.   Their marriage was like an iron
fetter, and it chafed severely.   It might have been a flowery
wreath but for the scorpion lurking in pride, to annul every
suggestion of compliance; to infuse poison when there should
have been healthful peace.   Love takes his flight when the

stern reign of pitiless Duty begins. Their differences were
not often wordy, but they seemed to surround themselves
when together with innumerable points of steely obstinacy,
which, coming in contact, invariably clashed. I do not think
such conflicts left them ashamed, or even repentant; but to
me it seemed as though the air was freely strewn with nettles,
multiplying their noxious products with fearful rapidity.
" When I speak I mean it, Cornelius," my mother would say,
in her most decisive tone. And then her brow would be
suddenly seamed with wrinkles.

It always brought the retort, " I expect to be obeyed,
Caroline. It is your place to submit," with irritation and
flashing eye, as the door slammed behind his hasty exit.

Leaving this dreary waste of dissension, there slowly rises
the vision of a dismembered home ; of a forsaken woman,
who, bowed to the very dust, yet disdains all sympathy, resolutely casts off humility, and, cut adrift from the sheltering harbor of home and a husband's protection, the roaring cataracts of
public gossip, scandal, and sneers to stem ; unfeeling questions
to evade ; a mighty sorrow to be concealed ; a helpless child
to be supported ; and the wrecks of a handsome fortune to
be laboriously gathered in,—mere stranded spars of illusive
hope, looking substantial enough in the distance, but melting in the avaricious clutch of attorneys' bony fingers, like
an avalanche under summer skies and showers,—yet lifts a
bold front to the storm, and resolves to weather it cheerily.

The panorama of grief shifts rapidly. There seems a species of freemasonry behind the scenes ; a banded brotherhood,
each dragging after him a fellow-sorrow.

My mother never told me the cause of my father's sudden
departure. Whether debt and the consequent disgrace
—debts to such an extent that no prospect opened of future

repayment—or crime, and the fear of punishment; or weariness of domestic bickerings, impelled his flight, I am left to
iudge. The desertion was complete. He never returned;
neither did he send back any message of farewell; or leave
a clue, whereby he might be traced. Three months after, my
little sister was born to an heritage of sorrowful poverty.

I have a sickening sense of frequent movings; of seeing
the grand old furniture sold piecemeal to supply some pressing need. All this changed my mother. The imperious
dame, whose will was law in her own estimation, vanished.
In her stead rose a pale, saddened woman, toiling the live-
long day to gain a decent sustenance; whose health gradually
sank under the weight of these privations; and whose unavailing penitence caused bitter, wakeful nights, plentifully
bedewed with remorseful tears. Her restlessness frequently
awoke me; I dared not speak or move in answer to her
murmurs; but her sighs and constant refrain, " Oh, Cornelius,
Cornelius!" cut me to the heart. This was only at night.
With the morrow's light, her calmness dawned anew. Such
a nature as my mother possessed could quaff unflinchingly
the gall and wormwood in her cup—but no curious eyes
must look on when she drained it. Had she known of my
sympathy she would have scornfully repelled it.

A low sound broke the spell, conjured in silence and gloom;
routed contemplation of the ideal, and sternly thrust before
me the actual. This then was the scene I beheld as I turned
reluctantly from the window. A low-ceiled room in the
attic of a third-rate boarding-house. It was very dingily
furnished with scant remnants of former days'. belongings.
A smouldering fire in the small box stove. A cradle with
a sweet rosy incumbent—this last item the darkness did not
reveal, but I knew the fact well before—and a low cot

whereon, pale and wasted, writhing uneasily on the bunchy, uncomfortable straw, lay my mother. It was her voice which roused me. I sought a moment for matches, lit the low night-lamp, which gave out but a flickering gleam, fed with too scanty a measure of oil. I added a stick to the dying embers, regardless of the prudent sigh with which she half raised her head to watch me; kneeling on the uncarpeted floor, I fanned it into flame with my breath, and watched it slowly kindle. "Well," I reflected, "things might be worse. Thousands have *no* fire. I pity them. This is my weakness. I like to see the flames leaping and crackling their fierce tongues over their victim; dancing such grotesque shadows on the gloomy walls; and giving out such a cheerful roar of delight: but alas! we have but a few sticks left, and after the box is broken and burned, I see no prospect of more fuel. You are too extravagant," I added aloud to the fire; "make all the noise you like, but you should really consume more slowly."

"What in the world are you talking about, child?" inquired my mother, in amazement.

I laughed: "Giving sensible advice to the stove, little old boxie here." I got up and gave the rusty damper an affectionate kick.

"Don't! you make my head ache," said my mother, sharply, "you are *so* heedless."

"I know it," I humbly responded, feeling deeply repentant: I had not meant to make a noise to add to her suffering.

"Then why don't you stop it?" she asked, querulously. "I really believe sometimes that you *want* to kill me; when you haven't any mother, perhaps you'll think of these things."

At this dreadful idea I came near sobbing. "Oh!" I

ejaculated, convulsively; then a great bunch rose in my throat, precluding the possibility of getting out any more words. I wanted to tell her how much I loved her; how anxious I was to make her better; and how surely I should die if she did —for I really thought so then—but I could not utter a syllable. My mother probably took my silence for sullenness, for she said no more. A long time after, I approached and bent over her pillow. "Do you want any thing? Can I do any thing for you, mother?"

"I only want to feel better. I suppose you can't give me *that*, child," she moaned wearily.

"Mother! I wish I could."

"Well," she said, fretfully, after a short pause, "don't stand here *looking* at me; don't you know any thing?"

I started back—cut to the heart: she presently resumed:

"I should think your aunt would come, if she's coming at all."

"So should I, mother."

"Don't repeat my words so, Ruby; it isn't the way to do," she said, irritated at my response. "I suppose you can't make yourself useful for once, and tell me how long it is since I wrote that letter?"

"Oh! yes I can, mother; it was a week ago last Monday; it went in that afternoon's mail; so the postmaster said."

I was glad to think I could render her this unimportant service: I looked eagerly at her for some signal of approbation. She gave none, however; on the contrary, she seemed vexed that she had forgotten the period; she never relished being reminded—even in an unconscious way—of any infirmity; and would have been much better pleased had I failed to remember the time, and left her therefore to recall it, and to exaggerate its length; but this I did not then know;

so I again timidly petitioned to be allowed to do something.

" Dear me ! it seems to me if you really wanted to, you'd find some way quick enough," was her cold reply.

" I do want to ; but you won't tell me what," I said, desperately.

" Yes, I suppose I'm an awful creature ; but you won't have occasion to find fault much longer." I was silent from self-upbraiding. " You see how your poor mother is failing," she went on, in a softened tone. " Memory is almost gone ; Time indeed stands still with me ; the hours seem days ; the days seem weeks : I should have said it was a month ago that I wrote."

" Then you would have said wrong, mother," I remarked, with delightful simplicity.

" I dare say you think so," she rejoined.

I was puzzled at this remark. " I make no doubt but that my aunt will come when she gets the letter," I ventured again.

" Don't you, indeed ?"

" No," was my answer.

" Your reasons for such remarkable credulity ?"

" Why, isn't she your own sister, mother ?" I asked in surprise. She rolled her head to and fro on the pillow, eying me suspiciously. " You've got a deal to learn, Ruby ; you don't know human nature as well as I. They're all alike, kith or kin and strangers ; all selfish ; when they have any axe to grind they're ready enough to be of service."

" I suppose so," I said, doubtfully, " but do they grind axes ?"

My mother laughed ironically, and resumed, talking apparently to herself. " Now there's Hannah ; I wrote to *her*

first, and she never has answered it—much less come herself
—I don't suppose she would take the trouble to come to my
funeral; nor Rhoda either; they are precisely alike.   Well,
if it wasn't for the children——"

During my whole life my mother had never talked to
me so freely.   I liked the change and sought to prolong it;
though nothing more seemed needful to be said on that sub-
ct.   "Shall we go home with her, if she does come: that
is, when you are stronger?"

"Pshaw!" she ejaculated, impatiently.   "There's little
danger of her asking us, so don't go to putting nonsense
into your head.   When I get stronger—if I ever do—I
shall find you a place somewhere: so think of *that* instead."

I *did* think of it.   In my ignorance I wondered if it might
not mean a school.   But that idea, common sense at once
rejected.   "The place," clearly, must be some servant's work.
Instead of feeling thankful for such provision, I could have
wept at the bare suggestion.   Some contrite thought moved
my mother: she looked down on me sadly, and her voice
lost its fretfulness.   "Poor little girl! you haven't had a
pleasant time lately, have you?   I don't mean to be cross:
but I cannot help it.   I believe I should do better if I could
live my life over again.   I *began* wrong, you see, and it's so
hard to change now: but I cannot go back if I would.   No!
that can never be, child."

She raised herself—beat up the pillows slowly—seemed
to be considering something,—and her face wore an half-
ashamed expression;—then she sank back and said, deter-
minedly, "I wonder if I *am* so near; get the Bible, Ruby,
and read that beautiful Psalm—you know it—about the
valley of the-shadow of death."

I found and read it.   "Am I *not* in the shadows?   Oh!

most merciful One !" she murmured, turning wearily to the
wall, " *will* thy staff support me ? Oh ! the waters are so
cold and dark, and my faith is but meagre."

" Mother ! what are you saying ?" I waited a moment for
her answer : then she was so still that I concluded she slept.
In sheer want of something to do I began to rock the cradle.
Hours elapsed thus.   The fire-light faded to gray ashes : for
fear of rousing my mother I had not renewed it.   The lamp
blinked ghostly at last, and slowly expired.   Then the clock
in the hall below solemnly swung out the hour of midnight.

CHAPTER II.

Although only ten years old, I watched nightly with my
mother ; catching a few hours' sleep towards morning, as I
sat in my low chair, or on the floor by the cradle.   It seemed
natural and right that it should be thus.   Mrs. Potter—our
landlady—was a sharp, practical, though not unkindly woman;
who looked in daily to inquire mechanically after the invalid.
She never sacrificed her own interests in this solicitude.
Knowing that we were unable to pay for a doctor's services,
she carefully refrained from suggesting the need of one ; for
that would have appeared, in her eyes, a tacit admission of
her own responsibility for the sums expended.   Provided we
scraped together the rent for our poor garret, she was satisfied, and never troubled herself to inquire whether, in this
endeavor, daily food was sacrificed.   She was tolerably civil-
spoken, too, for a well-to-do landlady ; and if she addressed
my mother as " poor dear," and carried her bottle of pity

rather too offensively uncorked for one of my mother's temperament to like, I always set it down to her kindness of heart ; my mother, to her ignorance.

What did I not suffer in those days—those lonely watchings ! Some say, children soon outgrow sorrow. I know better. In those solitary vigils, with naught to break the dreadful silence ; with those still spectral lineaments, starting white from the surrounding gloom ; with a vague consciousness of some huge, impending evil, crouching by my side ; not to be frightened away, nor cowed by resolute facings— I experienced pain—sharp and enduring as any a woman can suffer. They yet haunt me, with their nameless grip of terror—at times a keen realization of an invisible peopled world enveloping me, and a shuddering dread lest the sable folds part, and my straining—yet unwilling—eyes catch a glimpse of its shadowy inmates.

This evening, in the midst of the driving rain, was borne to my ears the faint rumble of wheels over the stony pavement. They drew nearer ; they stopped. A moment after, the door-bell violently rang. The noise woke Annah, who began to cry. My mother also roused to a listening attitude : "Who can be coming so late !" she muttered. "Ruby, can't you still that child's noise ?" she said, peevishly. "It's worse than bedlam. Hush !" she added, as I lifted her from the cradle and commenced a pilgrimage around the room to soothe her. Hearing footsteps in the hall below, I softly opened the door, stepped out on the narrow landing, and peered down the carpetless stairway. As I peeped through the rickety railings, I beheld a tall woman—very masculine in her proportions—toiling slowly up. She paused midway— at every step she had exclaimed, somewhat in this fashion : "Goodness gracious me !" "Lord a massy !" "For all this

world !" " I never see the beat on't !"—" I believe this ere's
a bee-line right straight to the garret," she said meditatively.
" It needs an injine to run up and down these stairs : I should
think it'd wear a body all out, a doin' their work up here,
'specially as there's no man to help along with the chores :
Joel said I'd git tuckered out," she muttered, " a comin' on
sech an unsartin errant too ; but sakes alive ; ef I stand this,
I'm good for the next pull, I guess ;" and she recommenced
her journey.   I felt too crushed in spirit to laugh ; besides, I
could only think she had lost her way—and I debated within
myself the propriety of setting her right.   She gained the
topmost step.   " Let me see," she muttered musingly : she
nodded her head slowly.   I drew aside into the shadow and
watched her curiously.   " I calculate I've come up four pair
o' stairs ; I must have missed my reckonin', for Car'line never
could a bin brought to this pinch, never ! sech a proud sper-
ited crectur' as *she* was too."   No wonder her ascent was so
laborious.   She had dragged up with her an enormous willow basket, with leaves in its top tied down with green quality ; and a respectably sized antique valise, bulging with
articles.   These she set decisively down, while she lifted a
corner of her blue bombazine dress, disclosing a gray quilted
petticoat ; from a pocket in it, she drew forth a stout pair of
steel-bowed spectacles : very deliberately she polished the
oval glasses, and adjusted them on her crooked nose—of
course, I noted the *details* afterwards : her motions I could
observe distinctly from my corner—at last she spied me out
in it.   " Here, you young one, walk up here, like a chicken
to a dough-dish, and tell me ef Mrs. Brooks lives here !" she
sharply ordered.

I advanced.   " Are you my Aunt Rhoda, from Northfield !"
was the answer she got.

"Sartain, sure; p'raps you'll have the charity to help me up with my kit, and show me to your marm—I take it you b'long to Car'line,"—with a look of inquiry. I hastened forward, and stooped to lift the basket. "Oh," she interrupted, "you've got a young 'un, have you? Wall, I guess I can manage these 'ere then: you haint told me what your names be."

I gave the desired information, and threw open the door to our room. "Them pesky cars hendered me so; I thought I never *should* git here," she said, briskly groping forward. "Massy! you're all in pitch darkness," she added, peering in.

"Yes! I'll have a light in a minute," I said. "You take the baby, aunt, and I'll run down for a candle; our lamp went .out ever so long ago." Down I went to Mrs. Potter's room, and—made fearfully bold by the emergency—borrowed a candle. She detained and questioned me about our visitor; then apparently satisfied in her own mind that she would not be a loser by an act of this nature, she handed me another. I lit one, and hastened back. My aunt scanned me closely as I received back Annah in my arms. "You ain't so skeery 'bout the dark, as our gals be; you wouldn't git them to set one minnit without a light, I promise you: wall, I s'pose ye have to make a vartue of n'cessity, don't you!"

"A *what*, aunt?"

"Oh! you haint a dreadful sight o'candles to burn, I'll be bound"—glancing around the cheerless room.

"No, only these."

"Humph! and them you got on my a'count. Wall, stick them up somewhere, and tell me how old this brat is."

"Fifteen months, aunt."

"Don't aunt me, yit; how d'ye know I *am* your aunt?" she growled, removing her things.

"You told me so," said I, simply, feeling very much disposed to heartily hate my new-found relative.

"A likely idee. Where's your clothes-press?"

"We havn't any," I returned shortly.

"Wall, any cupboard will do; anywhere to dump these duds."

"You'll have to leave them on the chair," I said, dryly.

Her look of dismay was amusing to witness, but she arranged it silently on the seat. First, the valise; her heavy blanket shawl went over it like a pall; a dove-colored shirred silk bonnet went on that; a pair of cinnamon-colored cotton gloves followed; then when a pair of serviceable yarn stockings were removed—I assisting in this process, taking firm hold of the heel and toe while, in her expressive words,. she "yanked it off"—and her thick, leathern brogans carefully retied in "a double-bow knot," she stepped forth a very respectable looking farmer's wife. I had never set eyes on one before, but I knew her directly. She carried the very smell of the dairy about her; the milky, cheesy smell that the long subsequent ride could not efface. She now moved with brisk tread to the bed; I out by the door listened curiously for their greeting. It was characteristic enough.

"Wall, Car'line, how are you? pickin up any yet?" inquired my aunt.

"I don't know, I didn't much expect you'd take the trouble to come," answered my mother feebly, as their two hands clasped, one browned with exposure, and hardened like flint with years of toil; the other, a fairy-like member, transparent as glass; wasted with sickness; colorless as the hue of death; the veins starting out like huge blue cords from its wasted fulness.

"You didn't, hey! Wall, you know I allers *was* a fool,
Car'line, so when I got the word, I says to Joel, 'I s'pose
she's rather spleeny 'bout it, but mabbe I'd better go down
and see her,' and law! Joel he put right in too, and I didn't
git no rest till I started."

"I wrote long ago to Hannah and she never answered it,"
said my mother—humbly, for her.

Her sister smiled, and coughed. "She and I are two persons, I s'pose you know; cf you don't, you oughter. She allers
was a selfish crittur, never cared a straw for nobody, nor
nothin', 'cept her own old lazy sides. I ain't no ways surprised to hear any thing of her in that line," she finished
stoutly.

"Oh, dear!" sighed my mother.

"Be you put to it for breath much?" inquired her sister.

"Oh, no."

A long pause succeeded. I hushed Annah to sleep, walking
up and down the narrow room. My aunt suddenly turned on
me: "Do you mean to tell me you set up all night, hey?"

"No," I faltered, feeling guiltily conscious of telling a lie.

"Wall, it's pretty nigh it, at any rate," she retorted.

"She is all the nurse I have," answered my mother for me.

"Humph!" she snorted disdainfully; "a pretty nuss *she*
is. I'll be bound she don't know tea from tansy."

My mother laughed. "You're odd as ever, Rhoda."

"It's no laughing matter, let me tell you, Car'line: you'd
a picked up long ago cf you'd been seen to a leetle. Here,
child, you didn't tell me cf you knew how to make penny-
r'yal tea, or saffern either. I mostly prefer saffern myself."

"No, ma'am," I answered, feeling still more guilty for my
ignorance of these mighty regenerators.

"Wall, what's a miss worth without that knowledge, I

should like to know?" she cried triumphantly. "I see it's
well I brought my tools with me. It's clear I should a
gone a-beggin to find any here. I've got oceans in that
satchel yonder; jest fetch it here, Ruby, and I'll show you
in a twinklin' more 'arbs than you ever dreamed of. There!
that's catnip—called so cause cats allers run for it when they're
fitty—it's grand for stomach sickness; and *that's* thorough-
wort, or bone-set, beats all the doctor's stuff in creation for
cleansing out the system, specially if one's humory. I'm
dredful choice of it; 't don't grow very abundant in our parts,
and ther's lots of it used. I allers git Polly Kitchum, who
lives in the Notch, to gather it for me; she's a master hand
at it. Why, I wouldn't be without it for *no* consideration.
I keep a bowl on't standing, the whole during time, on
the butt'ry shelf, and jest take a swaller ev'ry time I
go by. *This* is spearmint, Ruby, and this is sage, good
for one of them are pesky headaches such as the Lee
fam'ly allers *was* troubled with, and allers *will* be I
s'pose, for they're constitutional." (I wondered if she
meant the "Lee family" or the "pesky headaches.")

"What's in *this* bundle, aunt? it smells dreadfully."

"Oh, that's jest what I've bin huntin' for: its yarrer!—
grows everywhere; but it's proper good for 'most every thing.
Sure cure, I tell 'em, when ev'rything else gives out. I guess,"
she added musingly, "I'd better steep up a little, and give
her a cup, and see ef 'twon't start her up a trifle. What doctor do you have, Ruby?"

. "Not any, aunt: mother says she has no faith in them,
and she thinks it a needless expense."

"Jest so *I* think," she returned, with satisfaction. "I
don't b'lieve nothin' in none on 'em: now this ere'll fetch her
along quicker'n a cart-load of their messes."

She untied the small roll of pungent weed. "Verily," thought I, "if it tastes as bad as it smells, nothing will induce mother to touch it. She is so particular."

My aunt resumed, with vivacity: "I raly wish I'd a come afore: I'd no idee she's so run down, nothin' but skin and bones, is she? Wall, what can't be cured must be endured, mus'n't it? I s'pect the letter got kinder overlooked down 't the office; then agin I didn't think there's any hurry; but Joel says, 'Now, Rhody, don't put it off. Go down yourself and see how the land lays.' She glanced at the bed regretfully; "seems to me she's dreadful drowsy; does she have sech spells often?"

"She sleeps most of the time," I answered.

"Wall, we must fetch her out o' that, short order; now you start up the fire, and git me a basin, and——"

"Oh," said my mother, rousing suddenly, "I don't want any tea, Rhoda. Put Ruby to bed. I want to talk with you."

"Couldn't you force a leetle down now, ef I should make it and sweeten it?" persisted Aunt Rhoda.

"No, indeed! I feel better already: your coming has done me good."

I approached the bed to say good-night. She turned her gaze on my face, where it rested long and earnestly. Involuntarily I stooped. "Bend lower," she whispered. I did so. She raised her lips feebly to mine; she stretched forth her hand to pat my cheek fondly. Unusual the caress, unusual the words crowning it,—"My dear little daughter, good-night." Then she seemed half ashamed of the brief fond sentence, for when I would have lingered longer, she moved uneasily and said impatiently, "There, there, good-night."

A small "lumber-room" opened out of the one my mother

occupied, in which Mrs. Potter kindly allowed my poor bed
to stand. Its legitimate tenants—the rats—were a terror to
me, inasmuch as their constant noises sometimes suggested
the possibility of their taking position in my domain. For
this reason it was rarely occupied. Now I went to it, forgetful of my fears, in a maze of wonder at my mother's new
outbreak of tenderness. How the words thrilled me; I
repeated them to myself while undressing; sweet and smooth
as honey they flowed, and they looked to me as but the
harbingers of a plentiful future harvest. "Not in vain,"
thought I, "has been my quiet devotion, my unceasing care,
during these weary months. It has unlocked the seal, which
pent in too narrow a channel the clear, gushing waters." I
was meditating in this dreamy fashion when my aunt came
in and placed Annah in my arms. She left a kind word also
"Don't fret, child: I'll 'tend to matters and things now: go
right straight to sleep."

This good advice I suppose I followed after a time. I
heard the sound of low talking through the thin, plaster
less partition, but gradually it faded into indistinct murmurs; then it sank into whispers as my ear closed to all
sound, and, with my arms twined closely around the baby
form, the fresh, velvety lips pressed to my cheek, I slumbered.

*   *   *   I awoke—with a start—towards dawn from
disturbing dreams of a driving, pitiless storm. Hail, sleet,
and clouds of snow beating my defenceless head, as, shorn of
bonnet or cloak, with feet sorely benumbed by the intense
cold, alone and unutterably weary, I wandered in an aimless
search over an unknown wilderness. Wide barren wastes
surrounded me. The wind moaned and shrieked among the
dry, leafless trees. It rose, sobbing with the suppressed

2

fury of the coming gale. Storm-spirits hurled by me, shriek·
ing. Invisible forces lifted me in their arms, and, helpless
and frightened, I was borne upward. Anon, the vast void
called space, claimed me for its sole inhabitant. Sound was
no more. The power of speech was denied me. For the
vision was only endless night. My limbs—shrunken with
terror—essayed motion in vain. For crimes uncommitted—
or at least unknown—my soul was doomed to eternal solitude. Not so. Motion—suddenly asserted—seized me. I
was falling through the drear vacuity; whirling, as I plunged
downward, with the speed of the revolutions of the planets;
faster and faster as I neared the earth, which loomed in
sight—measureless, boundless. Its dark surface arrested my
flight; I awaited in terror the inevitable concussion.

Was I awake, or dreaming? I was in my own little cot;
Annah was still in my arms. The silence of night wrapped
the room—its *silence*, but not its gloom. No lamp or candle was burning, yet a tender radiance shone mild and clear.
By my bedside sat my mother, her gaze meeting mine smilingly. In former nights I had often waked to find her
restlessly pacing the sleepless hours away; so this vision
neither startled nor alarmed me, and I silently surveyed her.
It was the same, yet how transformed the image! She looked
not wan and wasted, as I remembered her a few hours since,
but well and happy. Happiness, full to overflowing, could
alone have generated that smile, wreathing her lip,—tender,
self-reproachful,—with which she watched me, while my
tongue trembled for utterance.

"Mother," I whispered softly, "how came you here?
Does Aunt Rhoda know?"

Still mute and smiling, the vision (if such it was) rose.
How, or whence, she vanished, I know not. I had never

once taken my eyes from her. The door had not opened; but she was gone.

As I lay, awed a little and wondering, a deep-toned voice broke the solemn stillness. It was my aunt's voice in the outer room, reverently uttering these words of holy resignation—"The Lord gave, and the Lord taketh away ; blessed be the name of the Lord." Then, after a pause, "Car'line was the youngest of us all, and she's gone the fust. It's trouble's done it."

"No," answered another voice ; I recognized it as Mrs. Potter's. "It's the will of an overruling Providence. That's clear enough to my mind. Her time had come ; and we ought to be submissive. Perhaps she's been took from the evil to come." My aunt gave a heavy groan. Presently Mrs. Potter resumed : "Your sister was a proper nice woman, but she's better off now."

"Yes," assented my aunt. Not confident of having yet struck the right vein of consolation, Mrs. Potter continued : "It's no use repining at our afflictions ; it won't bring her back; besides its flying right square in the face of Scripture. Be you a professor, ma'am ?"

"I hope so," responded my aunt, quickly, "I wouldn't give much for myself, ef I wasn't. My earthly course is more'n half run, and 'twould be a burnin' shame and disgrace, not to have my lamp trimmed and burning. I *hope* I don't b'long to the foolish virgins; and there's no tellin' how soon the bridegroom'll call for *me*."

"Yis, to be sure, we've all got to come to it," regretfully sighed the landlady. "We can't realize it, though, till it strikes home; *you* know that, Mrs. Martin, as well as I do. There's a beautiful hymn somewhere—I don't know but it's in the Moravian collection ; and I don't know *as* 'tis—but it's

about, 'We'll lay our armor down.' I always feel kinder consoled to let what *will*, happen, when I hear it sung in church,
but the trouble is, it don't *last* long. It must be a great comfort, Mrs. Martin, to reflect that your sister was a member."

"Yes;" absently responded my aunt; and a decent pause
followed. Then the landlady said briskly, " Well, well, Mrs.
Martin, 'twon't *alter* nothing to wait any longer. What shall
it be? Merino, or muslin?"

"I ra'ly don't know," said my aunt, thoughtfully.

"I suppose I may as well tell you," said Mrs. Potter, feeling her way to a bargain, "that I've got plenty of book-
muslin in the house; and as good book-muslin, too, as any
one could wish to be laid out in. I keep it a purpose for such
occasions. Them who keep a boarding-house, ma'am, don't
never know when these things *won't* happen. This is a dying world, you know," she snivelled pathetically.

"Yes, that's true," interrupted my aunt. She was too
sharp not to understand the woman thoroughly.

" Well, now, Mrs. Martin," sinking her voice impressively, " I feel free to tell you, that I've had *my* shroud made, and
packed away, nigh upon ten years. When I go a journey
I always take it along, for fear of accidents, you know. My
mother did so before me; she pinned every thing up together in the sheet, and when her time *did* come, all I had to do
was to go and put my hand right on to 'em; 'twas all ready;
I could a got them in the dark."

"You don't say?" observed my aunt, coolly.

"Yes; and there was my grand'ther too! Now what do
you think he did? the strangest thing! He went and got
his grave-stones, and his wife's too; had them marked—all
but the date, you know—got the foot-stones, and had the
initials put on."

" Mercy !" said Aunt Rhoda, " where did he keep 'em ?"

" Oh ! under the bed for a long spell ; but he found that they was getting too dusty there, so he carried 'em off to the graveyard, and set 'em up. He had picked out the place long before, where he wanted to lie, and he said he was determined to suit himself about the stones ; he didn't want his heirs to quarrel over his bones. Poor man ;"—she sighed—" he didn't live long after it. Some kinder thought it was tempting Providence ; getting ready so, to die ; but law, *I* never did. I don't think the Lord'll take us any sooner for being prudent. I don't believe in forerunners of death, either ; do you, Mrs. Martin ?"

" No," said my aunt, solemnly. " The Bible says : ' For he cometh like a thief in the night ;' I believe *that.*"

" Well, now," responded Mrs. Potter, " I'll just run down and get that muslin ; you can see if 'twill *do*, you know, and if it will, why, we can go right to work upon it ; there's no need of calling any one else in, as I know of."

I caught the sound of an opening door ; then of feet descending the stairs. Soon reappearing, there ensued a gentle bustle. I am ashamed to record of my aunt, that she objected to the *price* of the muslin so strenuously, that an altercation seemed pending ; but she was finally overruled by the landlady's decisive arguments. I knew instinctively the meaning of these preparations. I had never in my life looked on death, but now, through every nerve of my soul quivered the unresisted conviction : You are orphaned, and desolate.

Oh ! Reader, if you have ever lain thus—in a darkened chamber—dark indeed to your eyes and heart—with a loved form lying near to your warm clasp, cold and speechless ; with the hum of voices over the work of robing that form

for the tomb, sounding fearfully distinct, and almost palsying
sorrow, in spasms of indignation at their heartlessness; every
rustle of the snowy robe sending over you chilly terrors;
every clip of the scissors cutting your heart-strings, then indeed I pity you : still warmer glows my pity if, to the sufficient bitterness of the present, Retrospection adds a sting.
If memory pushes up from her charnel-house many oppor-
tunities, by you slighted, of adding one comfort, diminish-
ing one pang ; if she continually tortures your ear, by sounding through it the sad refrain: Repentance *now* is of no
avail; you can do these sweet offices no longer; naught can
benefit the dead.

I was devoutly thankful when, at last, the voices ceased ;
when the broadening dawn imperatively told me to rise, and
quit my room, even though it brought me face to face with
this strange visitant; even though it added the torture of
the funeral—another strangeness—and the succeeding long,
sleepless night.

CHAPTER III.

SEVERAL days elapsed, filled to the brim with loneliness,
It is so hard to grow accustomed to miss the object of our
daily love and care ; so hard to stifle longing with vain reflections. What a desert Life looks to us henceforth! In
vain we pierce the blankness for some oasis of precious
hope, to guide and comfort us. The scales of ignorant selfishness lie too thickly on our eyes, for us to see that there
is a pathway; and that God sends other travellers beside
ourselves, over the same sunless journey.

I roused myself at last from the contemplation of my own desolation, to soothe Annah's grief. She did not cry, but she fretted constantly. This stimulated my womanly dignity; it throve wonderfully. It seems unnatural, and ludicrous *now*, to recall my efforts to assume maternal functions; then, it thrilled me with an earnestness, effectually precluding mirth from its beholders.

Those quiet days to me were busy ones to my aunt. With the efficient promptness which characterized all her movements, she packed, and repacked, articles destined for moving; the few pieces of furniture were sent to certain auction-rooms in the vicinity, and thus disposed of; the landlady's bill ostentatiously called for, and settled; and a shabby suit of mourning hastily improvised for me,—"for the neighbors'll watch, as sharp's a brier"—my aunt observed in answer to Mrs. Potter's remark, that "she thought it a useless expense." The contents of the little brown hair trunk, thickly studded on its cover with my mother's initials in brass nails, were thoroughly overhauled. It held a number of my father's clothes, which my aunt unceremoniously bundled together, averring, "They'll do for carpet-rags; they ain't fit for nothing else." She muttered also, *sotto voce*, "I'd like to strip up the wearer on 'em too; heartless, good-for-nothing wretch. I'd never a b'lieved it of Corny Brooks."

. Twilight was slowly deepening into a bright moonlit eve as we neared Northfield. The heavy stage lumbered up to the tavern. Several acquaintances were lounging on the outside "stoop," who came up cordially to shake her offered hand. She seemed glad to get home again; glancing at their faces, then around at the dusty street and the well-known dwellings lining it, with unmistakable satisfaction.

The worthy farmers seemed fully aware of the nature of my
aunt's late journey, and by a few curious glances they guessed
the result. (It's astonishing what a shrewd faculty this
"guessing" becomes among the villagers. With its inquisitorial edge—keen as a hatchet—it hews for its owners a way
right into your household affairs; it adjudges your social,
religious, political standing; inventories your wardrobe—as
well as any mental, moral, or personal defects you possess,
and naturally desire to keep secret. What *one* knows, all
soon discover, and by the use—vigorously plied—of the same
legitimate means.)

One of these neighbors, whom my aunt called " Uncle
Jesse," offered to " harness up," and take us " down t'the
Hook."

Aunt Rhoda opposed, at first, a faint show of polite
resistance. " 'Ta'nt no trouble at all," he returned, " my
horse is hitched right under Deacon Brown's shed yender."

" I can walk well enough yit," began Aunt Rhoda, tartly,
when Uncle Jesse decisively interrupted her:

" Now, Mrs. Martin, I 'spose 'ta'nt nothin' for *you* to foot
it a mile or two arter ridin' all day; but this leetle chick
can't stan' it no how. Can you, sissy ? What's your name,
leetle one ?" He finished by kindly stroking my head.

" Ruby, Sir," I answered, timidly.

" Speak up, child; and don't be 'fraid of your shadder,"
sharply interposed my aunt.

Uncle Jesse gave her a queer look; then responded to
my answer, " Ruby, hey ! a proper pretty one 'tis, too; and
you're as nice a leetle gal as ever trod shoe-leather."

" I can tell you *one* thing, Mr. Warner; you'd better not
go to puttin' notions into her head," retorted Aunt Rhoda,
nodding at him most mysteriously.

"Tut, tut! praise don't never hurt nobody; I wish there was more of it in the world. Now you wait a bit, and I'll jerk up the old mare. I hav'nt used her much latterly, and she feels her oats, I tell you," and off Uncle Jesse trotted.

We stood in the tavern porch during this brief colloquy, and there we waited until the mare appeared, reined in with the utmost care by Uncle Jesse, whose sonorous "whoa's," and "there stiddy, stiddy now," woke expressive nods and winks from the other farmers. Indeed, I saw no signs of friskiness; on the contrary, she indulged her fat, nut-brown, sides in a very moderate trot, and meekly dropped her head on stopping.

"This is a dredful likely child, Mrs. Martin," remarked another neighbor, lifting Annah "to heft her," "a two-year old, I reckon?"

"No; only fifteen months," corrected my aunt.

"You don't say; well, I never;" and the whole group nodded emphatically at Annah—I suppose for a sign of approbation.

Uncle Jesse now gathered up the lines in his great brown hands, and turned the horse's head.

"We'se a talkin 'bout you this blessed mornin'," said he, "and says sister Siny, says she, 'I guess the reason why Mrs. Martin stays so, is that's she's goin' to nuss up Car'line and bring her hum with her; she's a good hand at it.' 'Yis,' says sister Crete, 'but there's no tellin': if she's foreordained to git well she will; and if she's foreordained to die, why she will, and all Rhody Martin's nussin' won't alter nothin''—and it seems it's so." He paused, with a soothing cluck to the horse, which I tried in vain to interpret.

"Where's Miss Charity now?" asked my aunt.

"Oh, teachin', as usual: she's commenced a s'lect school

2*

now, down to Scrabbletown; don't see her only once a fortnit. How does *she* take it?"—meaning me—his voice sank
to a confidential whisper.

"That's mor'n I kin make out jest yit," she answered. "I
'xpected to have a dredful fuss when she found it out'n the
mornin', but she didn't take on none, nor nothin', and I'm
'fraid she didn't feel it as she oughter."

"Ye can't allers tell when folks sense it," he returned.
"Some shows it one way, some anuther. Did Car'line go
hard?" was his next inquiry, glancing at me cautiously.

"No; she jest dropped off as easy as a baby goin' to sleep.
I *thought* she was struck with death jest as soon as I set eyes
on her; I wa'n't 'xpecting to find her so low. She talked a
consid'rable spell arter I got there, but she kep' breathin'
shorter and shorter, and 'fore I rightly knew it she was gone."

"Wall, that's somethin' to think on, ain't it?" said Mr.
Warner, thoughtfully patting his knee. "Why, here we be,
all safe and sound, and there's 'Mandy a sparkin' it in the
front door: wall, wall, young folks *will* be young folks, you
know, Mrs. Martin."

Uncle Jesse brought us up in fine style before a low-roofed
building, cozy, comfortable looking, and rather more tasteful
than is wont for a farm-house. A piazza stretched along its
southern side, over the framework of which clusters of wood-
bine saucily swung their dark, glossy sprays, and delicate
vines of 'morning glory' just showed here and there their
shrivelled pink and blue bells. A large "yard" enveloped
the mansion—thickly studded with dandelion and white
clover blossoms. In front rose-bushes were planted, just
bursting into bloom. A bed of pinks, none-so-prettys, four-
o'-clocks, and star-of-Bethlehems occupied a conspicuous
corner; patches of sweet-clover and southern-wood planted

their fragrant feet at consistently short distances; an enormous snow-ball bush drooped by the well-curb. Lilac-trees also crowned each window front. From the narrow picket-gate which swung heavily open—owing to a huge stone, depending from a stout rope inside—a walk of uneven flags led to the green-painted open door. Two figures rose somewhat hastily, the gentleman slyly removing a supporting arm from the waist—neither trim nor slender—of his companion.

"Amandy," called my aunt, "come and take the baby;" and having dropped this burden into her outstretched arms, she promptly offered each a hand. The gentleman shook it as if unacquainted with the friendly ceremony, and his color rose painfully under Uncle Jesse's good-natured smile.

"How are all your folks?" asked Aunt Rhoda.

"As well as common," he responded, indifferently; he seemed intently occupied in kicking a caterpillar off the flag-stone.

"Wall," said my aunt, wearily, "sech a tug as I've had, this last week. I declare, hum's hum, ef it's ever so humly, ain't it, Iry?"

But that unsympathetic gentleman had turned away after Amanda; my aunt gave me a meaning nod.

"Hum'm," coughed our escort, regaining his seat with effort, "I s'pect it's all signed, sealed, and delivered; ain't it, Mrs. Martin?" While she exchanged last words with him, I turned to look after the lovers—neither of whom had spoken, or in any way noticed me. An ungainly pair, they looked to me. Ira, lank, lean, light-haired, and freckled. Amanda, fat, with hair of a redder tinge, and eyes to match, just dashed with blue. She swung the disengaged arm by her side; she kicked her dress up behind in walking, in a

fashion nervous to beholders. No amiable look crossed her
brow when she received into her arms the unwelcome addition to the household. I felt the slight; I saw the look;
and, child as I was, I resented it. My aunt interrupted my
observations. "This way," she said, adding confidentially,
as we went along, "Iry's a clever man, and'll be well off one
of these days. He's prudent as any one need ask for. He's
steppin' up to 'Mandy, you see." Turning a corner of the
house, we came suddenly upon the milking-yard. My aunt
let down the bars, and we went in. Milking was not yet
over. Aunt Rhoda went around, and patted the sleek heads
of her favorites—a gentle twain, 'Bessy' and 'Mooley,' received her attentions with intelligent delight; lowing, and
rubbing their sides lovingly against her extended hand.
"They know me, the creeturs do, 'cause I'm their milker,"
she explained, as I stared around. My whole life had been
pent up amid brick walls; my wonder at all I saw, if unexpressed, was unbounded.

"Well, Mark," as a fine lad came bounding from the barn
to meet us. "Well, mother," he echoed, laughing. "Pshaw,
Mark, don't make a fool of me," said his mother, as he suddenly stooped and kissed her, with a mixture of merriment
and earnestness that provoked me into a laugh.

"So, ho! you've got fun in you, sis, it seems; how dare
you laugh at me, you city manikin! I could make a dozen
of you in size, Miss Betsy."

"My name is not Betsy," I said, indignantly. He threw
up his hands in affected horror. "Perverse, sacrilegious
wretch! deny your Christian name? I should think you'd
be afraid a judgment would follow. Betsy's a good name,
and a beautiful one. It belonged to your ancestors. Take,
eat it, and be thankful."

"I don't like it," I faltered ; believing him in earnest.

"I don't see how you can help yourself,"—and he grave-ly watched my working features. "It's wicked to repudiate it, though by paying a good, round sum, we might get the Committee on changes, to alter it ;—ever heard of the Com-mittee ?"

I was silent from indignation. "Oh! don't tease the child," broke in his mother, sharply. "You'll get her a cryin' in a minnit. What do you allers want to be a pickin' on some one for? I should think you might be in better busi-ness. Don't mind him,"—she added, to me. "There's your Cousin Demis, down by the gate," pointing in the direction indicated.

It appears the little romp, herself, saw us. A race was the consequence ; a race destined to be luckless. She shook her thick fringe of hair over her eyes, and started one of the peaceable cows, at the outset ; and on they came, the domes-tic cavalry and infantry together.

"Halloa! Demie, I'll bet on the cow," shouted Mark to her.

"And *I'll* bet on the gal," answered a voice from the barn-door. In her headlong course, not noticing, or heeding the fact that a figure was crossing the yard to the dairy, she brought up against that worthy, with an emphasis which precipitated both to the ground, and sent the white foam flying high in the air. The empty pails flew away on the trampled grass ; the cow lumbered on.

"Hurrah!" cried Mark, "I've won the bet; for here comes the cow. Father, you've lost." A hearty laugh answered him.

My good aunt looked on dismayed. "Did you ever?" she ejaculated. "Demis Martin, ain't you ashamed of your-self? Ef *you* ain't, *I* am, *for* you." The culprit came slowly up. "What a plight you're in; just look at your pant'-lettes; you may bile 'em, and bile 'em, and that's all the good 'twill do ; only turn 'em black. Grass stains never *will* come out o' bleached cloth." Demis looked heartily mortified, but she received her scolding meekly. " I declare for't there never *was* a woman so tried afore," despairingly added her mother.

"Never mind," broke in Mark, laughing, " practice makes perfect, you know. Lift your trotters a little higher next time, my dear, and say ginger and saleratus, over vigorously, and who knows but you may win, yet ! Our little Betsy has bet heavily on your running," he added, soberly.

I gave him an astonished glance. " Now, Mark, stop *that*," said his mother, severely. "Speak the truth if you *can*. You'd better go to work, ef you haint nothin' else on hand. Demis, come and shake hands with your cousin."

" How do you do, Cousin Betsy ?" she said, somewhat embarrassed, and she offered to kiss me, but I pushed her away roughly. Mark was full of suppressed fun. " My name is not Betsy," I cried, angrily. " I won't stay here if you call me so."

" I thought Mark called you so," she pacifically returned, with an indignant glance at her brother. " How could you ! Marcus Martin."

"It is Rubina," I returned, chokingly. "Mother called me Ruby—"

" Don't be angry with me," said Demis, plaintively. " I never do any thing right; I'm always in hot water, mother says." She took my hand, and under her auspices, I entered the kitchen. We met Deborah, the "help," on the threshold, thoroughly drenched. She said not a word, but darted sullenly severe glances at us, abashing me somewhat, but which Demis relished hugely. "My sakes alive," she whispered, " ain't old Deb mad though? I spilt two pails of milk, as clean as a whistle." Sitting down on the doorsill, she burst into convulsive laughter. I could not join in it, and she presently looked up in my face, " How tired you do look," she said kindly. " You're as pale as a ghost. Now sit right down there, by the window, and let me take off your things." This she did. She placed a stool under my feet; she treated me, in short, like an invalid. Going off for the baby, she returned, tossing it merrily; then placing it in my lap, off she flitted to the pantry for milk with which to feed her. " I'll have supper ready in no time," she added to Debby, who muttered angrily, " You'd better, ef you know when you're well off."

I surveyed the kitchen—a long, low room, fashioned after the manner of country kitchens of those days. Great iron hooks fastened securely in the plaster above, supported parallel poles, on which hung freshly-ironed garments of all shapes and sizes; a goodly array, telling—better than mere words—of the family numbers. Around the room, on convenient nails, branches of asparagus hung; not for ornament merely—though that too was considered—but as decoy resting-places for troublesome flies, who were supposed to be not indifferent to these delicate green couches. Indeed, they buzzed furiously around the feathery sprays, and settled finally in little black colonies for a night's repose. Two perpendicular wooden slabs, fastened at top and bottom with cross-pieces, thickly notched adown their sides, stood back to back with the fireplace. A few strings of quartered apples—the relics of winter stores—rested in these notches. A stove in front performed the drying process. No musty carpet covered the floor; that shone resplendent in a fresh

coat of yellow paint. Such chairs I never before saw : tall,
carved " fiddle-backed"—with seats of narrow strips of listing,
thickly braided, forming a couch soft and yielding.   On
the white-washed wall, in a narrow black-painted frame, hung
the serene face of Thomas Jefferson. As companion picture
to this, appeared a truthful vision of "The Prodigal Son
returned to his Father." I could scarcely take my eyes
from it. I thought this illustration of the beautiful parable
most wonderful—the very seedy young man, in ragged
broadcloth, long-tailed coat, of the true Continental type,
with his bundle (containing, doubtless, a change of linen)
tied up in a red kerchief, slung over his shoulder like a
peddler's pack, rushing furiously toward his home in the distance—a substantial two-story house, with green blinds,
through which peep the "invited guests," bidden beforehand to celebrate his return. His poor, old father, with
long, white locks streaming in the wind, hastens with outstretched arms to embrace him. His two sisters are also
starting from the door, dressed becomingly in yellow frocks,
with pink sashes. I fancied I could almost smell the " fatted
calf" roasting away in the back kitchen. Then I fell to
wondering why the artist had omitted the mother from this
family reunion ; unless, indeed, his undutiful conduct had
long ago brought down her gray hairs with sorrow to the
grave. I ventured to mention this to my Cousin Demis.
She stopped her work a moment—pondered, then merrily
answered, that "she was probably washing the dishes, and
did not know of his arrival." I liked the kitchen. Every
one of its clean, homely details met my full childish approbation. Neither did a peep into " the buttery" diminish it.
I caught glimpses of mingled rows of dark blue crockery,
pies, and cakes, which Demis was swiftly transferring to

the large square table. She spun to and fro like a top, with a cheery, buoyant motion, altogether new to me. Her clumsily-made calico dress, could not disguise her graceful form. Where did she get that oval face, with its rich dark color? the crimson cheeks and the perfect mouth ; the jetty hair, and eyes large, soft, and mournful? Where the pliant swiftness of motion ; the slender shape ; small feet and hands, which her sister lacked? Not from her mother, certainly. Occasionally she came to my side to playfully chuck Annah under the chin, or to give her a toss and a kiss. These meteoric flights were soon checked by her mother's voice issuing from an inner room with, " Flax right round now, Demis Martin, and see how quick you can git the vittals on the table. The men-folks'll be in afore long."

The invisible monitress now appeared ; having prudently doffed her best array, and assumed in its stead a huge-flowered calico frock, and blue-checked apron—the latter garment made in an odd fashion, with a high waist, and broad shoulder-straps. She came out rolling up her sleeves to her elbows, preparatory to an onset among the treasures of the dairy. Thither she briskly posted ; and I heard her sharp, coarse voice shortly after, greeting the " men-folks" as she skimmed the milk, and set the curd for the morning's cheeses, and related her late adventures in " the city."

A man now came in, whom Demis led up to me and introduced as her father. Uncle Joel was a tall, portly figure—slightly obese—with a fresh, good-natured face, and large, dark, dreamy eyes—the counterparts of Demis's. He stooped a little with much labor, but he had not the usual shuffling gait of country people. I liked him at the first glance ; so kindly beamed his eye as he took my hand, a hearty welcome quivering on his full, red lips. He did not utter it. There was no need. "Actions speak louder than words." He lifted us both on his knee, and passed his rough hand very fondly over the baby's silky curls. Very musical the words which followed sounded to me, in his soft, silvery tones. "She's as pretty as a pictur'," he said, smiling at her; at which the little one cooed, and threw up her chubby hands to clutch his dark, curling hair. "I shouldn't blame her a bit for cryin', so many new faces 'bout; but she don't seem to have an idee on't, does she? I hope you will like to stay here, my dear," he added, kissing us both, and setting us down rather hastily, as Aunt Rhoda entered the room.

Demis announced supper. Deborah placed the chairs, and marshalled the family to their places. She deserves a word of mention. She was fat,—not fair, and certainly not *less* than forty. (I ventured one day, long after, to ask her age, and was punished for my impudent silliness: she turned on me, snappishly retorting, "Most a hundred; and you're a sassy minx!") She had lived at my uncle's since Mark was born—seventeen years ago—and was, consequently, very much attached to all. She always offered advice on doubtful questions, and not unfrequently decided mooted cases. She was considered by them, and also considered herself, quite one of the family. This evening she appropriated the baby to her own lap, telling me "she was used to bringin' on 'em up, and I warn't;" pointing to the stalwart group surrounding the table for illustration of this assertion. Little Natty, a blue-eyed, curly-haired rogue of four years, claimed most of her devotion; but they were evidently *all* the pride of her heart, and if you taxed her with partial fondness for *one*, she indignantly denied it. On all their short-comings she looked with lenient eyes, and treated them with alternations

of parental authority and humble deference, curious to witness'; allowing none to blame or find fault with them—save
herself—without sturdy vindication, often angry defence.
She often exercised this unbestowed privilege, and rated
them roundly, pouring out on some trivial fault the whole
contents of her vial of wrath. They usually took this good-
naturedly, as a piece of no unseemly interference. Then,
after she had thus given her opinions an indignant airing,
she always made haste to palliate their severity, by some
especial act of kindness, which amply atoned for "hurting
their feelings." No wonder they all liked her. She was an
affectionate creature; and would cheerfully have laid down
her own life, if, thereby, theirs could have been saved from
any peril. She surveyed her infant charge this evening with
a broad smile. "I don't see, for the life of me, what makes
all the babies take to me so, such a humly, ugly old crittur;
Dwight, if you're through, jest let me hev your cheer."
Dwight was a sulky-looking boy of seven, rarely speaking,
save when directly addressed, and even then replying by an
affirmative nod, or negative shake of the head. He was
always sending suspicious glances around the board to detect
a whisper or sneer levelled at him; if, peradventure, he saw
a smile on a lip, he imagined himself the cause, sullenly repelling proof to the contrary. That first night he never
looked at me. He rose at Deborah's request, somewhat re-
sentfully; and swung away silently. It was days before he
ventured to be civil.

But dear little Nat. I still see how he curled his tiny,
brown, bare feet into his chair, his eyes sparkling with fun;
how his soft, brown curls flew, when abruptly released from
the coarse, ragged straw hat binding them down. His chair
was close to mine, and after a shy peep at my face—which I

as shyly returned—he seemed to feel that he risked nothing by the venture, and cunningly slid one fat, warm palm into my own.

After tea was over, the large family scattered in different directions. Amanda stole to the "keeping-room," with a basin of soap and water, and arranged her yellow tresses. She wearied herself out in endeavors to coax " water-curls" around her thin temples. I was amused at her contortions of mouth and forehead during this operation. She certainly possessed one virtue—Patience; for the difficulties in her way were considerable. One lock was too large for her purpose; she divided it. It was now too thin; she added a few hairs, with frequent dippings in the basin of water to render it more pliable. Then she soaped it, and rolled the stiff, dingy tress over one freckled forefinger, adroitly plastering it against the spot desired. It would not stay, but came tumbling down in a series of fantastic twists. Again she twined it into one solid ring, and spatted it vehemently into place; and again it leapt back exultant. Mark sauntered in, and watched her, with a roguish twinkle in his hazel eyes. "Oh! cut it off a few inches; it's too long," he suggested. She caught at this idea, eagerly. Clip—the tress fell to the floor. Alas! it was now stiffer, harsher than before.

"Humbug! There's no curl in your hair, Amanda. That's the reason it won't go off," was Demis's ironical exclamation.

"Let's see *you* try, Miss?" scornfully retorted her sister.

"To be sure." Demis let down her heavy tresses, dipped a lock in the water, rolled it up carelessly, and it fell in a graceful ringlet. Mark pulled it admiringly. Amanda gave a defiant sniff.

"There's nothing like trying," encouragingly persisted

Mark; "don't give up yet, the world was not made in a day, you know."

"I know you're a hateful, disagreeable, ugly wretch," Amanda irefully retorted.

" I've discovered the reason of her perseverance," imperturbably resumed the family tease, " Ira adores curls, and especially likes " spit-curls; I heard him say so t'other day, —fact."

Amanda turned suspiciously red at this announcement.

" What in thunder are you blushing so confoundedly for ?" he blurted out, looking innocent wonder. " Have I said any thing, girls, to call out all that madder tint ? I wonder if *that's* what took Ira's heart by storm ? Such a lovely shade of red ! just the color in the carpet here !—curls and blushes ! Whew !" He finished with a long, low whistle.

" You're the most provokin'est feller I ever see," angrily interrupted Amanda, catching up the basin and hastily darting into the entry, just as her brother was resuming.

" Poh ! there's no fun in joking her; she flies all to pieces ;" and Master Mark seated himself by the open window, on the edge of the table, dropping his long legs outside. " Demie, *you* are better game; you keep your temper. I don't know yet as to Betsy there; she is fiery, I rather think; her eyes have a hard look to them, as if they might turn if you pushed them in their sockets. Come here and let me test it."

I declined soberly. He gave me a curious smile, and mockingly shook at me his fist.

" Well, Demie, I must content myself with teazing you." She gave his flaxen tresses a vigorous pull : "Ah! what a sad contrast to mine." He twined his arm fondly around her, " I vow you're a regular gypsy lassie, Demie; eyes

black as night, and tawny skin; my nut-brown maiden, I
wish Dame Nature had bestowed like favors upon me. A
man"—he erected himself proudly—"has no business with a
milk-and-water face. Amanda and you should have looked
alike, it's the natural duty of sisters; but *you* are so perverse,
you know."

"And so are *you*, Mark, or you would not persist in
hanging your great feet there, after mother has repeatedly
ordered you not to."

"I believe she *has* expressed her mind on that point," he
replied coolly.

"And you'll sup sorrer ef you don't attend to what she
says, now I tell ye," remarked Debby, putting her good-
natured face into the room.

"He is only making ready to go to singing-school when
Olive comes along," said Demis archly, "and here she comes
down the hill. Why, Mark, who is blushing now?"

He laughed, sprang to the ground, and went off singing.
From a side window I watched how deferentially he turned
toward her, as her little head nodded emphasis to his wag-
gish prattle. I thought she looked fair and sweet enough
to turn any sober lover's head, much more the heart of
my wild Cousin Mark. Her laugh rang out like a silver
chime. Her form was that of a fairy. "He thinks all the
world of her, and she of him," oracularly pronounced Demis,
peeping over my shoulder at the happy pair, "and oh!
there's Ira coming for Amanda, and I don't believe she's
ready." She darted away to summon her sister.

Looking back now to that first night among new-found
relatives, I can see that in those few hours there was revealed
much of their real character. My impressions were subse-
quently confirmed. *Then* I only was conscious of being

translated into an entirely new sphere. The deadly grip of
home-sickness clutched me. I swallowed the starting tears,
and tried—oh! so resolutely—to think of it as an old thing
with me; as if these were faces, forms, I had long, long
known. In vain. Busy life—eager, bustling, happy—filled
those hearts around me. The placid content of minds, yet
free from scourging care and sorrow, cast its sheltering
mantle over that peaceful roof. Having experienced both
care and sorrow, I alone felt the scantiness of its covering.
Though a welcome, genial and true, shone on every countenance for the strangers—ah, yes! *that* was the trouble—I
felt as " a stranger in a strange land." * * * It appeared,
a little later, that I was to share my two cousins' room. In
a lowly "linter" chamber, two beds occupied opposite corners. Demis proffered her active services in bestowing the
baby in one; she accomplished this most skilfully without
awaking her. We had a vigorous resistance from Deborah,
who wanted her for a bedfellow. She insisted that she
would keep *me* awake, but she herself was used to it.
"She's croupy too, I guess, and ef she's to be took with a fit
in the night what *would* you do?" I turned a deaf ear to
her suggestions, and Demis laughed her bodings to scorn.

Really, in spite of the sloping walls and low ceiling, the
chamber looked not unpleasant. Perhaps Demis's presence
brightened it into comfort. She was a perfect ray of sunshine. She unbraided my long hair, talking cheerily enough
to dispel a host of intruding tyrants of home-sickness. My
heart warmed to my bright, gay cousin, but I felt too dispirited to answer in the same vein, and I listened to her
prattle in silence. It was no consolation either to reflect on
the bitter, unwelcome truth, that I had really *no* home to
sicken and long for. I left no one behind me to await my

return, to comfort the present parting with thoughts of a
future meeting. My brief past was a chapter forever closed
Only a solitary grave in Greenwood beckoned my wandering
fancy; but my thoughts returned to that grave as to a home,
for it held the form, not yet dust, dearest to me; to cling
passionately to the damp mould; to bestow upon it abundantly the fruition of tears; to keep faithful watch over the
humble headstone—shining out in the clear moonlight, so
lonely and sad among the myriad stately monuments—to me
the only dead among so many sleepers. What a great chasm
had rent itself into my life in one short week? I vaguely
wondered if I should always be so wretched, so miserable, as
I felt now? Yes, I was sure of it. The answer came distinct,
ready. It seemed as if it must be morning before Amanda
came up, but in answer to my inquiry she said peevishly,
that it was only eleven o'clock. She dropped off to sleep as
those do who have no cause to be wakeful; who see only
brightness in prospect, and plenty of leisure in broad daylight in which to dream of it; when it is so much your own
that you feel no haunting fear lest it elude your grasp or
burst—an unsubstantial bubble—shrivelling in its destruction
your dearest hopes, purposes.

Demis sat up in bed a while, humming in a low, pure tone,
a fragment of some old hymn. Then she pensively chanted
quaint "Barbara Allen;" the dreary repetition at the end
of each verse, echoed itself into a mournful, slumberous
weight upon my ear. At last she ceased altogether, and to
all appearance slumbered. Sleep for me, was out of the
question. My tired eyelids drooped mechanically, but, ere
a moment closed, a nervous start relifted them. I raised
my head finally from the pillow, and examined the room.
Very little was there in it, to repay my interest. A bureau

and an old-fashioned chest of drawers, in dark wood, elaborately carved. A chest painted red, and on its front an immense green flourish—some vine—or merely an artistic finish, I could not determine which. A coarse print, labelled " The Playful Pets," hung on the unpapered, unwhitewashed wall. I looked long at it in the moonlight. It showed me a girl with very crimson cheeks, and unnatural curls, uplifting her pinafore swarming with kittens. Then my eyes fell on the counterpane, also a picture, or rather a succession of uniform pictures, stamped on a light brown ground of curtain calico. Blue lambs reclined under lighter blue foliage ; a brook purled along over intensely magnified pebbles. There sat a fond shepherd and shepherdess, hand in hand, while a dog guarded the listless flocks. The sun, very low in the horizon, shone with wonderful rays of white. I thought it a remarkable production. I lifted it, and looked at the one beneath. This ground was scarlet, with trees, and animals, and—yes ; it was the garden of Eden, and there was Adam and Eve, fearlessly twining serpents around their arms, while a lion crouched beside them. When I looked up from my survey, I almost shrieked in terror; a white-robed figure stood close at my side.

" Hush," it whispered, " don't be frightened, Cousin Ruby. You didn't hear me, you were so absorbed in that quilt, and no wonder. Debby says it's over a hundred years old. It was my grandmother's." I said nothing,

" Now, my child," resumed my cousin, " why don't you go to sleep ! It's very injurious keeping awake all night ! Are you warm ?" I should have laughed at any other time, at her comical assumption of maternal solicitude ; now I only looked wistfully up to her face, as she bent over me—a look which somehow made her beautiful dark eyes fill with tears.

3

She murmured something unintelligible; she crept by my side; she wound her arms tightly around me, kissing again and again my cold lips, chafing in her warm palms my own icy ones. Her loving sympathy charmed away my grief. It opened, with noiseless key, the hitherto pent-up floodgates of affection. The barren channels, unused so long, flowed free and full at last. No scanty measure filled it. A freshet threatened to overwhelm it. The rushing tide met an incoming one, as fervent: united, they formed a deep of love—measureless, soundless. From that night we were to each other more than sisters.

CHAPTER IV.

Out into the Future rolled Time's chariot wheels. Days sad, solitary, busy, happy; according to our changeful mood, wove themselves into uneventful weeks; these, in their turn, craving fellowship, made haste to join themselves unto months as monotonous. A year slipped from the calendar ere we were aware. The sudden change—from a vast, roaring whirlpool of Life; a very Babylon of sound; a ceaseless ebb and flow of humanity's tide; when, though not one of the outside throng yet in its very midst; gathering momently an unobservant consciousness of its myriad busy forces, to a Sabbath-like quietude, a perpetual, holy calm—as though I had left a world's day, and entered upon its night of rest—bred a brief feeling of lonely dissatisfaction, which I shortly exchanged for pleasurable content.

"Northfield Farms" was an obscure, uninteresting town, deserving no especial mention. There are many such towns scattered at intervals along the fertile valley's slope—for it *is* fertile, green, and charming—many of them dignified by names quaint and romantic; many also are the sweet, significant designations of natives of the forest; thus simply perpetuating, among the hardy sons of our grim Puritan sires, these solitary vestiges of a poetry and a language long since passed away. It was, as its name indicates, a collection of farms extending over a wide area. The village proper, was "The Centre;" yet radiating from this were groups of lesser colonies of more recent planting, distinguished—as is commonly the case in New England—by various characteristic sobriquets.

"The Farms" contained accordingly, my uncle's, and a few neighboring estates. To the west, loomed "The Factories." Here, a swift, rushing mountain stream, dignified with the name of "The River," added its quota to aid human subsistence, by turning the wheels of numerous mills along its banks. This was the thriving part of the population. Here were mills of nearly every description. Woollen, cotton, and grist mills; mills for making warps, batting; calico print-works, and a paper-mill, of every degree of outward show, from the rickety tenement of decaying, paintless wood—quaking fearfully with the constant jar of its machinery; waking ominous shakes of the sagacious farmers' heads, and long speeches in the village Lyceum, regarding its durability, and the safety of its operatives—to the firmly planted structure of brick, and massive erections of quarry marble.

There were besides, "East Northfield," and scores of minor designations, originating in odd seasons of mirthfulness. "The Hook," "Scrabble Row," and "Thunder," among these, enjoyed a proportionate degree of uncertain celebrity.

Prosaic enough, these colonies were, in detail. Old fashioned simplicity marked them for its own. The same sombre characteristics also tinged the inhabitants with a kind of
antediluvian aspect in manner and dress. It was as though
the sturdy independence of the surrounding scenery threw
around them its quiet reflection. Born, suckled, reared in
the cold, dark shadow of these grim, rocky ledges of undisputed antiquity; the grand old mountains fostered corresponding elements in their characters; and hardy endurance,
stubborn tenacity of will, immovable purpose, stalked forth
with resolute front at every turn in these secluded hamlets.
I liked well the uncompromising hills, gloomily frowning
from the dread depths of their rock-ribbed precipices. I
liked the pastoral beauty of the vale below. Fields of waving grain—dancing lullabies to passing breezes—encircled it.
Fertile meadow uplands—green, soft, and daisy-starred—
dotted with kine, lowing mournfully as sunset chimes its vesper-
bells; frisky with untamed colts, proudly unconscious that halter and bridle-rein await them—upheaved in gentle billows of
verdure, toward the distant mountains. In the haze of evening, these latter take on shapes mystical and dreamy. Its
kindly robe screens all startling deformities. Dreamily
leaning against the heavens, its own azure hue envelops
them; their summits seem to pierce triumphantly its vaulted
dome, and sharp, rough outlines melt into mist and space.

I liked to watch the gradual paling of the vivid sunset
fires; crimson, scarlet, gold, nestling for a night's repose in
the arms of pale purple and unromantic gray; and the
moon, as she cautiously lifted her bright edges above the
eastern mountain-tops, then—suddenly growing confident—
boldly displayed her whole, laughing visage, and serenely
ventured on her midnight march.

I should say "we," for Mark or Demis always shared my

rambles. At this hour we two marched homeward—speculating, as we trudged along, on our probable reception. We usually got a cool one. My aunt neither liked or approved of our excursions. She thought it a grievous waste of time and strength ; an unprofitable investment, returned to us in the shape of damaged clothing, and souls unfitted for practical work. In our large household was always a dreary abundance of this commodity ; house-work that never was—never *could* be finished; a monotonous daily round of duties—comprised in none so fully as in a New England farmer's family; for on none, save Pilgrim soil, are so fully inculcated the stern necessities of labor, that will admit of no repose. Every thing must be finished "straight to the mark." There must never occur a lapse of self-indulgent revery ; reading is not tolerated, save on Sundays, when the equally strict religious belief renders work a crime, and eschews all literature which can possibly be regarded as secular. So the days, months, and years roll on ; cooking, cleansing, ironing, mending, mark and stamp each, until distaste and disgust are their invariable accompaniments. Progressive development of mind is a myth; freedom of thought and action wilts lifeless as, sternly dominant, rises the spectre, saying, "This *must* be done; that must be attended to *at once;* clothes must be made, rents repaired." Besides, my aunt held to the thrifty notion that it was best to keep ahead of actual wants, and store in chest and cupboard garments for future need.

Boys reared in such a home often grow to receive woman's constant ministrations as their constitutional right ; they laugh and look amazed should you suggest otherwise. They amass manhood's full stature—strong, ruddy, vigorous—having worked faithfully for their sires until, "of age," a desire of independence seizes them—they nur-

ture the wish for a home of their own. If attained—do
you think it a modest place, fully cultivated, proudly paid
for, and joyfully taken possession of by the twain? (Of
course a wife is necessary for a share of the labor.) Nothing less than a hundred acres will suffice; on which dreary
patches of waste land are to be improved, and not an acre
paid for in money. This is the meaning of the unceasing
toil—the discharge of the homestead debt. Haply if either
live to see it accomplished. Ere that time arrives, youth—
the season of improvement—has flown; age chills the faculties; they are ripe for the tomb.

Aunt Rhoda was styled by the neighbors "a dreadful ambitious woman," and many prophecies floated to her ears
that she would "break down some day, and hev to give
up." Still robust and vigorous, she indignantly scouted
the idea, and bustled from garret to cellar on mysterious
errands, whose results were fruitless. She inherited (from
the "Purdys; her mother's folks," she would say, proudly)
a bone and muscle bred abhorrence of any thing in any shape
approaching laziness. Lounging about the room with no
specific object, was pronounced "so shiftless." Trifles, running counter to her busy mood, violently irritated her. She
went about the morning offices as though a treat were in
store—cooking homely cakes and bread with a relishing
zeal, which would have flavored the most intricate culinary
mysteries. Then, her step had such a way of saying, "Get
out of the way; *I* am coming;" firm, unswerving, with a
rollicking motion of the hips, and a shuffle of her "calf-
skin ties," decidedly unpoetical, and destitute of grace.
Woe to grimalkin, or puppy, who inadvertently got in her
way at such times. If a "shoo" sufficed not to clear the
track—whiz! they went flying across the room, in obedi-

ence to a touch of her vigorous heel-tap. Equally luckless
the wight who preferred a request, or communicated a piece
of news. The request was certain of denial : the intelligence turned sour, and was spitefully thrown back into his
ears, with a few caustic remarks about tale-bearing and gossip.
The whole household respected her moods. Her children
feared, rather than loved her; and I also, in time, learned to
choose the appropriate seasons for approaching her; watching anxiously that stolid countenance, as a mariner studies
the changeful skies for winds propitious ; for clouds, dark,
restless, sullen—swift and sure portents of storms. She was
a zealous worshipper at the old Baptist "meetin'-house."
Rain, hail, or snow never wooed her to a warm fireside, on
the occasion of the weekly services. Duty was the god she
worshipped : she awarded it the guest-chamber in her heart.
Love, charity, and their caressing graces were silently shown
an obscure corner. Her very glance was a terror to evil-
doers; with eager edge it searched the countenance, detect-
ing each sign of guilt, and instinctively repelling propitiatory
confidence. Let me do her strict justice. Though her
virtues were of a harsher tint than was altogether pleasing,
yet they *were* virtues, all the same. She was impartial in
her treatment, on the whole, though chance occasions indicated a preference for her eldest son and daughter. Hers
was a nature which could not be softened into grace and
beauty by childish caresses—by material prosperity. The
first she instinctively scorned and repelled ; the latter only
made the angular lines more rigid, with suspicions of a
speedily approaching downfall. Debby, in private, declared
her "dreadful conceity, and allers a borrowin' sorrer;" but
she regarded her with awe, nevertheless, and zealously
endeavored to please her.

She punished me, if in her opinion I deserved it, exactly
as she did her own brood ; and such punishments, once resolved on, could never be averted or delayed one hour by
penitent entreaties.   She wielded the rod, inexorable as fate ;
stern and awful her countenance looked.   She would have
made a step-mother after the prevailing opinion of such
second-hand dames.   Strictly, justice would have been ad-
ministered ; rigidly, order would have been maintained ;
and turbulent riot and anarchy would have fled affrighted
and appalled at the sound of her advancing footsteps.

CHAPTER V.

FROM one of these rambles we came home late—as usual.
In our absence the kitchen had received a new occupant. A
middle-aged lady—strange to me—sat by the three-legged
light-stand, busily sewing.   She impressed me, though in
what way I could not tell, for her appearance was not extraordinary.   She wore a black and white calico dress, a long,
narrow, black alpaca apron, trimmed with gimp, decorated
with ample three-cornered pockets ; from these she drew strips
of gayly-figured chintz which she sewed together.   She was
evidently in mourning.   The sight of black garments always
distressed me : to brush them with my hand gave me a creeping sensation, something akin to placing a finger on a cold,
dead face ; suggesting to my mind their near kinship to the
shroud and the pall.   Such symbols of woe then I shunned.
But *this* image attracted, instead of repelling.   Her pale
yellow hair was pushed back from her forehead ; around it
was wound—several times—a long strip of narrow black vel-

vet, tied in a bow on one side. It was a pleasant, pale face, wrinkled a little; age, or care, had tracked a few footmarks on it, but they could not have been called disfiguring. The eyes were large, full,—in color a kindly blue. The brow rose above them high and prominent; a self-asserting brow; causality and memory unusually developed. A phrenologist would say at once that it was a strong, steady, reflective brow; a logical, patient thinker; persistent in argument, unyielding in debate. So much for her brief photograph.

She looked up pleasantly as the door opened, transferred her work to her left hand, and held out her right, which Demis caught and shook heartily.

"Why, Miss Charity, when did you come?" said she in surprise.

"Ef you'd a staid to hum, you'd a seen," very grimly interposed her mother, looking with great disfavor at Demis, and hastily scanning her circumference to discover probable rents. Demis—noting this—saucily swung herself in front of her mother, confident, for once, in being able to endure the scrutiny.

"You have come to begin school, I reckon?" was her cool address to the stranger.

"Yes! I hope you are glad," said Miss Charity; "you have had a long play-spell; all play and no work makes Jack a mere toy, you know." There was a quaint tremble in Miss Charity's voice, as if from emotion or weakness, which made one's voice soften sympathetically. I have observed it since in none but very aged people. Demis made a grimace. "I dont know about the *glad;* I suppose I must grin and bear it though."

"Demis Martin!" severely said her mother, eying her as if she had broken the whole string of the ten commandment

3*

beads. Demis pursued placidly, shrinking away a little from her mother, "Did you have a good school in Scrabbletown?"

"Pretty fair; there were *some* hard cases to manage, but, on the whole, nothing to speak of. Children will be children, you know," she added apologetically, turning to my aunt. That worthy compressed her thin lips still more decidedly. She gave back one brisk nod, as if to say, "I know all about the class, Miss Charity, more than *you* can ever tell me," and her flying knitting-needles kept time to her sharp, restless glances.

"Ah!" exclaimed Demis, pouncing upon the "schoolmarm's" work, "you are making more hussys. Those are for the last day, Ruby; perhaps you'll get one if you behave yourself; those pink and green ones are the prettiest." She chattered volubly. Miss Charity laughed softly.

"Do you really give them away?" I ventured to ask, shyly turning them over for inspection; cunning little pockets filled one side; some were finished, rolled neatly, and tied with bits of narrow satin ribbon.

"To my best little girls," she answered primly; "they are very handy to keep thread and needles in. I dare say you will get one," she finished, with prophetic kindness.

I was far from feeling sure of it; they looked like miraculous achievements; my eyes gleamed with covetousness, I am sure. To pass it off, I inquired, "And what do you give to the boys?"

"Oh!" interrupted Demis, kindling, "you should see. The prettiest little butterflies, and birds of all sizes, robin redbreasts, and blue jays, and oh!—lots of things. You paint as well as Mark does, Miss Charity," she finished eagerly, intending a compliment.

Aunt Rhoda's face gathered an additional frown, but she

restrained herself. Deborah, who sat in one corner darning hose, her knees tightly placed together and an iron candlestick planted thereon, which threatened every instant to topple over, and which she steadied with frequent nervous jerks and much dripping of tallow, looked up hastily at Demis, took off her glasses, rubbed them with the toe of a stocking, replaced them on her short thick nose, and—pursued her work. Poor Demis looked bewildered; she seemed to have struck the wrong chord all around, for the schoolmistress turned her face to the wall and wiped away fast dropping tears. Obeying a natural impulse, Demis went up and put her arm timidly around her neck, "I am sorry," she began softly.

"Wall, then, set down! do. You heave round so," returned her mother, shortly. Demis dropped into the nearest chair as if she had been shot. As if it had not taken thorough enough effect, her mother added another ball: "You're so heedless; allers hurtin' *somebody's* feelin's, and doin' what you hadn't oughter do. I wonder ef I ever *shall* break you of't." If Demis was quelled before—now she looked positively blue. She dared not speak.

"No, no. It was not what she said," the schoolmistress's voice quivered out, in eager deprecation. "I was only thinking that sister Submit used to paint them for me, and now I must do it alone."

"Yis! poor Summit is gone;" dolefully sighed my aunt, "but we shouldn't wish her back ag'in in this troublous world: jest think how she suffered: besides, you've others left." She knit on more vigorously for giving birth to this element of consolation.

"I know it," was the meek answer. "I do not repine, and we know that it is well with *her*. But her place in the

old homestead is empty, and whenever I think of her dresses
hanging just as she left them, and her Bible with her favorite
passages marked, and the vacant seat at the table, and know
that she is gone forever, that we never, never shall—" She
gathered up her work hurriedly, and left the room.

"I do wish, Demis, that you could learn to act like other
folks ; seems to me you're old enough, ef you're ever goin' to
be," commenced Aunt Rhoda, coldly.

I stooped to Deborah. "Where is Mark ?"

"Up-stairs I 'spose." She whispered, "Don't say nothin'
'bout his paintin' bus'ness afore Mrs. Martin. She's terrible
sot ag'inst it, you see. If you do there'll be war in the
wigwam. Massy to me! how she does let in 'pon poor
Demis !"

"Yis," Aunt Rhoda was saying, in a loud, hard tone, "I've
about gin up makin' any thing on you. I do my best, but I
can't beat nothin' inter you. You're gitten too old to whip
all the time, and you oughter be 'shamed to be spoke to so
much. It seems strange to *me*. *I* never was so. I'm sure
I don't know who you take after, and for my part—" I lost
the rest as I stole softly from the room.

In Mark's room I found Annah, gravely watching him as
he stooped low over some—writing, I thought. He started up
hastily and drew a newspaper over it. Then, to cover his
embarrassment, he lifted Annah to his knee and teased her
unmercifully, until Demis coming in a half-hour later plucked
her from her uneasy elevation, and indignantly remonstrated.

"Demie, how you *do* assume control over my actions;
but I'll say nothing more now; you look as if you had
been receiving a lecture."

"What are you doing up here ?" she returned, evasively.

When questioned, Mark rarely refused a true answer. He

drew out the hidden drawing, surveying it with a heavy look
of dissatisfaction. "Tell me what ails it! I tried to sketch
the glories of the new-born day: Greybaul lifting its proud
dome to the western skies; and the lustrous clouds, which
rock over, but dare not stoop to cradle it. It baffles me,
after all my efforts. It is so weak, so characterless, beside
the grand original. I should make a better copy than this,
else none at all." He swept the paper impatiently away.
"The truth is, I want masters," he added, dejectedly.

"Give it up, Mark!" pleaded his sister, with a quick,
anxious glance at his bright, earnest face. "You may as well,
first as last; for mother says it's all humbug. You'll never
amount to any thing until you do."

He laughed bitterly. "I do not see the matter with *her*
eyes."

"She just now said that you would never make a living,"
said Demis; "she told me to tell you her words."

"Ah! the dollars and cents are paramount to all else. A
'living," he echoed, commencing angrily to pace the room.
"Art is too glorious for such mean calculations. I would
not debase it to such a level if I could." He returned a
defiant stare to Demis's mournful gaze. She thought him,
his chivalrous assertion, his thoughtlessness for the morrow's
wants—sure to come—mere visionary babbling. He resumed—" And it cannot be bought and sold. It is a coy
mistress, hard to please, rewarding constant exertion with—
at the best—very uncertain favors: yet the mere touch of
her hand, the merest smile from her eyes, how delightful!
As if—he went on rapidly —painting God's immortal limnings of earth, sea, and sky; reproducing, though in the
humblest form, shadows, on which the eye may linger with
pleasure and profit, be not immeasurably superior to the

paltry monotony of doling out snuff and tobacco to the
meddlesome old maids of the village, even if one starve in
the former, and wax vulgarly fat in worldly store in the latter,
employment.　What is *your* opinion, Madame Rubina?"—
he faced me so suddenly, and with such a martial air, that I
laughed.　"Speak!" he peremptorily ordered.　"No driv-
elling, half-way thoughts either.　Shall I be a 'storekeeper'
and dutifully go into partnership with Ira Pierce, as my
father wishes? a Baptist elder (a pretty one I should make)
shouting out close-communion doctrine and infant damnation,
together with a thorough cold bath as the price of admission
to the fellowship of saints, according to my respected
mother's programme? or a poor devil of an artist—minus
every earthly possession, save the shadowy hope of one day
achieving that which will bring them all to my feet—the
alluring prospect of Fame, to which my own headstrong inclination incessantly points the way?"　He did not pause for
my answer, but went on impetuously : " Gods, what a fool's
business this life is! what are our inclinations given us for,
if we must never use them?　What good does our own will
do us if we are forever to hammer and mould it to fit others'
wills?　Why isn't *my* thought to be obeyed, *my* purpose
to be consulted, as well as those of one whom by a chance I
call my father—mother?"

"Our inclinations *are* for us to use.　If I were you I
should paint;" came my prompt answer, as he paused
breathless.

"Good; here's a monitress after my own heart.　Faith,
such sensible advice should be scrupulously followed." His
brow relaxed its form; his eye beamed on me a kindlier look
than it had ever yet worn.

"Because it's your own advice to yourself.　If I had said,

Mark, you are an ignorant dreamer, or shallow reasoner, you would have thrust me in anger from the room." I had much better have said nothing just then; he was too excited to reason as to motives. It was impossible to convince him that a truthful, if friendly, opinion had swayed me. He turned his back to me, and was silent—but not for long.

"Is that why you give me such counsel? because it suits with mine? Truly, my wrath is formidable."

"I do not fear it, or you, or any one living," I retorted, nettled at his injustice. He did not heed me: though sunny-tempered usually, at times he could be most cruel; his mother's strong temper now came uppermost; his laughing eye gave a gleam—cold as ice, rigid as stone.

"Away with such an opinion; away with your puny yellow face; what are you to me? or I to you? Let us each work out our own salvation." He snapped his fingers in my face most insolently.

Demis interposed in season to prevent a quarrel. "Bah! you are too enthusiastic by half. Ruby talks just so about Fame, and all that rubbish; for my part I don't believe in it. If there *is* any such thing, rest assured that it will never come to the Martin family. Come, Ruby; quick, quick; or we shall never get out of the room alive," she cried, opening the door hastily, as Mark came slowly toward her, his eyes like flint, and his face pale with anger. She reopened to thrust her head inside, with a provoking laugh, and say, "Good-night, dear! don't lose your senses before morning, and fancy yourself one of the old masters; it will be such a hideous disappointment when you wake to the reality."

A pang of sorrow shot through me, as we closed the latch on him, and that more mighty self, his earnest dreams: born but to die, is written on the best of them.

CHAPTER VI.

Miss Charity ruled her pupils with absolute sway. She taught thoroughly. In the crowded school-room sounded a perpetual hum of voices. She especially affected the young; exercising over them an almost maternal care. In one corner was spread a few blankets, with pillows, for the use of the juveniles when too tired or sleepy to remain quiet. They were promptly transferred to this couch, at the first symptoms of restlessness; and there always was a row of heads on the pillows—limbs diverging therefrom, necessitating a frequent application of Miss Warner's method, of kicking them gently into order. Around them ranged the noisy classes: "bounding the States," or repeating, in powerful sing-song concert, that immortal stumbling-block to young minds—"the multiplication table;" keeping perfect time to the rising and falling of Miss Charity's willow wand, which not unfrequently swerved from its legitimate direction, to course slyly toward some dodging delinquent from duty. Her mode of instruction was peculiarly unique; consisting mainly of useful lessons from a book of her own arranging, though "Colborne" and good old "Peter Parley" were also her stanch allies. The road to learning is not essentially an easy one to travel. Still less delightful the unthankful task of turning back from the hard-won heights, to cheer on the laggard; to infuse life into the inane—the almost hopeless dolt. Miss Charity was an able general. She proclaimed war against sloth. She opposed a pale, firm resistance to the lowly wayside flowers, blossoming here and there over the stony path. She tolerated no turning aside from the plain duty of the school-room. This was—in her expressive phrase—"storing your minds with useful knowledge." Accordingly, the rosy-cheeked apples, which little Bessie Cole brought in her blue gingham pocket, thinking to munch slyly while conning her lesson, were, after one tantalizing bite, promptly singled out by the preceptress's keen eye, and transferred to the interior of the red desk. Up would fly the cover, a moment later, to admit a round handful of chestnuts, the abstraction of Eleil Pierce's pocket, while she looked with dismay at the pile of dismantled shells already littering the clean, white floor.

Oh! the treasures that inexorable cover revealed to peeping eyes, when momently uplifted! Jew's-harps lying, twangless, beside peaceable fish-hooks, destined never to be baited; huge balls, compiled from strips of rubber over-shoes, and yarn from ravelled stockings; bunches of stout twine, which often returned to their former masters in a shape not wholly agreeable; drops of reddish spruce-gum, from the tiny mouth-piece, which Demis had to stand and deliver, to the unmanageable one belonging to stout Robert Jones; popped corn; bits of slate-pencils; smooth, white pebbles; fragments of chalk; gay-ringed allies, given up with pathetic sobs. It was rather mysterious, what became of the fruit and nuts. Day after day, month after month, the uneatable articles remained under cover, with constantly increasing additions, while their ripe, juicy neighbors disappeared from the fold in the ratio of the fresh arrivals.

Miss Warner's crowning glory was the annual examination, when—the parents of her charges being present—she displayed to their astonished vision such an orderly array of jackets and pinafores as seldom dawned on Northfield; when, prompt to an intelligent nod or wink, up rose, noise-

lessly, the appropriate class, volubly reciting their lesson.
Admiring whispers greeted "The History of the Bible,"
successfully recited; closing with a "Hymn," repeated in
concert, and the "Ten Commandments." Then, "The Seasons," in like manner; "The Senses," and "Punctuation."
What trembling lips commenced the long list of "Abbrevia-
tions?"—learned with many flutterings of heart—lest, after
all our anxious labor, the memory hold insecure tenure of
the property committed to its care, and that woful happen-
ing "to miss" occur. Each countenance involuntarily
brightened when success safely bridged this doubt, and the
murmuring plaudits of the spectators swept away all misgivings for the grand, poetical close. Poor Phebe's mishap
with the blackberries was pathetically related by Demis:
to my lot fell the soothing answer. Another propounded
"The Golden Rule." One luckless wight—after a bewildering obeisance—with outstretched hand and frightened eyes,
was safely through ten verses of "Who made the Stars?"
when his star of memory suddenly set, and confusion overwhelmed the young orator. The most notorious truant in
town dutifully recited, "Early to School without Delay;"
and little Johnny Tucker glibly brought up the rear with—
"See me—I am a little boy, who goes to infant school;
and though I am but four years old, I'll prove I am no fool."
I heartily hope that he *is* proving it now, out in the world's
school of manhood, unless the great seal of silence has been
pressed on his lips, closing forever his earthly tuition. Then,
the presents were speedily distributed; the aforesaid "housewives" to the girls, the butterflies and birds to the boys.
The silver medal, with the blue ribbon, which throughout
the year had paid nightly pilgrimages to each pupil's home—
the reward for approved conduct during the day, was now

suspended around the neck of Avis Pierce, a gift for good behavior. She was reserved and melancholy in temperament, so she bore her honors, without betraying a single flutter of pride. Indeed, she looked as if she would unhesitatingly barter them—together with her naturally fine talents—for a meagre portion of the other's gay assurance. I have known her to combat with her overpowering bashfulness until her eyes glowed with a fierce light, wholly unnatural. She hated herself—and you for noticing it. At times, she seemed to loathe everything human, and, finally, grinding her teeth, she would mutter: "If I could only get away from it, and I *will* some day. I'll live alone." Then, the reaction, with tears silently falling for hours. When questioned she answered coldly. Nothing but real interest —pressed anxiously—would move the stream of sluggish confidence; then, with averted head, she would mutter, as if wholly ashamed of the weakness which led her to confide, and of the paltry nature of the confession: "I am *so* miserable; I wish I was dead." Yet, her mind was of the finest order; she easily mastered the hardest tasks, far outstripping her brother and sister in all mental races. To outward, dull perceptions, no ingredient seemed lacking to render existence palatable. What was the power which so cruelly dwarfed the social faculties, while it hurried on with headlong zeal the intellectual? It was not selfishness craving satisfaction— vanity beseeching admiration. A ray of genuine pleasure crossed her wan face when asked to bestow a favor—only to be chased too quickly away by some hidden, chilling suspicion. It was not the absorbed, student thirst, despairing of being quenched in repletion, which so distressed her, and rendered life a burden of evil: she prized not her easily won honors. Some morbid tendency in her grand intellect needed to be firmly—speedily uprooted, that utter waste be not spread over it. But whose the loving, tender, cautious hand to do it? How speak, and to whom, of a fear so vague? of a tendency apparently so groundless?

It was Miss Warner's custom to invite one of the older girls to pass a week at her own home when school closed. I was not especially pleased at being this time selected. A week's separation from Demis and Annah seemed endless. To increase this disinclination, Mark solemnly hinted of indescribable gnomes, haunting the great house, making hideous noises at dead of night, and suddenly retreating to secret hiding cells, at all investigating attempts: of horrid bats, flapping slimy wings on the walls of the sleeping-room, even profaning the old carved headboards.

"I have never seen them, and I have spent more than one week there," interrupted Demis.

"We may as well bid her farewell, with weeping hair and disordered eyes," he pursued, reflectively: "I have serious doubts—a presentiment, as Deb would say—about this visit. Strange, the old maids never ask boys to go—no timidity to scare away researches, &c."

"Boys are a very valiant race, I know," said Demis, with quiet sarcasm. "I am no hand at story-telling——."

"I hope not, indeed," he ejaculated, seriously; "bear in mind their awful portion."

"But I will recall one incident for Ruby's edification," she proceeded, not noticing his interruption. Mark commenced whistling as she related the story.

"You have set out your brother well as a coward, Demic, and made a good story for yourself into the bargain," he soberly began, when just at this critical juncture Amanda burst into the room.

"This is a pretty how d'ye do;" she said, snappishly—
"Here I've spent the whole of this blessed morning, slaving
myself to death, and what do you think I've got to show
for it?"

"Oh! oceans and seas of sweet cake, frosted and unfrost-
ed, plain and mixed, plums and no plums, and so forth, and
so on, *ad infinitum*," answered Mark, speedily rallying from
the effects of the narrative.

"I oughter have enough to be decent, and *did* have this
noon, but if you'll believe me, I can't find hide nor hair of
but jest two kinds, and one of *them* is gingerbread. I baked
five, as true as my name is 'Mandy Jane Martin," she angrily
spouted.

"Pray add, which you are hoping to exchange for 'Mandy Jane Pierce," laughed Mark.

"You're poking fun at me; you always do if I say a word."

"Not for worlds, my lovely sister. I was simply stating
a self-evident truth. Now, if you will relax that frown a
trifle—it's angle is too acute for your style of beauty—oh!
don't go,—I'll tell you about your cookery. I suspect it's
having two appreciative listeners, as the minister says, on
Sugar-loaf hill. I saw Natty go off with suspiciously full
pockets, and Dwight shortly after followed."

"I never!" she retorted. "I declare 'taint possible to
hide any thing in *this* house, so's *they* can't find it. I put
that cake in the big tin milk-pail, and set it under the north-
room bed, and smoothed the valance down ag'in. I knew
they'd hunt, 'cause they see me a picking over raisins; but
it beats the Dutch how they find every thing."

"You should be thankful that they left *any*," subjoined
the consoling brother.

"I wish they hadn't, for then I could have excused it to

the girls; now, they won't believe I had any more, and they'll go away, and call me stingy. *I* know 'em of old. It's too late to make any more. I expect 'em every min-nit." She banged the door, and went off muttering.

Demis laughed indulgently. Mark carelessly thrust his hands in his pockets, whistling Yankee Doodle. Uncle Joe, who was smoking out of the window, slowly drew in his head, closed the sash, knocked the ashes from his pipe, and while his dark eyes beamed with fun, whispered to me slyly " It's jest as I used to do. Strange now, how they all take arter me in mischief!"

Deborah was suspected of aiding and abetting these dep-redations; she could deny them nothing: she covered their delinquencies with a pall of excuses, never lifted save by their severe mother, for the bestowal of merited reproof or chastisement. Deborah called them " babies yet," incapa-ble of knowing better. Why is it that the youngest nurs-lings in the family flock, are, in our eyes, never grown up? Even if gray hairs streak the dark glossy locks, and shy wrin-kles loiter curiously round the once smooth brow, still, our memory, fondly dating backward, transmutes them to our visions as "mere young things;" their caprices to be pardoned, their whims indulged. In reality, these were no delicate scions of the parental tree; they needed no hothouse cher-ishing. Wholesome restraint, when away from their moth-er's eye, was shaken off, like a threadbare garment. No room was sacred from their reckless rummaging, except one the " parlor bedroom," in which lingered traditions of ghosts and corpses, there " laid out," which they dared not brave even by daylight, and in which repugnance even the older ones shared.

Natty led these searches for plunder, sharing the proceeds

with his soberer brother. He purloined Mark's sketches, to present to some favorite playmate; or to paste, as a figure-head, on a kite. He tumbled his sister's drawers, in search of a knot of ribbon, and boxes for angle-worms. He abstracted Amanda's love-letters, thereby producing great mental fluttering, and innumerable bribes of lumps of sugar to restore the precious papers. He invaded my scanty possessions. He dressed himself in Deborah's ample, blue checked robes,—filling out the loose proportions with bolsters and pillows,—at pleasure. Once, he even donned his mother's best cap, bombazine apron, and spectacles, and appeared to her horrified gaze, in the dairy. He sometimes wrought his courage up to the pitch of personating ghostly inhabitants, by the disguising aid of sheets and a floury face; and paid nocturnal visits, only to be quickly scared away by a view of his own apparition in the mirror. Innumerable the pranks with which he electrified the house; his adventurous spirit seemed ever on the alert to discover the germ of some new, promising frolic. How we loved and caressed him! How his merry spirit brought sunshine to chase away shadows, disposed to linger. Dear little Nathaniel! You tormented me sorely at times; many an alien pang you plunged, keen and glittering, in my side. Yet it never lingered long; no malice corroded it; no genuine unkindness turned its sharp edge rusty. It was only the glitter of fun's bright weapon; the unconquerable spirit of mischief's transient sting.

CHAPTER VII.

Miss Charity was not sent for from home that night. At the breakfast-table she descried " the grays " leisurely trotting down the long hill, sloping before and beyond the farmhouse, only to ascend in a steeper elevation. Over the summit of this second hill, arises the neat, white homestead of Farmer Pierce. Miss Charity finished hastily, and started up: " There's Brother Jesse ; he never likes to wait." She darted up-stairs with the agility of fifteen years. I prepared to follow, in more leisurely fashion.

" Bless me," said Demis, " you don't look much as if you was going a pleasuring, my child,"—she still assumed the maternal prerogative. Deborah here took me aside.

" Now don't look so down in the mouth about it. They mean well by you, and think it an honor; they'll feel dredful curus ef you come any high strikes on 'em." I interrupted her by an indignant exclamation, but she raised her hand authoritatively. " Mabbe 'twill be a leetle lonesome at the fust start ; they're a strange set of 'em ; but a week's soon over. ' Time and Tide wait for no man ;' that's true as gospil preachin', Ruby. It used to be set for my copy, as long ago's I went to school to old David Butterfield, and it struck me so, I ain't never forgot it. Now, go and put on your roas'-meats, for he's hitched his hosses, and's comin' in. He sets his life by them critturs," she added aside to Aunt Rhoda, as his heavy tramp resounded on the piazza.

" Uncle Jesse entered shivering, and greeted us with his own heartiness of manner. He advanced, and spread his great brown palms before the hot kitchen stove. "Wall, this ere's putty tough weather for spring, Square," said he.

"Yis, we may look out for *any* kind in March; she's a proper skittish month," responded Uncle Joel, "she come in like a lamb, and she'll go out like a lion, most likely. I never knew that are to fail."

" 'A roarin' lion,' " added Mr. Warner, with a humorous twinkle in his keen gray eye, " ' seekin' whatsomever it may devour,' which, in *my* 'pinion, means hands and noses; them's what suffers most in this keen wind. I tell *you* it cuts like a razor." He clapped his broad hands to his glowing cheeks to obliterate the stinging remembrance. "How's your health, Mrs. Martin, now-a-days? poorly, as usual, I suppose?" he added, with a chuckle. Uncle Jesse Warner always grew facetious with favorable surroundings.

"Yis, I hold out consid'rable well. Ef I didn't, I don't know what would become of us all: most likely we'd all go to the poor-house afore the year's out," she answered, darting a severe glance at her good-natured spouse.

"Poh! Rhody, we ha'int come to that pass yit, I calculate. Law! she thinks"—turning to his guest—"that nobody don't do nothin' in this house but jest herself. She's a dredful smart woman though, I admit," he added, as she tied on her long, woollen apron, and departed to see after her cheeses. "She gin'rally keeps up fust-rate sperrits, but she's a leetle down in the mouth lately—you see, we did'nt sell off our cheeses last fall; don't bring but four cent a pound in market, and so I held on to 'em; wall, it sort o' frets her, I see. Then, too, 'bout Mark—"

"Why, what about him?" asked his listener, anxiously.

"Wall, I don't want it to go no further; but seein's it's *you*, I don't care ef I tell," he answered, reaching down his

4

pipe, and pressing its cavity full of tobacco. "Have a smoke!"—he offered it to Mr. Warner.

"No," said the latter; "I smoked jest afore I left hum. I do that allers, to settle my breakfast."

"Wall," resumed Uncle Joel, slowly puffing great blue clouds out into the room, and placidly eyeing me as I stood, hooded and shawled, by the window: "you see she's sot her heart on our oldest boy's bein' a gospil preacher ever since he was—oh, *so* high! I've heerd her lot on it to beat all. She took a notion that he was called of the Spirit, and, like Samuel of old, born a child of God. I could'nt never see 's he was a bit different from the rest, that come along arter him; maybe he was fuller of his jokes, but *that* ain't no great recommend for a preacher. Wall, this is neither here nor there; the gist of the business is this, Jesse. The lad is crazy to be a painter: he's got some idee 'bout bein' a big man; makin' us all proud on him; and I don't know what."

"Do tell now," said Mr. Warner, agbast. "Law! I guess the lad is a leetle out of his head; I don't think painters amount to much. There's Seth Gibbs now, down to 'Thunder,' *he's* one on 'em, and he don't know much more'n enough to go in when it rains."

"Oh," hastily interrupted Uncle Joel, "I don't mean *that* kind o' paintin'; any body can daub over fences and housen, I s'pose——"

I broke in grandly, with a proud toss of my head: "He means to be an artist; to paint beautiful landscapes, and portraits; and I quite approve the plan."

"You do, eh!" said Mr. Warner, laughing. "Another rebellious sperrit in your house, Square. Sister Roby says you'll hev your hands full one of these days, a tryin' to bring 'em all under."

"Wall!" said Uncle Joel, simply, "I dun know as I want to; they're well 'nough; though Rhody does say sometimes that 't seems to her as ef Satan's broke loose."

"'Spose we hear our ambitious little woman's plans for *herself*," said Mr. Jesse, quietly. I laughed.

"Oh, I mean to be a teacher like your sister, but I shall not *always* teach, of course."

"Of course not;" he echoed. "How can we expect it? Children now-a-days begin life when *we* leave off. Eh, Mr. Martin?"

"Yis, Jesse; you see she's as bad as Mark. They've *all* got great idees; and the Lord only knows where they'll bring up. Amanda's the only one who sides with her mother. As for me I'd jest as lief the lad would settle down, near hum, in some likely trade. I don't want none on 'em to slave as I've done all my days; and I ain't no more fore-handed than I was thirty years ago."

"But you keep out o' debt, and that's somethin'; that's 'bout all I manage to do," returned Mr. Jesse, cheerily.

"I dun know 'bout *that*, neighbor. B'tween you and me and the whippin' post, I'm 'fraid I shan't make a raise of the int'rest money this year; and that are mor'gage looks like a mountain. Sometimes I think I may as well give up beat fust as last, for I shall never be able to lift it off, high and dry, in all this world."

"Pshaw," said Mr. Jesse, "your boys'll help you."

"Wall, it'll come 'pon me so by spells, though I don't never mean to let these things move me, as Rhody does. It puts her all out o' kilter. I tell her 'taint no sort o' use bor-rowin' trouble; it comes fast 'nough of itself; but law! ef 'taint *one* thing she's worryin' 'bout, it's 'tother. I tell her it's a long lane that never turns."

"That's true as the Book of Numbers, Square—what on airth can keep Sister Charity so ? I must git hum to do the chores."

"How are the girls ?" interrupted his sister entering, fully equipped, with boxes and bundles.

"Wall, 'bout so, so; Sister Crete's ruther down at the heel; had one of her poor spells last night——"

He broke off to tuck the worn buffalo robes carefully around us. "It seems kinder curus, Ruby, that 'twas *mo* you fust got 'quainted with here. Lordy ! how sorry I did feel for them two leetle gals that night, comin' 'mong entire strangers. Wall, wall, that's all gone by. Now look there," he continued, pointing to the great Warner mansion, rising bold and bare of enveloping trees, out of the keen, frosty landscape. We turned to the right, and we lost the view. "You'll see 'em all on the look-out, when we git nigh 'nough. That's their way. They look me out o' sight when I start off anywhere ; ef 'taint mor'n to go down to the village arter a pound of resins, or an ounce of salarostus, for sister Siny to cook with, and when I git back, there they be still."

Miss Charity smiled. "You know the reason, I hope, brother," she said, with a fond upward glance at his homely, heartsome visage, seamed and scarred, by the destructive forces of wind, toil, and care, which latter plant the deepest furrows. She proceeded softly, "You know you are all the one we've got; so it behooves us to make the most of you, and guard carefully our human treasure, lest, inadvertently, some covetous wretch see, long for, aud, in a twinkling, whisk it away. Now, if we had more of the same staunch article, you might never have occasion to complain of receiving too much attention from a pack of spinster sisters.".

He looked bewildered. "She's actilly a laughin' at me,

Ruby--*me*, the lord of the manor, as that Inglish feller down 't'the factories' says so often 'bout his old stun mill. I'll have to take her in hand, won't I?" he continued thought-fully, the smile fading from his purple lips. "It's a pack that melts through into single Injun file fast enough. There's many a true word spoken in jeest, sister Charity, and I don't b'lieve in handlin' such things very often; but I must say I'm glad there ain't no more on us, to go, one by one, down to the old fam'ly buryin' ground. There's enough now, to keep our hearts a breakin' slowly for more years to come than I like to look forrard to. Verily, it's a world of vanity, and vexation of sperrit; we only git red of one burden, afore an-other bundle, jeest as heavy, is piled onto our shoulders. I tell you we can't shirk sorrer."

"True!" answered his sister, sadly. "In Adam all die; how then can our household band hope to escape it? Con-sumption eats at our vitals, and poisons our life-springs. I suppose there is no cure for it; but we know for surety that 'in Christ all shall be made alive,' and our scattered family reunite on the farther shore of Jordan. *There's* where we must found our anchor, brother Jesse; the cold stream itself would wash it, and us with it, speedily away; perhaps its rushing torrent bear us onward to dreadful regions." She drew a little, hopeless sigh, which said plainly: "It is a hard, bitter, forced resignation, springing from necessity, not born of content. Under its stern decree, present separation we must submit to. Let us therefore summon what remains to us of Christian fortitude."

"Wall, I know it, but somehow it don't seem to go to the spot," resumed her brother, who was seldom long silent. "I'm nothin' but a selfish creetur, arter all's said and done. I laid awake the live-long night a hearin' sister Crete's dry,

hackin' cough; she was dreadful distressed for breath, by
spells, and made a sound in breathin' like raspin' files.
Wall, I couldn't git it out o' my head; it went through
and through, like one o' Satan's devices we read about, and
oughter to forgit, but *can't*, somehow, for the life of us; and
when I got up this mornin', and see how 'twas a wear-
in' on her out, I was clean discouraged; I felt as though
we's the most afflicted family in all Northfield town. I tell
you I swallowed a purty big lump o' rebellion afore I did
my breakfast. Arterwards I found that other folks hev *their*
trials and tribulations, too, even ef they *don't* come in the
same shape as our'n."

"What changed your mind, brother Jesse?" asked his
sister, a little curiously.

"Oh, a triflin' sarcumstance; nothin' to speak of," he rejoined, evasively. "But I discover, the longer I live, that
truer words wa'n't never spoken than these: 'Ev'ry heart
knoweth its own bitterness.' What makes *one* forlorn soul
weak and sore, another wouldn't mind a straw, and viccy
versey. I tell you, we are measured and fitted for trouble,
jest as Silas Peckham, down to the holler, measures me for
a new go-to-meetin' suit, once ev'ry five year; and what
don't b'long to us by right, is clipped off, ev'ry inch on't,
jest as *he* trims his superfine broadcloth; he don't give me
any more than my statur needs, you know. Wall! my
opinion is the Lord won't nuther," he concluded, earnestly.

"Yes," said his sister, with solemn slowness, "but death
comes to all hearts alike, as the most terrible, most dreaded of evils. Poverty, obscurity, ignominy, crime even,
are counted as naught before this merciless scourge. There
is a hope that we may rise above and beyond the reach of
the others, after a time; this pursuer there is no escaping.

On mountain-tops, in the green valley, in city and country, beneath the waves of ocean, he seeks and finds his prey."

" Wall," broke in Uncle Jesse, warmly, " I don know 'bout some o' that doctrine. I've seen some folks, now," he pursued, reflectively, " proper good neighbors, church members too, and all that, who I don't 'spect would come under that harness. They don't seem to think losin' their connection the greatest evil ; bear up under it 'amazin' easy and calm like ; mabbe it's the resurrection hope that spurs up their sperrits so soon ; afore they're cold in the ground, as you may say."

" At any rate, we are not to be their judges, brother Jesse," returned Miss Charity, half rebukingly. " Here we are at the turn," she added, after a pause. " Now, if you do not start up the grays, the girls will get tired of watching for their bonnie brother."

The brother complied. The grays pricked up their ears, mended their pace, and, rounding the corner, cantered into the great yard, in flourishing style. I stole a peep at the windows. I counted four heads peering curiously out, ere they darted into an obscure background. Only one ventured to the threshold. She greeted Miss Charity most affectionately, at the same time offering to take her bundles.

" Come, little Miss Brook," said my kind host, gayly, as I sat staring stupidly at them, " you're too venturesome a little woman to want to set here all day, *I'm* sure, so give a jump ; there you be ; feel a little cramped, don't you, a settin' so long." I laughed at his good-natured raillery. " Here, sister Siny," he sang out to his sister, who was looking after her sister's boxes, " I s'pose you've seen this ere young woman at meetin' lots o' times, so there's no need o' makin' you acquainted. To tell the truth," he muttered to himself as he unhitched the horses, "I never was no hand at them sort o' things. Siny, now, 's a master-hand at it."

Miss Sinai gave a cheerful little chuckle. "I see, Ruby, that we must manage without an introduction."

She looked about thirty: plump, fresh, wholesome, red-cheeked, with mild brown eyes, and hair to match—rather scanty, it is true—done up in a twist behind, crowned with a high-topped shell comb; dimples played fitful games around her mouth, and ripe red lips offered such attractions that I involuntarily put up mine for a kiss. She was busy, and did not see the action; her brother did, and laughed heartily. She turned quickly; I renewed the pantomime, and, stooping, she drew me close to her bosom, bestowing not one, but a dozen kisses."

"That's allers the way. They allers want a kiss from sister Siny, every chick and child in ' the Centre.' I kinder hanker for one myself," said Uncle Jesse, fondly.

"Do you indeed? Stoop then!" she gayly cried, and as he complied, they gravely exchanged a salute. She turned to me merrily. "Don't tell any one, Ruby, what a pair of old fools we are. You see how childish he is getting, and as he is all the one I have to spoil, I suppose I must humor his whims once in a while."

More good-natured retorts between the two; then she took my cold hand in her warm, soft palm, and led me into the sitting-room—from which, as we entered, we heard feet scudding hastily. Only "the schoolmarm" was sitting quietly by the fire; alternately removing her wrappings of sacks and shawls, and warming her hands by the genial flame.

"Now," said Miss Sinai, carrying off my bonnet and shawl, "my dear Ruby, you are *my* visitor remember, and I want you to make yourself at home. Go wherever you like;

we don't keep locked doors here, and you will find the latch-string out before every one."

How blithe and merry she was. I scouted the idea of her being an "old maid." No! that she was not, and never could be. How pleasantly her voice echoed through the corners of the great room : it was low and sweet; free from the nasal accent and strong pronunciation of her brother's speech, or the prim decisiveness of Miss Charity's. She was too buxom to be mistaken for a sylph. Dark "merrimac, warranted to wash," cannot be considered as proper robes for a romantic heroine. Romantic! she would have scorn-fully repelled the insinuation, as something of which to be ashamed. Daily, toilful care is a poor nourisher of senti-ment; the weak plant sickens and dies in such rugged soil. Luxurious ease is its best foster-mother. So, though Miss Sinai read "Thaddeus of Warsaw" by stealth, in her room, at night, and wandered through the fascinating pages of "Alonzo and Melissa," and conned—half awe-struck—the direr horrors of "The Children of the Abbey," she came out in the morning as fresh and blithesome as before ; as ready to put her plump shoulders to the wheel of work, and send it rolling merrily around the old domain. It was merely a peep at the fabulous world of the novelist, vouchsafed to the weary work-day spirit, to lighten a little the dull pressure of the material. She always closed this indulgence with an elastic shake of the head, and the ejaculation, "Stuff and nonsense, every bit."

I liked to watch her as she flitted from room to room, a sub-stantial, self-denying, handsome household fairy; her sleeves rolled to her shoulders, displaying *such* arms, round, white, and plump, with soft curves at the elbows, tapering slowly to the small, dimpled wrists, and losing their identity in the

4*

perfect hands—marvels of symmetry, small and fair. No
mawkish rings tarnished their soft outlines. Miss Sinai re-
pudiated jewelry. Her delicate ears had never undergone
the torturing puncture with darning-needle and black silk—
perseveringly wielded by a fanatical grandmother. Indeed,
the wearer of long, third-rate pendents she denounced as
"factory-fied," and treated to a species of unspoken, good-
humored disdain. Neither did a flaming circlet of red,
green, or blue stones, in a rim of shining metal, proclaim its
individuality from its appropriate throne : she laughed down
"breast-pins." Neat little silk-fringed cravats, tied gracefully around her slender throat, were her sole adornment.
We grew at once confidential. She had the rare faculty
of removing from a guest's mind the uneasy strangeness of a
first visit. Directly, she had invested me with a charming
sense of home-finding. I seemed always to have known her :
already I began to look forward with regret to the week's
close. She attracted, she magnetized me ; and I followed
her as she flew. in and out, about her work.

"Where are your sisters?" I asked, in the course of the
morning. She was stooping over the fireplace, preparing
dinner ; either the heat or my abrupt question sent a vivid
glow to her face.

"Well," she whispered, after a pause, "you see, they like
company to come as well as I do, but they are so bashful that
it takes them a little while to wear it off."

"That's why they ran away as you opened the door this
morning?" She nodded. "I saw them at the windows.
They need not be afraid of me," I resumed—philosophically
adding, "I'm nothing but a little girl yet, Aunt Rhoda says."

"Oh, they'll be sociable enough after they see you once ;
all but sister Crete ; she is no great talker at any time."

"She is the sick one?   I have heard of her."

"Yes!" she answered, sadly.   "She has got the consumption.   We shall all have it some day."

"*You* won't," I pronounced decisively.   "*You* haven't got narrow shoulders; Deborah says *that* is a symptom."

She shook her head dissentingly.   "That's all stuff, Ruby. It's an hereditary disease.   I have never heard of but one cure for it, and that is equal to none; nothing would induce one of us to try it."

"Does Miss Charity know of it?   She said there was *no* cure for consumption."

· "Yes, she knows, but probably did not count this a remedy, though I have heard marvellous stories about its success; but, of course, they are all moonshine: I don't believe them."

"What is it?" I asked, curiously.   She looked at me a little doubtfully, before answering.

"It's to open the grave, after a certain time has elapsed— I forget how long,—to take the heart from the body, and burn it."

"Oh! Miss Sinai," I exclaimed, in horror.

"Hush!" she whispered, "don't speak so loud.   Charity may hear us.   Their theory is, you know, that some material tie, or a sort of invisible cord, binds the hearts of a family together, which can only be severed in this manner.   They say the one who dies, draws the next after her, to the grave, by this means; and by rendering her powerless, the others live the longer."

"Why, it's worse than to be a cannibal," I exclaimed, vehemently; "do you think there is any thing in it?"

"No, indeed; it's too heathenish a code.   I had rather die to-morrow than know of its being practised."

Dinner was now served.   After several summonses, the shy

sisters entered the room, in a body. Miss Lucretia, who was emaciated, wasted to the consistency of a shadow, coughed constantly. Miss Roby, a tall, gaunt woman, who reminded me involuntarily of the "gnomes," at which Mark hinted, she looked so surly; her harsh, iron-gray hair, frizzled, uncombed, and unconfined around her hard, wrinkled face, lending it additional· sternness. She wore a dark calico gown, of an immense flowered pattern; a round cape of the same, trimmed with deep, full ruffles, was pinned around her shoulders; the gored skirt, destitute of gathers, save a hand's-breadth behind, clung curveless to her long, lank figure, and, terminating several inches above her leather shoes, left bare a pair of ankles not remarkable for beauty, either of shape or size. Miss Zilpha, who was likewise old, gray, and thin. She wore spectacles, to conceal her bleared eyes and their inflamed lids. She wore a string of huge gold beads round her red, pimply throat, for the supposed benefit—cure was out of the question—of a scrofulous swelling under her chin. She helped herself profusely to snuff, after seating herself at the table, despite a prohibiting sign from Miss Sinai, who played the part of hostess. Then she drew from her pocket a small square of blue calico, and smoothed it over her knees for a napkin.

"I like snuff, and I ain't noways 'shamed to let big bugs know it," she muttered, crossly.

Miss Sinai looked dismayed at Miss Charity; they both sighed, and said nothing. Uncle Jesse did not *say* grace; they all *thought* it; an interval of profound silence followed, at which I marvelled inwardly. They called it "considering." It was a custom borrowed from the "Shakers," of which strange fraternity their mother had been a member. Escaping, while yet young, from their tyrannical control, and marrying a sober farmer, she became, in form, one of the "world's people;" but a few old habits she still retained, training her children to their observance.

A more diverse family group I have never since seen; in face, form, speech, dress, and manner, none akin. And, as in outward traits, their thoughts and opinions partook no less strongly of this robe of individuality. They could never be reasoned into accepting each other's views of a subject under family discussion, though their strong family affection one to another, usually yielded a knotty point, accompanied with a knowing nod, which said clearly, " I *could* say a deal more if I chose; but if it gives you any comfort to have your own way, take it! *I* don't care." Not but that the debate *sometimes* grew hot; especially between Miss Roby and Miss Zilpha. Not unfrequently a pungent sarcasm peppered the opposite ranks, and produced temporary confusion and dismay among the ruffled cap-borders, causing the defeated logical belligerents to beat a hasty retreat from the field. These sparring tilts occurred only at their reunion at meals; at all other times they were marvellously agreed; or perhaps they were too busy to waste time in empty argument.

This dinner was my initiation into their ways; though Miss Sinai, by gay prattle, and constant attention to their wants, and beseeching glances to Miss Charity—who amply seconded her efforts—strove to ward off all topics which might induce controversy. Her eye sought Uncle Jesse's constantly; but his blunt, kindly orbs were unconscious of any feminine meaning. He unwittingly opened the Lyceum, while distributing to each a generous plateful of " parsnip stew," served on a mammoth round pewter platter, and emitting an appetizing fragrance. " Wall, gals, I was down to old Deacon Nortrop's, this forenoon. He's going to kill a beef critter to-morrow," he serenely observed.

"I s'pose you spoke for a quarter, as usual, Jesse; but we don't want any on't. I'll be bound it's as tough as old Golding, and *that* was mor'n anybody could make way with," put in Miss Roby, in a gruff, dictatorial tone.

She was the possessor of the gruffest voice ever bestowed on woman. Nature is a capricious dame. She fashioned Sinai in a freak of melting tenderness; over the white firm flesh she breathed life's rose-color. She whispered the vocal organs to life, and they woke grateful responses of soft, bell-like melody. Proud grace swayed each careless movement. To her sister had been awarded a more grudging legacy: she was moulded like a grenadier. The frisky dame looked at her offspring with disenchanted eyes; some utterance she must have certainly: she was not to be a pet and plaything: she was formed for action. A rumbling sub-base fell to her share.

And here was Nature's whim, transversed: Sinai, the anxious helper; Roby—the week *I* saw her—an idle grumbler.

"How do you know we don't want any?" jerked out Miss Crete—alternating each word with a spasmodic cough.

"*I* know, and that's enough;" chimed in Miss Zilpha, looking hard at me through her green glasses. She was conceited enough to imagine herself the family oracle. "If we ever git out of any thing in the house, come to *me*. *I'll* tell you, brother Jesse," she finished, with a complacent smirk of her thin, faded lips.

"You need't take the trouble," he answered, dryly. "You have more pressin' matters to see to; openin' and shuttin' that are snuff-box, that's got George the Third's humly old pictur painted on the led."

"He's a real pritty man," she affirmed stoutly, "and why shouldn't I have his pictur on't?"

"'Cause you oughter be a better Dimocrat than all *that* comes to," he said firmly. "All the Warners, ever sence the battle of Bunker Hill—where Grand'ther Seth fell by a British bullet—hev hated the very thought of a redcut worse'n pizon."

"Law! you git things all mixed up endways," she retorted with scorn. "He wa'n't shot at Bunker Hill, and a Whig isn't a Britisher."

He went on, not heeding the interruption. "And I remember when our father died, he called me to his bedside and charged me over and over again never to be a turncut; 'Stick to the good old Dimocracy, Jesse;' them's his very words; I haint forgot 'em, and never will. I've allers bin a Dimocrat, and I mean to live and die one."

"Do! for pity's sake," again shot out Miss Zilpha. Unheeding her, he still pursued: "I remember 'fore father died, he sent for old Cap'n Nortrop to come up'n see him; wull, he come post-haste. I wasn't in the room: I heerd him say to the Cap'n, 'I want you to be one o' my pall-bearers, and take charge o' my funeral: you're the only one o' my old cronies as haint gone over to the Whigs. I mean to die as I've lived—a good Baptist and Dimocrat, and I hope you'll do the same, Cap'n.' Wall, I wan't nothin' but a shaver, then, but I thought Cap'n Nortrop looked kinder conscience smit, when they shook hands on't—and he *did* begin to say somethin' 'bout who he voted for last town-meetin' day, but father didn't seem to care to hear it. 'Look here, Cap'n,' says he, 'I don't keer *who* you vote for, ef you're only a Dimocrat'—"

"Wall, I've heerd all that rigmarole afore," interposed Miss Zilpha, quietly.

"Oh," coughed Crete, "it's merely a change of subject"—cough—"feels kinder cheap, maybe"—cough—"'bout buyin' the Deacon's beef"—cough.

"Sister Siny's cook this week, I believe, girls;" responded their brother, good-naturedly; "I'll leave the question to *her* now."

"Well, brother Jesse, I guess we *don't* need any," she said, a little hesitatingly.

"No more do I; and I wa'n't a goin' to git any," he said, very gravely.

"You're the most desateful creetur that ever drew the breath of life then, Jesse Warner. What did you say you spoke for a quarter for?" chimed in again Miss Zilpha's sharp voice.

"I didn't! 'Twas Roby insinuated it: she's a proper suspicious critter; prides herself on bein' beforehand tellin' what a body means, and it gin'rally turns out like this: she don't hit nowheres within gunshot of the mark."

"What's the mark, then, in this ere case?" slowly put in the thunder tones; "I, for one, will be dredful obleeged to ye for postin' on us up."

"Wall, now," he resumed—spreading his yellow bandanna on his knees, and deliberately carving a semi-circle of mince pie, "I was on the p'int of sayin' somethin' proper agreeable to you wimmin folks, ef you'd only let me go on as I b'gin. You see, arter I took a look at the Deacon's stock—likely red heifer that of his'n, too—I jeest went in to chat a minute with Aunt Patty——"

"I'll warrent ye," broke in Miss Roby, sarcastically.

"Well, brother Jesse, how did you find them?" quietly interposed Miss Charity, in time to prevent another wordy tournament.

"Smart as usual. Mis' Nortrop was a flyin' round like a hen with her head cut off; beats all how she does hold out; bears her age wonderful, I think. Dolly was tyin' a comforter. She's all hoarsed up with quinsy; she says she hes to hev jest sech a spell ev'ry winter season. Sara Ann was rockin', as usual. They sent an invite for as many on ye as could, to come to a tea-drinkin' there this arternoon. Aunt Patty said 'twas to meet the new minister: he'd come—though I haint had a squint at him yit, for that matter."

"What'd you tell her?" asked feminine curiosity.

"Why, I told her you'd do as you'd a mind to, I s'posed, but I'd do the arrand," he answered unconcernedly. He rose.

"You might have told them, while you's about it, *I* shouldn't come," growled Roby, decidedly. "When you catch me there ag'in, you'll catch a weasel asleep."

"I wouldn't be hired to go!" coughed Miss Crete, "to see all the ministers in creation."

"No! *you're* not able to go," said her brother, affectionately, "but some o' the rest might, I think; for the *looks* on't ef nothin' more: though Dolly said she misdoubted ef any on ye *would*."

"Law! did she?" said Miss Zilpha. "Then *I'll* go, jest to spite her. I 'spose she hopes we won't come: haint got vittals 'nough maybe for a large party. Sister Charity, you'll go too, won't you?"

"That I will," she gayly answered, "after the work is out of the way. I must not leave Sinai to do it all."

Not being allowed to share in this work, I stood quietly by and watched their manner of doing it. Deborah often declared that "they were an odd set;" I thought so too, as Miss Roby—filling a pail with warm water, and producing from a closet a bowl of soft soap and a scrubbing-cloth—

slowly let herself down on the floor to wash it. She carefully polished one board its entire length. Her kneeling pilgrimage finished, she with difficulty rose, handed the cloth to her sister Zilpha—waiting for it—who also assumed the devotional posture, and in like manner finished another board. So they alternately labored, while Sinai and Charity washed, wiped, and put away the blue-edged dishes. These latter talked in an under-tone quite undistinguishable. Miss Lucretia loitered a while by the fire, then went off, coughing violently, to take her after-dinner nap.

" Why don't *you* go visiting?" I ventured to inquire of Miss Roby, as she rose from polishing the fifth board. She shyly averted her head ere she answered :

" 'Cause, I don't maybe like, over'n above board, some folks' sweet-cake—made out of mutton taller, or ham-grease. *I* can't go fried meat-fat, or pot-drippings, even if *'tis* cleansed. I ain't over fond nuther of eatin' up other folks's leavins of plum sauce; and mor'n all that, I don't want to freeze to death: do you blame me?" she demanded gruffly, suddenly turning to face me.

" Do they do all that at Deacon Northrop's?" I asked, curiously.

She nodded her head mysteriously. " I shouldn't wonder ; and that ain't half. The fact is, they're tight as the bark to a tree. It beats all," she said, reflectively ; " they're well-to-do in the world, and ain't obleeged to scrimp so ; but as true as I'm a livin' woman, I've known Aunt Patty Nortrop stop little boys, goin' to the store for a stick of candy, and persuade 'em to buy a stem of currants instead, and she'd pocket their copper as cool as could be—you know, Ruby, you can make children do most any thing, if you only set out. I've known of her keepin' their hired men on salt pork the blessed summer long—till they got mad and quit; and Sara Ann's jest as bad as the old folks. She used to carry 'love apples' to school and sell 'em to the other gals—done it oceans of times—for a cent apiece. You can find any quantity of 'em growing wild in the Nortrop woods."

"What's bred in the bone, &c., you know, sister," put in Miss Zilpha, handing her the soap and cloth.

"You are a little too hard on them, girls," said Miss Sinai, gently; "We should have charity, you know the Bible says."

"Wall, *we've* got her, *I'm* sure," laughed Miss Roby, facetiously. "I don't see what more you want."

"And," pursued Miss Sinai, with a deprecating glance, "we don't make ourselves; we are not born alike: they cannot help it."

"Don't talk to *me* now!" she grimly retorted, "I know they *can* help it; and I know, too, that the Bible says that 'Faith without works is of no avail.'"

"Speakin' of charity," said Miss Zilpha, laughing, and pausing in her labor to dispose leisurely of a huge pinch of snuff, "puts me in mind of the time old Mis' Pettibone went round gitten a new meetin' cloak for Elder Clark. 'Twant no enviable job, but she had tol'rable good success among the members, till she got to the Deacon's, about the last place. Some give a quarter, and some fifty cents; the storekeeper's wife give in the trimmins, and sister Roby and I was goin' to make it all off for *our* part—wall, she told Mis' Nortrop her arrand. Dolly never opened her head; but Aunt Patty took the paper, and read the names on't, all over, and handed it back without sayin' a word. Mis' Pettibone told me 'bout it herself—so if it's a lie you have it as cheap as I—said she never did feel so streaked afore in all her life;

'specially when Aunt Patty put on a mournful look, and said, kinder solemn, 'Charity b'gins to hum.'"

"What did Mrs. Pettibone say to that?" I asked, greatly interested.

"She said 'Yis, and gin'rally *ends* there;' and she got up and took her boots off quick. She laughed as though she'd split, when she told me, but she said she felt dreadful put out in the time on't."

"Wall, at any rate, they might treat folks civil," said Miss Roby. "I remember visitin' there once; 'twas when Sara Ann was a leetle girl—she's jest about *your* age, Siny, though she don't call herself but twenty-five; church member, too. I guess she skips that part in her Bible that treats 'bout Annias and Sophiry. I'd sent word we was a comin', the day before, me and Delia—'twas when she's alive—and as Dolly Nortrop was jest our age, and a great case to carry on, we lotted on a real sociable set down. Wall, when we got there, ef you'll b'lieve me, there wan't a sign of no fire in the fireplace, and the room was as cold as a barn. 'Fore we got our things off, Dolly come a runnin' in with a shovelful of coals, and Mis' Nortrop she brought a stick or two of green wood and put on top. 'Law!' says she, 'we thought maybe you'd give up comin'; it's so late ('twan't two o'clock.) Dolly let the fire git down; however, the room ain't got cold none, I guess (good reason why, 'twas as cold as cold could be afore), and it'll soon blaze up agin.' Wall, there we sot, the whole blessed afternoon, in a shiver, a waitin' for the pesky fire to blaze up, and, instid, it grew colder and colder, and the room got as blue as a whetstun. You see, the wood was hemlock boughs, and so full o' water it only smoked and steamed round the edges: it didn't make a mite of no headway towards burnin', and 'twouldn't nuther ef we'd sot there till doomsday. I didn't care none for myself, for I felt so full of Cain, I could hardly keep a straight face on ; but poor Delia felt it, I tell you : she whispered to me once that she felt all over goose pimples ; and the smoke set her coughin' terrible. There wan't but one rockin'-chair in the room, and that Delia took : she never thought, nor I nuther, but what it's the way to do. I see Sara Ann a standin' round—oh! quite a spell—and lookin' hard at us, but I 'sposed 'twas be-cause she hadn't no manners. Byme-by she went off, and putty soon her mother come in, and told Delia ' that rockin'-chair was Sara Ann's, and nobody sot in't but jest herself;' and so sister Delia had to histe out of it, and the leetle five-year-old brat took it as brazen as could be. I whispered to sister Delia that 'twas part of the play. You needn't look so at me, Charity ; I ain't a goin' to say one word 'bout the supper. Dolly come in jest afore the clock struck five, with the shovel, sayin', ' the kitchen fire'd gone out, while we's a visitin'; it kinder slipped her mind,' and so she up and carried off what few coals was still fizzlin' and sputterin' under the green wood, and I was glad on't, for I opened the winder on a crack, and let out some the smoke. After sup-per, Aunt Patty said, ' she guessed 'twouldn't be worth while to make another fire in the keepin' room, as we shouldn't stay long enough to pay for the trouble, and she felt ruther oneasy allers to go off to bed and leave a great roarin' fire all shet up.' Wall, that was the wust on't ; 'cause I'd told brother Jesse not to come for us 'fore seven or eight o'clock, as we thought, while we's about it, we wouldn't be formal. He didn't come till nine, and I declare my hands got so numb 'fore that time struck, I couldn't hold my knittin' needles ; they fairly turned purple. I rubbed 'em kinder sly under my apron ; then I made an arrand out to the kitchen, to git a drink of water, and tried to warm 'em a trifle by the stove. Wall, would you b'lieve it? *that* was out too. I hope Mis' Nortrop didn't keep awake *that* night, for fear the house'd catch afire. I'm sure she might a slept as tranquil as the babe unborn, for when we come away, there wan't a sign of no fire in the hull house, 'cept the flame of one leetle scraggly, dipped, taller candle; and the wick of *that* didn't look strong enough to stan' alone, kep' loppin' to one side, and Aunt Patty had to give it a poke once in a while with the pint o' her scissors to make it know its place. They had an.ile lamp on the mantel-tree, but 'twan't lit. Wall, Rubiny, the long and short of the matter is, that I made up my mind then that I didn't like to go visitin'. Poor Delia was laid up with rheumatiz the hull spring after. I thought then, and I do now, that 'twas a settin' half a day and night in that are cold room brought it on: she run down all that summer and we buried her afore snow fell."

Her voice sounded a little tremulous as she concluded. We had been left alone at the close of this recital. Miss Sinai had disappeared noiselessly. Miss Charity softly followed. Miss Zilpha peered curiously into the closet, after their departure, at the neat piles of dishes; dipped one skinny fore-finger under the creamy surface of a pan of milk; tasted it, and, apparently satisfied of its sweetness, helped herself to a pinch of her favorite comfort, and took herself off. It was torturing to watch her walk. It was like a screw; hither and thither she swayed—like a slender forest-tree driven by the wind. I felt relieved when she gained the entry door, and it had closed upon her receding figure. As for Miss Roby, it was like the hush after a tempest, the lull that followed. Her work was likewise finished; the kitchen floor made neat, and shining like glass. She turned, and shuffled heavily away. For the remainder of the day she was invisible in the sitting-room, being domiciled in Miss Crete's comfortable quarters across the hall.

CHAPTER VIII.

In less than an hour Miss Charity appeared, carefully attired in her best company frock—a lustreless black silk—with wrist and neck decorations of narrow lawn ruffles; at the junction under the chin, appropriately finished by a tiny knot of pale purple ribbon. These tasteful bits of ribbon, and her velvet head-band, roused the scornful ire of the grim Puritan dames in the vicinity, who looked upon all outward adorning, in one past the giddy period of youth, and also a "church member," as but sinful vanities of the world, and hardness of the spiritual life. However, as her sisters liked them, she paid no heed to others' frequently expressed disapproval. She looked and moved a lady, though a rather prim one. Drawing a chair to the fire, she quietly seated herself to wait for her sister.

Miss Zilpha's mode of entering a room was altogether peculiar. First, the door noiselessly turned on its hinges—a treacherous click of the latch alone sounding a warning of her coming. Then a sharp nose was thrust through the crevice, cautiously followed by the glittering green spectacles, taking a hasty survey. Then the long angular waist was inserted, and finally the whole figure wedged itself through the narrow space. A startled look rested upon her face at attaining her object so boldly. Her long, lean figure was arrayed in faded blue camlet; the scantiness of the skirt compensated for by the ample fulness of the sleeves. On one arm swung a huge, cinnamon-colored, silk work-bag, with her knitting-needles protruding through its mouth. A century ago it had figured at similar gatherings, depending from her grandam's sturdy muscles, as she donned her huge "caleche," and mounted the cream-colored pacer, old Bess. Miss Zilpha was proud of its history, and cherished it as a priceless heir-loom.

"That ere," she said—pointing to it with her withered finger, "could tell heaps of cur'ous stories ef't could only speak. I'd give a crossed sixpence to hear some on 'em, wouldn't you now, sister Charity ? 'bout when the church called a council, to turn poor old Elder Thatcher away ; the Lord only knows what for: grandmarm didn't, though she tried hard enough to find out the real reason : the deacons, for once, was close-mouthed enough. Some said 'twas for his carryings on with Phila Hurd, settin' up, and walkin' out with her afore his first wife died, and you know *mother* said he married her jest as soon as she *did* breathe her last fare-well—afore she was cold in her grave as you may say—"

"Come, sister !" interposed Miss Charity, serenely, "the horse is waiting for us ; brother Jesse will be getting im-patient."

"I must take my own time, sister. I can't be hurried," she responded, loftily.

Perched on her forefinger, like a nondescript bird pluming itself for sudden flight, sat her muslin, lace-bordered cap. She deposited it carefully on the table, shook out her hem-stitched kerchief—which smelled strongly of dried rose-leaves—and enveloped in its creases the antiquated coiffure ; tying the four corners in a firm " weaver's knot." " There," she said, complacently, donning shawl and bonnet, " I guess *that* won't ontie : I hate a 'granny's knot' above ground, it's always a slippin' out. Wall, sister Siny,"—stepping before her—"you hain't said whether I'll do or not. I thought, seein's the new minister's to be there, I'd put on my best bib and tucker."

Miss Sinai smiled. "You will do admirably," she cried, gayly. "Be sure and bring Ruby and I a favorable account of the new minister, to pay us for staying at home."

"Certain !" responded Miss Zilpha, opening the pantry door, at which both of her sisters laughed.

"My spice boxes are nearly empty," called Sinai after her.

"Enough here for me to-day," she innocently answered, opening the little oval Shaker boxes, and abstracting sticks of cinnamon, pendules of cloves, grains of allspice, and stems of dried caraway : these she placidly dropped into the work-bag's capacious hollow.

"It's easy to see why Zilpha likes that enormous bag !" remarked Miss Sinai, mischievously. "Sister Charity carries *her* work in her pocket, but then it don't have to hold spices too. I wonder it don't kill you, sister !" she continued; "you are always eating something."

"I feel a sort of goneness," returned her sister, "most ways afore meal-times. I 'spect I've got the heart-burn. Old Doctor Lovejoy told me a mite of caraway seed was good for that are complaint : and the cap sheaf is that I kinder hanker for something to gnaw away on." After a pinch of snuff, she declared herself "all in a flutter-budget to be off."

From a side-window I watched them, down the long white road, past its sweeping curve, and out of sight; their green veils fluttering, and their heads occasionally turning to note the objects they passed by.

A high wind sweeping over the cold, March landscape;

5

the cheerless contour of its skeleton trees; the monotonous dearth of life and sound without, made the large cheerful sitting-room within, with its glowing, crackling fire, and Miss Sinai's sweet face, the very embodiment of comfort. "I wonder what we had better do? "she said musingly, as I looked vaguely around. "What do you like best, Ruby?"

I glanced at my well-stuffed carpet bag in the corner. "Aunt Rhoda insisted on putting up my work; she said I must knit to the heel. I hate knitting stents! don't you Miss Sinai?" I cried vehemently.

She laughed at my rueful glances. "I believe I used to dislike it; but I got over that a long time ago. Suppose you unlock your satchel and let me see your work!"

I obeyed rather reluctantly. She scanned it carefully, and again sent forth a low, musical chuckle. "Sooth to say, you are no great knitter, Ruby; that's a fact." She smoothed it over her knee with one plump, dimpled hand. "Why, I don't believe you narrow at all—and the seam is very broken—and—mercy on me! do see the dropped stitches; they are making tracks for home as fast as ever they can."

I suppose I looked guiltily foolish under her raillery, for she suddenly stopped, and added, "I'll tell you what we will do, Ruby! You ravel the stocking—its only a moment's work—and I will knit it over for you."

I joyfully complied. She mended the fire, adding seasoned twigs to the huge smouldering back-log, which speedily provoked darting tongues of flame, up the wide chimney. This done, she opened the old-fashioned butternut writing-desk, and turned over its meagre hoard of books. Selecting "Food for Reflection" for her own perusal, she lingered thoughtfully over the rest—so long that—my imperfect creation being returned to its embryo shape—I tossed the white ball on the table, and returned to the window. The wind was lulling. A homeless ray of sunshine illumed, for an instant, the dark edges of swift-sailing clouds.

"What are you looking at?" said a voice presently, behind me.

"Is that a graveyard, Miss Sinai?" I pointed to a group of white objects, looking like marble shafts.

"Yes, Ruby! It is our family burial-place."

"Oh! I did not know you had one." I counted six stones: "How much trouble you have seen!" I said, pityingly.

"I was but a baby when sister Artemisia died: neither do I vividly remember my father's death. Sister Roby says that brother Jesse is his very image."

"But the rest?" I said, heedlessly.

"The rest," she echoed, sadly, "I have mourned as well as the others. My mother lies there; and my three sisters, whom I loved dearly—Delia, who petted me more than the others; she was my protector, too, if I got into mischief, or trouble; my nurse when I was sick, and I cried myself into a fever when she died. Sarah faded next—our beautiful snow-wreath, and the house grew very lonely; it hasn't got out of the corners yet," she said, with tearful pathos, "and only a few months ago, we laid sister Submit by her side."

"Don't it make you afraid," I at length ventured, "to see those graves every time you look from the window?"

"My dear Ruby!" she said hastily, putting her hand fondly upon my shoulder, "Afraid! of what! No!" she softly continued, without waiting for my answer. "There they lie; poor, harmless dust of our dead divinities; and we, whom they loved, and left sorrowing, keep faithful guard over them. There is something, to my mind, cold and comfortless, in burying the dear departed away from our sight, in a common cemetery. Where they have roamed on earth, there should they likewise sleep, and awake at the sound of the last trumpet—at home. There, where the old home violets and daisies blossom, and clover and wild-brier scent the air. Why should we banish them to the silence of alien graves, and weeds, and nettles? You should see their resting-place in summer, Ruby! It's the sunniest spot on the whole farm. A little brook winds through the meadow : the orchard lies beyond, where robins trill the mornings into noons. You can see the grain wave green and yellow in the field below, where crows caw loudly. Then, when the sun dips behind the mountains, the whip-poor-will sounds its vespers, and fire-flies light their torches. We, too, from this window, watch how tenderly the moon and stars bathe it in holy light: perhaps we also think, how soon we shall take our places beside them ; but we are not *afraid*, Ruby."

"You do not wear mourning, Miss Sinai?" I next inter-rogated.

"No! that is a gloomy custom. It will not bring them back, and it only saddens the living. I have too often seen it the ostentatious garb of hypocrites ; mourning in their robes, but rejoicing in their hearts. And you know," she added, smilingly, "we are part Shakers; they do not believe in it. Still, we all do as we please about it: each suits her own feelings. Sister Charity likes to wear it, and does ; we do not object, or ridicule it."

I was preparing another storm of questions, but she play-fully drew me away to the secretary, saying, "Now you have ruminated long enough ; see here! which will you have?" She reached down the volumes, reading aloud their titles. "'Young's Night Thoughts'—too gloomy, I suspect!" I nodded. She replaced it. "'Doddridge!' No. 'Pilgrim's Progress,' then?" I shook my head. "I know it by heart," I cried.

"How would you fancy 'Dick's' works, then?" and she gravely handed me a ponderous tome for inspection.

"It looks incomprehensible," I managed to say, after a doubtful survey.

"I am in despair then, Ruby! No; here is one I have not seen in an age" (she had artfully concealed it to the last): and she fished from a dusty corner a mutilated, ink-besmeared, dog-eared copy of "Robinson Crusoe."

I grasped the coverless volume eagerly. Aunt Rhoda allowed no such fascinating tales in her house: all such literature became contraband if discovered, and was speedily consigned to the flames. Mark managed to elude his lynx-eyed mother's sense of moral duty; and I once caught a glimpse in Deborah's drawer, of part of "Charlotte Temple."

Miss Sinai knitted rapidly as she read, bestowing no attention upon her work, yet fashioning a well-shaped stocking, without dropping a stitch. At intervals she raised her eyes to turn the leaves of her book, and to flash into my corner a sunny smile of pleased content. The short afternoon waned. "Five!" was solemnly knelled by the clock ere she stirred.

"You like that book, Ruby?" she inquired.

"I should think so, Miss Sinai! It's charming! I should like to live just so, and you should be my 'Friday.'"

She laughed. "Strange, Ruby, but I don't feel much flattered. He was a savage, you know, and the proposal implies that you consider me eligible for one also."

"Oh! no, indeed. I prefer you as you are. We should be a little more civilized, of course; have more to eat; and keep out of the reach of cannibals."

"I like to watch you, as you read," she said, smiling, "I've had that pleasure this half hour. You have such a way of smacking your lips at a relishing passage—just as brother Jesse does at any dish which especially suits his palate. He is an epicure: I suspect you may be a mental one."

I shook my head dubiously. "I never read any thing," I said.

"That's a dreadful state of things," she responded, with mock seriousness.

"I never had but *one* book, Miss Sinai, guess what that was."

"'Gulliver's Travels,' maybe, or 'Arabian Nights.' No? What then?"

"'The Young Woman's Guide.'" She laughed at my rueful air. "I shall never read it, Miss Sinai: I've tried more than once. Aunt Rhody says it's my duty to read it through: but I don't remember a word, when I try."

She turned to the window to conceal her merriment. "Poor child!" she said presently. "I may possibly hear some one speculating about your literary tastes, and come to the rescue with a word of advice, provided you tell me, you know."

"Oh no, *that* is improbable, Miss Sinai. 'The Young Woman's Guide' will go to my descendants alone."

"Stranger things than that I spoke of, happen now-a-days," she merrily returned, whisking out the tea-table.

"Crete ain't so well," said Miss Roby, gruffly, at tea, "dreadful plagued for breathin'. I guess I better steep up some 'izop for her. She's uncommon put to it for breath, to-night. I b'lieve, and allers *shall*, that she's more phthisicky than any thin' else."

"It's these cold winds that affect her so. I do hope we shall have settled weather soon," said Sinai, anxiously.

"Wall, we won't! ain't no prospect on't. It'll be dreadful tryin' all the spring, 'specially when the trees are leavin' out," said Miss Roby, gloomily.

"And there is no hyssop," pursued Sinai. "You will have to take chamomile."

Uncle Jesse brought his sisters home from the Deacon's, in due season. Miss Roby questioned them closely as to "What they had for tea?" "How many kinds of cake?" "Black tea or green?" "Sage cheese or dried beef?" "Whether the table appointments were scant as usual, or decent enough for hospitality?" Finally, "Who was there? what they wore? and what work they carried?" Sinai colored a little during this catechism, but maintained profound silence. Her intuitive refinement of character, controlled by powerful Christian benevolence, rendered these gossipy details extremely distasteful. She absolutely writhed in her chair when names were spoken, and Miss Zilpha's sharp voice weighed them in her balances, on each pronouncing judgment. "Do unto others, &c.," was the broad platform on which Sinai planted all her motives of thought and action: self-sacrifice was the predominant element surrounding her daily life. She would not have relished a neighbor's discussion of *her* household: she relished still less her sisters' method of overhauling *their* neighbors; but an expression of this feeling would have wounded these sisters—all her elders in age—so she compressed her lips in resolute silence. She looked up only when the minister came upon the stage; was turned around, familiarly discussed, and sent off with flying colors. Miss Zilpha pronounced him, "A

pritty man, and not a bit proud; I thought him real hum-
spun, didn't you, Charity ?"

"Sister Charity's as mum as a dormouse!" growled Roby.

"Oh!" broke in Miss Charity, " I'm sure Zilpha's sufficient
for the talking.   Your aunt, Ruby, invited him to take up
his quarters with her for a few weeks; as he will not move
his family here yet."

"I shouldn't a bit wonder, now," interrupted Miss Zilpha,
" If this tea drinkin' was planned for that very purpose; to
save the Deacon's folks from bein' obleeged to have him
there.   He's got to stay *some*where, you know, and they're
cur'ous creeturs 'bout some things.   Mis' Martin couldn't do
no less than ask him hum with her, the way 'twas brought
up.   What do *you* think, sister Charity ?"

"I think," she answered dryly, " that we have sufficiently
discussed our friends and neighbors for one sitting; so I
move an adjournment."

Seconded, and carried debateless; an unconsidered point
of domestic order faced suddenly the dispersing cabinet—
my bestowal for the night.   The sisters occupied apartments
wherever their taste dictated: not in contiguity to each
other, as more social instincts might suggest.   The great,
roomy mansion admitted of entire exclusiveness, of which
they availed themselves.   The house would no doubt have
quartered a regiment.   Perhaps it *had* opened its warm,
wide heart, in hospitable eagerness, to afford secret shelter
to sorely-pressed Revolutionary heroes.   Its doors may have
swung on reluctant hinges for bands of Tories, and King
George's soldiers; the lofty chambers re-echoing their brazen
orgies, with quivering shame.   Uncle Jesse had legions of
stories concerning "good old colony times," stowed away in
his memory ; which he was not loath to bring out for lengthy

airings, to appreciative listeners. In this fond pride he was neither silly nor childishly amiss. Who of us—looking back to the sad, yet glorious annals of that long, gory, desperate struggle; a heart to heart, almost a friend to friend strife, between the powerful, vengeful lioness, and her maddened offspring—that thrust not inquisitive fingers at the roots of our own forefathers' sunken graves, to delve amid its decaying lore; to clear away the weedy forgetfulness, which might over-run beyond pruning, and shroud in shameful obscurity, the patriotism and divine self-sacrifice of our own soldierly grandsires; to polish to a still brighter lustre the frail, corroding glimmer of human fame—human glory!

A shadow of these thoughts flitted through my mind. I shuddered at the idea of sleeping alone in the strange rooms, out of which opened numberless cupboards, presses, and doors communicating—by narrow passages—with other rooms, their counterparts. Not portentous things in themselves, in cheerful daylight; but trifles, light as these, often bespeak insurmountable terror to a timid spirit, thoroughly educated in superstitious lore, and ever on the alert to prove or disprove its own stupid imaginings.

I was to be spared such trial. Each spinster claimed me for her bedfellow. It was in vain that Miss Sinai, in answer to my appealing glance—insisted on the traditionary right of a hostess to apportion guests their quarters, and with her usual meek submission to her sisters' whims, she allowed herself to be silenced.

Miss Roby declared that, "I should try each of their rooms in turn." In order that fairness might characterize her proceedings, she stooped to the wood-box, selecting therefrom four splinters. These she arranged in her two bony palms, and requested her sisters "to draw." "*Mine*

5*.

is the longest!" she exclaimed, triumphantly; and, gruffly facing me, she seized a candle, and my satchel, and marched me off forthwith.

CHAPTER IX.

Up a broad, steep, winding staircase plodded Miss Roby's heavy footsteps—echoed by my fainter tread. Her pegged boots emitted a painful squeak, as she trod the oaken boards of the dim, shadowy corridors. A rush of cold air smote our candle, nearly extinguishing its flickering glimmer: then it rushed at a headlong pace past us; enveloping us thereby, and dissipating, in chattering teeth and icy shiverings, all sense of the glowing warmth and light of the family room below. Though I shunned, with curling lip, the idea of being afraid, my poltroon heart tacitly acknowledged the fact, by sending out a hand to clutch cautiously my grim guide's robe; and not for worlds would I have ventured a curious glance over either shoulder. I carefully abstained from pulling Miss Roby's gown lest she suddenly turn, and overwhelm me with derision. This was no easy matter, as her gait was a shuffling lurch sideways; sometimes hitting a shoulder against the white-washed wall, and compelling me to adopt the same style of motion. Once, her foot stumbled at a door, which—as if in answer to a preconcerted signal—flew open wide. It brought Miss Roby to a halt. "This was poor sister Sary's room," she remarked—plunging the flaring wick into the repellant darkness. "And there ain't a thing been touched in it—so to speak, sence she died. See here!" she added, entering and going straight to a closet-door, which she opened. It seemed the abode of dusty dampness; a vague, mouldy smell—that sometimes attaches itself to chests of long-packed clothing—exhumed therefrom. In it hung dresses, bonnets, and mantles—one, a scarlet cloak of broadcloth, with deep capes, in whose heavy folds those merciless ravagers, 'the moths,' had gnawed huge modes of entering. A goodly pile of counterpanes and quilts occupied one corner; wreathed over, with a spider's fairy-like tracery. Her shoes were also there, with creases crossing the morocco tops, as if just removed from the tired feet—now rapturously treading the golden pavements of the Eternal City. In the outer room was the bed; made up round and high with feathers, after the fashion of New England housekeepers: the soft pillows, in their long, narrow cases, having—above their hem—her initials worked in blue worsted "cross-stitch" The narrow-framed mirror—one-half a picture of a two-storied, prim country house, flanked by wings, and surrounded by a yellow fence; out of which seemed to rise—(a closer inspection led to the surmise that they took root in the garden behind) flourishing poplars, of unnatural blue-green foliage. Below this quaint little mirror was its accompaniment—still to be found in rural districts —a comb-case of red and black broadcloth, suspended from a nail, with the yellow warped comb faintly streaking its mouth. The light-stand underneath the mirror, containing a work-basket and its implements; a little basket of tiny shells, and yellowish white "lucky bones;" a Hymn-Book and a Bible. These mute surroundings lingered still at the maiden's shrine: the pilgrim frequenter, with penitential tears, had been rapt heavenward, to kneel at a higher worship. This room seemed the *real* grave of the vanished human presence; sadder, more solitary, more sacred by far

than the grassy, snow-covered heap in yonder meadow.
That seemed an empty symbol, erected to satisfy man's
love for a tangible form: *this*, the real cemetery.   Nay! it
seemed—the longer we lingered—as if the life that formerly
inhabited it still clung earthward; still trod the faded carpet, and looked into our eyes, or floated in space, around
and above our heads; in some mysterious guise, impalpable
to our gross eyes of clay, but making her presence visible to
our finer inward consciousness; just as Music, floating down
to us from the same unseen, immortal heights—itself no less
a breath of the same divinity—condescends to draw nigh
unto our earthly embodiment ; to claim kinship with flesh,
bone, muscle, and thrill our dormant spiritual fibres with
its vague, mesmeric pulsations.

I could not repress a shudder—which was partly of mental origin—at the icy dampness of the room, most tomb-like.
I even thought I could detect a lingering smell of the var-
nished coffin—borne from it so long ago—and I wondered
at the matter-of-fact complacency of Miss Roby's countenance.
She evidently was unawed by ghostly imaginings, as she
settled several chairs anew, and pulled the awry bed-spread
into place.   I was inexpressibly relieved when she motioned me out, closed the door, and again took up the line
of march toward her own quarters.   These were at the farther
end of the last narrow passage.   It was her whimsical fancy
to room here, where not a genial whiff of sound of the life
below stairs, or her sisters' distant chambers could smite her
cars.   If there be a charm in isolation, Miss Roby found
and enjoyed it.   In these upper rooms she ruled alone; no
recluse in his cell more given over to welcome solitude.   Her
solitary window looked on the garden—now a white waste—
and, afar off, the continuous gray mountain chain, from

which Greybaul towered—king among peers; undisputed prophet, among his followers.

Miss Roby paused at the door, drew a key from her pocket, and solemnly unlocked it. She pushed me in before her, and I imagined how a convicted, sentenced culprit might feel, traversing, in company with his jailer, dim prison-wards; ushered, in reluctant state, to his dreary cell. However, *my* turnkey followed me in, and closed the door with a heavy bang: the draught of air it created extinguished our candle, and as she again turned the key in the lock we were left in utter darkness.

"This is a pretty how-d'ye-do," she muttered, audibly; "nary a lucifer-match in the room, I'll be bound! though, for that matter, Lucifer himself is allers round, seekin' who he may devour, body and branch. Do you know *that*, Rubiny?" raising her voice to a sepulchral treble, as she searched—groping heavily around—for wherewith to kindle a light; evidently with the result she had predicted, for she unlocked the door, and saying: "You stay here, and I'll git it lit in a minnit," shuffled heavily away. I trembled like a leaf; for—in spite of my secret shame at the thought—I was an arrant coward. Her last remark conjured up the idea of his Satanic majesty. "She may be right," whispered my craven heart. "He may, even now, be marking you for his prey. What if he *should* seize me? I am no doubt a fit subject!" In despair at this horrible suggestion, I timorously crouched on the floor, and fell—in a happy fit of faith—to saying my prayers with vigor. I think I never rehearsed the familiar prattle with more energetic demonstrations, or in a louder tone. Such earnestness would season many torpid prayer-meetings, with a savor of warmth very convincing and melting to the cold snows of congealing sin-

ners' hearts, which never—by such suns—have chance to
thaw. I dared not put out a hand, lest I inadvertently
clutch what I most dreaded; "perhaps," thought I, "the
very cloven feet themselves, or the snaky appendage,
always honoring artistic representations of the destroyer of
Eve, in the Sunday-school books, which frighten credulous
children into early piety, precocious experiences, and early
graves." Cold chills ran over me. I felt my hair rise on
end ; that strange phenomena which so often thrills us :
often, while roaming heedlessly some green, sunny meadow,
or in a crowded street, or by the quiet home hearth-fire—
which Deborah explained by saying that we were on the
identical spot where, in the future, should rest our graves.
"Am I to be buried here? She has been gone long enough
to light forty candles. You're a fool!" I added, to my beating heart, which was thumping away like a sledge-hammer.
To quiet it, I began a good old Psalm, and had half finished
it, when the heavy tread again resounded, and a welcome
gleam of day shone on my night.

A malicious smile distorted Miss Roby's wide mouth, as she
comprehended my terrors. I verily believe she rejoiced therein, and would have relished exceedingly another trip down-
stairs, could she have summoned to her aid an eligible excuse.

"Why, child alive! you're as white as a sheet," she said,
putting down the candle. "You didn't see nothin' now, did
you, to scare you so?" she whispered, curiously regarding me.
"I tell *you !*" she added, grimly shutting her teeth, "I got a
rale lectur' from sister Siny, for leavin' you up here in the dark.
Jest's though any thing'd tech you *here* sooner'n down in *her*
room !" she said, with scornful emphasis. " I don't know how
'tis ; but somehow or uther she's took to you mightily; and
for that matter, she's oncommon 'fraid of the dark, herself."

"Is she ?" I asked, immensely relieved.

"Yis, Rubiny Ann! she is—ef that's any comfort; and I s'pose 'tis, for misery likes company, you know. I knowed you was scart awful; or you wouldn't strike up old 'Dundee' in that are way." She paused and shook with laughter.

"Are you glad of it?" I asked, indignantly. "I believe you blew out the light on purpose to try me."

"Law! no, child, I didn't; no such thing." She chuckled still to herself. "I was only a thinkin' how folks allers goes to singin' when they're scart; as if that'd help 'em any! When sister Siny was a leetle gal, she'd strike up 'On the road to Zion,' jest as soon as she opened the sullar-door, to go arter potatoes or apples. I've sent her down many a time, jest to hear her; and laughed ready to split, all the time. There's Benjamin Field, too, that lives jest above here: he's courtin' Sary Jane Wells, over on 'Stafford's Hill,' and he goes hum, Sunday nights, a-screechin' as loud as he can yell—a reg'lar Injun whoop; he hain't no voice, nor never had; or else he whistles, and one noise's bad as t'other. Great fool he is, to let ev'ry body know how late he comes hum: I lay here and laugh all to myself, knowin' he's as 'fraid as death—ef tain't moonlight—and he thinks nobody don't know it. "Now," she resumed, more gruffly than ever, "I should like nothin' better than to *see* a spook, if there *be* any: I reckon we'd come to an understandin' proper quick, and I'll resk but what I'd git the upper hand of 'em, in less than *no* time, if we did have a tussel."

Miss Roby's sleeping apartment was a museum of old-maidish hoards—dusty, useless lingerings from the Past's remembrances, which she piled into corners, chests, and cupboards; shoved under the high tent-bedstead—itself a cherished relic; and littered the tops of bureau and chairs.

There the high chair stood, in which all the Warner babies had been tied, and drawn to the family board, from time immemorial. By its side the heavy wooden cradle; its ponderous cliff shelving off to the high, straight sides, yet wearing a very spectral look; as though your eye—by too long gazing—might start to life its half-forgotten rock. Old stools were there, worm-eaten, hacked, and rickety, yet dear to Miss Roby's ancient heart, from the spell of some cherished reminiscence. Chairs, with patchwork cushions of red and black camlet—frayed and faded, but which told their own eloquent stories: a mother's and sisters' forms rocked to and fro in them long ago; a mother's and sisters' fingers— long since food for worms—had fashioned their diamond and octagon forms, and pressed them into service. There were wooden boxes of all sizes, full of odds and ends which no-body else wanted, but which Miss Roby prized; yellow, warped ivory combs, broken brushes, an empty box of black-ing, with the label, "British Lustre," smeared and torn, shrivelled ears of "pop-corn," rolls of gay calicoes "for piecing," small wooden bowls of Shaker manufacture, bits of shattered looking-glasses, dilapidated school-books, and num-berless round tin boxes. From one of these latter she whipped off the cover. It was nearly filled with pins, bright, straight and new, mixed with old, corroded, crooked monsters, and a sprinkling of black, tiny weapons. She plucked a few from her dress and added them to the stock, sententiously observing: "I never go by a pin, Rubiny Ann, without pickin' on it up; it's a sign ye'll never be rich if ye do. See! what a lot of 'em I git by this means. I hain't bought a pin in, I don't know when. I find plenty, out doors and in; other folks's droppin's. And that ain't all, nuther. Now look there! 'Waste not, want not,' ye know.

For *my* part *I* believe in bein' prudent, and layin' up 'g'inst time o' need comes along." She removed another cover. "I can allers find *here* the very identical button I want for brother Jesse's pants, cut, or wes'cut." In truth, it was a miscellaneous assemblage of brown, white, brass buttons, and covered moulds—all ripped from discarded clothing; very many with the threads of former service persistently clinging to their eyes—a taunting reminder in their present igno- minious state of dependence. "B'tween you and me, Rubiny Ann, the girls laugh at my savin' and prudence; but they're mighty glad to come to me for some on 'em, once in a while. There's jest the very thing now, for brother Jesse's galluses; I'll take that out while I think on't."

Though certainly not an alluring companion, Miss Roby was, in her odd way, both social and kind. Observing me shiver, as I drew around me the ample quilts, she reached to the bed-post for her red flannel petticoat, to spread over me. I slyly pushed it back. "You're a dainty piece, Rubiny Ann, as ever the Lord let live," she growled under her teeth.

"My name is not Ann," I returned stoutly.

"Yis 'tis, too; or oughter be," she insisted. "Wan't you named after your grand-marm Lee, I'd like to know?"

"Yes! but my mother did not call me Ann," I returned.

"Half a name ain't no name a' tall," she persisted, maliciously. "*Her* name was Rubiny Ann, so of course your'n is too."

I disdained a reply; and in the long silence that ensued I was lapsing off to sleep most comfortably, when her stentorian murmur again aroused me: "Be you sleepy, Rubiny Ann?"

"No!" I answered bravely, opening wide my eyes, and peering around the room to keep awake. As they became accustomed to the gloom, the objects they discerned looked strange and ghostly. Miss Roby's dresses hung around on pegs. As I looked at them intently, they seemed to move, swaying back and forth like living things. Her old black hood, from its lofty perch, nodded, and beckoned me to a like elevation. Her striped shawl fluttered proud defiance, and shook a tattered corner at me threateningly. Even the high infant's chair attempted a grand *chassez* with the cradle; and the cushioned rocking-chairs quivered ominously. These objects were not agreeable. I again closed my eyelids.

"What a mum leetle piece you be!" remarked Miss Roby. "You don't like me, I guess, for I heerd you chatterin' like a magpie this afternoon, to sister Siny."

I did not even offer a polite disclaimer. She appeared to resent my silence.

"You take after your mother, Rubiny Ann; *she* wan't no great talker."

"She never ran when she heard company coming," was my mental ejaculation. Miss Roby resumed—determined to unseal my lips—

"Your father, now, was a proper sociable body; he'd keep the hull room in a roar for hours upon a stretch——"

"You knew him, then, Miss Roby," I eagerly interrupted.

"What's to hender my knowin' on him, I wonder? He lived round here nigh 'pon three or four year—married here, you know."

"What sort of a man was he, Miss Roby? I mean, as he appeared to you."

"Humph!" she growled, "a putty chap 'nough, if he'd

bin a likely one—which he wasn't. I s'pose *you* know that
ere as well's the rest of us : he run away and left you, 'cause
he and your mother didn't draw well together ; served him
right too," she whispered, savagely.

" Yes," I responded, not quite understanding her allusion.

" Strange ! now," she went on after a pause, " the rest all
seem to overlook what's gone before ; but somehow, for the
life of me, *I* can't. Scriptur' doctrine does very well to
plaster over old sores, with *some ;* but with *me* they're
dreadful apt to break out, arter a spell, as bad as ever. That
are place where it speaks 'bout turnin' t'other cheek, if your
enemy hits you a cuff on one, and lettin' him have the same
chance ag'in, allers riled me consid'rable. I feel like givin'
on 'em back, as good as they send, don't *you* now,
Rubiny Ann?"

" Yes !" I cried ; laughing in spite of myself.

" You'll laugh out the other corner of your mouth one of
these days," she said solemnly. " I used to tell sister Sary
that are, and it come true, too, arter a time. She was the
liveliest of us all, and she'd laugh me right square in the
face, when I tried to sober her down—dear heart ! she grew
sober 'nough finally, and *then*, Rubiny—see what strange
creeturs we be—I'd a gi'n a new dime to a seen the old
smiles come back ag'in."

" Tell me about her, Miss Roby, I'm not sleepy."

" Nor I nuther. Wall, child, if I *do*, you mustn't breathe
a lisp on't to a soul down stairs. *They* wouldn't like it if
they knew it, and I s'pose it ain't much use rakin' up old
scores to live 'em over ag'in."

" I never will tell," I solemnly repeated.

" See't you don't; if you know when you're well off," she
growled ; then, after a moment's reflection, she resumed:

" You see, when your father come here, to set up shop down
't'the Centre', he was a young man, fresh from college, nice
lookin' too, and clever as the day is long ; and t'warn't a
thousand year 'fore all our young gals was arter him all sorts ;
they all sot their best lookin' caps for him. He was 'cute
'nough to sense it too, and he jest jined in the fun. He driv
all the other young fellers off the field, and he went with who
he pleased—fust with one, then with t'other. Bam'bye he took
to waitin' on sister Sary sort o' reg'lar, hum from singin'
schools and junketts ; and then he asked her for her company, and ev'ry Sunday night arter that he set up with her.
I allers thought she didn't set no great store by him at fust ;
she wanted to bother the other girls who all stood ready to
snap him up at a mouthful. But he had a takin' way, and,
arter a spell, she fairly sot her life by him : wouldn't hear nobody speak one word ag'inst him, in any shape whatever.
She give Seth Field up here (Ben's father) the mitten on his
a'count. You see he'd been shyin' round quite a spell—and
he was as likely a lad as ever trod shoe-leather. He fairly
worshipped the ground she trod on, and no wonder nuther,
for sister Sary, in them days, wus as handsome as a pictur;
looked more like Siny than any the rest on us. She wus
ruther rude, and rattle-headed sometimes, and brimful of
mischief, but true as steel to any one she took a notion to.
Wall, things run along so ; and ev'ry body looked at it as a
settled thing, and begun to joke us 'bout the weddin'. Seth
drew in his horns too, and to spite her, went off and married
Lociny Sweet, down ' t'the Holler' ; put his own eyes out, a
tryin' to put out other people's. She's led him a dog's life
on't all his days ; makes him toe the mark, I tell you. He
has to stay to hum and tend the baby, while *she* goes off to
sowin' s'ciety, or t'the ' Female weekly mission meetin' for

heathen.' He has to git up and cook the breakfast 'fore he calls her; does the washing and churnin', and helps do chores gin'rally, when he aint nothin' else to see to. Its broke him down turrible. Wall, as I was sayin', we b'gun to git things together for sister, 'ginst the time she'd want 'em; we'd keep askin' her *when* that was? She never made much of any answer, and we all thought 'twas cur'ous how bashful she'd become; but brother Jesse never would have her teased a mite, —You 'sleep, Rubiny Ann?"

"No, indeed!" I cried, starting up. "I am listening. What came next, Miss Roby?"

" A weddin', child; but not sister's," she answered drearily. " What'll you say, child, if I tell you that in all this time he'd courted her (over two years) he'd never said one word 'bout *that?*" After a pause she resumed. " One beautiful spring mornin', Jesse come in from the barn, and beckoned me out in't the cheese-room: 'twas eighteen years ago come next May, but it don't seem half so long. He looked dreadful cut up 'bout something, and he hem'd and hawed ever so long, 'fore he finally got it out: ' Roby, Cornelus Brooks wus married last night, down to Square Lee's, to Car'line. What d'you think of that?' Them's his very words. I never was so took aback in all my life. ' It can't be; brother Jesse,' I said, ' for he was here last Sunday night: he and Sary never had no fallin' out, I know.' ' I can't help *that*,' he answered. ' It's so, for Mr. Pierce jest went away from here; he come up to tell me: he said we ought to know of it. They've gone off t'the city, and I hope they'll stay there one spell. I'm a church member, sister, in good and regular standin'; I don't want to have hard feelin's to one of God's creeturs; but I *do* feel tempted to do somethin' awful to that are man. I'm glad—for *his*

sake—he aint here.' I s'pose, mabby, I looked as if I would
do somethin', for he said right off—'we'll leave him in God's
hands, sister Roby. His sin will find him out yit'—and I
tell ye it has, Rubiny."

" What did you do ?" I asked eagerly.

" Do ! what could I do ? Brother Jesse told me, I must
tell the rest, and have it over with; and he jest turned and
went off t'the barn again, 'fore I could open my head. I
can't b'gin to say how long I stood there. Jesse went to
threshin' the barn floor with the flail, as hard as he could.
I knew he was a tryin' to work off the chokin' feelin'. I'm
'fraid if he'd got sight o' that are man jest then, he'd a flayed
him alive. Wall, child, pretty soon Sary herself come out to
see what kept me so long. We'd jest tore up for house-
cleanin', and wus all in commotion. She looked like a June
pink as she come out a singin' like a bobolink, though the
tune was mournful like ; I can hear it yit—" Miss Roby attempted to sing it:

' 'Twas down in the lowlan's, where Mary Ann did wander!
   Twas down in the lowlan's, where Mary Ann did roam!
   She belonged to this nation, she's lost her dear relation,
   Cries the poor fisherman's little gal, whose friends are dead and gone.'

" Wall, it struck me kinder sad and sudden, and I bust out
a cryin'. She stopped and looked scart. ' Why sister, what
has happened ?' says she, kinder thick. I never saw *you* cry
·before.' "

" Well, Miss Roby ?" I questioned, for she stopped and
sighed several times.

" Yis, child! I jest put my arms round her and said,
' Thank the Lord, you haint lost *all* your friends. *I'm*
thankful on the whole that you've got red of the desateful

scamp.' Wall, she looked puzzleder than ever: she didn't
see no drift at all, and I jest had to speak right out plain. I'd
a thousand deal ruther cut my little finger off, child. She
didn't take it as I expected. She didn't faint away, nor
scream, nor cry, nor nothin'. She jest turned white as a
ghost, never made no sound, only turned away from me, and
went off t'the haymow, and there she stayed the whole blessed
forenoon alone—none on us dared go anigh her; but she
come into dinner jest as usual, and she worked like a slave
the whole arternoon. We never said no more 'bout it 'fore
her, nor she nuther to us.

"The neighbors pryed and peeked round consid'rable.
Some folks tried to make a great handle out of it; they said
lots of things, but there wan't a word of truth in none of
'em; no livin' soul ever knowed *jest* how matters stood: she
bore up so bravely, I wanted to break off with the whole
Lee tribe; they'd used her so pizon mean; but she wouldn't
hear a word 'bout it, and so we jest came and went as before."

"She died?" I ventured to ask.

"Yis! Eighteen years ago," said Miss Roby, "she went
like all the rest. She wanted to go, and we couldn't ask her
to stay in this troublesome world. She kep' sayin' over and
over to herself, hours afore she dropped away, 'where the
weary are at rest.' It's on her tombstun; Jesse *would* have
it on."

"You must all hate me," I said soberly, after the excitement of hearing a story had vanished, and I reflected on the
sorrow my father's conduct had brought to that peaceful roof.

"Massy, no, child; what be you a thinkin' of? I never
see brother Jesse so fond of ary child as he is of you. These
things all happened ages ago, you know; and they'd be
dreadful put ont if they knew I'd told you."

Still, the unwelcome thought hovered over me like a bird
of ill omen; it brooded in the pauses of Miss Roby's stream
of talk, poured now into inattentive ears; then, flapping its
black wings, it scudded noiselessly out of the locked door,
along the dark corridors, until it came to a room—opened
wide. Was it my fatality to forever see that deserted room,
with closed and open eyelids? thought I mournfully. It was
no fancy, after all, which made me feel her vanished presence.
She *was* there: she herself opened the door for us to enter.
Does she ordain *me* to do penance for a father's sin? Is the
robe of retribution now enveloping his head, to extend its
sable skirts over all these weary distances of time, space, and
repentance, to reach my unparticipating knowledge? Yes!
it was but implicitly vindicating the immutability of its own
law. I assented to its justice. My excited fancy was quick
to pursue, to picture awaiting scenes in the future. How
strange! thought I, that Miss Roby does not suspect this.

Miss Roby would not easily have been led to entertain this
idea; she would have scouted its wild impracticability; relentlessly pursued the gloomy fugitive, and finally laughed it ,
down, as the essence of all that is ridiculous. In her sensible
fancy floated no airy specks of doom, ripening to an impas-
sable border land of morbid imaginings. Fact kept the current clear. The material was in her nature, too ponderous
for these subtile threads of the spiritual to leave any definite
trace of their workings. Sooth to say, her mere aspect, and
one utterance in her stentorian tones, were enough to fright-
en peacefully disposed nocturnal visitants back to their unquiet rest. I could imagine her elevating that wide-frilled
nightcap in grim composure, to scan closely the shadowy
mystery; resting her chin in one hard palm, as she then serenely opened a conversation with the spectral dame from

Paradise. And the manner of this discourse, in which she would endeavor to "get the upper hand" of ghostly logic—unawed, a little excited, but not in the least frightened—it all rushed over me so vividly that I laughed. This unlucky giggle started her bolt upright.

"I don't, for the life of me, see nothin' to laugh at. It's what'll overtake all on us some day," she gruffly observed, evidently inferring my mirth was occasioned by her stories. I made no response, and she presently recommenced; flooding me with all manner of by-gone recollections.

"Wall, now," she remarked, settling herself comfortably among the pillows, "I ain't no b'liever at all in signs and wonders, and never *thought* much about them things, till arter Phebe Besely was took down with canker-rash, though I'd allers heerd, from a child up, as many stories as'd stretch from Dan to Beersheba, 'bout this very thing. Poor Phebe was dreadful sick. They had a council of doctors for her, from all parts. Old Doctor Ray was here, from Chispa, to see her; but t'wan't no go. They all give her up, sooner or later, all but Doctor Lovejoy; he stuck to her till he see there warn't a grain o' hope she'd ever pick up agin, then *he* told 'em too. They wanted he should keep a tryin'; so he'd jest give her a leetle somethin' to ease her along. She was fevery, and out of her head most of the time, ravin' crazy, as you may say. Her poor mother was most distracted. Wall, child, she was struck with death four days afore she died; didn't sense nobody nor nothin'; eyes sot in her head, and her under-jaw had to be propped up to keep her mouth shet. I don't know but she'd a been in that condition yit, if I hadn't happened to run in there. What to do they didn't know. You see they couldn't do nothin' for *her*, and 'twas awful to set and see her in sech a plight. Sister Zilpha'd been in that morn-

6

in', and she told me how she was. It was my week to do
housework, but I told her ef she's a mind to wash up the
supper-dishes I'd go in and watch, as I hadn't been over the
door-sill in most a fortnit; so I did. It was a bitter cold
night. I never see nobody change so as Mis' Besely had;
she looked proper old, and as thin as a shad—most worn
out a watchin. She catched holt o' my hand the minute I
sot foot in the entry, and says she, 'Roby, do see if there
can't nothin' be done for that poor child in there,' and she
bust out a cryin'. I went in, and Phebe lay there stupid
like, and mournin' jest like a dove when she's pickin' one
of her little ones to pieces. I've often heerd 'em in the raft-
ers, where they've nests, and it's the mournfullest sound in
creation; 'twould most make a stun weep to hear 'em.

"I stood there ever so long. All to once I happened to
think. Says I: 'What sort of a bed *is* this cre, Miss Besely ?'
'Why,' says she, 'don't you know a feather-bed, Roby,
when you see it afore your face'n eyes ?'

"'What *kind* of feathers, I mean,' says I, 'goose feathers
or hen's feathers ?'

"'Hen's feathers,' said she, looking kinder down'n the
mouth. You see, Rubiny, they wan't very well-to-do in the
world, and had to put up with sech as they could git—'that's
the reason she can't die,' said I to myself; 'it must come off
short order;' and it *did* come off, and she jest dropped away
as easy as a lamb. In less than an hour I was sowin' on her
shroud. I won't have a hen's feather bed in the house, Rubiny;" she presently added, "they're so soggy-like; it's
'nough to beat one all out to stir em' up ev'ry day. I tried
that once, when I took care of Aunt Chloe, and I got tuckered out putty soon."

I expected to hear Aunt Chloe's history, and as that

would doubtless suggest others, I anticipated an utterly
sleepless night, but, fortunately, Miss Roby had talked herself
into a sleepy mood, and, pausing a little too long after this
last sentence, some slumbrous weight obscured these memories, and, clipping the tangled thread of narrative, left grateful silence.

What a kindly magic lurks in sunshine's potent ray!
Though I slept uneasily, and woke early—a fitful start, from
direful dreams; though I hastily covered my poor silly head
with the heavy bed-clothes, hushing my respiration, to listen
anxiously for sound from above, denoting—I knew not what
dreadful apparition—yet, with night's sombreness fled likewise the tormenting host. A coward's evanescent courage
returned with the first stray gleam of dawn, peeping at me
from under the white cotton curtain's edge; its broadening
smile routed aught of a timorous nature, and scattered it
beyond recall. I dared lift my flushed face from its burial
in the smothering pillows. I counted Miss Roby's antique
garniture on their lofty pegs. I surveyed curiously the
wondrous wall-paper, of wreathed bunches of scarlet-leaved
poppies, alternating in rows, with strutting peacocks, elate—
mortal like—with an empty-headed estimate of their own
shallow importance and social magnitude. From the ceiling
they likewise lifted their heads, and spread their gorgeous
tails, the poppies blooming most naturally on the same soil-
less heights. Miss Roby suddenly stirred; awoke. "Bless
me!" she ejaculated, rubbing open her eyes, and viewing me
rather surprisedly. "Do tell if your peepers are open
a'ready! I guess I kinder oversleep' myself this mornin'," she
added apologetically. She rose with alacrity. "I most
forgot to ask you if you dreamt anything?" she said presently; "cause, you know what you dream in a strange

room 'll surely come to pass—least-ways the dream-book says so."

· "I hope not!" I exclaimed, shuddering; "do *you* believe in dreams, Miss Roby?"

She paused in the act of inserting a leg in a blue woollen stocking, and eyed me curiously. "T'want pleasant then, I take it!" she slowly answered. "Dreams allers go by contraries; if you dream of a funeral, it's a sure sign of a weddin', and you can most gin'rally tell right off whose t'will be. There's Ira Purse now 's been steppin' up to your cousin 'Maudy long enough for't to end in one. I like to dream too o' clear water, it's a good sign; muddy water 's a sure sign o' trouble, and a white horse bodes death; but law!" she hurriedly added, as if ashamed to know even any thing of this mystic lore, "I never laid up nothin' long I dreamed of; no dependence to be put on 'em, you know."

"Then you *don't* believe in them," I pertinaciously said.

"Wall, no! I don know as I do," she answered doubtfully, and resuming her toilette, "though folks do have proper cur'ous notions in 'em sometimes; and it beats all, how *real* they be. Now there's a house I go to—in a dream—ev'ry little while. I never saw one a bit like it anywheres else; but I've got so 's I know ev'ry door and winder, and the rooms look as nat'ral as life."

"Do you see any people in them?" I inquired.

"Wall, now, that's the strangest part of the hull," she answered quickly, "sometimes it's as still and lonesome as a tomb; furnitur all piled up ready for movin', and not a soul to be seen. Then agin, there's a queer couple there— old country folks I should think. I never see no other faces but them two. The woman don't wear a dress like our'n; it's short, and a frill round the waist (and that is blue stuff)

with a peaked bodice, and it's despit low in the neck: I
wanted to take holt, and give it a yank where it oughter go,
at first—the good-for-nothin' trollop—but I got used to it
arter a few times—'specially as I found out she's a married
woman. She's cumely 'nough, too, Rubiny; but there's an
evil look on her face, and she watches her man proper close.
He is dark complected, with snappin' black eyes, and the
whitest teeth I ever see; long and sharp, as I can make out
when he smiles—I should'nt wonder now, Rubiny—" continued Miss Roby, leaning forward, and whispering impressively, "if he'd been a man-eater once."

"Oh no! Miss Roby," said I, a trifle shocked. "That
can't be, you know."

"Wall," she said—her imaginative faculties at once sub-
siding into their ordinary calm—"'tant real, you know,
only seems so." She picked up her leathern shoe, turned
it over, and zealously blew out the dust.

"Miss Roby," I said eagerly, "I went there last night.
I know it's the very same house; the woman looked as you
say, but—"

"But what, child?" she said, smiling incredulously.

I felt myself turn pale. "Oh! you won't believe it," I
cried, "but let me tell you what I saw there."

"Sartain," assented Miss Roby.

"I saw that woman walk the house from top to bottom,
over and over again, and finally go to the open kitchen door
and stand a long, long time gazing down the dusty road. I,
too, went, and peeped over her shoulder, but she did not see
me. At first I saw nothing; but, away off, I heard the faint
rumble of wheels. They came in sight presently—a white
horse drawing a red lumber wagon, in which sat a man,
driving. He was singing, too, as he drew up across the

road, in front of the barn door—a song in a strange tongue;
I could not make out the words, but the voice was sweet
and powerful. He sprang out, and began unharnessing the
horse. As he turned his back full upon us, I heard a sound
behind me, which made me suddenly turn. There stood
that same woman—her eyes ablaze with fury—holding in
one hand a pistol, which was smoking and snapping, as if
it longed to go off. I thought she was going to kill me,
and started back, almost dead with fright. She never noticed
me at all. She stood a moment in the door; I heard her
mutter something as she raised the weapon at the man
opposite, and fired—not once, but a hundred times. It
seemed as if she would never stop. Even after she had flung
it down—as if it burned her hand—it kept on firing. Then
she hastily picked it up, ran to the well, and dropped it in;
but it never ceased firing, and it gurgled, as if a human
being was drowning."

"Did you see anything else?" queried Miss Roby, with a
knowing nod.

"Yes! the man staggered to the open door, and leaned
against the post. The woman came up to him quietly, with
a satisfied look on her face, as though she had at last accomplished a long-waited-for deed. He spoke to her mildly.
She fiercely shook her head. I did not understand the
words, but I could *feel* what they were saying. He told her
she would gain nothing; she would yet swing for it. She
replied that she would first cut her own throat; and, walking coolly away to the stove, she stirred a kettle of porridge.
The man turned white as death. I ran and brought from a
little bedroom its bed; I spread it on the kitchen floor. I
got some pillows. The woman never saw me; she still
stirred the porridge; but the man smiled into my face most

gratefully. He laid himself down; I covered him with a sheet."

" What then ?" asked Miss Roby, eagerly.

" Oh! then I awoke, cold, uncomfortable, and very much frightened," I answered.

" Wall, child," said Miss Roby, solemnly, " I've seen that are, all acted out jest so. I couldn't a described it better myself; and I've seen more too. You woke too 'arly; but," she added, after a thoughtful pause, "it's clear beyond my reckonin' how *you* should see it too ; I never tell no one my dreams. I'm 'fraid, child; we none on us knows too much 'bout this ere life of ourn. It's a proper strange thing, at the best on't," she said, as we descended the winding stairs, and entered the kitchen.

CHAPTER X.

Miss Sinai was busy with breakfast. The coffee steamed fragrantly from the quaint Britannia urn, surrounded by a colony of pink and white cups and saucers ; in each shallow cup rested a tiny silver spoon—the handle so slender, the bowl so diminutive, that it might well have been an heir-loom from ancestral fairies. The maidenly initials on each shield-like top were, with nearly a century's use, almost ob-literated ; a few faint whirls of tracery remained, ornamented along their lines with numberless dots, in which " M. S. W." were almost lost sight of. These, my hostess signified with gentle pride, were the former property of one Mary Sinai Wade, her great-grandmother, for whom, in part, she was named.

The pewter platter this morning supported luscious slices
of smoked ham, with eggs surrounding its marge; and a
"Johnny cake" was nearing the perfection of browuness on
a shingle before the fire. Uncle Jesse entered, with a pail
of sap from the maple grove, to use in our coffee, in lieu of
sugar. . He gave me a pleasant nod and smile, then stopped
short. "Seems to me you look ruther pimpin' this mornin',"
he said kindly; "guess you didn't sleep the best kind, did
you, Miss Brooks?"

"Miss Brooks, indeed!" chimed in Miss Sinai, quickly;
"and .that puts me in mind, Ruby,.that you are just to call
me Sinai in future. I am missed enough by other people."
("*I* can't afford to *miss* her; I think too much of her,"
laughed her brother;) "unless," interrupted she, "you
choose to adopt the sisterly prefix, like the rest of us. I
mean to *be* your sister, Ruby."

I could only pass my arm round her neck in a close caress at this proof of kindness to a stranger, an orphan and—
Miss Roby's story *would* unwelcomely thrust its visage before me. Sinai stooped to inspect my face. "Oh! *I* know
what the matter is." She darted a questioning look at her
sister Roby, who innocently returned the glance. "I see it
plainly. I was afraid she'd talk the child to death. Sister
Roby never knows when to stop when she's once on a story-
telling track." This she whispered to her brother, and he
good-naturedly retorted: "Wall, you know 'twont answer
to put out sister Roby, and she can steal a nap this forenoon to make it up."

The day sped delightfully. I visited the woods, where
the sap was slowly gathering for the sugar-making. From
massive trunks of maples, hoary with age, and garnished
with many a scar, down slender wooden channels, the sweet

liquid dropped musically into waiting pails, bowls, pans of
tin, and from these was emptied into a huge caldron, which
smoked and steamed over a blazing fire of fragrant pine
knots. Uncle Jesse superintended it. "It's commenced
to run putty bravely, I tell you, Ruby, for this time o'
year," he observed in the pauses of his labor. "This ere
thaw is jest the right thing to help it along : freeze nights
and thaw days is what we want."

"Shall you make much?" I queried innocently. He
struck the seamed trunk of the nearest tree with his horny
palm.

"Can't tell, you see. All depends on this ere. I
shouldn't wonder ef we *did*," he said, with a knowing twinkle in his keen eyes. "One year we fetched 'bout five hundered weight; that's putty fair for a *small* grove."

"Isn't that nearly done?" I pointed to the boiling mass.

He laughed. "I guess you hanker arter some on't.
Wall, when it's ready to sugar off I'll call you, and show ye
how to eat it; don't one in fifty know *how!*"

He kept his word, some hours later. Rolling a ball of
snow, he dipped it in the cooling sugar, and placed it before
me. "There, Ruby, that's good for sore mouth," he said,
artlessly, watching me; "take right holt now, as though
you meant it."

Towards sunset I returned to the charmed exile of poor
Crusoe. I vented a ludicrous sigh as I finished, and restored
the volume to its musty nook in the desk, at which Sinai
bit her lip, to repress a smile. I watched her, as she worked,
in the bright fire-light. The shining rods flew in and out of
the smooth, firm texture—clinking faintly against each other
a sort of tune to the monotonous flow of voices. Insensibly,
drowsiness assailed me, but I indignantly warded it off, feel-

6*

ing my dignity in some degree imperilled if I should be
caught napping before my wide-awake seniors—that tena-
cious dignity of a dozen years, which tries, so ludicrously to
beholders, to suppress the ways of childhood and to ape the
ways of womanhood. I opened my eyes unnaturally wide,
and rubbed them vigorously with the back of my hand, as I
thought, quite unobserved. Another childish delusion. At
the third repetition of this involuntary pantomime, Miss
Sinai surprised the unwary sentinel. I was vanquished in
my own citadel. Almost, without knowing how or whither,
I found myself tucked warmly into Miss Zilpha's high bed,
in a cosy room, on the first floor. Sinai bent over and kissed me. "It's too bad," she said warmly, "going from pil-
lar to post, in this fashion. I wanted you, but sister said it
was *her* turn; but after to-night—" and she nodded her
head smilingly. "I shall charge her not to waken you," she
added, as she drew a shawl around her shoulders, seated
herself by my side, and softly knitted away, gazing at me
meanwhile with good-humored fondness. My memory thus
confusedly sketched her, ere it closed its portfolio for a
dreamy ramble. I did not like Miss Zilpha. Her sisters'—
Sinai and Charity—pleasant attributes only rendered more
conspicuous her lack thereof, amounting even to deformity.
Even Miss Roby, gruff, uncouth, plain, and shy, was thoroughly kind-hearted. Not willingly would she have
wronged a fly of its inheritance. Her character had a malicious aspect sometimes, but subsequent actions always
proved it to have been only surface deep. She scorned
hypocrisy; she never feigned a friendship she could not
feel. Miss Zilpha was both plain and shy, with an unseason-
able addition of selfishness, showing its face constantly in
little things; conceit of her own mighty self, and intense

love for fault-finding and slander; she had other points scarcely more precious, but these shone in a prominent light. Miss Roby revelled in gossip of former days; but she never deliberately sat down to devise evil prophecies regarding her neighbors, to dart groundless insinuations into the fairest lives. Miss Zilpha frequently smote thus, with merciless zeal, merely because her nature was too warped to view the sunniest aspect of sayings and occurrences. She had a hard, stony look in her inflamed eyes, which her spectacles transformed into a species of sly cunning, not a whit more agreeable. This evening she entered her room, cautiously, I suppose, for I did not hear her. Why, then, did she approach the flame of the light she carried so close to my face, that its warmth, mingled with her fetid breath, smote me into wakefulness? If that was her intention, she accomplished it admirably. However, I purposely kept my lids closed, and as she turned from her survey I peeped from them covertly. She trod on tiptoe across the room, in a short, quick manner, making thrice the noise of her usual footfall. She opened her closet door, and gave a searching glance round its narrow interior, then under the valanced bed. Her maidenly nerves thus reassured, she opened the door into the hall, and peered cautiously down its dark space; afterwards closing, and placing a chair-back against it —a truly formidable barrier. I thought she never would have done with her nocturnal preparations, useless as they were; and she crowned them all by hanging a shoe on each tall bedpost, as a surety for pleasant dreams. No! she had not *yet* finished. She knelt at the bed's foot, for a short silent prayer.

Trifles touch us in early years sooner than a miracle in later. The heart ossifies its emotions with growing knowl-

edge and experience. That mute, humble posture of the
gray old woman woke in me a momentary thrill of pity for
her infirmities, and of respect for the piety which it seems
her breast harbored, as well as others, more worldly favored.
This transient solemnity was completely dissipated by her
subsequent action. " Prayers first, snuff afterwards," I ir-
reverently muttered, as I watched the pungent incense, in
mammoth pinches, rise to and disappear devoutly within its
fore-ordained receptacle.   She enjoyed it with relishing
sighs, after which she shoved the box under her pillow,
placed a clove in her mouth, mounted cautiously the creaking couch, and, in a few moments, was sound asleep.

   I lay, dreamily pondering many things ; curious vestiges
of impossibilities, which *will* flit vagrantly through immature brains, and depart as speedily to make room for their
successors.   As I gazed at the suspended shoes on the bed-
posts, to my astonishment, their owner calmly arose, tied
them on, seized the unlit candle, and—displacing the guard-
ing chair—opened the door.   "Where are you going?" I
cried in dismay.   She gave no heed, nor even appeared to
hear me.   I spoke once more ; but she was now out of both
sight and hearing.   " Very likely she has forgotten something she will need in the morning, and has gone to seek
it," I reasoned ; but I thought it extremely odd that she
did not light the candle.   Noiselessly as she went, she returned, after a short absence, empty-handed of aught save
the iron candlestick.   This she deposited on exactly the
same spot it stood before ; she hung the shoes again in their
former position, and crept into bed.   If she slumbered, it
was in the strangest form of this refreshing unconsciousness.
A shimmer of starlight stole through the uncurtained windows,—a weak solution indeed—just sufficient to dispel utter

gloom, and enable me to define certain objects. It showed
me Miss Zilpha's face; always colorless, it now looked of the
hue of death, yellow and ghastly. Her eyes were opened
wide, but she respired regularly. Presently she threw her
hands up over her head, with an uneasy motion, and they
remained close locked together. Her parted lips emitted a
moan, as of a sufferer in some deadly peril. She straightened her limbs, and they remained so; the muscles tense
and rigid. Always repulsive, she now looked doubly abhor-
rent. I summoned enough courage, however, to endeavor
to waken her, which seemed at first an impossible task. I
shook her with all my strength, but it barely sufficed to turn
her on one side, only, afterwards, to roll back like a log.
This I thrice repeated; then I drew down her hands. They
were cold as ice, and almost as hard. I vigorously conquered my loathing, and chafed them until my own fingers
ached; she did not arouse, and she moaned still louder. I
remember feeling a vague fear that she might be dying. I
had heard and read of people being stricken as suddenly,
and with this fear came also a thought of my own responsibility. I endeavored to pluck up a little needful spirit, to
summon help, ere it prove too late. "Perhaps it already
is," I whispered nervously, as I sprang to the floor, and
made a desperate grasp at the candle. Then, either the
coldness of the painted, carpetless floor, or my own cowardice, struck such a chill upon my unusual courage, that it
all exhaled, and—still holding aloft the iron candlestick, as
a trophy of my hardihood—I sprang again amid the sheets.
"Miss Zilpha," I cried bitterly, repeating and prolonging it,
which she did not heed, and I had no hope of its reaching
other ears, so many rooms intervening. Alas! I lacked the
simple fortitude to slip hastily across those rooms, and sum-

mon her brother, whose room was adjoining the invalid's; so I fell to shaking more energetically than before; one more vigorous roll than the others sent her beyond my control, and over she tumbled to the hard, cold floor. I was both relieved and frightened at this unexpected result; frightened at first, but relieved when I saw her move feebly, then hastily rise, and rub her eyes in bewilderment. I drew a long breath; "Oh! I am so glad," I cried, as she stared, first at the bed, then at the floor.

"Massy to me! how'd I come here?" she asked, presently resuming her rightful quarters.

"I pushed you out," I replied.

"You did, hey?" she said severely. "And what for, pray tell? It's mor'n half to own it; that's a fact."

"Dear me! Miss Zilpha," I said hastily, "you acted so strangely. I thought you were dying. I spoke to you, then I shook you, and I suppose I pushed á trifle too hard."

"Oh!" She seemed relieved. "I s'pose I had the nightmare. It takes me powerful hard sometimes; seems so I's bound hand and foot, and couldn't stir for the life of me; sometimes I look up and see a lot of wild critturs all ready to spring at me, and I can't git out the way, nor holler, nor nothin'; and sometimes it's a crazy man on the tight run arter me, with a hatchet; and sometimes I'm a goin' like a perfect harrycane; sometimes it's one consate and sometimes a'nuther."

"But you moaned, as if you were sick," I said. She looked surprised.

"Did I? I didn't know's I made no sound. I'm glad you woke me out of't, child, though I 'spect I'll be black and blue to pay for that are jounce. Sister Delia used to tell me, too," she went on, "that I walked in my sleep, but I allers thought

that t'was some o' her gammon. I never remember cuttin'
up any sech capers," she added confidentially.

I told her of her walk this night. She laughed incredulously. " I guess you made that are up out o' whole-cloth,"
she ironically retorted. "We'll see, now, if everything ain't
jest's I left it, to-morrow mornin' ; and 'twouldn't be, you
know, if I.did as you say." She spoke positively, and I had
no desire to contradict. " This tellin' fibs is a dreadful bad
practice," she resumed, severely, "leads to the gallers in the
end. Strange, now, how some folks'll put up with sech
things ! I've seen them that thought 'twas all good milk porridge ; but if *I* had children, I'd whip it out of 'em if there was
a possibility I *could.*"

I knew she was alluding to me, and I felt indignant at her
base suspicions. I abhorred and dreaded a falsehood more
than the whole catalogue of other sins. There is something
so mean, so abject, in the countenance of a liar ; it singles
him out at once from the rest of mankind, and proclaims.
him decent only in solitude ; fit for no other office than to
serve as a world's opprobrious football ; and were their paltry bodies as elastic as their consciences, they would outlast,
in this menial capacity, scores of generations.

" Be you a Christian ?" resumed my judge, " 'cause I think
it's high time you was a thinkin' on sech matters, and 'layin'
up treasure in heaven, where neither moth nor rust doth cor-
rupt, and where thieves do not break through and steal.'
That are's a mighty solemn question, child !"

I felt a little sulky, and would not answer. She went on:

" Now, I used to have sister Siny sleep with me when she
was a little gal, I used to be pestered in them days 'bout
sleepin', and I'd wake up Siny, and larn her the beautifulest
hymns. She'd rouse right up, too, the minute I wanted her

to, and say 'em all over as nice as ever you see. I remember
one went like this—'twas mother's favorite." She struck up
in a doleful key the following :

> " 'There is a flower, a holy one; it blossoms in my path,
> It needs no dew or daily sun; nor falling showers it hath;
> It blooms as brightly in the storm, as on a cloudless day ;
> It rears on high its humble form, when others fade away;
> When others fade away, when others fa-ade a-way.'

"Know what that is, Ruby? Wall, listen now; the next
varse'll tell you :

> " 'That plant is *Faith*; its holy leaves, reviving odors shed
> Upon the lonely place of grief, er mansions of thee dead;
> God *is* its sun, its livin' light; an happy hour he lends,
> When silently in sorrer's night, religion's dew de-cends,
> Religion's de-ew de-cends; reli-gi-on's dew de-cends.'

" Sister Siny was the best behaved little gal ever you see ;
you don't come across no sech now-a-days. When *I* was
young, children didn't know more'n everybody else ; they're
sassy 'nough *now*, goodness knows. *My* mother used to
tell me 'children must be seen and not heard!' and I was
fool 'nough to believe it. I used to take Siny out with me,
when I went neighborin'; I'd put her in a chair, and tell her
she mustn't stir. Law! she'd no more think o' gettin' up
than as though she wan't made. She's a dreadful cunnin' little thing. I remember once, I had to go over to the pond for
a pail o' water—our cistern was dry—there wan't no one in
the house, as it happened, but just us two, and I couldn't be
bothered with her a taggin' along ; she wan't but four year
old ; so I set her up in the high chair, and told her to fold
her hands ; now, says I, do you set there till I come back ;
if you don't, I'll cut ye in two. Wall, I asked if she'd

minded me, when I come back? 'Oh,' says she, as pert as ye please, 'some one knocked, and I jumped down and opened the door. It was lame Joyce, the peddler, and he took me up and kissed me, and set me up in my chair, and gave me this little tin cup!'"

"Annah would have been dancing around the room," I said.

"Most likely," she assented. "She's a good-natured little thing, when you've done set all, but a reg'lar fly-away; she wants holdin' in. Sister Siny was one of a thousand though. Let me see," she mused, "what was't I was goin' to say? it's slipt my mind intirely. Oh!" catching a clue, "I was goin' to tell you how we'd wake up in the night and count over names; did you ever do it?"

"I don't know what you mean, Miss Zilpha."

"Wall, say we take Maria now for one," she explained— "you must think over all you know in town by that name, and I'll keep count. There's Maria Reeve's one," pronounced Miss Zilpha, "and Maria Lovejoy's two"—and so on, until she had sifted the village pretty thoroughly of those bearing that interesting cognomen. Then she suggested the Amandas, and afterwards the Albinas and Elizabeths—including the abbreviation Betsy—and Charlottes; also a timid census-taking of happily unconscious Davids, Thomases and Israels. Miss Zilpha's old heart leaped again to the tune of early recollections. Her repulsive frigidity thawed more and more. She vouchsafed towards me a more condescending familiarity, relating for my edification numberless anecdotes of her sisters. I have an indistinct remembrance, too, of feeling her arm inserting itself under my heavy head, to draw me in closer proximity to herself—an act of fondness I was too sleepy to repel, and which I was

glad of afterwards, if it gave her but a transitory pleasure.
In my dreams our late intellectual exercise still pursued me.
A panorama of familiar faces glided past me; the entire village population loomed out in solid phalanx; blithe lads and
merry lasses, the blind, the sickly, the old and young, bearing huge placards of painted names, which I was serenely
counting.

CHAPTER XI.

On our homeward drive, Uncle Jesse drew from his
pocket a little package, neatly folded in brown paper: "This
ere's for a gal called Ruby Brooks. You take keer of't, and
when you light on that chick, jest toss it over to her."

"A book!" I cried delightedly, feeling its shape through
the wrappings; "how good of you, Uncle Jesse——!"

"Don't know nothin' you're sayin'!" he interrupted; "I
ain't noways 'countable for that are. Sister Siny slipped it
into my overcut pocket, jest's we come out of the porch, and
whispered to me what to do with't. Now, don't go to
thankin' on her, when you come acrost her; she won't like
it. Here! you may's well take this in .with you too, 'n
divide it all round the board," and the good soul piled in
my arms a huge cake of maple sugar.

"Oh! come in, Uncle Jesse."

"I guess not!" he answered doubtfully. "T'aint egg-
zactly friendly, I know, to sneak away agin so, but I see the
domine in there, through the winder, and I ain't in jest the
trim to scrape a 'quaintance with him; not that I mean to
be proud," he added quickly, " but I may's well be trottin'

back. The gals feel ruther peaked to stay alone long; so
many stragglers round about, you know, and Sister Zilpha
allers *was* a spleeny piece. Good-bye!" he repeated kindly.
" Come 'n see us agin afore a thousand year—Hallo there !
leetle frolicsome," he suddenly shouted, as Annah came
bounding down the walk, with shouts of transport, Demis
following, in but a trifle more sedate fashion, and Mark bringing up the rear. " You think you're hull-footed now, I
'spose," he said good-naturedly to the merry trio. " Law !
ef *she* ain't dancing too. Wall, hum's hum arter all said
and done ; and dance away young creeturs ; frolic to your
heart's content, 'cause you're seein' you're happiest days now,
and you don't know it." He checked a sigh, which action
struck us in a fresh mirthful vein, and again we laughed.

" Bless me ! Uncle Jesse, I like to stay anywhere else better than at home. Then I can do a little bit as I like.
Now, its 'Demis Dorothy Martin' (I hate middle names,
don't you ?) ' I *should* think you'd be ashamed of yourself—
most a young woman grown.' Law me ! what's the use ?"
continued Demis, peering into Uncle Jesse's puzzled and
amused face, then—very unexpectedly to us—cutting an entirely original "pigeon wing" right in the face of the window. Two pair of horrified eyes gleamed from it, as I took
a hasty survey. The sash lifted a little. " Come inter the
house this minute, ef you can't behave yourself," screamed
her mother's shrill tones, and she shut it with a bang.

The wheels slowly craunched around, making deep ruts
in the spongy soil.

" I should like to bury my perplexed cranium in your
garret, Mr. Warner, for—well, say a week or two," said
Mark, rather gloomily. He commenced whistling to the
impatient grays. " That's a nice bit of horse-flesh," he

added, more cheerfully. Uncle Jesse, in turn, eyed him sharply.

"I guess you'd be sick o' your bargain in less'n half that time, my lad," he put forth slowly; "them quarters was gin over t'the rats and rubbish—to say nothin' of spooks and spiders; great black fellers's big's my fist—'fore even *you* come along. Now, my boy," he mused audibly, "what's to pay, I wonder? traces broke, eh? out o' joint a peg? don't hitch, mabbe, with strangers. I've heered mother tell the gals, oceans of times, that 'too many cooks spile the broth;' I guess there's a good deal in't too," he added, in the lowest of cautious voices, with sundry covert winks, for Mark's enlightenment. I threw Mark an astonished glance. A moment since he had been merry as a lark. I could not comprehend the sudden change to the extreme of soberness. Mr. Warner leaned his fat elbows on his fat knees, and seemed lost in thought, as he leisurely tapped the end of his riding-whip against his yellow teeth. He evidently expected some answer to his numerous surmises. Mark smiled in the dear old man's kind face; gave a comical twist of his mouth, and said—nothing.

"Wall, wall!" observed Mr. Warner, carefully gathering up the reins, and turning in his seat to give a scrutinizing look at an approaching team, "that must be the deacon's pacer," he soliloquized softly, "by the way it siddle's along; I'll have to jog on, 'cause he can't turn out here. I was goin' to say," he added earnestly to Mark, "that the old homestead's allers to hum. Come up any time. You can lodge in any room you take a notion to, and, furthermore, I'll give you as much maple-sweet as you can lay your jaws to." He drove off, softly humming the first bar of "Old Hundred." Mark slowly strolled up the opposite hill.

" Dear me !" whispered Demis, with a comical little sigh, as we stepped on the broad piazza. "*Such* a time as we've had, Ruby ? I wish the new elder, that they made such a fuss over, was in Bungay. Mark called him a lunk-head last night to mother, and she was *so* mad." She pinched my arm to enjoin silence, as I was about to answer, for the door opened, and her mother's face looked out, fairly purple with suppressed wrath. She darted me a scornful look. " Why don't you come in the house ?" she asked sharply, " instid of hangin' out round it, like a sneak. Nobody won't harm you, I guess not, if you don't give 'em occasion," she finished, sarcastically. Certainly this was not the greeting I had been picturing to myself, the livelong day. More than passive kindness I never looked for, at any time, from my undemonstrative relative ; but this thrust was so unkind and uncalled for ; I was so grieved and astonished, that I passed her by without answering. I looked back instinctively, to see her reach out her bony fingers at Demis, who lingered behind ; she caught her by the arm and shook her roughly. " Let me catch you a cuttin' up sech didoes agin, if you dare," she fiercely whispered. " Do you hear ?" " Yes, marm," meekly answered Demis. " Wall, do you mean to mind your P's and Q's—*that's* what I want to know ?" asked her incensed parent, treating her gratuitously to another impressive shake. Demis again dutifully responded, repressing a cry of fear and pain.

." Right b'fore my face and eyes, and the new minister too. I'm mortified to death. You ought to have a guardeen put over ye," added her mother, sternly—gradually relaxing her hold, then finally suffering her to enter. Demis threw her apron over her head, and darted up stairs, sobbing bitterly. Annah patted softly away after her.

In the atmosphere of the kitchen some elements seemed
strangely displaced; though, as far as housewifery went, all
was perfection.   Every separate article in it shone, from the
effects of the usual Saturday's scrubbing.   Uncle Joel sat
by the stove, an unusual thoughtfulness on his rotund
face.   He eyed the coals awhile, ere looking up at me, as I
went and stood by his chair; then he patted my head kindly, and an expression of real pleasure caressed his face; his
eyes sought mine wistfully, but he said nothing.

I followed Deborah into the pantry.   "There's war in
the wigwam," she muttered, with a cautious glance.   She
tried hard to muster a smile, but it was not at home, and
made but a brief tarry—brief, indeed, for the most scrupulously genteel of such callers.   Used to her moods, I detected
a scowl on her forehead, betokening displeasure; her thick
lips, too, gathered in an ominous pucker.   She was brimful
to the muzzle of explosive matter, and waiting only an ignit-
ing word for a commotion, such as frequently swept across
her pathway, to ensue.   Meanwhile the unconscious divine
rocked to and fro in "the keeping-room" alone, while the
preparations for supper, under the sullen Deborah's care,
were slowly progressing.   The door was ajar.   Through the
narrow crack I stole peeps at the latest Northfield novelty,
until my aunt's re-entrance to the kitchen warned me away.
I bethought me then of the sugar, and produced it; at sight
of which, the constraint visibly lessened its rigor, and Uncle
Jesse's donation received hearty encomiums, both on its superior quality and its generous size.   It seems that the minister had an appreciative taste for the sweets of life, done up
in this convenient shape; for, unasked, he came out to see
it, at which Deborah sniffed irefully.   She looked unconcernedly *over* his head, when he approached her with a

question. When, after a time, she lowered her optics to bear duly on his, and condescended sufficiently to reply, her answer was so indifferent, disrespectful, and widely short of the mark, that it evidently galled the parson to the quick. He retreated hastily from the table.

Deborah had an incurable habit, when offended, of showing her wrath in this and similar ways: in roundabout but pertinent questions, propounded with apparent innocence, but owning a malicious originator; in often totally omitting to answer a civil question—though, if you casually remarked upon her growing deafness, she would retort, hotly, that "she could hear as well as she ever could, thank heaven!" Often she would covertly uncover the cause of her anger, by insinuating speeches, directed to any inanimate object in the room, but cutting keenly the one for whom they were launched. This unlucky evening the arrows flew thickly—guardedly, it is true, and abruptly ceasing whenever Aunt Rhoda—of whom she stood a little in awe—entered, or came within hearing distance.

As it was Saturday evening, all work was suspended after tea—the family Bible brought into prominent service, while the members alternately read a selected portion of its immortal history—usually the familiar story of Samuel or Joseph, or, perchance, the exploits and death of the strong man among the scoffing Philistines. On Saturday evenings we were expected to retire early. Going to my room this night, after these exercises, I found Demis musing dreamily by the open window. I commenced to rally her on her taste for solitude. She answered me abstractedly. "And you got specially mentioned in prayers too," I went on, gravely.

To my surprise, she burst into tears, impetuouslywaving

me back when I approached to console her. She gasped, and sobbed hysterically. "I hate the weasen-faced, red-haired little puppet above ground," she cried vehemently. "He has no business to burn up Mark's pictures, as he does." Seeing my puzzled look, she hastened to explain, between her sobs, how the minister incited her mother to destroy Mark's sketches—calling them "temptations of the evil one"—as the only way to turn his inclinations to the ministry. She described the scene which followed, with a burst of indignation, and frequent ejaculations of hatred to the instigator.

"And what did Mark say?" I asked.

"Not a word. He has got beyond talking, I think. He put away his brushes and pencils, and locked them up."

"Where is Amanda? I hardly missed her, she isolated herself so completely from the family."

"She went up to see Olive this afternoon. *She* hasn't any feeling. She sides right in, against Mark; says 'it's good enough for him; he must be sick, to care so for his daubs, useless things as they are.'" She closed her lips with scornful emphasis.

CHAPTER XII.

THE Rev. Silas Fuller was a dapper little man; spry as a youthful cricket, and seldom as long quiet. He squinted horribly, therefore wore spectacles — gold-bowed ones — which produced a profound impression upon his congregation, and helped decidedly toward conversion. His gait was rather peculiar—midway between a walk and a trot, as though he was perpetually trying to keep even pace with some invisible longer-striding companion. That he ever stumbled into the pastoral office was the great mistake of his life. Such are not the men whom Nature selects, as rightful generals over armies of pilgrim souls. She does not so maltreat her offspring, by sending them, as teacher, a narrow mind, a hopeless bigot, a pretentious dunce. But here he was, in all his self-styled glory; his dapper head fitting to his dapper body, by a slender isthmus of neck, which revolved, like an inquisitive weather-vane, for a perpetual survey. We have seen such men before; the type is not uncommon; and their outward seeming is, to a certain extent, a sure index of their mind. The brisk little white-washer, who comes, on sunshiny days, during the troublous reign of the annual spring-cleaning freshet, with his brushes and bucket of lime, belongs to this fraternity. How he flies around the barrel of slacking lime, peeping needlessly into the hissing, steaming mass! How nimbly he mounts his stool! How deprecatingly he absorbs praises from the gratified, smiling mistress, as the smeared smoky surface leisurely grows into one of purest white! How anxiously he sucks his nether lip, when perverse drops fall from the uplifted brush, and spatter the bare, scoured floor! If familiar with the regions, how briskly he trots away for a towel, wherewith to remove the spots, as footsteps approach the door! How admirably he flatters fretful housewives, and dodges the impending fault-finding! And for all these virtuous qualities, he remains to the last only " a clever little man enough."

And the dapper clerk. How spotless in attire! how unfledged in looks and knowledge! what commercial verbosity! what an enormous seal ring—not to speak lightly of

7

carbuncle studs and the massive watch-guard; what salaried arguments melt into persuasive smirks, and smooth the pathway of free trade!

Then there is the dapper doctor, in the first stages of incipient manhood—where he always remains; with school erudition swelling dangerously in his plastic mind. How pompous his strut! how scrupulously he embellishes the most ordinary chit-chat with staggering medical expletives! He lugs about him, as companions to these—unswerving in their fond allegiance—marvellous reminiscences of "what I did in college! among the Fresh', you know," how adroitly "I fooled the prex, an old fogy, you know." They are —where he lingers long—familiar as "household words." "M. D." wreathes itself indisputably round his pretty whalebone stick, which swings luxuriantly to and fro from his kidgloved fingers, with a hop, skip, and a jump, and an occasional dexterous summersault. Then, in fits of thoughtful abstraction as he walks the streets, it knocks its head meditatively on his teeth, or curls up comfortably under his arm, like the unwelcome umbrella, which one is compelled to carry on an April day, when, though the sun smiles, it cannot hide the treacherous thunder heads in the west; in fact, it assumes fifty different quirls and modifications, but a professional cane it remains for all that. One would think it mesmerized, in a manner, as, apparently of its own accord, in its master's most absorbed moments, you may still see it keeping up its gymnastic feats—leaping franticly in mid-air, swaying softly by his side, or peacefully keeping time to the brisk pit-pat of his little shining boots. Witness the thrust of this M. D.'s fingers through his locks—which exhale an odor stronger than agreeable, of whipped lard, scented with bergamot—ere approaching a patient's bedside; and the un-

varying smirk on his downy lip, as he counts the wrist's pulsations, or desires him to thrust out his tongue ; and the
lofty erection of the medical brain, as he hands the nurse a
powder, with the usual solemn injunction, " It *must* be taken
precisely at the moment, sleeping or waking, or I'll not be re-
sponsible for the *consequences*." This is the physician whose
fraternal sympathy for the sufferings of the whole human
race you can pack away conveniently in a filbert-shell, with
ample room for a counterpart. He grins delightedly at the
accession of a new patient ; and, if the disease is contagious,
" thinks there is no need to exclude from the sick-room" the
other members of the family. " Be careful, and there's not
the *slightest* danger (but that you'll take it), he subjoins
mentally. He is never puzzled at any unusual developments
of the disease ; consequently he rejects, with a touch of insulted dignity, all anxious suggestions of " counsel." He
gloats over surgical operations as a legitimate field for ex-
periment, and stands ready to amputate all your limbs, or
your head either, at but a hint from his precocious instinct,
" for fear mortification'll set in." And at the crisis of your
earthly fate, when your life quivers eager, yet reluctant, betwixt two worlds, and a rude sound may decide the delicately
poised scale, he walks cooly to the window, and taps airily
on its sash, or enjoys, with keen relish, a lunch in the chimney corner.

The physique of the dapper minister is not one whit more
alluring ; and the same extraordinary assurance supplies but
poorly the constitutional deficit of mental ballast ; the same
arrogant egotism lifts him to a preponderance of power, wit,
and learning in his own eyes, as, with rolling eyes, affected
speech, and agonizing gestures, he paints yawning pits at the
pulpit's foot, with pious incantations, filling them to the brim

with the summarily selected, writhing, never-to-be reprieved or pardoned black sheep of God's immortal fold. Then, by a mysterious twist of saintly logic, he transports the complacent "believers"—the paying portion of his congregation tacitly included—himself at their head, into the New Jerusalem, claiming them, of course, for "gems in the crown of his rejoicing." A comfortable enough doctrine for the blessed *white* sheep, if they can forego all human feelings of pity for their unhappy brothers and sisters below. Is heavenly pity more merciless than earthly? and will not sore disappointments await some of us at the judgment-seat? How will our pettiness quail and shrink appalled into involuntary self-condemnation, as the record of nobler deeds, purer lives, than ours by far—unknown to us on earth—lift those we rigorously sentence, condemn, *here*, above us *there*, in an inaccessible niche of reward. A quiet little text in holy writ tells us that "the first shall be last; and the last first."

However, it is not of the Rev. Silas Fuller *in* the pulpit, who comes under notice now, but when he doffed his ludicrous attempts at ministerial dignity, with his glib sermon recitation, and descended from his vainglorious stilts to mingle familiarly with his plain farmer laymen. Deborah, after one week's trial of his company, lost her patience, and never afterward recovered it. She scornfully dubbed him "Miss Nancy"—a cognomen she spread far and wide among her clique of acquaintance, when, in the dusk of evening, she threw her checked shawl over her gray head, and went "neighboring." She declared roundly, one morning, that "he needn't think to come it on her in *that* shape; she knew when she's imposed upon, as well's the *next* one, and she wan't goin' to put up with't much longer, nuther."

"Why, not put up with our minister?" inquired Demis.

"No, indeed!" she snapped out; "he's the nearest nothin' ever I see, if he *does* hail from Boston; he treats folks pizon mean, *I* think, and if this's the way he's goin' to carry on, I for one'll quit. I never was used to no sech doin's," she pursued hotly, a flush mounting to her gray cheek. "He marches right into my room mornin's, without leave or license, and opens the winder, jest's soon as I come down stairs; no matter how cold 'tis, or if it's rainin' pitchforks. When I go up to make my bed, I'm sure to find it open. I put a fork over the latch one day, and stole out'f the clothes-press door; didn't make a mite of no difference; he found that are out, and I found my winder open jest the same. I declare for't I won't stan' it! *I'll* settle his hash for him!" she screamed shrilly.

"He wants the house well ventilated," put in Mark, archly; his eyes twinkling with fun. "To tell the truth, I caught him at his tricks, with the girls' window, this morning, and I ordered him out in such a tone that I think he'll *stay* out one while. I told him, moreover, that hospitality had bounds, even for a minister."

"Why, Mark!" exclaimed Demis, delightedly.

"I declare, my boy! I'll make you a batch of Injun pancakes for that are, and a spongecake too, for ye to whet your bill upon," said Deborah, with the broadest of smiles. She chuckled softly to herself at intervals; and when she spoke again, it was in a greatly mollified tone. "It's cur'ous, now, to see the way he manages; if't didn't put me so desp'rate out o' sorts, I should laugh ready to split. He allers gits up 'arly, and he'll be down here 'bout as soon as I be, a hangin' round to see me git breakfast, and a puttin' in *his* oar ev'ry time Mrs. Martin tells me anythin' to do. Then, ag'in, he seems to think he knows mor'n ev'rybody else—

jest as if *I* hadn't cooked all my life, ever since I's knee high
to a toad. He says the coffee hadn't oughter bile up but
jest three times; it's spiled if 't does; and he'll twitch it off
on't the h'arth, if I aint lookin'. I have to watch the crittur
as close! Wall, when he does so, I'll put it *back* ag'in; and
—you never see nothin' to beat it—he'll set as oneasy on
his cheer; and the fust time my back's turned, off he whopps
it ag'in. Now, if *that's* Christian, I don't want nothin' to
do with it."

"I saw him directing you how to cook fish, yesterday,"
remarked Mark, mischievously, thus starting her on a fresh
track. Debby flushed up again.

"Yes! he stuck to't that it must be cooked jest so many
minutes, whether or no, and he tuk out his watch to keep
count. I told him I allers let it bile till 'twas *done*, minutes
or *no* minutes, and, furthermore, that I guessed I knew
'nough yit to tell when 'twas done, without none o' his
watches. Wall, he was real muley, and insisted *his* was the
right way to have it healthy; so, for once, I thought I'd
humor him." Debby tossed her head scornfully. "He
told me *when* to turn it over, and I turned it over; and he
told me when to take it out, and I took it out. What'd I
gain by it, I want to know? Come dinner-time, Mrs. Martin scolded terrible 'bout the raw fish; wondered how'n the
name of common sense I come to be so heedless, and all
that; and when I told her 'twas cooked 'cordin' to orders,
she shortly told me to cook it over ag'in. Wall, I took off
a piece for Elder Fuller 'fore I put it back int' the spider,
for, says I to your mother, '*he* likes it so, it's so powerful
healthy.' Now, if you'll b'lieve me, he didn't eat a morsel
on't it. I see which way the wind blew. Says I, 'Elder,
you don't fall to much; what's the matter with it? You

don't seem to be very fishy this meal; don't be 'fraid on't; it's clean."

" Yes!" interrupted Demis, mimicking his mincing tones. " My good friend, a half minute longer would have brought it to perfection."

" It's all minutes with him," added Debby, with a sigh. " I wish he'd clear out and leave the sapworks, for my part."

I believe the good soul regarded him, sometimes, in the light of a trial, sent to inculcate patience. There was a good deal of reason for her complaints; he fairly persecuted her with eternal suggestions, infesting cupboard, buttery, and dairy, at all hours, with the pertinacity of a hound. There was no domestic office—even to the trimming of a lamp— which he could not show one to perform in a better way; and though Aunt Rhoda was, as Debby quaintly phrased it, " all clear quill with the Parson," I sometimes thought she heartily wished the end of his tarry would come.

One Monday morning he hovered zealously around the wash-tub, where Debby was busily rubbing. He peeped into the pounding-barrel, and observed: " Clothes only need pounding five minutes; it answers the same purpose as a longer time, and does not wear them as much. That *you* must perceive, my friend; though—you must allow me to say—I never met a female, before *you*, so bigoted to old ways, so extremely difficult to convince of rational changes."

" Don't call *me* your friend," retorted Debby, calmly. " I'm pesky 'fraid I *aint*, and I'll 'low you to say any thin' that weighs on your mind. Speak right out in cov'nant meetin', I say, if you've got any thin' special, 'cause, you know, Elder, that bym'bye comes *my* turn."

" I cannot help feeling a human interest in the labors of

women, and endeavoring, as far as possible, to alleviate them," he philanthropically remarked. " I know the views which some of my clerical brethren entertain; but *I* don't consider it at all derogatory to my dignity to help my wife."

" The wimmin's much obleeged to ye, I'm sure; but they hope you won't put yourself out the way none to 'leviate them," answered Debby, demurely proceeding with her work; " though, I must say, I'm proper glad on't, if you *do* take holt to give your wife a lift; she's a weakly body, I've heerd tell."

" Now, Miss Deborah," he pursued, briskly, " let me convince you of the superiority of *my* plan; you pound, if you please, and I'll keep count, five minutes, and we will see if the clothes are not quite as clean as when *you* pound an half hour, wasting your strength needlessly."

" Nay! *you* pound, and *I'll* keep count; I'll rest me a bit," proposed Debby, hastily slapping her suds-covered hands on the washboard, with such unction that the foam flew in the Elder's face; she wiped them on her woollen apron, and reached out for the watch. The abashed divine colored a little, but reluctantly handed it over, and grasped the pounder.

Mark cautiously opened the keeping-room door, and peeped out, brimful of laughter, at this reversion of proceedings.

" What if mother should come in now and spoil the fun! she always does," whispered Demis, as Annah tottered up to the perspiring church functionary, and asked him, innocently, " if Debby mustn't pray for him if he worked for her.'

He pounded vigorously. " My good friend, I think it

must be five minutes," he said at last, pausing to wipe his streaming forehead.

"Oh, massy, no!" answered she, looking down at the watch, "it lacks some time on't yit. You go too hard," she added, "you'll tucker yourself all out, at this rate."

"Never fear," he replied, resuming his labor. Debby turned round with an expressive gesture, signifying "she'd got him there; and there she meant to keep him one spell."

"By Jove! that's the richest thing I've seen," ejaculated Mark, taking extraordinary attitudes to retain his laughter. He also began a series of eloquent gesticulations to Demis for paper and pencil, wherewith to sketch the scene, when the door opened, and Aunt Rhoda entered. She stopped short before the tableau, glancing suspiciously at Deborah, who bore the scrutiny with apparent unconcern. "What's all this?" asked aunt, sharply.

"Dear me, sus," said Debby cosily, "he's a showin' me how to wash. That's all. Nothin' to make a fuss about, is there?"

"Oh!" returned her mistress, unconcernedly, as she passed on.

"Now, my friend, please tell me the time!" again demanded the little washerman. He looked around inquiringly, showing us a face of the color of a beet, and deluged with perspiration.

"Wall," replied Debby, "it's near 'nough to five minutes, I guess; but *do* you s'pose them are pounded enough? Hadn't we better make sure on't?"

"Oh! I'll warrant those," he rejoined glibly; and he ran to the towel and dried his hands. Debby restored his watch. He colored to the temples as he glanced at it; then turned as

7*

white. "You've deceived me," he angrily cried; "I have pounded fifteen minutes!"

"Wall," rather sharply retorted Debby, "I wan't goin' to hang out dirty clothes for you, nor no man livin'. I guess they hain't took no hurt by a few extra rubs. That's 'bout the time *I* allers give 'em, though I must say I never measured it afore."

"Ah! you are more difficult to manage than my wife," he returned. "*She* is willing to hear to reason."

"I pity her!" said Debby, shaking her head, "I do, indeed, from the bottom of my soul. She's a dreadful afflicted creetur, I b'gin to think."

"How so, madam?" he inquired, waxing wroth. "In what respect, pray?" and he endeavored to look at her sternly. But Debby had suddenly grown deaf. She resumed her interrupted rubbing, without even looking up to catch the withering fire-fly gleam from the insulted parson's small, yellowish-blue eyes.

"I think you'd a made a heap better hand to a hired out for housework than you be for preachin', though *I* don't want hide nor hair on ye for either," she muttered, as he picked up his hat and cane, and went out to air his vexation.

"I declare, children, I made somethin' out on't arter all," she presently said, putting her frowsy head in the keeping-room. "I ain't his 'good friend' no longer, I'm 'madam,' and—don't say nothin'—I'll fetch him to his porridge afore I've done with him."

But though this *uncivil* warfare was persistently waged, with extremely short intervals of peace, by these unequally matched combatants; though domestic quiet was attacked, routed, and sent flying almost daily—affording ample amusement to at least three of the household—yet the masculine

citadel showed no signs of surrender. The solitary garrison
never arrived at that point of submissive obedience so hopefully anticipated by his feminine enemy. He was never forced
by penitential hunger toward the "bowl of porridge" in
waiting store for him ; for, to her chagrin, defeated on one
field, he invariably returned to fight loyally on another.
Humiliated by his ancient foe he often was ; but, to do the little
man justice, he seldom bore malice longer than one entire
day, and he seemed utterly unconscious that his interfering
habits were at all unusual, impertinent, or offensive to pre-
siding domestic geniuses ; that they were derogatory to ministerial dignity, or irritating to dominant New England independence of spirit. Deborah was in error from the beginning,
in spreading abroad, among the members of his flock, grossly
indignant bulletins of his odd doings. Her listeners were
amused. edified, and curious to absorb her recitals, but extremely cautious about supplanting her in her position.
They suppressed all invitations to sojourn with them longer
than to assist at an ordinary afternoon tea-drinking ; and as
it is no part of a hospitable host or hostess to hint of an unwelcome prolongation of a visiting term, and as he seemed well
content with his quarters, he remained—Deborah's tormentor.

Uncle Joel was a conscientious church member, and so full
of charity towards every one, that he tried to be lenient to
all shortcomings of those both in and out of the sacred en-
closure ; but it is doubtful if he ever perceived the elder's
failings. An odd mixture of the simple and reverential pervaded his whole nature. He was often obtuse to that which
deeply touched others ; to the most ludicrous of human
manifestations ; and to the plainest of logical perceptions he
remained mute and inattentive. But in recompense for this
deficiency, if such it was, he had dreamy apprehensions of

feelings and thoughts immeasurably exalting. When these outlines—dim at best to the wisest and purest—were revealed to him, his soul shook off its petrifying slumbers, and stood out, ardently worshipping. *Then*, and then only, he was strong enough to breast the waves of scornful defiance, and ridicule of his intuition. He was a good man and a sincere Christian, though doctrine puzzled his simple brain sorely, and election and foreordination were logs over which he stumbled, and for that reason usually avoided in his spiritual travels. He peered curiously sometimes at his new spiritual guide, as if vaguely seeking to discover by his countenance the perplexing source of an ever-haunting deficiency. He looked distressed at Deborah's abrupt parrying of the elder's thrusts at her cherished country ways, and sighed at her unhesitating retorts when criticised by the elder in his cold, wiry tones, but he never once ventured to check her.

However, there comes an end to all things. In accordance with this universally conceded law, there came a close to this visit. May flowers were blooming in forest hollows, when the much-vaunted patient wife came among us, bringing all necessary equipments for housekeeping. It was a blessed day for Debby; and her eyes fairly sparkled when he bade her a civil farewell. She dropped a courtesy, and handed him from the pantry a good-sized bundle of pies, neatly wrapped in towels of her own spinning, weaving, and bleaching, for a parting gift, with the curt observation: " Wall, Elder, forgive and forgit's the motter in this ere world, and I don't lay up nothing 'g'inst nobody. I hope ye'll find them pies eatable, though I didn't make 'em 'zactly as *you* said I oughter ;" and she then discreetly withdrew.

Strange promptings of the affections, prejudices, and antipathies lead and rule us unaccountably. Several days later, when the minister's daughter—sweet, rosy, merry Kitty—came to see us, Debby conceived a violent fancy for her; and as peculiar a friendship dawned between the two, as existed hatred between herself and Kitty's sire.

CHAPTER XIII.

THREE years weave many changes. Light and shadow trail along their web and woof. In this short period, not a human heart, pulsating with life, but which erects and demolishes a hope, a fear; not one, fully awakened, but which smiles with newly born blessedness, or pales and quivers in the throes of mortal agony. Their imperceptible development transforms crude childhood into serene, conscious youth. Youth ripens into the mellow flush of early manhood. Age gathers an added wrinkle; and a village history a few more chronicles. But, after all, old landmarks along life's highway seem not materially displaced or obscured. Miss Charity's rule in the schoolroom is temporarily abandoned. She is suffering from a cough—"slight," she calls it; she thinks "she caught cold the day of the funeral"—which was chilly and rainy—and an edict has gone forth from Miss Roby, that "there's no two ways about it; she's got to stay to hum a spell and doctor it up." In the great warm mansion there is another silent corner; another soul has reluctantly exchanged incompleteness for fruition and tearfully groped heavenward; another grave swells the group ·in the green meadow cemetery. Miss Lucretia sleeps the dead's dreamless slumber. The final rupture of the golden bowl occurred but a few weeks since. A lengthened scene of suffering fell to her lot, but the silver cord is loosed at last, and in its wake follows divine

peace.   The day after the burial, I strolled with Demis
and Kitty to her grave.   It was summer; but no sods covered it,   All around lurked luxuriant, green uniformity.   The
waving grass almost concealed the shape of the surrounding
mounds rendering this new corner more sadly revolting.   This
high round mass of yellow gravel, belched from depths under blooming verdure by the stolid sexton's spade, with por-
tions of its surface crumbling off, and rolling down to hide
in the weeds at its feet!   In looking at a new-made grave
there seems no reliable evidence of immortality.   Faith struggles to believe, and tries assiduously to render into consoling
practice, her doctrines ; but the bare cold earth, speaking so
eloquently of the silence of desolation, blankly refutes them
all.   We gaze, instead, into the hopeless vault of our dear
buried love.   It stares at us *so* unanswerably.   We are dumb
before its mute logic.   But when noiseless battalions of unseen forces have crowned it with affinity to nature ; when
seed-times and harvests have bloomed, and waned over it,
and constant vigils of our common mother have bathed it in
resignation, *then* our scattered senses reunite and rend the
veil, and we catch a bright view of the immortal life beyond.
And hope grows anew, that in the hush of recent sorrow lay
cold and torpid.   Then we begin to realize that we have but
planted the seed in that green flower-crowned mound, or rather
the useless husk of the seed, germinating in death; its flowers
smiling for us beyond the stars.   *Now* Faith's prophetic eye
springs upward, into invisible but not unfamiliar realms.

   Demis and I have been drafted into household duties, and
may consider our schooldays ended.   I am sorry; and so is
she.   We are just beginning to love study ; to appreciate its
importance ; but we cannot help ourselves.   Her mother is
generalissimo of the household forces, and she says sharply,

that, " when one can read, write, and cypher to the Rule o'
Three in 'Rethmetic, with 'nough Jography to bound the
States, and Parsin', so's not to make no mistakes in talking;
that's eddication a plenty in her opinion : it's all *she* had, and
what answered for her'll answer for *other* folks." Besides this
fiat, the committee issued another at the annual " school
meetin'," and Uncle Joel came home from it with the announcement, that, being over fifteen, we could " draw no more
public money." "Whose notion is *that*, I wonder ?" cried
Debby, who was vigorously rocking Annah in a kitchen
chair, and pensively humming, " Hi, Biddy Martin."

"Lawyer Prince first started the idea, I b'lieve; they're
goin' to hire a man teacher, too, for the winter," he placidly
returned.

The committee came down soon after, to engage Mark,
but he unhesitatingly declined; whereat his mother looked
much displeased, and his father as much bewildered.

" Why not make a ventur' at it, my boy ?" inquired Uncle
Joel, raising his head after a long survey of the glowing fire.
" I think it'll be a good sight easier than helpin' me haul out
lumber this winter, and I'm sure your larnin' need'nt stand in
the way."

" Wall, all *I* have to say is, I think it's high time you was
settling on *somethin'* or other; you don't earn the salt to your
porridge," put in his mother, a good deal nettled at his
prompt refusal, " and sixteen dollars a month don't grow on
every bush, let me tell you!"

"I dont b'lieve I should like teachin'," said his father, slowly.

" Stuff !" cried Aunt Rhody; " Joel Martin, you don't
know what you're talkin' about, you haint never tried it."
She put down her knitting and steadily regarded him, until she appeared to consider him sufficiently awed to

keep silence, after which she resumed her work and argument.

Mark interrupted her. "I tried it a week for Ned Peabody. He was down with the mumps, and I'll not try it again."

"Do tell!" exclaimed Deborah, in a pitying tone. "I wonder if he tried a mustard poultice; though some do say that slipp'ry elem is better!"

CHAPTER XIV.

It was Monday morning. All in our little household were astir long ere the stars waned, clear and cold, from the western horizon. "Wall," said Deborah, pushing back from the breakfast-table, and putting her chair plump against the wall with an energetic snap, that made the listing quiver, "I s'pose that are washin's got to be did, so the sooner I tackle it the better."

"Yis," assented Aunt Rhoda, "and Demis you put over the fat-kittle, and then go up chamber and help 'Mandy sweep up. You know the teacher's comin' to board to-night—there's oceans to do. Flax right round now, and see how smart you can be, if you've a mind to. Now Ruby, *you* may mix up some doughnuts, and when the fat's hot I'll fry 'em." She closed, and sealed these rapid orders with one of her characteristic "hems!" which, lest you may not translate aright, I may say, meant instant obedience. No lingering of a moment; no foolish chat on the stairway; scattering remnants of jest and laughter, which pleasurably season the scene of labor. When we worked in Aunt Rhoda's presence, all must be grim determination. Much talking provoked her ire.

She affirmed that "it made us heedless, and she wanted us to b'gin to appear *like* folks." If she surprised us in a merry mood, she instantly assumed a shocked visage, dolefully inquiring "if we knew which end we stood on?"

"Mother!" said Demis some hours later, as, her sweeping finished, she stood by the door with a basket of damp clothes in her arms to be hung on the line outside, "seems to me Amanda's mighty chipper lately; shouldn't wonder if we had a wedding here before long. High time, I think. *I* won't wait seven years for a Laban." No one replied. Her mother raised a flushed face from the hissing kettle, in which were slowly browning great puffy twists of lightness, emitting a strong odor of cinnamon. She stood fork in hand, turning them rapidly over, that both sides might take on exactly the same hue. Occasionally she favored me with critical glances and sharp irritated expostulations, as I vigorously rolled out the soft dough, conscientiously trying to imitate precisely her own method of doing up the long spirals into just the right shape. It was a hopeless task. She found fault assiduously, from time to time throwing out hints "that no one in *that* house tried to please *her*, and, for her part, she'd long ago gi'n up expectin' it."

"I do my best," I at last said desperately.

"Wall, your best is very poor, indeed, Ruby," she severely retorted. "There! turn it over *this* way; then give it a twist, *so*-fashion; and then it don't fly apart in the kettle." She motioned with her fork these directions; her face cleared a little as she watched me. "They come up beautiful, if you *did* make 'em," she added by way of encouragement. "I'm most afraid you put full short'nin' enough in 'em."

"Ruby can cook as well as the next one if she's let alone,"

interposed Debby. " *Nobody* can't do nothin' when watched like a lynx. It flustrates *me* all sorts."

" Wall, Deborah, you just attend to *your* work," condescendingly said Aunt Rhoda. " Nobody asked you to speak. I spose I can do as I see fit in my own house ; when I can't I'll let *you* take the reins o' government."

Debby dared not contradict this assertion ; she bent her head in silence, commencing a vigorous rubbing. But this state could not continue ; being thus put down did not suit her, as she phrased it ; " she wan't goin' to be browbeat by nobody livin' ;" her face grew every moment more sullenly angry. " Deary me !" she presently said, pausing in her labor, " my wrist's gittin' lamer and lamer every day I draw the breath of life. I can't work so much longer. It's as much as I can do now to wring these great heavy sheets ; and *sech* washes as we have, to be sure ! *No* need on't nuther ; havin' so many things jest to make work." No answer. So she presently resumed, with a preliminary sigh : " I was a countin' the pieces over last week to Miss Purse ; she said she didn't see how I stood it ; she shouldn't think I'd hold out as well as I do."

" I'll be hanged if *theirs* ain't jest as large," asserted Aunt Rhoda ; " there's eight of 'em in the family, besides the hired man."

" No they ain't," said Debby, positively ; " an' they sleep in flannel sheets ; *that* saves a sight, for you know you can't wash 'em, they full up so."

" Wall !" crustily observed her mistress, " you needn't take the trouble to go roun' to the neighbors complainin' how hard you work. Nobody obleeges ye to do it, *I'm* sure. If you *can't*, you needn't, only don't be everlastin'ly twittin' 'bout it. I'm sick and tired o' hearin' it, for *my* part."

Deborah at this retort dissolved in tears. When she spoke

it was in a voice decidedly husky, with a pathetic whimper.
" Wall, I'd never a thought it, Mrs. Martin, turnin' me away
arter livin' with you over twenty year, and bringin' up the
children for you. I'm jest as fond of 'em as if they's my own.
And why shouldn't I be, I'd like to know? never slept a wink
all that season they had the measles and canker rash. Ah!
you'll never git any one to slave as I have for 'em all my
days. I've allers been an underlin'; but I can go, I s'pose. I
know plenty that'll be glad to have me. I'll finish the work
first, and mop up, so's you won't, none on you, have *that* to
do. It looks as if it wanted to ride out—this room does. I'll
resk but what I can git places enough."

As during my residence in Northfield, I had heard this
threat almost weekly, when any thing went wrong with the
domestic harness, I felt quite tranquil as to the result. As the
short afternoon waned, the mental skies cleared encouragingly,
and when evening set in dark and bleak without, the domestic
horizon shone mild and clear. With Dwight and Natty, came
also home to tea, the schoolmaster. A blazing fire in the
keeping-room roared and sparkled in welcome. This room
had been made especially neat and inviting, by much sweeping
of the gay striped carpet; prolonged anxious searching after
truant atoms of dust, which, instead of flying orderly after
their fellows out of the open windows, rebelliously nestled on
the rounds of the stiff-backed, cane-seated chairs, on the broad
top of the massive mahogany bureau; and in the recesses of the
oval carved mirror-frame. The gilt eagle on the pointed top of
this mirror, the brass rings in said bureau, were freshly polished, and glittered in the cheerful fire-light like burnished gold.
As they were my own handiwork, causing me nearly the afternoon's labor, I surveyed them with a degree of pardonable
pride. The coming of "the teacher" to board, is, in a

New England family, considered quite an accession to the
social circle; and Demis, as she busily plied the brush over
the already shining surface of the fireplace, and gave the
glittering balls on the andirons a few lingering touches,
rattled volubly on the interesting theme.   Her mother
appeared to think that the talk exceeded the labor, for
she suddenly opened the door from the kitchen, put her
head inside, gave a critical survey, and asked rather shortly,
" What all the rumpus was about?"   She did not look particularly charmed or satisfied with the vague answer she got;
so she peremptorily ordered Demis off to the " spare room,"
to "straighten it up."   "Be sure you put quilts enough on the
bed," was the parting injunction.   "Stay!" as a chance thought
crossed her mind.   " Demis, what spread's on that are bed?"

"I believe it's the one I pieced when a little girl," said Demis.

"Wall, wall, if that's on, you may take it off, short order;
I remember the quiltin' aint nothin' extra on that; you *would*
have a quiltin' bee, and do it all yourselves, and, massy to me!
some of them stitches are long enough to hang a person.   I
felt as though I should fly, when I come to look at it."
Demis looked disdainful.   "I wonder if you think, Mother,
that the schoolmaster will inspect the quilting of all the
spreads on his bed?   It's as good as he usually gets, I'll be
bound!" she finished hotly.

" Wall!" her mother calmly retorted, " 'twould be dangerous sort o', to put it under; he might get caught in some
o' them ere stitches; and as for havin't outside, there's no more
to be said 'bout *that;* so get right square along."

" You look in that chist in the north chamber; and I guess
you'll find one that's decent," she called after Demis, who
had started on a gallop up the stairs, " sech a headstrong
piece," she muttered crossly; " I do wish I could make her

do as I want to have her; she's enough to try the patience of Job. But, then, as the minister says, we must all have our crosses, and take 'em up and bear 'em;" and she sighed complacently. My face flushed, my voice quivered, as I asked her "if she considered Demis a cross?" she eyed me in astonishment. " What's come over you, all of a sudden?" she asked sharply. " You look mad enough to snap my head off. What's the reason, I wonder, you two gals never can bear to hear the least word said ag'in one 'nuther? 'Twon't *allers* last, I'm 'fraid. You'll fly off the handle one o' these days. I never knew't to fail when folks are so thick."

" Why don't you answer my question, Aunt?"

" Wall," she said peevishly, inclining her head to listen, " hear that screeching now," (I heard an uncommonly sweet voice warbling an old-fashioned ditty, above our heads,) ".it's nothing but hootin' and tootin' from mornin' to night, and for *my* part, I'm sick and tired o' hearin' on't." She turned fretfully away, adding piously, " but it's all in this life, and that's one comfort." She looked in again presently to inform me that my work would " answer well 'nough," and she detailed me forthwith for duty in the kitchen. Here much remained to be finished: the straggling odds and ends of the day's labor to be concentrated to one focus and briskly dispatched. Then ensued a great deal of running from the table to the pantry. The yellow shelves of the latter place suffered a sweeping robbery; an incongruous regiment of edibles were marched in Indian file upon the waiting board. Then there was the necessary descent into the chill damp cellar; minus a candle—my aunt never tolerated one in those regions, for fear of fire—I dreaded encountering the ominous darkness, and when possible, always shirked this duty on some equally unwilling shoulders. Many a goblin form lurked for me in a post rising gray in the gloom ; or in a newer barrel than the rest : often my cowering terror played me the most fanciful tricks; and darting frantically towards the locality of the sweetmeats, I would seize the first bowl which my hand encountered, and retreat—with expectant glances over either shoulder—to the stairway. When company was expected Debby was not trusted with setting the table. Her intentions were excellent; her efforts untiring ; but in her cranium the phrenological bump of order was totally wanting ; no amount of quiet instruction and example, or multitudinous hints—to most persons a sufficient, because mortifying reminder, would inculcate carefulness. She always left the butter-knife trailing awry on the white cloth ; the cups and saucers sprawling awkwardly in all directions. Debby had finished her " mopping up " ere sundown ; but, instead of the threatened departure, she had changed her dripping garments for a new blue calico gown, and dry leathern boots. She had smoothed her thin gray locks—amply wetted with cold weak tea; which hair invigorator always stood at hand, in a cracked blue teacup, replenished every morning—and then ensconced herself by the roaring kitchen stove. She looked the embodiment of homely peace and comfort. Taking Annah upon her lap, and gently trotting her to the cheery whistle of the steaming tea-kettle, she offered to tell her a story about—" when I lived down East." "Wall, when I lived down ' t'the nine Pardners'—You see, Anny, there was nine brothers and they was all in bus'ness together, so the place was named arter them." This explanation, as well as the story that succeeded, and the ensuing " voyage to Savoy," had been told to Annah's wondering ears, scores of times before ; but she never wearied of hearing them, and, provided Debby ran always in the same tracks, was satisfied and delighted. If she attempt-

ed changes in the narratives, the little auditor speedily set
her right. Debby's stories were lengthy, usually inducing a
drowsy languor, which she roused and dissipated by the
query, " I wonder now if Anny wants a song !" Then a voice
rose over the kitchen bustle—strangely pathetic, as it quivered through the sad minor of the love-songs of her early
girlhood.

A sapless forest tree slowly wrenched from the soil ; turning and twisting with every rush of the wind, groaning
heavily with every angrier sweep of the blast, and for many
days chanting thus its own forlorn dirge, is a sad sound to
hear. Scarcely less ominous did Debby's singing seem ; the
grace and pliant sweetness gone from her voice, oozing out of
its every spiritual pore, along with its twin sister Youth. Age
stopping the wheels with the rust of the body's infirmities ;
turning music into cackle. In weird tone arose the unredressed
plaints of dying swains (which Debby prefaced with " it's said
to be a *true* story,") happy if the object of their affections
but visited their slumbers, and smoothed their passage tomb-
ward ; and the fortunes of luckless navigators who—like the
illustrious Genoese—scoured the seas unweariedly ; but, unlike him, in quest of faithless fair ones.

> " He sail-ed east, he sail-ed west,
> He sail-ed to a foreign shore,
> Where he was taken and put in prison
> Where he could neither see nor hear."

Deborah's store of these quaint ballads was inexhaustible.
She revelled in the marvellous ; and these sole relics of a time
long since vanished into the " sere and yellow leaf," still sung
her old withered heart to a renewal of those lost days of
youth, warming its paling ashes with a flash of the old fire, not
the less comforting, that it was only a transient glimmer. Her

stories were largely dosed with the strong flavor of the
supernatural. Mysterious sights and sounds which happened "away down East," when she dwelt in that enchanted land. She was called "a witch" by some, because she
frequently predicted impending evils, and they not unfrequently verified her prophecy. She possessed a natural shrewdness which she turned to good account. "*She* could see
through a millstone as well as the next one; specially if
there's a *hole* in it," she was fond of observing, though she
liked to be looked upon as one possessing the key to hidden
knowledge. Accordingly, she impressively told fortunes,
when it so suited her mood; either in deciphering the lines,
which a perplexing Fate causes to be written on the palm,
or by the more popular method of sifting the shadowy future
from the little pile of tea-grounds remaining in the cup. She
said "she was born with a veil over her face,"—and I once
heard her stoutly maintain to a doubting neighbor that "it
was a *green* veil;" and could tell, by any one's countenance,
when any thing was going to happen to them. She saw
"sperrits," too, and was a devout believer in omens—some
of which her own eyes had seen, and many more of second-
hand origin : of shadowy coffins gliding over the ceiling, obstinately transfixing themselves over the person whose doom
was thus sealed; of luminous hands waving mysteriously;
and of foreshadowing signs in the atmosphere, as well as the
no less truthful nature of dreams, of which she was always
the eager positive interpreter. She ceased her song with the
summons to supper, and devoted the rest of the evening to
a persistent scrutiny of the schoolmaster. "What a puttin'
through ! for nothing !" she muttered as she slowly let herself down into her chair.

Uncle Joel good-naturedly started the conversation into,

as he supposed, congenial channels. As for the new preceptor, for a time he sat stiff and silent in his chair, thus unconsciously repelling our persistent scrutiny. Thwarted in fathoming the spirit animating the frame, I had a malicious pleasure in singling out each personal defect ; in watching the ungraceful motions of the tall thin figure. I slyly gave Demis a reassuring nod ; evidently we need stand in no awe of so quiet, so bashful a man. Yet, though slight his form, it somehow gave me the idea of strength ; though low his brow, and retreating, one insensibly associated it with intellectual attainments—albeit followed by a smile at the folly. Not pleasant that face ; but sturdily strong. The mouth compressed its lines into cautious selfishness ; yet its smiles were most genial, as subsequent interviews revealed, in spite of the cold, *hard* eyes ; they shone, too, but with no tender brightness. Their glittering gaze relentlessly impelled one to do his bidding, instead of winning ready, cheerful acquiescence. Yet, though they brooded in a sea of repulsion, at times they strangely attracted— by what charmed attribute I never could define. In these rare seasons a vague impression of manifold heavy sorrows bravely borne—the parents of glorious aspirations,—of a heart, sympathetic, generous, true, eager to succor the helpless, to warm and cheer with the true elixir of encouragement the despairing and the faltering, suddenly beclouded my previous estimate of his character, and induced an apparent accession of friendliness to my manner. It was far longer before Demis dropped her reserve in addressing him.

It was evident this evening, from his replies to Uncle Joel's good-humored questionings, that his sway over the rough village boys, would be no arbitrary government of the detested ferule, or the still more tortuous raw-hide. He denounced it as infamous, just calculated to breed insurrection ; and his

8

eyes gleamed resolutely, as he said that " he had come to put to flight such lingering traces of barbarism in Northfield. Not that I am the pioneer in this good work, or expect to be manufactured into a martyr if I fail. In several of the States, the system of instruction has manifestly taken a higher grade than formerly, and the pupils are appealed to like rational beings, not flogged into a dumb, surly show of obedience."

"I don't know," said Uncle Joel, increduously shaking his head ; "I wonder how a body can tame em 'n any other way ! There's some plaguy hard critturs in our deestrict, and it don't do a mite o' good to turn 'em out, 'cause they *can* draw public money, and they *will ;* go hum maybe, and git sent back post haste next mornin'. If I'se in your place, Mr. Hume, I'd lay in a whaler or two, and then you can use it or not, as you're a mind to, only, in case the reasonin' process didn't go down the way ye expected, 'twill be mighty handy to have a *stronger* dose of physic handy."

" I'll try my method first, and then I will remember your advice, Mr. Martin. Will force is sometimes stronger than muscle, you know," said Mr. Hume.

" Wall, I hope you won't have no trouble ; but the fact of the business is, the school's got a bad name. You see they kinder run over wimmen folks, and once they git the upper hand they're dreadful loth to let go. Them big boys of Stephens's are making their brags, how they'll cast you out of the winder in short metre, if you don't carry your carcass to suit 'em. I heerd 'em in the office to-day, and there's plenty o' scallywags round just mean enough to hoorrah 'em on, only to see the fun. They'd like to see a college chap took down a peg or two."

Mr. Hume smiled, and nodded. "I shall make it my especial duty to oil their consciences a little ; the wheels are rusty; don't work smoothly, but a good engineer soon sets that all right. They must be converted."

" Lordy!" ejaculated Debby, rising precipitately, and leaving the room.

Uncle Joel looked contemplative. " Wall," he said slowly, " when *I* was a shaver I used to get tanned awfully sometimes. Mother used to say that her boys was *all* full of the old Nick, but Joel was the cap sheaf; and grandmarm used to pray over me, time and time agin: she'd whine out that I was on the right road to ruin, and nothin' but a mericle would ever stop me; and I'd come to the gallers, and all *that,* till I got to feelin', arter she begun, as if I raly *was* a slidin' along a greased track, right down to the bottomless pit, and couldn't stop for the life of me. I allers thought the old woman was ruther disappointed arter I sobered down all of a sudden——"

" Now, Joel Martin," broke in Aunt Rhoda, "don't you b'gin to tell over afore these boys how *you* used to carry sail; they'll be tryin' the same pranks, and, goodness knows, they're bad enough now."

" Wall," persisted her phlegmatic husband, " I must say, I don't believe so much in sparing the rod and spilin' the child, as some folks not a thousand miles off. I've heerd the school-marms say, sometimes, they'd ruther take a whippin' themselves than to see Joe Martin come into the school-house; wouldn't think it now, would ye ?" he added, laughing.

" 'Taint *all* been rooted out of ye yit, I guess," remarked his wife. " The scriptures warn us to watch and pray, and to strive without ceasing; and if you don't do it, I'm bound to do it for you." With this affectionate harangue she rose from the table, with the serene, self-satisfied air of one who has dropped a word in due season, on particularly stony ground, and has so much less to answer for at the Judgment-seat.

"Demis, show Mr. Hume into the settin'-room; and Mark, you fetch up some apples. I want to pare up them windfalls, and have 'em a dryin'." Thus speedily, pious Mary vanished, to make room for her active, worldly-minded sister.

Those two weeks passed swiftly. The lengthening evenings flew on wings of random, cheerful chat, seasoned with the usual family labor. We formed a ring in the large kitchen, its centre occupied by baskets of early apples. Tin pans comfortably crowned each sitter's knee, which slowly exchanged their bounteous measure, for one of curling rings, and dissected cores. Mark, perched Turkwise on the table, solemnly strung together the separated quarters. And —how or when I do not remember—we became pupils of Mr. Hume; ardent, if ignorant, seekers after knowledge. He came nightly, after he had left us for another boarding-place, and we spent long hours in the good work of improvement. With Mark's entrance, study usually vanished, and a series of romps attempted—soon and surely checked by Aunt Rhoda's decisive voice issuing from the kitchen: "Come, come, now, none of that ere; you're enough to craze a nation!"

It is not to be supposed that we escaped village gossip. One evening—it was a raw, blustering one in early January— we hurried our tea, as usual, to go to our room for some trifling addition to our usual dress of homespun woollen. These additions were merely a knot of ribbon at the throat, and the hair freshly braided; they were soon completed. We returned again to the kitchen. In the entry, leading from the stairway, we stopped involuntarily on hearing our names mentioned. It was Amanda's voice, in no amiable tone, repeating malicious assertions. "It's so," she concluded, "positively, for Ira says so, and I guess he wouldn't lie about it."

"Of course not," echoed Debby, somewhat ironically. "But, to tell the truth, I've heard the same thing, oh! oceans o' times. It's got to be an old story with me. Law! suz, I never laid it up to bring hum, for *you* know, Miss Martin, it's an old sayin', that a ' crow that'll fetch a bone'll carry one.' Well, if it's a lie, you may have it as cheap as I, but they *do* say that Mr. Hume is a sparkin' one of our gals. They won't b'lieve nothin 'bout the lesson business; say that it's only a kiver for courtin', and want to know if *both* on 'em are in the room the whole during time."

" Wall, what do you tell 'em ?" inquired Uncle Joel.

" I won't tell 'em nothin'," she answered shortly, "only to find out by their wits, if they've got any; and to guess, and come ag'in. It's none of *their* business; and I, for one, don't take sass from nobody, not even if 'twas Queen Victory herself. Old Miss Prince's as high as nine 'bout it. Says it's takin' his attention from the school; and that the deestrict might jist as well throw the money in the fire as to waste it that way. She says, too, that he don't keep his hours, and there'll be a fuss made afore long, if he don't haul in his horns: and I don't know what all. I can't b'gin to tell all she said."

"Why, I'd no idee on't," said Uncle Joel, dismayed.

"The other day," pursued Debby, and we heard her set down her teacup with a spiteful rattle, " I was a goin' by there, and it seems she got a squint at me, for she up and thumped on the winder for me to come in. I made b'lieve I didn't hear her and kept right square along, but rap, rap, went her old thimble ag'in in the winder pane, so I give up the p'int, and went in. Wall, they appeared dreadful pleased to see me. I haint been there in an age before—not sence that scrape in the house 'bout the peaches, you know,

Mr. Martin —— and the way they rattled on 'bout one thing
and 'nuther was a caution. Mind you, they didn't come right
out and out, but *I* could see what they's drivin' at. Arter a
spell, Malissy says something 'bout it, and seemed awful put
out, 'cause I would'nt let on that I knew what she meant.
'Law!' spoke up her mother, ' you musn't b'lieve *all*
you hear. If you do, you'll have your hands full. *I* don't
not mor'n half, and not *then*, unless I *know* it's so.' 'Nor I
'nuther,' snapped out Malis, as short as pie-crust, ' but I heard
this myself—I'se in the store, and one of the men asked
him who he thought was the best-looking girl in the
place, and it didn't 'pear to take him long to consider, for he
spoke right up and said, 'Miss Martin.' ' Wall, he p'rhaps
meant Mandy,' said Mrs. Prince. ' No, he didn't, nuther,'
said she. 'I guess he don't think sandy hair and freckles
over and above beautiful. B'sides, she's spoke for already, I
spose !' "

" The old vixen !" muttered Amanda, wrathfully.

" I sot still and heard it all, and never opened my head, for
I thought, now I was in the scrape, I might as well be killed
for an old sheep as a lamb, you know."

" 'Fore I'd change places with *her* as to looks !" scornfully
observed Amanda.

" Wall, wall," said Debby, calmly, " I never should a spoke
out only you begun on the gals, and I can't, nor *shan't*, set by
and hear 'em 'bused. You know, I don't fellowship Meliss
Prince any mor'n you do: she's cut out for an old maid,
if there ever was one. She'll be one, too, unless I miss
my guess, for she tries so hard to catch a man ; now, mark my
words !"

" I shouldn't wonder if she'd set her cap for the schoolmaster," thoughtfully remarked Uncle Joel.

" Wall, Mr. Martin, I guess you needn't guess ag'in ; you've hit the nail on the head," chuckled Debby.

" We will stop this," I exclaimed indignantly. I was vexed to feel my checks burning painfully, but, turning to see how Demis was affected, I was a little consoled at finding her face likewise flaming. In her case it heightened, instead of detracting from, her dark beauty. Without one miserable pang of envy ; with naught save one solitary, irrepressible sigh for my own plainness, I stood several moments—my hand on the latch—silently regarding her. My bonnie, brave New England girl ! My royal gypsy queen ! she was far too simple to notice my gaze, or to guess its meaning. No vanity sillily compressed into a smirk the full red lips ; none showed its detracting light in her soft dark eyes. She turned towards the door, smiling mischievously. " Never mind ! we won't care what malicious spinsters say. As Elder Fuller is so fond of saying—Let us rise above all such grovelling considerations, and march on—to our lessons, to victory, or failure—and oh! there's the schoolmaster's knock."

CHAPTER XV.

APPARENTLY these rumors did not trouble Mr. Hume, for he continued his visits. It is more than probable that he was in ignorance of their existence. I think, had he been thus enlightened, our lessons would have ceased abruptly. Never have I seen a man so shorn of independence. The world's opinion ruled him ; was his guiding star. It may have been a necessity to thus defer—in his secret thought ; his fortune was still in embryo shape ; perhaps he needed the world's

lever of approval to develop it to maturity. I know not. I
only know that he sedulously deferred to all, of every grade;
that he sought—sometimes by covert flattery—their good
opinion. Shrewdness usually accompanies this quality, but
here again was a marked deficiency—reluctant as I was to
admit and cherish the truth, constantly, in numberless little
ways, crowded home upon my perceptions. He was a good
student; but his attainments he owed not to natural abilities;
rather to eager, patient, persevering effort. And with all his
reserve—difficult, indeed, to penetrate; with your consciousness of his faults, and they were numerous, you
steadily grew to trust, to admire, to like the man. What the
charm was I could not tell. Ungraceful the manner, it was as
surely magnetic. This reserve, too often mistaken for diffidence, would not succumb to other influences, but it slowly
unwound the most persistent coil of the same attribute in
another. He was never confidential; of his antecedents we
knew nothing; of his purposes, little. Yet he thawed,
seemingly without desire, the frostiness of other minds' seclusion: he grew acquainted—by your own act—with every family secret, with all your extravagant hopes and ambitions. And
what did he do with these seemingly unsought confidences?
He thrust them coolly aside; he treated them with silent
indifference, or with that inexplicable stony gleam—it may
have been triumph—in his eyes. He liked to impart knowledge. We progressed rapidly. Sometimes Olive joined our
circle. The study hours were short when she came; and
though Aunt Rhoda persisted in opening the door, occasionally to—as she phrased it—"put a quietus on us," and
took poor Uncle Joel up in the most vehement manner when
he good-naturedly suggested that "she better leave the young
folks alone; they wouldn't take no hurt, he guessed;" she

was always counterbalanced by Debby, who, imitating to the life her mistress's manner—would slyly look inside to whisper gleefully, "Go on with your bird's egging! I'll bear you out in't. If I was nimbler I'd jine in too," and then suddenly vanish, with a wholesome grinning face, lest she, too, incur a sharp reproof.

But joys decrease, as well as pains. February closed the winter term of school. Our evening lessons closed also. Mr. Hume made a round of brief farewell visits, and rejoined his class in college.

The days slowly lengthened. March, hoary and jubilant with tempestuous winds, cutting the flesh of the luckless traveller, like tiny weapons of steel; searching the very bones and marrow with relentless fury; its occasional treacherous calms but the shrinking prelude to wilder bursts of passion, shrieked itself hoarse at last, and passed with lamblike calmness from the year's calendar. April, too, has fled—sweet month of alternating smiles and tears; in ages past, and ages to come, the victim of an excess of admiration; putting on the glory, like an every-day garment, of poets' rhymes, and decked in the doubtful splendor of sentimental school-girl essays. What need to praise thee, when the violet and daffodil push their fresh faces from their snowy beds to greet thy coming! When, out of the love they bear thee, delicate forest blossoms struggle manfully to the sunlight—mute, fragrant flatterers! A busy housewife thou art, excelling all the seasons! There is so much rubbish to be cleared away; the frozen soil loosed from bondage; roots to be warmed into life by clear, unclouded suns; seemingly dead forces to take on their resurrection, and blossom abundantly. Nature's allies throng fast and furious, to prepare for the summer's campaign.

8*

May coquettishly wafts us a breath now and then from the tropics. Pinks sleepily open their white eyes, hidden among their grassy spears. Honeysuckle bells quiver, tremulous with fragrance on their slender necks. The lilac flings abroad its sweetness, and sends up a colony of shoots around its base. The air is vocal with feathered emigrants, wooed and won back from southern skies; content, it would seem, to exchange orange groves for maples and elms, as they flutter noisily back to their old nests, and by their cheerful twitter tell us, "there is no place like home; no land like that of the Puritans; no air like that of freedom."

A languid charm pervades and softens the clear sunlight, and disposes to indolence. Even the toilful farm horses share this mood, standing meekly in harness for hours, in apparent contemplation. And when the carts are at last filled—with sand from the highway, with stones from the field, or decaying sodden leaves from the orchard—and the word is given them to jog onward, they do not pretend to muster a trot, but walk lazily alongside of their lazier masters.

Here, too, the ever-recurring gray firmament of colder months changes to a steadfast arch of cloudless blue—Nature's perfect morning wrapper, worn unsullied, unwrinkled throughout an entire day; or a more lovely, because less monotonous picture, snowy glaciers of clouds looming portentously in the southwest; then, forgetful of their threatening errand, as the glorious sea spreads out before them, come rapidly onward, so gently ploughing their feathery keels through the billowless sea, that their motion is scarcely perceptible, and, like a flock of homesick pigeons, they halt with reluctant misgivings midway on their airy passage. And yet another, when dense, white continents, joined to others as vast by narrow stretches of isthmus, discover themselves to the upturned eye—opening, as we watch them to show us peeps at blue lakes, over which anon a fragment flits—a cloudy pebble which does not sink, but rests on the surface, a veritable island. Silvery barges scud across the heavens, full-freighted with shadowy Cleopatras. Ay, familiar faces beckon and smile to us also; and the longer we gaze the more confused we grow, and scarce can tell whether the blue or white be uppermost, or whether ourselves or the clouds are stationary.

However, May, to the thrifty housewife, is more suggestive of the annual scrubbing of the domicile; of sundry winter garments to be packed away, and lighter gear replaced in wardrobes. To the farmer's wife it is more suggestive of the coming toils of the dairy, the hot, sweltering, haying time, than of natural beauties. These latter are taken for granted; enjoyed with that dull perception which cannot conceive of any thing occurring to check or prevent their annual reappearance; they are there for all time to be gazed at in the interstices of ardent labor; but the daily round of this same toil must be looked after.

With the advent of summer I emerged from the chrysalis state and fluttered confidently forth, a village " schoolmarm." This important post was obtained for me chiefly through Uncle Jesse's kind representations. Then followed the indispensable official visit from a solemn-looking constellation, —one sun, and three lesser lights content to bask in the splen dor of his beams. The sun was the minister, of course, and the satellites were the lawyer, deacon, and " town field-driver." My heart fluttered tremulously on being summoned to this august presence. I remember, such was the stress of my anxiety, pausing a moment, my hand on the latch, to offer up a brief prayer for a happy result, and to summon to my aid an air of unconcern. I felt no addition of faith after the petition ; neither assurance after the struggle for it. As I entered, the field-driver accosted me : " Take a settin' on the longe, won't ye, Miss Brooks ? Ye needn't be afeared of *me*, 'cause I can move along and make all the room you want." He vented his mirth in a facetious chuckle. My cheeks burned at his insolence, powerless as I was to resent it. What more natural in such an emergency than to hide the flaming offenders. I turned to the window, just as Demis came tripping by, her apron filled with radishes fresh from the garden for tea. A quick sign with one hand asked me if they were there ? I nodded. She threw it up in pretended astonishment, and mischievously held up a scarlet radish to indicate the similitude. Then she clinched her tiny fist, and shook it expressively, just as Elder Fuller's little figure crossed to my side and peeped curiously over my shoulder. I chose a seat, and " Brother Storts" opened the exercises, with a request to the " Prudential Committee" to settle the terms of hire. The minister retorted, that " as Brother Storts himself was *that* committee, doubtless he would proceed at once with that duty." He was answered by an inquisitive nod in my direction and this query :

" Wat do you think's about the fair thing in the matter o' wages ?" and he doubled his tongue together, thrusting it between his great yellow teeth.

I considered, which pause was only for looks; I had pondered this idea previously, long and well. Speculating with commendable hopefulness on the probable amount of my earnings, my estimate, I thought, extremely moderate. Mr. Storts dissentingly shook his head. " So, so !" he gravely pronounced, glancing meditatively at the carpet, then quickly up at my face. " It's too much for the fust. onset !" He

glanced appealingly at the elder. The divine, wiry, dry,
rustling as usual, came to his aid and eyed me severely.
" I believe, Miss Brooks," he coldly observed, " this is, as
our brother well and truly observes, your first essay at
instilling the precious seed of knowledge into the youthful mind." I reluctantly assented. " We feel the awful
responsibility resting upon us, individually and collectively, in
this great matter of education." Looking me full in the face
to impress me with its momentous consequences, he slowly
added, " We are not in the habit of engaging inexperienced
instructors. No ! One who aspires to this proud title should
possess experience, age, dignity, and wisdom. Have you
these prime virtues, Miss Brooks ?" I grew a little indignant
at this, and found my tongue: " Pray tell me how one can
have experience except they teach ? and as for age—"

" Excuse me," he interrupted, " you have yet to hear me
out." He proceeded as though I had not spoken. " Yet,
at the instance of our mutual esteemed fellow-citizen, Mr.
Warner, who recommends you warmly, we, after due de-
liberation, and frequent implorings for Divine assistance, in
this, as in all other weighty matters of the law, have concluded to award you a fair trial. If you succeed, you open the
way to a station of future incalculable usefulness ; if you fail
—" he left this blank to be filled by all the ills and calami-
ties my imagination could devise. " You will, therefore, perceive that a reduction of your exorbitant demands is an im-
perative necessity, until you have proved yourself competent
for a station which is our country's proudest boast." The
little man had probably learned this wonderful flight of eloquence, for, after its delivery, he relapsed into profound
silence. His subordinates wisely remained mute. My response came more meekly. " That's the ticket," approvingly

remarked Brother Storts—I felt any way but fraternal—
"we've ciphered it over, and I reckon 'bout a dollar and
twenty-five, for sech a business, 's the fair thing."

"It ought to be sufficient satisfaction to work for the love
of it. That is reward enough to any right-minded person,"
placidly observed Elder Fuller. He put on his spectacles, and
peered at me over them—by this means preparing to put his
mental laboratory into working order. Then followed his
grand wave of the hand, whereby he thus waived all prior
claim—by reason of superior talent and office; and the reinstal-
lation by his humble luminaries, who "couldn't think o' sech
a thing, raly," and the final arrangement, whereby each in turn
should invest themselves in inquisitorial robes, and sound
the shallow depths of my acquirements. Deacon Marabee
came last, and he had decidedly tough work to summon his
arithmetical forces. After a protracted hemming for needful words, he said desperately: "Miss Brooks, what's 'Rethmetic?—I'm gun to b'gin at the b'ginnin', and go straight
through," he explained *sotto voce* to his fellow-laborers. "Did
you arnser that question, Miss Brooks?" his glance returning
to my face. I replied in the affirmative. "Wall, say it over,
if you please, I'm a little hard o' hearin'." I repeated it accordingly. "Yes!" assented he, with a meditative air, resting
his lean elbows on his shrunken legs, as he stooped forward
and plunged his long fingers through his grizzly locks. "It's
the art o' numb'ring though, rayther than the *science* of numbers, and it's a wonderful art too; learns us to cipher and
keep a'counts. It's the usefullest of *all* time-serving arts, take
it all round. Grammar, I never could see the use of, nor the
sense on't, and though the art of jography is all well enough,
it can't hold a candle to figgers. You notice, my young friend,
I call it a *time-serving* art. Can you tell me what I mean?"

Seeing from his manner he expected me *not* to know, I hastily proclaimed my ignorance.

He nodded his satisfaction. " It's a servant of time, Miss Brooks, therefore I call it *time-serving.* It's of the earth, earthy. What a thought it is, a grand and wonderful thought, I may say, that in another world we shall need no sech arts and sciences. No studyin', or teachin', or nothin'; no committee men to look after the int'rists of the young, no nothin' at all, but praisin' and givin' glory to the Lamb who was slain from the foundation of the world; only castin' our golden harps before the great ' White Throne,' and jinin' the colony of the saints; the hundered and forty and four thousand, who are the redeemed."

How much longer the worthy man would have pursued this exalted strain it is impossible to say. It was evident that he had lost all sense of present duty, in this rapt communing with the waiting glories of immortality. He doubtless fancied himself flanking his long pew in Sunday-school, filled with attentive Bible scholars. Elder Fuller récalled him, very shortly, to sublunary things. " Deacon Marabee! You'll hardly ' get through' the book to-night at this rate." The deacon started bolt upright.

" I b'lieve I kinder lost myself," said he. " I'm famed for it, specially when I git to dwellin' on the wonders in store for them that love and fear the Lord. Wall, Elder, if you think it ain't best to put any more questions to the subject, I'm willin' to express *myself* satisfied with things as they be."

" Glory, Hallelujah," shouted Demis, bursting into the room immediately the last had vanished from the ' yard.' " I never saw any thing like it in all my born days. Here they've stayed, and stayed three blessed hours, and I wanted to go strawberrying. I declare, it is too bad," and she energetically gesticulated to such an extent toward the retreating figures, that the spying orbs of her mother caught and transfixed her; she told her to "stop *that* in short order; she wondered if she wasn't afeard to show sech disrespect to aged Christians. *She* should *expect* a judgment to foller. The Lord didn't tolerate irreverence to his followers,"—concluding by an urgent recommendation to read the Bible story of the bears, who destroyed the boys for insulting the aged prophet, Demis laughed.

"What now, Miss Sauce-box ?" angrily interrogated her mother.

"Oh, nothing! I have my misgivings on some of those stories you are always quoting."

"Yis, I dare say, and I have mine on some others," rejoined Aunt Rhoda, nodding her cap-border ironically; "one is, that *you'll* never come to no good end, Demis Martin, and the sooner you know it, the better."

CHAPTER XVI.

MONDAY morning found me fully equipped for my new station; with the approved rudiments of learning done up in blue covers, and packed away in my satchel. I had a deal of gratuitous advice from Mark, and sympathy from Demis, with promises of sundry visits, and fervent hopes from Deborah, that "I shouldn't git starved out, for," she observed, "you know them fact'ry bugs ain't much of any hand at cookin'; they do as well's they know how, I s'pose; poor creeturs, they ain't to blame for what they don't know; we none of us be. Now !" she decisively added, "I've

put up some doughnuts and cookies for you, to whet your
bill on when you git hungry, though you must make a show
of eatin' when you go to the table, else they'll be as high as
nine 'bout it. Them kind o' folks are so dreadful 'fraid of ·
bein' slighted, you know; allers on the watch to see if somebody a *leetle* better off don't look down on 'em. *I* know 'em
of old. Now, I don't expect you'll have much but griddle-cakes
and brown sugar; the butter '!l be frowey, too, see if 'taint !
But if you're cunnin' 'bout it, you can manage so's not to
swaller one morsel. I remember Lovicy Lovejoy's tellin' 'bout
goin' to sowin' s'ciety at one of them housen—Miss Hicock's,
I b'lieve 'twas. At any rate she was a church member, and
she'd tended up putty regular to the others, and asked 'em
to meet with her. What to do they didn't know. They
put it off and put it off as long as they could; fust *one*
would speak for it, a little grain ahead, you see, Ruby, and
then another, till they couldn't put it off no longer, and they
finally 'pinted a day for't. I see Lovice that day. She felt
like death 'bout goin'; they're so pisen nasty at Hicock's.
She laughed, and said she expected to eat her peck o' dirt
afore she died, but she leetle ruther pick out the kind, and
she'd a good deal rutherer not eat it with her eyes wide open.
Wall, only three of the s'ciety went. They all had 'company come' *that* day. Kinder unexpected, you know. 'Twas
in the spring o' the year, and some was all torn up a cleanin'.
Mrs. Martin was among *them* kind; so tuckered out that she
didn't feel able to ride up there. I must say I never knew
her to stay to hum on *that* a'count, afore or sence. Wall,
what to do they didn't know; but they finally fell to and
sewed till dark, and then was invited out to tea as crank as
ever you see. Lovice is a sly crittur. *I* never should a
thought o' comin' the game *she* did; more likely than not I

should have been tuk with a powerful headache, or a sour
stomach, or somethin' o' *that* kind; but, no! She was well
enough, and started up as spry as a last year's cricket, as if
she was *so* hungry she couldn't wait, and dreadful 'fraid she
shouldn't git t'the supper-table afore the rest. She's told me
sence it did her a heap o' good to look round and see the
others a worryin' down the vittals. They couldn't do no
otherwise, you know. Miss Purse said she thought she could
take a stiff lobelia 'metic when she got home, and so *she*
put in and eat. Wall, what'd Lovicy do, but take a piece
of ev'ry thing that was passed round; four kinds of cake,
and three biscuits, great, yeller, sour-milk things, as big as
your fist, and a whoppin' piece o' mince-pie in t'the bargain,
and when supper was through there want a scrap of nothin'
under the sun left on her plate; she finished it as clean as
the Shakers could ask for. Walkin' hum that night the ladies
was a speakin' 'bout it, hopin' they shouldn't have to go there
ag'in right away, and so forth, and so on. 'Dear me!' says
Lovicy, 'How *could* you eat so? For *my* part I couldn't
swaller one morsel, and I'm as faint as I can be. The fust
rush I make when I git hum'll be for the butt'ry.'

"'Do hear her!' says the others. 'She eat like a pig.
She better talk of folks bein' nasty. She seemed to relish
every thing pritty well, I thought.'

"'Me!' says Lovice. '*I* didn't eat nothin'; see here, if
you don't b'lieve me,' and she pulled her hankucher out of
her pocket, stuffed jest as full as it could hold of crumbles
of ev'ry thin' she'd took at table.

"'Oh, oh! why didn't you tell us, so's we could a done
so too,' said Miss Purse.

"''Cause I didn't want to git caught, as some o' us would
a been if I'd told you. You see *you* eat and *I* kept talking

all the while, so they mistrusted nothin'.' You can try it if you git brought to sech a pinch," concluded Deborah, with a sage nod.

The whole family turned out to see me off. Uncle Joel, from the meadow below the piazza, waved his yellow bandanna. Mark held the horses' heads while Mr. Warner clumsily mounted to my side. Deborah stood at the end of the piazza, polishing her forehead with one corner of her checked apron, and smiling at me encouragingly; while Demis assiduously endeavored to hush Annah's cries; perched upon the gate-post, she clamorously entreated to be taken. Even Aunt Rhoda paused a moment from breaking up the curd, and, looking through the open dairy door, nodded almost pleasantly as we drove away.

There is such an exulting sense of importance in the first home-leaving, when the fruition of a cherished purpose shines surely and steadily ahead. My dignity developed wonderfully while riding slowly towards that little grove-hidden schoolhouse, the target for all the eyes in the village. They were levelled at me along the street; they twinkled from doors, and peeped cautiously around lifted edges of green-paper curtains, as I *then* thought, *enviously.* A condescending almoner is pity; abundant, uncostly alms I bestowed upon those unconscious recipients.

"Dear me, sus!" sighed Uncle Jesse, as we neared the place. "Sister Charity was a sayin' this very mornin' that it seemed so strange to think that one of her old scholars was steppin' inter her shoes. It shows there's no stannin' still. We're gittin' older and older ev'ry day. Sister Charity's putty poorly: she don't pick up *very* fast," he added, reflectively. "See, Ruby, ain't there a swarm, now?"

We had stopped in the midst of a noisy throng of lads

and lasses : the former suddenly beginning tree ascensions
with brown, bare feet ; the latter, bright with pink ruffled
aprons, and green gingham sun-bonnets, whose strings they
were industriously chewing.   I determined to organize my
kingdom precisely after the manner of Miss Charity's old
régime ; so I placed a piece of paper on the corner of a
spelling-book, and, leisurely tapping it with a pencil, walked
up the rows of faces for a timid census-taking.   It was decidedly a work of time and patience.   One youngster gave
answer that he was "old Joe Brown's boy;" and, upon
further questioning, replied, "Dad calls me ' skesicks,' and
mam calls me puddin'-head ; yer can take yer choice."

The boys all laughed, and the misses giggled.   I inquired
his age.   "Mam says I'se born in the year one, and I ruther
guess she knows," was the curt reply.   Again the boys
laughed.   As I steadily pursued my task, I now and then
caught wondrous pantomimes on all sides, liberally greeted
with appreciative mirthful sounds.   Then the girls, one at
a time, darted at me with wistful looks and eager beseechings
for a pin, until I wondered if they thought me a pin-
cushion, and, looking narrowly into their quarters, found
sundry shawls turning rapidly into infant forms, and undergoing a vigorous care.   They tore leaves from spelling-
books to plait into fans, and curled dandelion stems into long
ear-rings.

The days wore away drearily, seamed with little golden morning gleams in the shape of fresh, queer little bunches of violets
and daisies ; of striped grass, southern-wood, and sweet peas,
laid sweet and cool upon my desk.   Debby's anticipations of
the meagre fare to which I should be subjected were realized.
Often no roof would admit me, when my sole resource was
Uncle Jesse's, where a hospitable welcome was sure to await me.

The summer waned slowly. July passed in intense heat. Its sultry burnings breathed upon me almost intolerable languor. I grew to loathe my long walks at morn and even over the scorched sandy roads. My pupils, too, caught the contagion of restless indifference to study. Away off, on the hill-sides, were patches of forest. Viewed through the narrow panes of my school-room windows, they looked tantalizingly suggestive of coolness; the cattle sleeping under the scattering trees seemed, indeed, enviable.

Utterly exhausted, one sunny afternoon, I fell asleep—my head resting on my wooden desk—when a sudden uproar startled me. A new scholar was the cause—a tall, red-haired, lusty lad, with small gray eyes, rebelliously twinkling around the room, and returning to meet my sleepy gaze. He voluntarily informed me that his name was Andrew Jackson, and saucily inquired if he should " set on the floor ?"

I pointed to a seat. He shuffled along the floor toward it, and this banished my drowsiness. I was alert and vigilant to detect mutinous acts, but all went smoothly until the close of school. Then, as the last class arose, the big boy remained in his seat, surly, inattentive. To my mild inquiries, he returned dogged answers.

"You will at once take your place," I confidently remarked.

"Not ef I knows myself, I guess," was the serene reply. The class eyed me curiously; a few smaller pupils set up a titter. As I stood, meditating what course to pursue, surveying him with some disgust, pride urging me to conquer him—he favored the assembled class with a knowing wink, and dropped this remarkable observation: "Some apples are green when ripe, Miss Brooks. I'm one o'*them* sort, ye see ;" then, after a pause : "I ain't none afeard of my granny," at the

same time rising, and slowly turning pivot-like on one heel,
a hand grasping his other ancle.

His insolent coolness exasperated me. I felt suddenly,
through all my veins, the strength of a tiger. Once fairly in
my grasp, it seemed as if I could crush him like an egg-shell.
A thought seized me. I advanced cautiously, and slyly
putting out my foot, as he continued his careless swinging
—anon, leering at the silent class, he tripped and fell headlong
to the floor. Having once got the advantage, I retained it;
calling one of the larger boys to my aid, we bound him
securely. His rage, his mad struggles, were, for a time,
furious. Oaths rang out loud and fierce, accompanied by
sullen threats and promises, with eyes of flame, of future
repayment.

Then, as no one replied, or noticed him, he ceased to
struggle. Shame trod closely on the retiring heels of Ire—
shame at the unprovoked contest. The sullen quiet of submission succeeded to the tumult. I sought and transfixed his
eyes with a steady gaze. They quailed. Sarcasm is the
discipline for this nature, thought I. His prestige is gone
among his former subjects: I must make the victory complete.
In cool, measured accents I addressed him. I spared no sting
which I thought could wound and humble. As I ceased, the
class signified approbation by one universal murmur, with
pleased looks at each other, and expressive head-noddings. I
caught a few observations, in an undertone, such as—"I'm glad,
for one;" "He allers was a plaguey bully;" "I reckon it's
the furst day in the year that he's been took down such a peg."

"Shall he stay on the floor?" I now ventured to ask.

"Yes!" "Yes!" "Yis, marm," came the responses —some
of them from sturdy, full-fledged rogues, who merited an almost equal treatment. But youth always takes the side against

the physically weak and helpless, the mentally inferior, or the conquered. They are fast allies just as long as admiring fear carries a compelling might, and no longer.

Andrew, by this time, was as submissive as a lamb. All bravado had vanished; he was actually crying. My eye steadily seeking his, compelled him to ask my pardon for his insults, then, of the scholars, which he did humbly. I released his bonds, and allowed him to rise, and the lesson passed as · orderly as usual. This incident—so trivial in itself—was an era of hope for the future good behavior of the whole school; and, as for Andrew Jackson, his respectful deference was marked; his devotion was unbounded. He usually remained after school, to walk home with me, and one evening we thus encountered Mr. Warner.

" Wall, who'd a thought it ?" he exclaimed, with a wondering look at my satchel, which Andrew carried. I took it from him, and turned back with Uncle Jesse.

" Thought what ?" I asked.

" Why, I heerd that are Jackson feller a makin' his brags t'other day, that he wan't goin' to be ruled by a woman, a milk-and-water face too. I say, what'd you do to him, Ruby ? it's took the starch all out," he added. I merely laughed. " The biggest, meanest, young rascal that ever trod shoe-leather; wants to be sent t'the house o' correction the wust way," he said with emphasis. " There never *was* one of his kith and kin fit for nothin' under the sun but to sarve as a scare-crow; *won't* work, do your best. Work an' they had a fallin' out once and never got over it, I 'spect. I was in hopes this one'd keep away from you. You'll get 'nough of him 'fore the term's out."

" You see," he resumed, meditatively, "they're *so* conceity. Can't tell 'em nothin'. They know it all beforehand. Now

I think that conceit's like chickweed; it takes an amazin' sight o' pullin' up and hoein'; you've got to be etarnally at it, and *then* you never know whether you've got red of it for good or not."

Midsummer passed. Broad fields of yellow grain fell in serried ranks at the wide sweep of the reaper's cradle—formidable-looking, but powerless, opposers. Over hill and dale floated musically autumnal signals. The flail merrily resounded. Apples began to drop from the trees with a mellow sound, suggestive of ripeness. Squirrels ran nimbly along the zigzag lines of rails that fenced in orchards from the highway. November wreathed in mist and haze the too vivid landscape. The nights grew cooler, and left crisp dew on the still green foliage. December, though not yet come, blew upon us from afar his frosty breath.

Those days released me from bondage. The august Committee again visited me on the last day of my service. The children came decked in holiday attire, with brilliant nosegays of asters, ostentatiously presented, and full of eager anticipation respecting parting presents.

Elder Fuller made a speech, impressive and original. "He was astonished, and, he must say, confounded, at the wonderful progress of all the pupils in their several branches of knowledge. It showed great perseverance and unflagging industry on the part of the pupils, and great efficiency on the part of the teacher." Here he showered the praise until I felt amused and then indignant. "Education was a great and a glorious thing; indeed, he might say, the only thing worthy to engage the attention of the young." He elevated above his head a dictionary. "Here, my young friends, is the lever which moves the universe. This is the keystone to all knowledge; the foundation of all the arts and sciences. Show *me* a

Plato, a Cicero, a Newton, a Washington, and I will show *you* a zealous, earnest student of this book. Master it thoroughly, and you will see the channels of wisdom and learning open to admit you, and overflowing with living waters. It is a golden link in the vast chain of books, which binds our land round and round, and through and through." The children cast reverent looks at the battered volume, and wondering ones at each other, as the minister's voice sank impressively to its lowest key, while he solemnly added, " Let us pray."

CHAPTER XVII.

It appeared tha·, with the advent of winter, Demis's prophecy was destined to find literal fulfilment. She informed me immediately upon my arrival, that Natty had domiciled his chubby form under the "great room" sofa the preceding Sunday evening, for the express purpose of " finding out all about it." " Such a fright as he gave us !" said she. " We didn't miss him till nine o'clock, and then what an ado, to be sure. Debby was half distracted, running around the house, and shouting with all her might.· Finally, Amanda heard the commotion and looked out to inquire the cause, and after a moment we discovered him, curled up fast asleep. Such a shaking as mother gave him. I know she would have whipped him, if father had been away. I don't know why, but she never did whip one of us before him."

" And when does it come off ?" I asked.

" Natty said about Christmas time, and Ruby," she whispered, " Mr. Hume will be back in time for it. He is coming to teach again this winter."

9

"Does that make any difference?" I inquired half jea-
lously.

"Of course not, my darling. You *do* take one's words
up so. Only, the more the merrier, you know."

Dear Demis! She was open as the day. Her frank,
guileless nature saw no reason to conceal the pleasure with
which she looked forward to the schoolmaster's return. I,
too, felt a strange sweetness surging through my heart, but
I strangled it at its birth; if cruel to myself, yet a kind
mother toward an illegitimate offspring. For why should I
nourish the shy stranger, and feed it daily with promises of
a golden future, only, when it should have grown to manhood's strength and sternness, to be crushed to atoms in its
fierce endeavors to be free from unwarranted thraldom?—
only to gather thorns at life's meridian, when, in its blessed
morning, I had sown foolish trust; the sting of secret shame
following closely the slightest departure from the solid track
of Reason's footsteps.

Not many days after, upon going into the keeping-room,
I perceived a change. The cherry table with its blue and
orange woollen cover had disappeared. The dimity curtains were twisted away from the windows. Chairs were
huddled into the centre of the room, upholding four long
wooden frames, fastened together by pegs in their corners,
on which was spread the surface of a gay "album quilt."
As I silently regarded it, the owner thereof appeared, her
form dilating with pride, and pointed out the most precious
squares.

"There's pieces of all the girl's dresses," said she. "I shall
take lots of real solid comfort lookin' at 'em. They wrote
their names in the centre, you see, and give 'em to me to set
together. It's the fashion here, when a girl gits married."

"Then you have made up your mind to be married," I said, prudently averting my gaze to the autographs before me.

"Yis! I don't mind tellin' you. Demis is such a hector, I never can tell her any secrets; she'll laugh you right in the face. It's comin' off Thanksgivin', an' father says, that, bein' the first to go, I shall have a real rouser of a weddin'."

"Why didn't your friends here have *one* write their names?" I asked, pointing to the straggling hieroglyphics; running " up hill," and "down hill," and into corners; some bravely starting near the centre of a block, with bold capitals; but, getting cramped for finishing space, dwindling gradually to letters of fairy-like minuteness; others, dwarfed at the starting point, but swelling to a fatness truly aldermanic, as they ran along the white centre; some with extravagant twists and quirls, as if just at that juncture the authors thereof had been suddenly seized with colic, and unable to prevent the letters from assuming sympathetic contortions.

She gave me a surprised look. "I like it a thousand deal better as it is," she said. "Its jest *as* they write. I guess none on 'em ever saw the inside of a writin' school, though; none. but the Purse girls. Look there! You can't ask for harn'somer writin' than that of Olive's name, I'm sure," and she bent a searching glance around the frame. "Rubiny," she continued, "I don't want to draw you inter harness, as soon's you step foot in the house, but—" she hesitated so long, that I looked up in surprise; she was not often chary of asking favors. "Oh! only to make a silver cake for me. I want a nice tea; the girls always tell what's on the table, when they git home. Have you seen my settin' out?" she abruptly inquired. "Come on, and I'll show it t' you. I s'pose the girls'll have to have a squint at it too."

She proceeded on up the stairs into the "east chamber,"

and opening a capacious chest, proudly lifted out for my inspection, piles on piles of the whitest imaginable linen, the laborious accumulations of years, fragrant of sweet cloves, spices, and
dried rose-leaves, with her name in full, marked in colored
cross-stitch upon each. She appeared to take immense satisfaction in my looks of pleased surprise, and replaced them with
lingering fondness, pausing to settle and smooth their strong,
glossy folds. Then, she opened a closet door, and pointed
to the shelves, laden with blankets and quilts. There were
" rose counterpanes," in blue and white, and red and white.
There were blankets, in coarse check, fine check, and plain ;
and thick-padded " comfortables," tied with great knots of
blue yarn ; and quilts, in " basket" pattern, with handles, and
without handles, to suit the most fastidious taste ; in large
stars, and small stars, stars with four points, and seven points,
and with rings in their centres, and one, " Lone Star of
Texas." There were " chains," and " wild goose chases,"
and rose-buds, and one of a zigzag pattern, called " herring-
bone." And one huge sunflower pattern, looking, as Debby
declared, " as nat'ral as life :" and also a " butterfly"—
emerald green and " turkey red," insects of a shape unknown
to Audubon, skimming over a field of pure white, fenced in
by a yellow binding. And lo ! " the Mississippi Valley" was
there ; and a grand old " Irish cross," and " a circle round.
the moon," besides other suggestive titles, too numerous to
specify ; and the first, on which she tried her undeveloped
powers.

    " Who'd ever a thought I'd a made such a piece o' work
on't as *that* is ?" she said, surveying it scornfully ; " it'll do
though for the hired man's bed, if we ever have one," and
she tossed it to the topmost shelf.

    There were white spreads, with heavy tasselled fringes, and

netted fringes, and thick knitted " edging;" piles of dimity "valances," and pillow-cases, and "ticks" for straw and feathers. In short, all that a reasonable girl could desire. To please Amanda, I gave the articles a lengthy survey. " It's tol'rable, I think," she complacently observed. " About as good as most girls git. Mother'd feel streaked enough if it wan't; and I hain't asked no odds of nobody. I made 'em all myself."

" That's the reason you keep your room so much, I suppose."

" Certain! mother wouldn't have all these traps roun' down-stairs. I've taken sights of comfort up here, mor'n I shall ever see again, I'm afraid." And she gave a sentimental sigh. " Mother's goin' to make me a carpet, and then I shall be whole-footed."

The quilters assembled early. "Fust and foremost," growled Debby, as Miss Harriet Ann Carr, arrived.

She may be truthfully described as a maiden, tall, tanned, and skinny, of doubtful age, poor memory, and decided leanings toward the state of matrimony. By the persevering saving of "milk money" she had attained to gold spectacles, becoming "near sighted with waning youth;"—a fact she freely lamented, averring it to be "a great pity that young folks couldn't git along without glasses; it makes 'em look so old-grannyfied, you know," always ending piously with, " Wall, what can't be cured, must be endured." She was fond, too, of smelling of any one's open snuff-box, remarking the while, " Mother laughs to beat all; but, I do really, and always *did* like the smell of black snuff, with a bean in it; jest a whiff ye know." Mellissa Prince was there, with her insinuating glances, and perpetual " they says," and envious constructions of innocent remarks, accompanied by her sister "Frances

Awgusty," bold, rude, and disagreeable, given to constant head-tossings and giggles. Olive, with her pale oval face, and deep hazel eyes, reflecting earnest truth, set them all right occasionally in their wanderings. Amanda, silent as usual, went from side to side, assisting to roll, and marking minute diamonds with a card dipped in a saucer of starch, highly colored with indigo.

Toward sunset, Deborah came in to inspect the quilting. As she peered curiously over the noisy girls' shoulders, she. was eagerly importuned to tell their fortunes. A shadow crossed her face, as she looked around the group. "Law's sakes, gals," she said, "I've told 'em to you dozens o' times, and married you off, and that's all the good it does; you won't foller 'em, so what's the use?"

" No !" interrupted Kitty, " you never told mine."

" 'Cause I think you're clear quill, you know, and can git along without it, fur'zi know."

" Nonsense !"cried Miss Kitty, " and you won't tell Ruby's."

" Well," said Debby, slowly, " I've never had the heart to tell Rubiny her'n ; for the fust night she come here, goin' on seven year ago, I saw in her countenance a long life of trouble ; I hain't seen nothin' yit to make me alter my mind. See here !" she eagerly clutched my hand, and spread open the palm, " Did any on ye ever see sech lines as them before ? so deep ! hundreds of 'em, crossin' and crossin' each other ; the line of life is long and deep ! she'll live to be old ! then, see where others cross it. I tell you, gals, when you see that—which you won't very often—it says, as plain as plain can be, trouble and worriment and care. I can't tell ye *nothin'* pleasant," she shortly said, flinging away my hand, as though it stung her. " I see, by yer looks, ye don't b'lieve nothin' in't, but that don't make no differ-

ence. 'Tain't Faith as makes our fortins come true. Ye never
can be prepared for it nuther. It takes ye onexpected; when
ye think ye've got clear o'one p'int, it'll come in anuther. I see
it as plain as day. You'll make friends, maybe, but you won't
keep 'em; 'twon't be *your* fault though. It *is* to be. Some'll
die. Them you love best, o' course; that's allers the way.
Some'll desert you, and it'll seem to *you* for jest nothin' at all.
You'll be as poor as Job's turkey all the days of your life;
live alone, and sorrowful, and, like's not, die in the poor-house.
There's more, too, and worse; want to hear it?" she asked,
suddenly.

"No! that is sufficient, I think," said Kitty. "You're
gloomy as the grave, Debby. Ruby, though, don't look as
if she put much faith in your prediction. That's one comfort. Now beware, in telling mine, how you make it up out
of whole cloth. It must be true as the Gospel, and not half
as tedious; and if you forget the marrying part, I'll never forgive you. I'm bound not to be an old maid." The little
hoiden shook her fists at the seer, and hummed lightly, "Oh,
Canaan, 'tis my happy land."

"Do you think I *make* fortins, Miss Kitty?" said Debby,
scornfully. "If you do, you're much mistaken. I only reads
what's writ for me in the book o' Fate. When I tell 'em, in
'arnest, they allers come true. Them flyaways," she added,
contemptuously, "I talk nonsense to; there's nothin' remarkable in *their* futur'. They'll, some on 'em, git married,
most likely, and have nine or ten young ones apiece, mostly
boys and gals, and they'll die when their time comes, and
that's good enough for anybody, I think."

"Well," said Kitty, laughing, "I always knew that I was
remarkable, but strangely enough no one at home will agree
with me in that opinion. Much obliged to you, Deborah."

Debby stooped quickly, and lifted the black sparkling eyes
upward. "Poor child!" she said, foudly; "who could
have the heart to give you one sad, painful moment?" and
she turned to leave us, but Kitty caught her by the hand: "I
demand to know it, whatever it is," she cried, with crimson
cheeks and startled eyes. We suspended work, and watched
the pair.

"I wish to heaven I had not come in here this afternoon,"
said Debby, solemnly. "But I'll tell, if tell I must. In less
than a month, Kitty Fuller—now mark my words—somethin'
awful'll happen to you. You'll be stark livin' alone too. I
see a brook, as plain as plain can be. It's red too; red as
blood. Oh! dear, how glad I'd be to help you, but it's strong
and sudden, and nobody nigh to see it. I can't tell you
more; but be careful; do be careful." With these words she
vanished into the kitchen. A silence fell on us all. Kitty
turned white as death, and whispered brokenly, "Oh, girls,
what does she mean? Am I to be murdered?"

"A pretty idea," indignantly interposed Demis, as the
noisy tongues caught up and reproduced this supposition with
commiserating glances at the victim. "Kitty hasn't the
shadow of an enemy in the world. I'm astonished at Debby.
She feels gloomy and has vented her spleen in the usual way
with her. I never believe her. She may keep her fortunes to
herself for all I care. To-morrow she would tell you one
quite different, if she felt so inclined," and she looked angrily
at the whispering girls. Thus encouraged, Kitty shook off
the unusual feeling of sadness, and became once more her own
bright, gay self.

"For all Demis's disbelief——" began Olive to me, in a
whisper, then mused absently.

"Do you credit it?" I asked.

"Oh! I was thinking of something which she prophesied once, stranger still than this, and it *did* happen just as she said. It's very strange ——-" again she mused.

An uncomfortable feeling crept over me, making the merry voices seem strangely discordant. Happy unconcern lit each face. The released tongues flew wildly. Olive, alone, kept me silent, thoughtful company.

" Laws, gals!" said Aunt Rhoda, "after tea, fold up the quilt and put it away; there'll be somethin' else to tend to, I 'spose."

The "something else" arrived soon after, mustering by twos and threes. We—suddenly grown sedate—overheard their agitated whispers ere entering. "*You* go in first." "No! *you*—you're the oldest," &c.

It takes a long time to thaw the ice of New England reserve, in these secluded districts. It is as hard as that wreathing the surrounding mountain summits; but when spring forces surge within—as they do surely, though tardily—lo! the crust cracks and quivers, and through the fissures you catch a gleam of the social fires smouldering there. So these rustic swains ventured cautiously, with prolonged, embarrassed pauses, toward the genial conversational fire, rattling and sparkling merrily among the girls; then they began to get their courage up, and to hitch their chairs a little in that direction, and to change their locality, and to walk- about with less and less restraint. From this stage there was but one desparate leap to the rollicking fun and clatter of later hours. " Plays" followed in eager succession. " Judgments" were performed with a celerity unsurpassed in criminal annals. Jokes mingled freely, whetted to an edge so keen, that the dullest could not fail of perceiving and applying the point. Through it all drifted down to us Debby's mournful tone, wailing through an old song:

9*

> "When last I saw my Love to the church she did go,
> Bridegroom and bridesmaids they made a fine show,
> And I followed after with my heart full of woe
> For to see how my Love she was guarded."

How distinct and sad the words came to us, by the rest unnoticed. And when she came to the last verse her voice rose, as if with prescient fear, and swept outward in a wilder echo, midway between a dirge and a shriek:

> "I'll dig me a grave both long, wide, and deep,
> I'll cover it over with roses so sweet,
> And I'll lay me down in it, to take my long sleep,
> For Love's been the cause of my ruin.
> For Love's been the cause of my ruin."

But it ceased at last, and as the old clock slowly chimed the midnight hour they began to grow quiet, and to speak of leaving. As they waited for the teams to drive up, sundry whisperings floated dreamily round the dimly lighted room, from couples blissfully hand-locked, standing in corners and window recesses. I stood alone by the fireplace, filled with painful reflections, when near me I caught Mark's voice prudently lowered for Olive's ear. There was a fond, eager question, and a timid, tender response; and then he added a little louder, and I fancied regretfully : "I have made up my mind, but no one knows how hard the struggle has been to give up——"

"Who?" queried Olive, archly.

He finished. "The hope of being something very, very different. I feel no special calling for the Church. I have a dim notion at times that it is perjury."

"You *will* love it beyond every thing, when you fairly begin your career," she answered, with enthusiasm.

"You would make the better minister," he responded. "For you love the office, and I do not. However, the past is buried. I burned my brushes the other day. Let what will come, I never will touch paint or pencil again. A grand bonfire they made. I hope mother will be satisfied. I am;" and he bent a fond look downward.

I went up to them: "I heard you, Mark!" I thought it best to say simply.

"The devil you did!" he replied, hotly. "And what business have you to be around listening?" His brow cleared directly. "Oh! well, it's no secret," he added, as if recollecting. "This little maiden has promised to be a minister's wife some day; poor taste in her, I must confess, but I won't grumble." His old, gay manner assumed away again. I gave him a look full of pity. I could not comprehend such an ignoble withdrawal of buoyant, glorious aspirations to the level of the common-place; it looked to my eyes but dust for gold, no matter if the dust were real, and the gold very far away in the future, and very uncertain. Hope affords more and better nutriment for a longing soul, than present possession of something undesired, crowned by bitter discontent.

However, I merely said: "You have been a long time in deciding."

"Well, I am but a vacillating dog, after all," he said, sighing. "I suppose I shall be what I *shall* be, however," he added slowly.

"That is incomprehensible; or does it signify a theological mystery?" He did not hear or heed me.

"Olive," he pursued thoughtfully, "I am not eloquent; I never can be. You will blush, with deserved mortification, at my wretched failures in that line."

As I turned away I heard her solemn response, low, sweet, and trustful: "Dear Mark, power cometh with grace from on high. I am not afraid, neither need you fear."

CHAPTER XVIII.

ONLY two weeks remained to Thanksgiving, weeks of unceasing activity. A silk dress arrived from Chispa, in a brown paper wrapper, duly directed, with the proper shop flourishes, to "Miss Amanda M. Martin." This was an event in the household; and the delicate lavender and white brocade when unfolded and hung over a chair-back, fully justified our extravagant phrases of admiration. Debby was of the opinion that "'Mandy would look like a June pink in her roas'-meats; though," she added, with a view to utility, "she never can step foot out-doors in that are gown in all this world; never! Seems to me it's a dreadful foolish business. If it'd 'a been black now, it'd 'a been worth somethin' quite a spell."

"She can color it after the wedding is over," demurely observed Mark; and Debby instantly acquiesced, with an after rueful suggestion that "'t'won't never be so shiny after it."

Animated conferences were held as to the style of making. Demis insisted on a surplice bodice with elaborate puffings of lace. Aunt Rhoda stoutly maintained *her* point, the "mellon waist," producing the argument that "her'n was made up so, when *she* stepped off," meaning her sister Hannah's. I being a novice held no opinions,—a fact all novices would do well to note. The final result of these discussions was the sending to town the bride-elect, to put herself and belongings into the hands of the experienced.

Violent snow-storms heralded the approach of Thanksgiving. Huge drifts, firmly crusted over, lay on vale and hill, and in the moonlit evenings rang far and near the merry shouts of the coasters. The pond, too, wore a glittering surface, but was pronounced as yet unsafe for the skaters. Days of melancholy, yet cheerful waste, when the sky was one vast white plain, and the earth another; when the rugged mountains wore a white veil, and the hill-sides lay swathed in a winding-sheet, and the vales were raised to a level with higher land by means of this kindly material; when every tree and shrub did its slender part toward wearing the wedding raiment; when even the birds who linger with us change their brown plumage for white, and only the matter-of-fact things of man's creation, upright brown and red sides of barns, sheds, houses, hold out a sturdy belief in their own better hue. But Nature does all she can for such obstinates, dropping a snowy ridge on eaves and chimney-tops, and along the fences, to keep them in countenance with her —far and wide—pure surroundings.

Dwight and Nathaniel spent their evenings coasting, and Demis and I frequently accompanied them. Many an exhilarating race we had down the long hills. We were the ungrateful recipients of sundry tumbles and bruises, as, despite skilful guidance, our steel-shod sled would frequently veer like a worn-out weather-vane, and send us whirling down the frozen surface.

Uncle Joel looked up from his paper rather thoughtfully one evening, upon our entrance to the kitchen—" Boys, where do you go to slide?" said he.

"Why, down by the Alum Rocks," answered Demis, quickly.

"Wall, I mistrusted so," said her father. "I don't want to spile your sport, but I wish you'd jest go some'ers else; there's oceans of hills all round us, so you can't go fur out o' the way." After a pause—"I'm 'mazed you should go there, Dwight. Natty don't know no better. Don't you know what a dangerous place 'tis! Rocks right below you hundreds and hundreds of feet, and at the bottom a pool of water, I don't *know* how deep; guess 'taint never been sounded. Wall! to stan' down there and look up, it's as perpendicular as that are stove-pipe, and no mistake. When I was a youngster," he resumed, with a retrospective glance at the ceiling, "I remember well 'bout the Alum Rocks; 'twas there little Sammy Miller was drownded—went off like shot while slidin', and when they got him out—poor little feller! I never see anybody so hack'd and hew'd. I stood roun' while they searched. *You* remember it, don't you, Rhody?"

"Yis, indeed!" said she; "'twas an awful Providence; and his father was killed in the fullen' mill, right away after; got ketched in the belt, and couldn't stop; went over and over the big wheel. Poor Widder Miller's had a pretty hard time on't, take it all round; allers been as poor as Job's turkey, and allers will be. I remember it well, Joel, 'cause Elder Lee preached a powerful affectin' discourse. Le'me see! I haint forgot the text, I guess: 'The ways of the Lord are wonderful, and past finding out.' I shan't forget it to my dyin' day. Though, comin' hum from meetin', Miss Purse said that 'twan't a primin' to the one he preached when her grand'ther died, down in Chicopee Valley. He was brought here, you knqw, Joel. Everybody said 'twas foolish to send so far for a minister, and then come right back with the corpse, but 'twas his request, and them things should allers be attended two."

"Wall, wall," said Uncle Joel, uneasily.. "Mind you don't go anywheres near that place agin. I shan't take a mite o' comfort ef you do."

"I must say," remarked Aunt Rhoda, the next morning, coming into the keeping-room, where Demis and I sat placidly sewing carpet-rags—long strips of gay colors, and winding, as fast as we joined the ends, into a huge ball— "that are copperas sets beautiful; 'twon't fade nuther, I guess, an' it don't crock much, do *you* think it does, Debby? I s'pose you know," she went on, "that there's lots to be done this week, and we may as well go 'bout it fust as last. After prayer-meeting last night, I run up hum' to Sary Purse'es, and she giv' me her rule for plum-cake. She says she allers has good luck, but the best people miss it sometimes. Mine *used* to be fust-rate, but I don't know what; somehow, latterly it don't work right. It *ought* to be good, for there's enough good things in't. Deborah says I've lost my knack, and sometimes I think so too. Now, one of *you* try, and see how *you'll* make out. I thought that mabbee I could prevail on Lovicy Lovejoy to come down an' stay a spell, and chore it; she's famous for wedding-cake, so I up and run up there too. I was sorry afterwards; it's sech a stretch to Biscuit Hill; for I had my labor for my pains. She'd gone over to Cyrus'es, in Little Falls, and nobody knew when she'd be back."

"It's curus how that woman does gad," put in Debby. "I should think in some o' her travils she'd pick up a man; but she don't seem to, does she?"

"Perhaps she don't want one," observed Demis.

"Humph!" and Debby significantly nodded her head.

"Never mind!" said I, impatiently, "we can make it, I should hope. How many kinds are there to be, Aunt?"

She meditated a moment, resting the rolling-pin on the table, and her arm on that. "Le'me see; there's plum-cake and sponge-cake, an' pound-cake's three, and cup-cake's four, and Washington-cake's five, and there's a new kind that the Purse'es was tellin' 'bout. Olive see some on't down to the Mills'es at the Harbor. It's baked in round tins, and put on top one 'nuther, with jell' spread between. We'll try it, I guess, and that's six. That's enough, a great plenty; with cookies and ginger-snaps, and a few sech like, in the way of small ammunition."

"I guess," said Demis, archly, as we got fairly at work pounding loaf-sugar and seeding raisins, "your thoughts were more on receipts than hymns, mother, at meetin' last night, according to *your* tell."

"I guess you don't know every thing, Demis Martin," rejoined her mother, quickly. "It wan't a Sabba'-day, so there's no killin' crime in neighborin' a little after meetin's out." She took up an egg, and tapped it gently with an iron spoon. "How many does that resate say ought to go in here, Ruby?" she thoughtfully inquired, as she vigorously whipped the broken yolks into yellow foam.

She re-commenced: "We had an oncommon interesting season last night. I never see sech a subdued look, as you may say, on all the faces. I don't know how 'twas, but all seemed to feel as if the Spirit was strivin' in our midst, and a callin' on sinners to give up their stubborn hearts. Elder Fuller spoke very affectin'; he said he thought he saw signs of a revival of the faith. Deacon Sweet, too, made a very feelin' prayer. He said he was willin', for his part, to give up all arthly idols that might hender the work of Grace; and he besought the Lord to come and show forth his salvation. I tell you, there wan't scurs'ly a dry eye in the room. I couldn't help thinkin' that p'rhaps he was the ordained instrument to bring about what he prayed for; for, as soon as he finished, some riz for prayers, and a good many more looked as ef they wanted to, but dursn't. And then the Elder, he got up and prayed that pride might be utterly consumed, and all carnal desires, and a heart of flesh given 'em for their hearts of stun."

"Of course!" impatiently pronounced Demis. "That's what they always say. But who rose?"

"Le'me see," she reflected. "There was Avis Purse, was the first one who got up; she's the only one who ain't a professor in the Purse family, and I tell you her mother's eyes glistened, when she stood up on the Lord's side. Then Ki Cramer got up, and arter a spell Lorany Sweet, and then Natty, and then—"

"What! our little Natty?" cried Demis, in amazement.

"To be sure," placidly returned Aunt Rhoda. "He's old enough. I felt like gettin' right down on my knees, to give praises. I wish Dwight had been there. I s'pose its useless askin' you two to go," she said sadly; "Ye will not come unto me, that ye might have life."

"Don't talk to *me!*" said Debby, briskly filling patty-pans, "nobody won't make *me* believe, if they stand over me with a drawn sword, that Lorany Sweet 'll ever git religion. I don't care if she *is* a deacon's darter. I mean the rale gini-wine article. There's a sight o' professors now days; but I don't come across no practicers. I 'spose there *be* some, only I don't happen to light on 'em."

Here she paused to taste the mixture she was putting into the oven, and to observe doubtfully, "Massy! Ruby, I'm 'fraid you hain't got pearlash enough in this ere. Seems to me it don't taste jest right; but I don't know, I'm only a passenger." She gave it a submissive look, and shoved it into the oven.

"Wall," she resumed, "arter she came a flyin' int' the sanctuary, that ere Sabba'-day, a rigged out in the manner she *was*, and so brazen-faced about it, too; I jest made up my mind that all hands might as well save their breath to cool their porridge with, as to try to convert *her*. You never heard o' that, did you, Ruby? Why, you see 'twas in the dead o' winter, and bitter cold. It seems some one dared her to do it, so she up and said, she jest as lieves as not. She marched in after Elder Lee had got through the heads of his discourse, and begun on the application; right down the broad aisle she streaked it, straight to the deacon's pew. The strangest looking mortal ever you sot eyes on. She had on a pink calico gown, low neck and short sleeves, and *sech* a scrawny neck, my stars! and a black bombazette apurn on; she didn't wear no shawl, only a black lace veil throwed over her ears to keep 'em from freezin'. I never see, in all my born days, anybody so beat as her father was, when he looked up and found that apparition waitin' to be let int' the pew, lookin' jest as innocent as if she's in the nicest plight in the world. He looked mad enough, too. I bet she catched it when she got home; but law! what'd *she* care for that. I guess she'll have to haul in her horns if she actilly gits int' the church. She ought to have a guardeen put over her."

"I remember it as plain as day," added Aunt Rhoda, "she got an awful cold, jest worried through it, and that's all. I'm glad Grace has laid hold of her at last."

"Humph! Grace has got a powerful tough customer," muttered Debby.

"There's no tellin', but she may be a bright and shinin light yit. The wind bloweth where it listeth, and ye heareth the sound thereof; but where it bloweth, or whither it cometh, who can tell?" solemnly said Aunt Rhoda. "Well, Miss,"—rather curtly—"what are you so smilin' about? I hope you ain't laughin' at Scriptur."

"No! mother, I was only thinking of the prayer-meeting for young converts at Chloe Scott's. Olive told me all about it. I don't know how Loraina came to be there; but she knelt and prayed with the rest; she prayed for every thing, and everybody, and finally wound up by wishing they might all have a foretaste of perdition, and Chloe Scott a double portion, and she went on in the same strain until Mrs. Scott came in, and sent her home."

"The massy on us!" cried Deborah, with uplifted eyebrows. "I should say as much."

"I wonder she wan't struck dead," rejoined Aunt Rhoda.

"Chloe says, she never can forgive her in all this world, never!" pursued Demis; "she can't bear the sight of her."

"Wall, she oughter," said her mother, decisively. "It ain't showin' a Christian sperrit; forgive till seventy times seven, the good book says. But Lorany's a different creetur now."

"I hope she'll stay so a spell; long 'nough for us to see how she looks," rejoined Debby, carelessly. "Lordy! gals, how this cake has riz up. It'll do for 'em to whet away upon, I guess."

Thus the week passed, filled with work from morning to evening—void of incident, save the fulfilment of Debby's sad prophecy. All Northfield was startled to hear of poor Kitty's premature end. It cast deep gloom over the village— saddening the approaching festivities. On hearing the tidings, I threw on my shawl and ran up the road, to see if it could be true. I met Olive Pierce coming down to tell us.

"Yes!" said she, "it is true. I was down there yester-day. She was in high spirits as usual, and said that she was coming here this afternoon for a visit; she should ride Bessy, and give Annah a ride before she went home. I presume she started with this intent, for they found her down by the red bridge dead; her pony standing quite still, whisking his tail, and looking down on her, as though wondering why she did not get up and mount him."

"Have you seen her parents, Olive?"

"Yes! I went there as soon as I could, to see if I could be of use, but the house was full and all in confusion. I could only get into the entry, so I came away. I saw her mother, through the open sitting-room door. She appeared very wild. Two or three ladies were grouped around her. The Elder, they say, is very calm."

"It is a terrible shock to us all, Olive. Poor Kitty! So full of life, and health, and hope. To think she should be snatched from it all so suddenly. Come in." We had neared the gate.

"No, not to-night," she answered, "as I've seen you." However, she seemed in no hurry to turn back, and we stood leaning over the low pickets, pursuing the sad theme, until our voices grew husky and silent. My hand rested on the fence; she gathered it tightly in her warm palms. "How cold it is! It is like death itself," she said, starting. "Do you feel so chilly?"

"Not in the least. It is constitutional, I think. They are always cold." She gently chafed it, until it glowed under her magnetic touch. Her voice sank to a caressing murmur: "My dear, you know what Mark said the other night?"

"Yes! He intimated that——"

She interrupted. "But somehow I don't feel its truth.

I cannot tell you why. I see no reason to doubt, but something will surely happen. There *may*, you know. It will be so very, very long before——"

"Nonsense!" I said stoutly. "Don't let us have any more presentiments of evil. It's natural—your gloom tonight. I, too, feel it, but no sibylline foreshadowings. A night's rest, Olive, will effectually strangle them."

"Then you don't credit your evil stars:" she looked searchingly in my face. "You don't look as if you did. I don't think I ever saw you sad but once; that first night you came here. You had a woe-begone face then; thin, pinched, and sallow, with great dreamy eyes. When next I saw you, it did not look the same face at all."

"Demis wrought the change, if any there were, by giving her rich, generous heart in exchange for my dwarfed, sickly one."

"And you have no sadness now?" she interrupted.

"Indeed, I hope not. If trouble *must* fold her sable wings in my domain, the quickest and surest riddance is to smile her out of the open door, and bid her a genial 'God speed.' I don't want her. She is a guest as unwelcome as a superannuated, imbecile cousin of the fortieth remove, and poor at that, quartering herself uninvited in the house of a rich relative. Is the comparative tension too tightly strained? I think not. I am rich—not, perhaps, as the people about us estimate riches, in house, and lands, and safe bank-stock; my indigence there might gratify the bitterest enemy I am ever like to have. But that does not trouble my sleep at night, I assure you. In youth and its wealth of vigorous hope; in bodily—and, I hope, mental—health; in undaunted energy and perseverance, I count my fortunes."

Olive smiled. "Yes," she said. "Your wealth in *that*

species of property is undoubted and reproductive. I never knew a more hopeful character. If it could go on forever thus!" she added, dreamily, as if to herself; "forever planning and anticipating. What will she do when youth has departed, and health flown on the wings of exertion? Hope will never beguile them back for another trial. And old age comes slowly but surely. Independence and fame are habitually shy of approach."

"I will earn them long ere that time arrive," I confidently answered. "When they turn to mock my eager pursuit, and flutter from my grasping fingers, I will again give chase. Olive, you bird of evil omen, I will overtake the fickle dame and bring her to terms right speedily. The slough of despondency shall never furnish me with more than a night's lodging." She was silent. "You little know," I pursued, "how much I think of the future. I am an orphan, with a child to rear and educate. I *must* do it. I *will* do it. How, when, and where, is still a mystery for that friendly future to solve. If I could leave Northfield! I can work my way to the light, slowly, slowly; or if my father would come back and help to make the task easy. Alone! that is a trial, Olive, you know little of."

Despite her sweetness, a look of scorn crossed her face as I mentioned my father, but she quickly suppressed it. "That is true," she answered, sadly, "but every heart must fight its own battles, and weep for its own sorrows; my lot is neither so bright or peaceful as you think. Hush!" as I was going to reply. Looking up, I beheld Mark standing in the path. She leaned forward and kissed my forehead—thus tacitly sending me in.

CHAPTER XIX.

THE auspicious morn rose bright and clear. Great golden banks of cloud scudded across the eastern skies, paling to clear white before a flood of brilliant sunshine.

" Bless me !" ejaculated Demis, sleepily rubbing open her eyes, " there's a wedding on the docket."

" There's a wedding on the docket," echoed Annah, imitating her exact manner. Children mould their standard of excellencies in character by one or two persons. They are not alchemists, to single out from individuals solitary traits of goodness. It is rather complete attraction or repulsion. Win fully their childish fancy, and forever after you may walk in its innocent devotion ; there is no speech so perfect as yours, nor manners more elegant, nor learning to surpass *your* scanty attainments. Thus Annah doted on her cousin, scrupulously following every action, repeating, parrot-like, her quaint expressions, until one day Demis awoke to the fact and set a guard upon her lips, while it made her love the child more dearly.

Breakfast was soon dispatched. A fire kindled in the dark, solemn, " great room." Debby said that " the bewfut needed a turn or two with the wax," so she polished it until it shone like a mirror. Thrown open, it ostentatiously revealed glittering white china, overrun with gilt sprigs, and a silver teapot—my aunt's wedding portion, and never used. Bunches of " Live for Ever" and " Bitter Sweet" glowed on the high wooden mantel, in diminutive glass mugs—the latter adorned with a painted wreath, and the injunction, " Remember Me." There were also a pair of vases, declar-

ing themselves "A Present to Maria," and "For Demis," in
blue lettering; a peach of colored china, and a companion
orange, which Debby threatened to "take Annah in hand"
for touching; a whale's tooth sufficiently ugly, and an alum
basket containing cards : artistic affairs they were, of wreaths
and scrolls, testifying to the legitimacy of "Friendship's
Offering," and signed by the donor's name. On either end
of the mantel towered in polished pride a veritable silver
candlestick. The ponderous table supported the family Bible
and the "Life of Adoniram Judson," rather ludicrously
flanked by sundry diminutive profiles of the Martin family,
cut in black silk, and pasted on white paper; looking, for
any thing the impartial observer could discover, like an ego-
tistical repetition of one set of features; and a pair of white
rabbits, composed of soft, furry flannel, with brown straws
for whiskers, and twinkling black beads for eyes.

Heavy freights of uncles, aunts, and buxom cousins, "on
the Martin side," arrived—all especially invited to the late
Thanksgiving dinner. As evening closed in over the glittering road, rang fast and faster the tramp of hoofs. The
house was full when the minister arrived. The dense crowd
opened right and left with sympathetic reverence, and upturned faces involuntarily saddened at sight of the broad
mourning band on his hat, and at thought of the lonely,
bereaved mother at home, weeping out her holiday.

Words are inadequate to picture the serene content of Aunt
Rhoda's face, as she bustled from room to room, performing
with anxious care the part of an attentive hostess,—or Uncle
Joel's jolly complacency—which nothing could fret; his
jokes—followed by scores from other gray-haired sires—not
witty always, but certainly harmless, and hailed with raptur-
ous bursts of merriment,—nor of the abundant table with its

row of the six kinds of cake—each a snowy pyramid—and
the "small ammunition" doing duty at corners. Space will
not permit me to chronicle the favorable criticisms from
thrifty matrons; each was declared superior to its prede-
cessor, and "the best they ever see:" nor the sly allusions of
young men and maidens, as they wrapped bits of the bride's
loaf into tiny parcels to "dream on:" nor the momentous
hush, as the whisper thrilled through the throng, "they are
coming:" nor the solemn prayer that rose, and the simple
ceremony, diluted with sobs from tender-hearted damsels;
and the longer following prayer, in which the young couple
were dosed with the usual quota of desperately good counsel: nor of the riotous fun of the succeeding hours. The
last sleigh of "old folks" sounded its departure. Uncle Joel
and his weary wife retired after seeing Annah, who resisted
sturdily, dragged away to bed by Debby.

"Now!" said Eliel Prince, "now's the time. Mrs. Martin
said we might stay till midnight, and it'll soon be here."

"Well!" remarked Eben Skinner, "I fetched it along with
me; but I left it in the cutter. I kinder misdoubted, if,
arter all, 'twould do to bring it in. I can git it in a jiffy, if
you say the word."

"I don't know," said Mark, rather doubtfully. "Mother's
opposed to dancing. She will send you all home. I give you
fair warning."

"I guess I know *that*," retorted Eliel, with a chuckle.
"However, a few good old country dances won't kill anybody. I'll risk it."

"This room is on the other side of the house from
mother's," observed Demis, encouragingly. "I'll close the
doors between, and if you play low, Eben, and can omit that
horrid squealing at the beginning, she won't hear it."

10

"Certain," assented Eben, "I tuned it all up as slick as a mitten, 'fore I left home; so form for Money Musk, if you please, gen'lemen and ladies, or ladies and gen'lemen, which-ever way you'll have it. I'll call off."

"Low! call low!" cautioned Demis.

I did not dance; but I found ample amusement in watch-ing the rest. How they flew to the muffled tones of the little violin, and Eben's shrill whisper, commanding them to "swing once and a half round;" "forward in lines," and "ladies chains." We got a fright once, and the dancers stopped, as the door quaked suddenly; but it was only Deborah, who happened to like music as well as any of us, and, after the first ejaculation, sat quietly down, holding her delighted peace.

"A leetle trifle lower, Eben," she said coaxingly; "I heard it way up-stairs. It's so shrill, I should think the dead in their graves might hear it, much less Mis'. Martin, who's got pesky sharp ears. *She'll* settle your hash for you, if she *does* hear it."

"Now for the Twin Sisters," called the master of ceremo-nies as they paused, flushed and breathless. "Balance all! Down the middle, and up the outside," shouted Eben, who was getting excited. Demis looked hard at him: "Wall, we'll rest a bit," said he, wiping his streaming forehead. "Gi! how warm 'tis. I s'pose though, there's no such thing as opening one o' them doors," and he took up his bow with surprising resignation; "so take your places for Op'ry Reel," he sang out in seamanlike style; when round went the mad gambols more furiously than before.

"Bravo!" whispered Mark—also a spectator—"if mother cannot hear this she must be growing deaf. She would spin it off pretty quick if she did—"

"Do se do," chimed in Eben, "Down the outside," he

whistled, "Back to back! all primenade! seat your par-
deners."

"And form for the Tempest," added Eliel, breathlessly.
"Quick, boys! I have a dismal foreboding, strengthened by a
sound which smites my unwilling ears. We'll finish *this*
though," he cried, triumphantly.

"There's many a slip 'twixt cup and lip," muttered Debby.

It was indeed a tempest; seemingly inextricable convolu-
tions, revolving themselves clear at last, intermixed with impromptu "pigeon wings" from the masculine row, and the
unruly violin piping shrill defiance to prudential motives, as
round spun the whole troop until— Suddenly Eben dropped his bow as if it had been red-hot, for the door was flung
quickly open; filling that space stood Aunt Rhoda, with irate
brow, and flashing eyes, and—peeping over her shoulder—
her more amiable husband; his face sober with amazement.

"What's all this?" she sharply asked.

"The Tempest," meekly replied Eben, scratching his head
in bewilderment.

"The tempest!" she echoed scornfully. "I should think
so. A pretty how-d'ye-do this is. I never thought 'twould
come to this in my own house. Never! Dancing! And
most on you professors, too!" She turned with a sudden
movement upon Mark. "I'm astonished at *you*, Sir. A
blessed example this is; and 'fore I'll submit to be put upon
so, and by a ——"

"Now, now, Rhody," interrupted her husband, anxiously,
for mother and son stood steadily confronting each other.
Her face absolutely glared with passion; his—calm and
white—was full of the look of a long-hunted beast, fairly
turned at bay. It was the first time I had seen resolution
stamping itself on those mirthful, gently-defined features. I

liked the change. A moment they stood thus in perfect silence, his eyes riveted to hers, waiting only for her lips to finish the sentence. They quivered; parted to speak; closed again—compressed with strong resolve.

Uncle Joel forced a laugh. "Pshaw! Now, mother, don't be hard on the young folks. I haint forgot the day I'd a' walked four miles and over for a chance o' shakin' my heel. I ruther dance than eat when I'se hungry; that was 'fore this rheumacy took hold o' me so. It's a good joke, though, stealin' the march on us old folks, arter sendin' on us off to bed," and he laughed this time heartily.

"A good joke, indeed," she exclaimed, hotly. "I don't see what there is to laugh at, Mr. Martin; and during a revival too. It's the wiles of the devil, more likely. At any rate, it's a joke that's played out; so pack up your traps Mister Ebin Skinner, and march. Quick! I don't stir from here one foot till you do."

In spite of this abrupt termination of festivities, all seemed to consider the past pleasure worth the present price, and as they drove from the door I heard them laughing heartily at their abrupt dismissal.

CHAPTER XX.

THE week following was *too* quiet. It begat almost intolerable ennui. Ira and Amanda commenced housekeeping. The transient excitement this step occasioned—the packing and moving successfully disposed of one entire day—exhaled with the last departure, and we relapsed into irksome solitude. Debby, Demis, and myself filled the afternoon hours with listless sewing, while Aunt Rhoda made neighborly visits, and attended meetings. One day we sat thus as usual. From the eastern window a wintry prospect spread far and wide. Twilight was prematurely descending. The leaden sky gave promise of approaching storms.

"I declare," said Demis, abruptly, "I never would have supposed that we would miss Amanda so much."

"I knew we should miss her," replied Debby, in a satisfied tone.

"Yes," I said, "especially after so many weeks of sport. Our sliding is over. Your mother has discovered, Demis, that 'young wimmen grown did'nt slide in *her* day.' However," I added, after a pause, "if we play, Amanda's carpet will never be finished."

"I think it'll be a han'some one," observed Debby. "Just you ldok now at this ere stripe," holding up a huge ball of shreds, all colors and textures, sewed indiscriminately together. "This stripe's called hit or miss, and it's well named too. It sets off the orange and red powerful." There was another dispirited silence, which Debby broke by saying: "I think it's downright gloomy latterly, and 'taint all because there's been so much junketing, as you gals seem to think. I tell you somethin's goin' to happen."

"I wonder what?" said Demis, tartly. "You are always harping on that theme, Debby—'Something to happen!' I'm sure I wish there would. I wish the schoolmaster would come, if nothing more."

"And what more *could* there be?" inquired Debby, maliciously. "You'll miss it one o' these days, lottin on that are man so, let me tell you."

"I don't care one straw about him," said Demis, hotly.

"You do, and you know it. Ruby knows it, too, if she's got any gift at all."

"It's December, and time for the school to open," I hastened to observe.

"Wall, set your mind to rest; he'll haul in next week; I heard the deacon say so yesterday. What good'll it all do ye, gals? You know enough a'ready," said Debby, with scorn.

Demis laughed. "I should want to die at once if I thought so," said she wistfully, "should you not, Ruby?"

"I don't think so *now*, Demis. I cling to life. It will take a great sin, or suffering, to bring me to that desire. And then I believe I should prefer joining the Sisters of Charity, to contribute my mite toward assuaging human sorrow. God bless the holy sisters! They deserve the meed of saintship hereafter. Their ranks are never too full; their hearts never shut and double-barred against the erring. Their hands are not too delicate to minister to the victim of a loathsome disease, nor too white to wipe away the bloody stain from the criminal. When good orthodox Christian dwellings refuse to receive the outcast, and the pampered expounder of Christ's words on earth puts on a severely rebuking face, and frowns at her in holy horror, *then* she turns to the unostentatious cell of human sympathy in Popish bosoms, and is never denied admittance."

"But they end by converting the heretic," observed Demis, triumphantly.

"'Pears to me, if I was one o' them critturs Ruby's been speakin' of," interrupted Debby, "I should be amazin' glad to get converted over to their ways. Ev'ry body'd oughter jine 'em right off; there's no two ways 'bout it. I hope they dont have hard work to git 'em over. Sech folks never'll git very fore-handed *here*, but they lend to the Lord. Elder

Fuller, now, talks a great deal 'bout proselitin', and sech trumpery. *I* don't b'lieve the Catholics do it any mor'n the Baptists and Methodists and Bluelights; and if I was goin' to be put through the proselytin' business a'tall, I'd bet I'd go where I could git some benefit from it. Talk to *me* 'bout ——" She paused, looking incensed at Demis's ring-ing laugh, and subsided into a reproachful silence.

"Go on, Debby," said Demis, wickedly.

"Oh! you can poke fun at me if you've a mind to, I'm nothin' but a passenger," said Debby, meekly.

"Nonsense!" I cried, "You're the conductor of this train."

"No," she said, still in a meek fashion, which never re-mained long.

"I remember, Demis, going once with my mother to visit a hospital. I recall every detail of the well-ordered building. There were vast airy rooms, hung around with Romish pic-tures, and liberally supplied with plaster images of the cruci-fixion. The patients' cells were models of neatness. Sister Agatha showed us around. She had a sweet fair face, which even her ugly flapping bonnet could not spoil. I fell in love with her directly. She laughed so pleasantly when I told her 'I should like to come there if I ever should be sick.' "

"I thought nuns were shy and gloomy," said Demis.

"Sister Agatha talked very freely. There was a cabinet of articles for sale in the refectory—crosses, Madonnas, rosaries —the proceeds to go toward defraying the expenses of the institution. She wished to give me a little crucifix, but my mother motioned it back. She gave me a lecture upon *for-wardness*, when I got home, saying it was wicked to worship those things."

"Hark!" cried Debby, suddenly, as there came a rap on the outside door.

"That's a welcome sound!" cried Demis, springing up hastily, and sweeping her lapful of woollen bits into the basket. "I'm glad company is coming at last. I began to think that our friends had all deserted us. Well!" was all she said, as she came slowly back, and resumed her seat.

"Who was it, Demis? A peddler?"

"I wish it might have been," she retorted. "I havn't seen one in an age. No one was there."

"I certainly heard a knock," I rejoined, as positively.

"I thought so too," said she, "but it seems we were both mistaken."

Rap, rap, rap, distinct, positive, leaving no room for doubt. I flew to the door ere the last vibration, fully expecting to catch our mischievous visitor, but started back in amaze, for no one stood there.

"Well! why don't you ask them in?" cried Debby, ironically.

"It's one of the boy's tricks," I remarked, coolly returning; "and they doubtless are hidden in full view of the door, laughing at our surprised faces. It's an old joke; let them have it to themselves." They *did* have it. Apparently, they resolved to be not easily disheartened. On the front door, on the kitchen door, and, when we were not looking up, on the windows. The vibrations of one hardly ceased ere its fellow sounded.

"Those foolish youths are giving themselves needless trouble," said Demis, at last, looking up, and dropping her work wearily. "I'm tired of hearing it." She cast an annoyed glance at the door.

"Them ain't the boys' doin's," solemnly responded Debby, I've heerd 'em afore now, when no livin' soul was by, and I knowed they'd come ag'in. And they *have*."

"Of course," retorted Demis, scornfully. "They will come until they get sick of it, or until mother comes home from covenant meeting. I'll warrant they'll stop then."

"Maybe, and maybe not," stoutly maintained the seeress. "One might as well talk to a stun as to try to tell *you* anythin', Demis. I tell you—you may b'lieve it or not, as you've a mind to—I've heerd them noises off and on for ever so long. Furthermore, I tell you that 'taint nothin' new to *me* to hear 'em; but they never come—no, never! but what some one died soon after. *I* know what 'tis. It's a warnin' call. Now," she pursued, as if relieved at having spoken her mind, "I think it's downright wicked, and a temptin' of Providence, to make light o' sech matters"—we were smiling—"mabby you'll think on what I'm tellin' ye, one of these days, if anythin' *should* happen."

"It would be strange, indeed, if nothing ever happened," I said. "You know, Debby, that Elder Fuller says it's a deceitful and a dying world."

"*He* don't know nothin' 'bout it," she retorted, with scorn, "but, we'll drop the subject, for there comes Mis' Martin, hum from meetin'; and if she *is* a clever woman, I must say she's dreadful sot against *some* things. I declare, it's time to git supper too; after five o'clock, as true as preachin'!" and muttering something about "seein' to startin' up that are fire," she trotted off to the kitchen.

"Mother, were there any new converts?" asked Demis.

"No," she replied; "no new ones. Some told their experiences, and some on 'em was quite lengthy, but desp'rate interistin'. Hesekiah Cramer said he was struck with conviction when he wa'n't mor'n twelve year old. It's a sign we never ought to give up laborin' for sinners, and I've hopes of you yit, girls. He said he was down sullar one day, sortin

10*

over apples ; 'twas jest after a revival meetin', and all to once
somethin' come across him like a flash of lightnin'. 'Twas
that are passage of Scriptur, where it speaks of sep'ratin' the
sheep from the goats. Said he to himself—'that's jest what
I'm doin'. I'm puttin' the sound apples car'fully in a barrel
by themselves, to keep ; but the old rotten ones I throw
helter-skelter in a heap, and carry 'em off anywhere to git
red of 'em. They are good for nothin'. Why shouldn't
Jesus do as he please with his own, and where shall I be
when he sorts his apples? Many the windfalls, I spect, or
worser yit, the rotten ones, that have been, or might have been
good for suthin'.' Wal, he said it overcome him so that he
sot right down to think ; and he made up his mind that he
wan't on the right track to salvation, an' he up and made a
string o' good resolutions ; but, after a spell, they sort o' died
away, and then come another call. Like Jacob of old, he
fought sorely, and wrestled long with the sperrit for the vic-
'try—and he *did* overcome it. Then—he said—he was a
backslider. He had stuck to the faith through all, but he
didn't enjoy savin' grace as he used to, and now he'd had a
third call. He broke down, right there, and for the life o'
him, couldn't say another word. I declare 'twas a solemn
scene. I didn't know afore, that he was engaged to have
Kitty, but they say he *had* been keepin' company with her
a year, and over. Nathaniel's evidences, too, was satisfact'ry.
I'm 'fraid Dwight's gittin' hardened ; he didn't appear affected none while his brother was talkin'."

"Aunt," I broke in quickly, " were the boys there until
you came away?"

"Sure. I'd like to catch one on 'em leavin 'fore meetin's out.
I'd show 'em how to ride on a fullin-mill, I warrant ye."

"And Mark, too?" queried, Demis incredulously.

"Why, yis. Seems to me you're uncommon cur'us. Mark spoke quite a spell, and made as good a prayer as you'll often hear. He come right out afore 'em all, and said he'd dedicated his life to the cause, to be a gospil minister. Arter meetin' Mis' Purse asked him hum to tea. I guess," she added, bridling her long neck, and untying her cap-strings, " I guess they think he's good enough now. An elder, you see, ain't to be sneezed at, and—they'd be loth to own it— but they allus *did* seem to think Olive a *leetle* better'n common folks."

I slipped away to the kitchen to assist in preparing tea. Debby was in the " buttery," with a huge loaf of bread in her arms. She took up the carving knife, and, pressing the loaf firmly against her bodice, began hewing off thick slices, nodding her head at every vigorous lurch of the knife, as if to assist it in working its passage. " Wall, child," she observed, "this ere's a strange world we live in,. ain't it! There's a dreadful sight a goin' on all the while. We make a great fuss about our goin's out and comin's in, and after all—come to sum it up—what does it amount to! Nothin' under the sun, but jest bein' borned, bein' afflicted, and then dyin' jest when you git reconciled to livin' a spell longer. We don't have our say 'bout nothin', from beginnin' to end : no mor'n they do at school."

" Who knows but it *is* only a school, Debby !" I ventured to say, " preparing us for that which is in reality — Life. It's a severe school sometimes. It's hard to learn the lessons it imposes ; and harder still to give up our friends when, their tasks finished, they graduate to a higher class than ours. These material ties are so firm. Our selfishness would fain keep them forever in its lower grade."

" Wall, it's human natur' to set by our kindred, Ruby.

Them that don't are brutes. No! not that either, for brutes
are fond o' their kind; they're worse than heathen. To be
sure, I 'spose *our* loss is *their* gain, and we can see 'em ag'in, *some*
time. I don't know though, 'bout this resurrection business.
I don't swaller it all. It's a putty slim prospect o' seein' them
to *my* mind, to be obleeged to wait 'till the judgment-seat, and
by that time mabbe they'll git over hankerin' to see us, and'll forgit all about us, that sech folks ever existed. That ain't weekid,
is it? Then, too, I can't see what we're goin' to do with these
old concerns when we git 'em up there. Why, ain't we jes's
well off without 'em if we only think so? I, for one, when I
git red on't, wouldn't pick out my humly old picter, and ask to
git back to it ag'in for all etarnity. It's bad enough to tote
it round in time." Here she broke off abruptly, to hold
up before me the loaf, which revealed a huge hollow in its
centre; and to put on a very mournful countenance, as she
obsérved, in a low tone, " That's a grave, Ruby! I never
knew that sign to fail!"

" Nonsense, Debby!" I shook my head incredulously.

" But we've all got to come to it," she sadly pursued. " For
my part, *I* think it's the best way to think on sech things,
so's it don't come too sudden like. Now, child, that's what
I was a goin' to tell you this afternoon, but Demis won't
never hear no word 'bout it. It's all true as the Book of
Genesis; what I told you them raps was. Here! you set the
tea a steepin', while I run down sullar for some plum-sass."
She soon reappeared, panting and muttering crossly : " Them
stairs are the unmercifullest stairs I ever *did* see; I don't
b'lieve Jacob's ladder could be much steeper; if so, I
wonder the angils didn't git all tuckered out a runnin' up
and down 'em. Wall!" she continued, setting the plate on
the table, and running her finger around the edge to wipe

away a few purple drops, making ready for a leap to the
cloth. " I wan't to tell you somethin' that happened when
I was a gal. You musn't breath a word of it to nò livin'
soul, for I don' know but they'd put me in prison. I was
knowin' to't in the time on't. I guess I couldn't a been
mor'n fourteen year old, at the outside, when I went out by
the day to spin or work, jest as they wanted, and one week
I went up t'the holler, to Lawren Carr's. I staid eight weeks,
though I didn't dream o' sech a thing when I went; but you
see, Abram, his son, was took down with summer complaint,
and it settled into a slow fever, and his folks prevailed on me
to stay and do chores and see to things, so's Miss Carr could
wait on him. Wall, he was expectin' to a been married that
very fall to Prudy Perry ; as likely a gal as ever trod shoe
leather, and han'some too's a pictur'. She come up when he
was the sickest to see him, and watch with him, 'cause he
was out of his head most the time, and he'd keep callin' for
her the wust way. Wall, after a tedious spell, he begun to
pick up some—I'd told 'em all along the fever'd have to have
its run—so's he was quite chipper, and put in t'the chicken
broth as if he was possessed. They want very comf'rt'bly on't
for things, but they contrived to make a live on't. Come in t'the
butt'ry, while I cut some cheese," said Debby, pausing, to height-
en my interest in her story. I followed her in. She closed the
door ere proceeding, in a mysterious tone : " One night, Prudy
thought she'd go to bed, as he was so smart. There was two
beds in the room, Prudy slept in one and I in t'other. I
was mighty tired. I'd been helpin' Miss Carr 'bout the
washin', and I wan't used to it, and I s'pose I dropped right
asleep, for Prudy woke me up. I must have slept as sound
as a log, for I remember I was dreamin' of gittin' my day's
work done, and goin' off to meetin' in a blue bonnet and

yaller gown, tied round the waist with red ribbin, and feellin',
you may depend upon it, as if I'se the biggest duck in the
puddle. 'Debby, Debby !' says Prudy, ' what you up for ?'
'.I ain't up, nor *been* up nuther,' says I, a leetle out o' sorts,
and tryin' to keep on with my dream 'bout my Sunday
fixin's. I jest got underway ag'in, and was puttin' on my
white knit mitts, and shovin' up my new parasol, when
Prudy at me ag'in. ' Debby, Debby ! do keep in bed. I
can't sleep a wink, for youv'e been up, off and on, the hull
livelong night. I guess your'e a sleep-walker, if there ever
was on'. I tried to catch hold o' ye, to pull you into bed,
when you came nigh me, but it's so dark I couldn't see you.
It's dangerous to haze round so ; you might hit somethin',
and. knock your brains out.' I couldn't make the crittur
b'lieve I hadn't stirred out one foot, 'till I lay still and
listened and heered the sounds too. They'd come to
my bed, then round the foot to Prudy's, and then they'd
kinder die away, and then they'd come back ag'in. We
didn't know what to make of't. I couldn't sleep no more,
and we didn't dare to git up and strike a light, so we jest lay
with our heads kivered up till mornin'. I tell you we was
glad enough to see daylight, and we popped our heads out.
Wall, Ruby, the doors was all shot, and the winders down,
jest as we left 'em ; but on the floor—t'was a sanded floor
—all round the room was the strangest tracks ever you see ;
nothin' mortal about *them*, and that ain't all nuther.
Abram grew wuss and wuss ev'ry day, and went into quick
consumption, and he finally up and died the very day he was
to a been married to Prudy Perry. 'Twas all explained
then, you see, 'bout them tracks. I never told a livin' soul
but you. I shouldn't *now*, only I want you to think on't,
and not make light o' sech things. I don' *know* as any-

thing'll happen; and if I did, I wouldn't tell anybody," and Debby shut her lips persistently.

"What became of poor Prudy?" I asked.

"Wall, now, between you and me and the whippin'-post, it was ruther queer about that," she replied, looking reflectively at the plate of cheese before her. "You see, Simeon Cole lost *his* sweetheart 'bout this time. He seemed to feel dreadfully; wore a weed on his hat, and all that. Prudy, too, put on half mournin' for Abram, and seemed to take a realizin' sense o' *her* loss. Wall, Sophi Paddleford spoke up one day, and said she thought they ought to make a match; and would you b'lieve it? they happened to meet there one evenin' and he went hum with her—mis'ry likes company, you know—and that very Sunday night he called—there's plenty of folks ready to watch for sech things, you know, Ruby—and the long and the short of it was, that he courted and married her in less'n a year. It seems as if 'twas to be, don't it? It made a good deal o' talk in the time on't." She paused suddenly, "Hear that teakittle now; mournful-like, but not loud. I don't like to hear it sing so, Ruby. It's a sure sign we shall hear of a death *some*where. I never knew it to fail. It goes all through me. I know you don't b'lieve nothin' in signs, but I *do*, and so'll you some day, when you've heard and seen as much as I have."

"Why, Debby, you speak as if that was certain."

"Wall, so 'tis. You've got the look in your eye; kind o' filmy, you see. You wait, and see if I don't speak truth. It'll come suddin. It allers does. But *'twill* come."

"And so will my aunt, if we don't make haste," I retorted, as the door-latch clicked ominously. "Here she is now," and Deborah closed her mouth, and drew in her features into an innocent expression, as if to thereby protest her utter guiltlessness of ever alluding to these contraband subjects.

The good soul was firmly wedded to her belief in the supernatural. Those mystic tendencies she inherited, in part, from a sight-seeing mother; and, fondled in the lap of a credulous neighborhood, ever alert to credit the marvellous, that which rightfully belongs to the simple, they had grown with her growth, and strengthened with her strength, until they inextricably wove their subtile fibres through the web and woof of every mental tissue ; to eradicate one, the whole structure must be demolished ; and it is questionable whether, out of such helpless ruins, enough sound material would have remained for re-erection. At all events, as she apparently derived much comfort from the harmless superstitions, and for the most part, nourished them in secret, none sought to deprive her of them.

Before my uncle and aunt, however, she was compelled to hold her peace. They considered her visions, omens, and prophecies as controverting Scripture, which inspired testimony, expressly declares that, "He cometh like a thief in the night;" and offering an inducement to Providence for a judgment to follow in the wake of her irreverence. In these later years, with our developing faculty of classification, she would be immediately labelled a "clairvoyant," enthusiastically bottled in a sensational sphere, and corked with flaming programmes, paragraphs, and advertisements. What a difference a few years make! Deborah, owing to the extreme simplicity of the times she lived in, was only a fortuneteller on the sly ; and an absurdly credulous believer in crude dreams and omens.

CHAPTER XXI.

SUNDAY came and went like others, full of holy calm. The baptism and reception into the Church's maternal care of the six young converts stamped it with memorable interest, as the first-fruits of a hoped-for revival. Natty was the first to descend to the icy bath; his fresh young face flushed with holy enthusiasm, and the light of a deep, peaceful joy in his dark eyes.

At this junction Annah set up a furious lament, and we were compelled to withdraw, despite Aunt Rhoda's frowns. This relative of ours believed devoutly in infant conversions, and had hoped the scene might have been the means of bringing the child into the fold. Her piety was never passive. She greedily devoured indigestible memoirs of remarkable infantile converts, who, sickening mysteriously, and making rather lengthy exhortations to surrounding impenitent friends—had been rapt from their little weeping worlds to an heavenly inheritance. She adored stories of nice little Sunday-school girls, by their touching prattle converting a dram-drinking parent from his evil ways; and she judged Annah of an age sufficient to define *her* position in the moral and religious universe. I scouted this idea; hence frequent clashes.

In *her* creed, infants, only a few hours old, were ruthlessly dispatched to endless torture for being too bodily weak to live. "As in Adam all die, so in Christ shall all be made alive," she was fond of quoting. "Christ has imperatively ordained this ordinance. He descended into Jordan; and

we cannot get to him by any other way. 'For ye are condemned already.'"

Oh! finite limiting of infinite grace. Poor weak humanity daring thus resolutely to define—Divinity; to pronounce
upon the utmost verge to which "Our Father's" cord of
compassionate loving-kindness extends: to scan the receding circle of the merciful remembrance of our frailties. From
the chaos of perplexed reasoning, in which such a stern, pitiless dogma hurls the intellect, rises in light serene the comforting assurance: "For *His* ways are not as *our* ways;
neither His thoughts like our thoughts." ·

Aunt Rhoda came home from church this day with a more
uncompromising front than ever; and as she divested her
head of its green caleche, she thus delivered herself: "I declare for't, it completely spiled my meetin' for *me!* To think,
that a child, most a woman grown, shouldn't even be decent!
I overheard Mis' Prince whisper to Nancy Carr, that 'for her
part she thought 'twas heathenish; livin' in sech a Christian
community, and settin' under the very droppin's of the sanc-
tu'ry;' and Nancy said back, that 'she hoped *she* shouldn't
abuse her privileges; but, then, we didn't none on us know
what we might be brought to do.' *I* know what Annah's
comin' to," pursued she, decisively. "She's going to meetin',
rain or shine. She's old enough to give her heart to the
Saviour. I don't b'lieve she can repeat the very first answer
in the Catechism." ·

I stoutly defended her knowledge in this respect. She
persisted in doubting. "Bother!" cried Demis. "Let us
talk of Nancy Carr. I know what she never will come to."

"Well, what?" asked her mother rigidly.

"Matrimony," and she soberly vanished. Annah was
summoned, very much frightened at the prospect of a lecture.

"What is the chief end of man?" slowly and solemnly inquired her aunt, peering at her over her spectacle tops.

She stood bewildered, apparently endeavoring to summon the reply from her treacherous memory. Aunt Rhoda gave me an exultant glance, and solemnly repeated it. All at once the child's face brightened. "Keep what you've got, ' get what you can; hold up your head, and look like a man," fell glibly from her lips.

Her aunt dropped the primer in horror, and blushed with indignation. "Did you ever?" she inquired of Uncle Joel, who bent his head suspiciously low over his book, and remained mute. "Sech wickedness," she went on, "sech irreverence is awful. Then, this is the way you learn the Catechism; them sacred words, printed by servants of the Most High. I don't wonder, poor child, you don't know nothin'!" she said pityingly.

I interrupted her. "Do you think I taught the child that?"

"Where'd she pick it up then?"

"I don't know, aunt."

"I don't b'lieve you," she said, hotly.

Annah began to cry. "Cousin Demis told it; it's pretty too!" ceasing her tears, to defend her favorite. "She knows ever so many more!" and she flashed at her aunt a defiant glance, which made the good lady hop uneasily in her chair, and clutch her fingers, as if she longed—yet was not quite sure of the propriety of finishing off the day's exercises by a matter of so secular a nature as a whipping.

"Wall, wall," muttered Uncle Joel, "never mind! What's the odds, Rhody? Makin' such a fuss about nothin'!"

"Indeed! I don't call it 'nothin', Mr. Martin!" she said, angrily. "It's Gospel truth."

"Wall, wall, the child don't know no better! She thinks Demis is law and gospel. Lectur' Demis, if anybody."

"Suppose *you* take her in hand, Mr. Martin. It'll be new business for you. *You* let them run right over you, and never say boo."

"Oh no, I don't, Rhody," he rejoined, meekly.

"Well! if you know best," she sarcastically observed. "You can go, Annah. I won't ask no more. I don't want to git sech another start." She folded her spectacles into their case and rocked herself, complacently. It appeared, also, that she meditated; for she presently observed: "I'm sure we ought to feel thankful, Joel, that the Lord has inclined three of our children unto his ways! As for Demis, that child allers was different from the rest—dreadful hard to manage. I'm 'fraid it'll take a mighty solemn providence to turn *her* heart to the testimony. I declare I tremble all over, like a leaf, when I think what's in store for her!"

"I don' know," replied Uncle Joel, thoughtfully. "I don't find no fault with none on 'em. I guess, on a long hull, Demis'll come out with the rest,—and Ruby and Annah too," he added, with a kind glance at me.

Aunt Rhoda, with an incredulous sniff, wheeled around to the light-stand, and opened the great family Bible, with a jerk. Slowly turning over its leaves, with one long forefinger, she paused finally, and buried her eyes amid its comforting pages.

The next day brought the schoolmaster. He came down directly to see us, and announced his intention of remaining to tea. Uncle Joel's hearty hand-clasp and resonant "How are you?" sufficiently testified to his pleasure at the reunion, and my aunt's rigidity visibly decreased with every moment of his stay.

Strong, manly, and cheery he looked, one worthy to win

confidence, and incapable of betraying it. The hard glimmer
in his eyes, which formerly I had thought so repelling, I now
sought for in vain. The sneer—too often wreathing the thin
bloodless lips—had broadened to a smile, more genial. He
looked one placed, by some sudden turn of Fate, on better
terms with his own nature than in former days, and consequently in more improved relations to all mankind. Then
his laugh rang out more freely, devoid of clogging affectation
in its tone, and that I was not alone in feeling the change,
witness Debby's greeting as she entered. "Law ! Mr. Hume,"
accepting his offered hand, and holding it like a little toy,
" *I'm* well as common. How be you? And proper glad to
see you. Your paw don't look much like mine," she added,
relinquishing possession ; "mine's brown as a berry, and hard
as flint. It's seen work, and a good deal of it too." He made
some pleasant observations.

"That's all right," remarked Uncle Joel; "but a leetle
work wouldn't hurt you : make you tough. Work'll never
put nobody out o' jint, I guess."

"I practise, daily, in the gymnasium," said Mr. Hume.

"What's *that* to the pint ?" demanded Debby. "Don't
'mount to nothin', does it ?"

For answer, he seized the heavy iron mortar, kept standing
in the corner for pounding salt, and held it aloft, with one
hand, triumphantly. Uncle Joel, good naturedly, chuckled,
"Didn't see nothin' wonderful in that—thought anybody
might," essayed to make the trial a success, and signally failed.
" It *is* a purty consid'rable heft," he admitted ; and was going
to try again, when his wife serenely observed : " Law, now, Joel,
I would'nt be drawn inter no fool's play, if I'se you. " You're
too old for sech doin's." He dropped the weight, looking
as if a damper had been put upon his rising cheerfulness.

" I wonder where the boys be ?" said Debby, anxiously, some time later in the day.

" I met Dwight going to mill, at three o'clock," said Mark, " and Natty was sliding with Cyrus Wright. Very likely he has gone home with him."

" He hadn't oughter be out after dark. He aint very rugged latterly," she remarked.

" I guess 'twont hurt him none," observed Aunt Rhoda, placidly.   At which lack of maternal solicitude, Debby muttered under her breath, " I'm glad I'se got more feelin' than *some* folks, if they *be* mothers."

Twilight deepened into dusky evening. At six, Dwight entered alone, staggering under a huge bag of meal. He threw a look of surprise around the table, and sank wearily into a chair. " Why, where's Natty ? I thought he would come and help me draw this home. I told him to. It's mortal heavy."

" That's what I should like to know; and I'll find out," cried Debby, starting up hastily ; upsetting her teacup, which rolled with a crash to the floor. She threw a shawl over her shoulders, and, lighting the lantern, went out. Uncle Joel seized his hat and followed her. We heard the gate click after them, and the craunch of the crisp snow under their feet, and then there was silence. A strange suspense settled over us; Demis and Annah began to cry, until hushed by Aunt Rhoda's sharp voice: " I'd act like fools an' done with it : jest as if somethin' was the matter. Deborah allers was ravin' distracted if one on 'em was out a minute after dark. I don't want no racket, for my part." They stopped speedily.

" Perhaps he is in one of the neighbor's," observed Mr. Hume, hopefully. " He may have gone to Mr. Pierce's, or home with this Cyrus, whom Mark saw with him."

"Of course! But, to satisfy you, I'll go after him," said Mark, leaping to the door. I, too, strolled out, when I could no longer bear the silence, and Demis followed, clinging to me closely.

"We will walk up to the village," I said. Our search was fruitless. We approached every door in hope, but turned away saddened and disheartened. Nearly all had that day seen him, but that was the extent of the information gleaned. At the last house we encountered Mr. Wright, likewise out on a mission of inquiry. We looked at each other in dismay. "I don't know what to make of it," said he. "The lad was never from home after dark before. He has been gone since morning; but we did not feel alarmed."

"Oh! my poor brother! my poor little brother!" shouted Demis, franticly wringing her hands.

I tried to speak hopefully. "But he may have gone home with Eleil."

She shook her head. "He never would have gone by the house without telling us; besides, he had his sled to put up first."

"Well," I said, desperately. "There is but one place more; the Alum Rocks. It's possible they may be still sliding, though your father prohibited that place."

"We will go," she said huskily. "Come, Mr. Wright. I can't go home yet."

It was at least a mile to the Alum Rocks. I thought it extremely unlikely that he had ventured there in defiance of his father's command. But action, however misapplied, was better than quiescence, so we pushed on bravely, keeping a kind of running pace with Mr. Wright's heavy strides. Not a word penetrated the wintry silence. It was intensely cold. Our rapid motion served to keep us somewhat warm; but vapor froze upon our mouths and nostrils, and the stinging blast cut keenly into our exposed faces. Demis suddenly stopped.

"Ruby, I believe I have frozen my hands. They are numb," said she.

"Swing 'em! swing 'em!" shouted Mr. Wright, pushing forward. "So!" he added, violently swinging his own arms by way of example. "That will keep the blood a circulating."

I bethought me of a pair of mittens in my pocket. I had dropped them there in the morning, and utterly forgotten them since. Now, I inwardly blessed the chance, and I drew them on Demis's chilled fingers, in spite of her feeble remonstrance.

"We are almost there," she shivered. "Let us push on."

"Good God!" ejaculated Mr. Wright in horror. "What a place for sliding. God forbid that they should have gone down *there*," he muttered to himself, approaching and peering cautiously over the edge of the precipice. "I see no signs of 'em," he added aloud. "We must come back the way we came."

"There they are!" cried Demis joyfully, as far up the snowy slope, we descried two dark objects moving.

"No!" I said. "It cannot be, for one has a lantern. Why, it's your father and Deborah! It seems they came directly here."

"Oh dear! I can't go fast enough," she cried, despairingly. "Come, come," and she fairly flew up the long hill. The figures had disappeared, but, looking carefully around, we caught the lantern's glimmer among the leafless forest trees, down in the darkness below.

"Now, girls, you must stay here," said Mr. Wright, sooth-

ingly. "It's too slippery and steep for you to venture by
yourselves down there, and I can't stop to help you. I'll
call, if we find any thing."

"*Any thing!*" I shuddered at the ghastly forebodings
implied by this word. He did not wait for an answer, but
picked his way swiftly down the dangerous ledge.

"I can see his footsteps. Come," whispered Demis, and
we followed him mechanically. We reached the bottom.
Uncle Joel turned. The two men looked at each other
gloomily. "My God help us!" burst from Uncle Joel's lips;
extending one hand, which Mr. Wright grasped firmly; with
the other he pointed to a huge break in the icy pool.

"Well, Martin," said Mr. Wright, brokenly, "do you think
they made that hole?"

"I don' know neighbor. The ice isn't so very thick, and
comin' from way up yonder'd be a powerful blow."

"Yes," returned the other, drearily.

"I wish we'd a had our wits about us, enough to a fetched
ropes and hooks along," said Debby, coming up. "I may
as well go after some, and I'll send some men to search the
pool."

"There is no trace anywhere round to tell us," said Mr.
Wright, holding aloft the lantern to peer, fruitlessly beyond
him. "I suppose the sleds have gone under the ice."

"Stay," cried Demis; "I see something out there."

"Why, so there is. Give me the lantern and I'll get it."
I said eagerly.

"Oh no!" returned the men simultaneously. "The ice
won't hold you up, and you can't see the air-holes in it."

But I was already swinging down the rocks. I advanced
cautiously—searching by the dim flicker of the lantern for
treacherous cracks. I reached the article I sought, lying on

11

the jagged edge of the icy rupture, as if a last agonized token; thrown upward for the help—which never came.

It was simply a little striped mitten.

There was dead silence when I handed it to Uncle Joel. He softly pressed it between his palms, as if to *assure* himself of its tangibility, turned white, and silently handed it to his neighbor, who likewise pressed and passed it to Debby. "Well," she said sadly, caressing softly the unconscious token from a watery grave. "That ever I should live to see this day! I s'pose this is evidence enough, Mr. Martin; I knit it myself," she broke into dreary bewailings.

"And *my* poor lad left nothing," said Mr. Wright chokingly.

"Demis snatched the mitten, hugging it convulsively, kissing and talking to it as though it were a living thing. "Oh dear, dear, dear," she murmured, "What *shall* we do?"

"Do!" I echoed, forcing back the coming sobs. "Get them out, of course. I am going after help. Will you come with me?" She assented, like a broken-hearted child; placing the cold little hand in mine to be led away from the sad scene.

In spite of the unremitting exertions of the neighbors, three days elapsed ere the bodies were recovered. During this period the saddest of silences—that of agonized anticipation—reigned throughout the house. Few came near us, and we walked the rooms, solitary, voluntary prisoners, listening to Deborah's heart-broken chanting of the dead boy's early years. There was also an old eastern death-song, which she wailed continually. I should make *one* exception. Aunt Rhoda kept on her calm, even round of duties much as usual. She prepared the meals regularly—which no one ate,

and she rose as early as ever. Amanda came home; but never very efficient, save when controlled by selfish desires, her dismal reproaches at every one present were quite unendurable, and at Mark's request, her husband came down one day and removed her to her own home.

"When the bodies were brought down the hill, stark and stiff, their pale hands firmly grasping their sleds by the runners, crowds came out of their dwellings, and following after, filled the house. Out of these, who came chiefly to observe countenances, and watch curiously how each took it, and then, repairing to Mr. Wright's, there repeat the analyzation, there were some sympathetic friends, full of genuine, hearty kindness.

"In the midst of life we are in death," said Elder Fuller solemnly that evening, after the busy hands had departed. "It ought to be a comfort, my friends, to reflect that he was prepared to go. I see the hand of an all-wise Providence in this dispensation. It's another lesson to the young."

"Yis," shudderingly observed my aunt. "What if it had been Dwight? He isn't fit to die, and stand before the judgment-seat of God——"

My uncle rose here, and abruptly left the room. I softly followed him into the keeping-room. There he was, sobbing as if his heart would break. Reader! did you ever see a strong man weep? One not easily moved? A woman's tears flow easily, and are as easily quelled. A rivulet of gusty passions, which clears all dust from its channel; finishing the sacrament with a few gasping sobs, and leaving behind refreshing sweetness—the pebbly bottom, white and clear in the returning sunshine. Man's passion is the turbid torrent; swollen to overflowing by unusual rains. A de-

vastating freshet, as it slowly subsides, leaving scathing desolation in its track. Dumb terror seized me, as I helplessly
gazed on the convulsive shivers of his broad shoulders; the
passionate throes heaving his breast, and the intermittent
sobs. He lifted his head at last, with a piteous glance.
"Oh! I can't set and hear sech stuff as that," he murmured. "It makes no difference *which* is taken. *I* can't spare
none on 'em. Come here, children;" we were all weeping
unrestrainedly, kneeling at his knee; he passed his strong
arms round us, and gathered us all to his great loving heart.

"Oh, father," whispered Demis, affrighted, "don't, don't
take on so. It hurts me."

"Child, I can't help it," he sobbed. I'm an old man, well
stricken in years and infirmities, but I never cried afore. I
didn't know as I could; and now I've got a goin', I can't
stop. 'Pears so I'd got to cry for all that ever happened
afore. If he had a been sick and died, I should thought it
God's will, and been submissive, but sech a death is awful!"

" Have you seen him?" softly inquired Olive, who had entered unheard. He shook his head. "I can't bear to!"

"Come, all of you," she said, persuasively, "and see how
sweetly he slumbers," and as we rose to follow her, he came also.

"O Death, so full of terror! Why canst thou not lift the
hideous veil from thy features, and show poor, weak humanity the Divine splendor which lurks beneath?" murmured
Olive, reverently uncovering the still, waxen features.

" Yes!" said Mr. Hume, coming forth from a window re-
cess. " For now we see, as in a glass darkly; but then, face to
face. Think, my friends, what a glorious vision now greets his
eyes; face to face with immortality, and life, and light divine."

Uncle Joel wiped his eyes, gazed awhile in silence, and
withdrew somewhat comforted.

"The sting of death is sin," said Olive. "That is all one need fear; and what *is* our life? It is but a vapor soon exhaled; but a shadow which fleeth away. Oh! girls, we should make the most of this transient season," she concluded earnestly.

"You think this the only probationary state;" I ventured, "but who can tell, but that in the region beyond may exist repentance and pardon of sin."

"This is no place to discuss such a doctrine," she answered coldly. "You will do well to read your Bible more." She refolded the damp cloth over the white face beneath us, and left the room.

"Wall!" mused Deborah, swaying herself to and fro on her seat, "it ain't a mite of no use to try, if the sperrit don't move you. If you're foreordained to be saved, you *will* be; and if not, you won't be, 'cordin' to some folks tell. Maybe *your* time ain't come yit, Ruby," she added, consolingly.

"I don't want to be one of the elect if all my friends are not," said poor little Demis, mournfully. "I couldn't be happy in heaven, if those I love were not there," she added.

"You will lose these natural feelings then, in the superior love that shall kindle in your heart toward the Author and Preserver of all—the Righteous Judge. So God is glorified, *you* will be willing that all else shall be lost. You *will* be willing to be damned, yourself," said Mr. Hume, gravely.

Demis looked doubtful; she shook her head slowly.

"No," muttered Debby, giving him a strange look. "Come to the pinch, and he wouldn't himself. It's easy enough to talk! I'm sick of sech figerin' roun' common sense, among the whole ke-boodle of 'em."

Here Olive opened the door. "Elder Fuller wishes you

all to come into the kitchen for family prayers. I cannot get Dwight down; he is up in his room in the dark, and he won't listen to a word. Mr. Martin won't go either. Some one *must*, for the looks of it."

"Wall!" muttered Debby, wrathfully, "it won't be *me.* Catch *me* stirring a peg to hear that ere man hold forth, an' you'll catch a weasel asleep." Mr. Hume opened the door, and signed to me to follow.

After prayers, we returned to the parlor. "Who is to watch?" asked Mr. Hume. "I am," returned Debby, lifting her head. "It's the last thing I can do for him. You can all stay up, if you've a mind."

"Is the funeral to-morrow then?" inquired he.

"I s'pose so," rejoined Debby, sadly. "It's too soon, *I* think; but I heard the Elder tell Mis' Martin, that they'd better both be buried to-morrow, as 'twas Sunday, and 'twould make the day impressive. That man ain't got no feelin's," she said curtly. "All he thinks 'bout is makin' a figger among folks, and Mis' Martin and he's as near alike as two peas. She's 'mazin' calm; takes it just as he did poor little Kitty's death—I don't know how folks can do it, for *my* part." A pause followed. She resumed. "Somehow, I can't feel to kneel when he's prayin'. I don't fellership him a'tall. His prayers don't reach the spot. I don't b'lieve they ever do git higher'n the chimbly's. I'd a heap ruther git'n a corner som'ers and say, "Lord be marciful to a poor creetur' like me! Oh, Ruby!" she broke forth— "What'd I tell you? I felt it in my bones, that something was goin' to happen; but I never thought of the baby's dyin'. Poor little boy!" She covered her head with her apron, and moaned dismally.

Mr. Hume looked distressed. He went up to her, and

kneeling noiselessly, pulled the apron gently down. "Be ye
comforted, my poor friend," he whispered. "Ye have done
for him all that ye could. Let us pray together," and then,
with a voice almost inaudible from emotion, arose the schoolmaster's first public prayer. Debby lifted her straining eyes
at its conclusion. "Oh dear, Mr. Hume," she said, "I'm
'bleeged to ye, I'm sure ; but there's no peace for the wicked,
is there ?" and ere he could rise from his knees, she placed
her hard, heavy hand upon his head, and solemnly blessed
him.

CHAPTER XXII.

THE winter passed slowly. Heavy shadows settled down
upon the dwelling, creating a mental listlessness, which no
activity of body could dissipate. Uncle Joel sat entire days
by the kitchen fire, resting his head thoughtfully on his
broad palm, listening to the singing teakettle, and gazing
absently at the maker's name; in raised letters on the stove-
hearth. Then he would rise suddenly, put on his hat, and
walk slowly in the direction of the village. We knew his
destination. We knew that he stood for hours in the waning daylight by a snowy mound in a distant corner ; but no
one remarked, in words—upon his going out, or coming
back. Finally his visits ceased ; for, standing so much in
the snow, brought back his old enemy the rheumatism—always ready to assail him. At first, it treated him to a few
irritating twinges ; then, finding the citadel sufficiently weak-
ened, it boldly assumed an inflammatory character, and stretched him helplessly upon a couch of intense suffering. What
time Aunt Rhoda—placid as ever—could spare from nurs-

ing him, was given to the Church. A wide-spread revival followed the recent "calamitous visitations of Providence." Meetings for prayer were held five nights out of the seven, at the Baptist and Methodist Churches, alternately.

For, the latter sect—not to be outdone by their neighbors —had also spiritually awakened ; and oh ! fact most worthy of notice—constitutional animosities of belief; jealous bickerings, for once were merged in a hand-to-hand clasp of Christian brotherhood. Each minister came to labor with our slumbering consciences. Demis listened in proud indifference, especially to Mr. Love, the Methodist pastor. Indeed, I found him personally repulsive. He was a tall, coarse man ; bitter in his hates, which were easily excited, and relentlessly vindictive. He often sorely belied his amiable patronymic, for he never forgave what he deemed an insult. All angry threats he scrupulously fulfilled to the letter. He carried his partisan zeal to. excess. He also deemed it derogatory to Christian dignity to descend so far as to win souls to Christ. The pathetic was out of his line. He revelled in the denunciatory. He commanded your attendance at church, and, once within the sacred inclosure, fastened his keen eye on you like a basilisk. If by any chance you were betrayed into a smile during his sermon, he endeavored to make you bitterly repent it—and vow never again to place yourself under his tutelage. At such times he would pause abruptly, and, pointing at you his prodigious hand, solemnly rebuke you for irreverence. You were happy, indeed, if you escaped hearing your name loudly called before the whole congregation; their entire battery of eyes was quite sufficient punishment. He was slovenly in costume; invariably appearing in public with disordered hair and filthy linen, soiled hands with black-rimmed finger-nails. Deborah called him " A mortal nasty crittur;" but he described himself as "being not worldly minded"—bringing up the fishermen of Galilee as illustrious precedents. I suspect he would have failed of proof that they eschewed decent cleanliness, even in the pursuit of their calling. A disgusting scent of bad tobacco, both chewed and smoked, polluted his presence; as a consequence, the shining stove-hearth bore sad witness to his visits. When a fit of religious converse seized him, he drew a chair to your side, staring full in your face with impudent bravado, and resenting as a deadly insult your instinctive shrinking away from him and his teachings.

One could scarcely be blamed for vanishing into the nearest hiding-place, at the unwelcome sight of his loosely built, shuffling figure, filing through the little gate leading to the kitchen. Elder Fuller also awakened one unhappy day to a consciousness of his criminal neglect of needful pastoral duties, and forthwith inaugurated an energetic round of visits. On these dreaded occasions all work was suspended, and a semi-circle of prayer formed, in which Debby—though strongly pressed —would never be initiated. She glowered through the open pantry door at her old enemy, until—his duty finished—he departed. " The husbandman soweth his seed in sorrow and care, but he reapeth a glorious harvest," was his accustomed finish to these spiritual programmes; or, for a variation, " Paul may plant and Apollos water, but it is God alone who giveth the increase." He gave this last word a relishing smack in conclusion, as if, in some mysterious way, tasting its prolific flavor.

He stopped sinners in the street. He waylaid laborers going to their work, to warn them of the wrath to come. In roaring caldrons of factories he plunged his fiery zeal, and over the machinery's continuous hum, rose resonant

11*

his terrific exhortations to the pale-faced operatives. He palsied their reason, with graphic limnings of a speedily approaching judgment. He overwhelmed their tired souls and bodies with dramatic gesticulations of the wrath of an offended Judge. He pointed to the ceaselessly revolving shafts; thus intimating their bodily danger, and then suddenly hurled before them the fearful question, " Where would your souls be then?" Not one word was dropped into grieving souls, of God's infinitude of mercy and love: no hope held out of future repentance, when drawn by universal laws, each and all should some day find a home in the bosom of the Father. " Now! Now!" he greedily cried, " *Now* is the accepted time; now is the day of salvation. It is the last call of the Spirit. Hearken to its merciful cry, or remain *forever* given over by His grace."

People laughed at first; then grew serious. Their combined labors kindled the slumbrous embers of religious excitement into a glowing.flame. Of course, I attended the meetings. In accordance with earnest entreaties, I rose for prayers. I visited the "anxious seat," in turn with my seeking sisters. I successively tried all the special localities pointed out as means for obtaining grace. The genial shower descended on the thirsty pools in my neighbor's hearts; filled and refreshed them. Mine, it left dusty and barren as before. Deceive, I would not; so when the nightly question came, "Do you feel a change of heart?" as usual, my answer was a negative shake of my despondent head. " At least, you feel yourself to be a lost sinner, deserving especial condemnation?" I did not, and I said so. Then my heartlessness and ingratitude were commented upon, and publicly held up to the gaze of the scornful. I was used for a warning to other awakened sinners, lest they, too, protract the period of delay, and likewise

be given over by the Deity. I was pronounced a fit vessel
for Divine wrath, and awarded a place with outcast swine;
their unsavory husks, and putrefying morsels, freely doled
out as my only inherited sustenance.

It was too unpalatable fare. I sickened and fled from it
and its administrators in heartfelt disgust.

"Wall," said Aunt Rhoda, one evening, tying on her black
silk hood, as usual, "Ruby, it's high time we're a startin'." .

I made some excuse for not leaving Demis alone.

"She needn't be alone," she retorted with a cutting
glance. "I'd be glad to have her go in *my* room. But there's
no use in askin' her, and I shan't let you throw away this
chance of salvation." She looked at me as if *that* settled the
matter; no more words need be wasted. All I had to do
was to meekly rise, open the press door, take down my own
black hood and shawl, and follow her. Demis eyed me
askance, to see if I would yield the point so tamely. My reply came resolutely: "I have done. I grow more obdurately
indifferent the longer I go. Then, their falling to the floor,
struck with 'the power,' is more disagreeable than all else."

"Those are the Methodists," she said.

"Yes. But they are all under the same influence."

"Very well. Suit yourself, and you'll suit me," she retorted curtly. She opened the door quickly and shut herself
out. Demis eyed me archly.

"So you're a sinner, still, Ruby. I'm glad of it, I like you
better as you are. I used to go; and many a time I've plunged a darning-needle into the flesh of those lying like logs
on the floor. They started quick enough, I assure you." · ·

Our lessons suffered slow decapitation. First one branch, then
another, was relentlessly chipped away—ostensibly, from want
of time; really, from sheer disinclination for study. In this ·

cowardly abandonment Demis led the van. She said "she
was too tired;" and when the schoolmaster brought out the
books, drawing up a chair beside her, she would draw back
a little, take up a volume, listlessly, and, after trying in vain
to give her attention to its contents, lean her head thoughtfully on the back of her chair, and sigh wearily.. I often stole
from the room, leaving them alone thus for hours, and they
never seemed to miss me. Neither did my well-meant absence appear to do Demis any good; for, on coming back to
it, she would still be gazing thoughtfully into the air, while
the schoolmaster would have opened and become absorbed
in any chance volume. One day, when this pantomime had
been successfully repeated, Mr. Hume threw down his book,
and turned to me laughingly. "What is the matter with
me, Miss Ruby?" I was so astonished that I did not answer.
"Because," he went on, "your cousin is evidently afraid of
me. I must have seriously changed."

"No," she stammered, awkwardly.

" She treated me, a year ago, like a human being. I havn't
forgotten the apple wreath—" He started up and went to
her; for she had burst into violent sobbings. He took her
hand. She did not answer his concerned inquiry, and he
looked down on her aghast, but presently rallied. " What
a tiny hand," he cried, cheerfully. " I believe, Miss Ruby,
that it belongs to the fairies. She evidently got it by mistake." He pretended to whisper this wondrous intelligence.
She hastily withdrew it to cover her face.

" Ah! she thinks a poor mortal not good enough to touch
it," he cried, with mock fervor. " I wonder if the other one
is similar! Oh yes, I see it now! It's the other's mate,
and therefore not for me," he added, meaningly. She ceased
sobbing instantly. A flash of cold pride swept over her

face with lightning fury. He had turned to me, and did not see the token, as he still pursued—in a bantering tone—"I must, then, have recourse to one of earthly lineage "—and seizing mine—" I believe firmly in electric affinities. Now when my electricities are too redundant, I seek to dispose of a few in this manner. You perceive——"

I lost the rest in watching Demis. Her eyes flashed scornfully, and she threw us a jealous glance—a reproachful one it was to me. I forced a careless laugh. " Oh ! pray go on, Mr. Hume. You are rapidly verging toward the transcendental. 'Redundant affinities'—Demis, you may have my share."

He went on, unheeding. " Now this is something tangible," surveying my long fingers, "tolerably well-shaped; not destined for show at all; run in the right mould for trills and quavers, and scales on the piano-forte, which fairies are never expected to perform. Are they, Queen Demis ?"

She smiled, mockingly, the jealous fire still slumbering in her dark eyes, and humored his bantering mood. "Oh yes, child of earth; but it is too exquisite for mortal ears ! Thy grossness cannot catch the soundless vibrations of the melodies from my ancestral home. Its speech thou canst not divine, oh, fragment of mortality !"

He retorted pleadingly, " Oh ! Queen of the beneficent fairies, torture not our expectant ears by such words of discouragement ! Rather salute them with a gracious sample of that ravishing music. Thy servant is unworthy, but will be grateful."

The " beneficent queen " remained sulky and mute. " Do you sing ?" he said suddenly.

" No ! I went to singing-school a few times, and zealously did my sweetest sounds on do—re—mi—I thought myself progressing famously. Then imagine my horror one evening, when our worthy chorister suddenly brought down his fiddle-bow on the black-board with a rap that made us all start nervously—"Stop!" he thundered. "I want to find where those horrid sounds come from ;" and he coolly proceeded to try the voices, separately, on the blissful rise and fall of the eight notes. In serene ignorance I essayed my turn at ascending the musical ladder. I didn't return the way I went, and there my voice remains to this day, perched on the topmost round of high ' do.' I have never had courage to bring it down by myself, and I suspect, long ere this, the poor outcast has perished of starvation, cold, or affright."

"But what was the matter with it ?" cried Mr. Hume, smiling.

" 'Miss —you—what's your name ?' asked the crusty old chorister. ' Brooks,' I repeated, demurely. ' Well, Miss Brooks, you'll never learn music. You have about as much voice as a tree-toad ;' and he turned away, laughing as he resumed his fiddle-bow, at once restored to good humor. Such discipline was not to be repeated. I managed to sit the evening out, tranquilly, in spite of sundry malicious winks and sneers from my melodious neighbors ; but it was a cruel disenchantment I never again ventured."

"I cannot help thinking," said the schoolmaster, thoughtfully, "that it is but an instance of what we must look for constantly in this life ; and it is far better that our ignorant illusions should be torn to tatters, than to carry them around constantly, and so, never at liberty to seek for the real. I call it a kind hand that robs me of mine, and though it may be meant in malice, I will bless it, nevertheless. You are, certainly, divested of *one* delusion, and at liberty to turn your devotions elsewhere. Miss Demis,"—pretending to consult an imaginary document—"you are next on the.list for musical experiences."

"She has none of that nature," I interrupted; "she sings like a lark."

"Ruby," she began, deprecatingly. Mr. Hume interposed with fresh entreaties. After a little hesitation, she complied.

The schoolmaster looked enchanted, as she finished, tremulously. "I never heard a sweeter voice, Miss Demis."

Oh! magic of praise! Demis's languor vanished; her dark eyes brightened with pleasure. She drew herself up in stately pride, and her voice took a fuller, richer, cadence, as it broke into another old ballad. She rendered it with touching pathos. She felt it to the quick, with sympathetic intuition, every word of that passionate song. The plaintive air brought tears to both of her listeners' eyes. Hers were earnest and clear, with a strange, absent expression, as though she—in, to us, invisible realms—saw with vivid, spiritual ken, that despairing, unhappy lover. This time, the schoolmaster was silent.

I suggested another, and yet another. Wrapped in the soothing atmosphere of such music, the hours sped too quickly. The singer had, apparently, forgotten her audience. She roamed from song to song, as fancy dictated—like a butterfly choosing his flowery couch; as a bee daintily gathering honied juices. Now, she gave us a verse in sad minor; then, suddenly changed it to a lively Tyrolese air; then, grave, Puritan hymns, which her dead grandfather had taught her when a little child—floated out into being, with stirring martial neighbors: then we failed to recognize the words. She was improvising both words and air, as she leaned her head on her hand, and gazed dreamily out of the window. Sad, unearthly warblings of magical beauty!

Did she catch the refrain of the angels, that she looked with
such intensified gaze into space, pouring forth the plaint of
a bruised heart, that, bending slowly, but surely, with its
weight of care and sorrow, gets courage to lift itself at last
above all hopeless loves of earth ; courage to tread the airy
heights heavenward.   Sweeter it grew, and more ethereal.

It shook us off, and dropped us far beneath, as we essayed
to grope after.   Far, far in the distance it sounded.   No
earthly element, *now*, could hinder its exultant flight, as, reft
of detaining chords, the once caged earthling beat against
the very gates of Paradise ; knocked, and demanded admittance.

It was perhaps strange, but in those few brief moments I
had a feeling as if Demis was actually dead ; her body rigid
in her chair.   As if I had been watching the immortal spirit's
flight, instead of her voice.   As the last bird-like whisper
died in silence, I rose and went to her.   She started into
her usual self immediately.

"I never heard such singing before," said Mr. Hume,
softly.   "I could listen to it forever; and I could quarrel
with Ruby for dissolving the spell."   I sighed, and looked
at Demis anxiously.

"That voice," he resumed, admiringly, "would make your
fortune."

"I am glad you like it," she said simply.

"Like ! I adore music," he cried with enthusiasm.   "But
I could never learn its rules.   I cannot wait for them ; the
slow plodding things.   I want to give them wings, and
mount upward—as · you did just now, my sister."   She
winced a little.   "I disdain preliminaries,"· he added laughingly, "so you see I was not 'cut out' by good mother
Nature for an artist.   But *you* are, Miss Demis."

"Does she often sing like this ?" he inquired, turning to me.

"Yes. And not exactly like this either; but our little room is made vocal, almost nightly. In the still, solemn · midnight, I wake with a start to find her dreamily gazing out of the window, and softly sighing to the clear moonlight —not loud enough to waken the household—these unutterable melodies."

"Why do you not write them down for the piano ?" eagerly inquired the matter-of-fact schoolmaster.

"I never saw a piano," she answered calmly, "but I have imagined one. These sounds I never try to remember. They come and go of their own will. Sometimes, I have a feeling, that I am repeating them after some one; who, I cannot tell. Sometimes they surge up so stormily in my heart that I cannot sleep, and then I find no rest until I give them vent."

Inexplicable mysteries surround us; mould us to their will. "What becomes of these, our mental offspring, born amid throes of reluctant compulsion, and vague, silent throbs for sympathy ? In darkness, in weariness, in misapprehension; in cruel unkindness, and bitter, scathing neglect; in winter's frosts, and amid the tropical glow of summer, struggling equally with frantic haste for their birthright: compelling us, earthly parents, to do their imperious bidding, and give them expression. For, every word, and every sound, is but the birth of an idea; and the human swarms infesting this globe are the willing or reluctant progenitors. What state receives them as they float away from our lips ? What higher life crowns them with permanence, before so · inert, so powerless ? Or, do they retain an immortal spark of gratitude for their birth, and constantly haunt our vicinity, invisible to our dull perceptions ? Ah ! Heaven and hell are not the only mysteries which our disembodied souls shall encounter, if, in the state beyond, our rightful expiation for sin shall be to religiously trace, to its very core and minute ramifications, the effects of our *spoken* words and deeds.

After this, Demis frequently sang for the schoolmaster. Lessons were tacitly abandoned, with few and far between days of repentant resurrection. He cleared the books all away one evening, bringing down, instead, an armful of lighter literature.

"Though not a devourer of novels," he remarked, while arranging them on the table, "there is nothing, to my mind, that relaxes overstrained mental tension like a good story. Of course, I don't allude to those of an exciting nature. Something calm, sedately humorous, with a keen tinge of irony flashing here and there, provoking mirth, like this good old 'Vicar of Wakefield' for instance. We will read it again : it is always new. Now, my pupils," he resumed, glancing around, "you have had a plea *for* novel reading, I suppose you should rightfully have one *against* it. Though I cannot tell a tale of its effects—'drawn from sad experience'—I should think there would be nothing more effective than a severe bodily task to counteract the evil of *too much* romance reading—especially if your imagination appropriates the woes of the heroine ; endeavoring to put all it reads into practice. Fill the hands with something necessary to be done for a human being ; once earnestly engaged in doing it, it is astonishing how quickly the baleful imps flee, leaving the storied brain once more fresh and clear. None of your wearing away either. A spring for the hat ; a violent wrench of the door-latch—not even a civil good-morning— and you are well quit of them. But we are not arrived at that point yet, and we will have alternate reading—unless, indeed, you are tired of your preceptor, and his dictatorial ways, and court solitude, or have some important samplers to embroider—senseless work! allow me to say. The letters in the alphabet are so much prettier; but I don't see any," and he looked with a relieved air, around the room.

Moses being tricked out for the fair, especially pleased Demis. Her humorous fancy caught the scene immediately, and wove round it fertile flashes of merriment; though she had read it before. I was not, therefore, surprised when, a few days later, a small engraving, representing his return with his bargain of spectacles, appeared mysteriously upon the table, addressed to Demis. She was delighted. She carried the picture to her room at night; for aught I know, she slept with it under her usually sleepless pillow. At all events, she did not sing that night, but lay quiet and motionless till morning. One trifle also more. She forgot that the wrapper was the coarsest of brown paper, and, in a temporary aberration of consciousness, folded it carefully, and thoughtfully placed it away in her drawer. And in the succeeding days her cheeks grew bright again, and her light step flitted round the house as freely as ever. And hope, which never utterly dies from out the human heart, until that heart itself lies cold and coffined, sprang once more into newer, fuller, fresher life than ever. And a thousand green, dewy possibilities flung out a gorgeous foliage, under which she blissfully sat, and wove them all into fond. fervent realities.

CHAPTER XXIII.

THE genial spring-time chased away the frosts of winter.
Mr. Hume still lingered in Northfield. His school was ended.   The short college vacation had also flown on the
wings of this strange delay. Indeed, the ensuing summer
term had just commenced; yet, here he was, recklessly
squandering the precious hours in a round of visits among
his pupils, and in long readings to us at home, with no apparent thought for other duties. If I wearied myself in
conjecturing causes, that imperturbable countenance instantly
negatived them.   No impatience corrugated that smooth
forehead into thoughtful frowns; no anxiety—real or suppressed—wreathed one trace around the smiling mouth.   It
seemed only the undisguised aversion of an indolent nature
towards speedily assuming a new harness of labor.

To Demis, his presence brought new life. In the days
which he passed away from her, she visibly languished;
wearily complaining of the murky dampness of the atmosphere, and the hours of uninterrupted monotony; but with
his return, her health and spirits again flowed back to their
former even channels. This change was so apparent, that
it seemed almost impossible but that her father and mother's
serene obtuseness must be quickened thereby into vigilant
life and action.   Debby, only, looked thoughtfully conscious.
She muttered strange sentences, while going about her work;
casting the schoolmaster sharp glances of dissatisfaction.
When they were alone in the keeping-room, she frequently
contrived the most improbable errands as an excuse for entering, until warned to keep away by Demis's inquiring look.

"I don know nothin 'bout sech truck," I overheard her mutter after one of these voluntary expulsions.

"Seems to me now, ef I'se in her shoes I'd gin him a dish of arb tea, and tell him to start his pegs for hum, short order; but I don know. Mabbe I should up and do jest so myself; gals *be* fools 'bout some things. I haint so much of'n opinion o' him as I *have* had. Don't seem good milk porridge to *me* ; but mabbe 'tis ; I'm only a passenger."

Toward Demis, the schoolmaster's manner daily assumed a more caressing tenderness. His thoughtful care for her health and comfort was assiduous, though unobtrusive. His face wore a perpetual smile in her presence ; if it ever saddened with self-reproach, it must have been only in solitude. But, if *he* drew daily nearer her heart, in closer communion, *I* as surely retreated—waved back by the influence more powerful than mine ; the will—to mine—antagonistic. His love for her was less pure than mine ; I felt, I knew it, and I resisted sturdily. Inch by inch I was fought from the occupancy of those pleasant pastures, mine, I thought, by virtue of long years of inhabitancy, until, in the outmost verge, one more vigorous thrust placed me beyond the pale, and bolts and bars closing after prevented any forcible re-entrance.

And I! Oh! in those leaden April days, I grew to hate them both. Already, saddened by neglect, and sneering indifference, jealousy prompted another sting, and it plunged deep in the festering wound—quivering there, as only the barb can quiver that sucks the life-blood of your dearest; best. Do you think, however, that I thrust up the gory spectacle as a feast for their eyes? as a lure for needed pity? I felt no such pusillanimous emotion. I longed for no such remnants of charity. Had pity been mingled in the fare I received, the cup—overflowing—would have been

dashed back in their faces, regardless of consequences. I
suffered—for it is the bitterness of death for a woman to
be so cruelly misunderstood—and neither read me rightly.
To Demis my heart steeled, because I saw that, in spite of
her jealous injustice toward me, in spite of our unhappy
estrangement, happiness for *her* woke to a new, a diviner
experience, and vividly flushed her future.   Alas! mine rose
up before my shrinking eyes, blank and barren as a desert
isle; and it is an added drop to misery to turn thus from
inward desolation, and, gazing out on broad, fair plains,
reflect that they lie forever beyond our reach.   Yet not an
useless drop; for the eye, sharpened by suffering, pierces
below the veil of surface forms and professions, beholding
—as clearly as the material eye the pebbly bottom of a
brook—the real soil, bearing the guiding motive.

Elliot Hume, then, I beheld, as a cold, careless experimenter.   At the first revelation, scorn and indignation froze
love and regret to silence.   I could now watch their apparent
devotion; their obliviousness of my presence.   I could specu-
late upon the reason for his often involuntary repulse of her
too evident preference for his society.   I could smile inwardly
at her signs of distress, and at the reappearance of the moth
around the flame—his coldness never lingered.   "Be it so,
if you both will it," thought I, "I can bear my own ap-
portionment.   The end will surely come, and, Elliot Hume,
it must bring you but a bitter triumph.   I would walk through
seas of pain, fiery tongues consume me, ere I stoop from
my safe, sure foundations, to give you one helping word."

Demis writhed at his railings against women; his un-
founded, sweeping accusations; but she dared—or could—not
set her love aside, to array herself in arms against him.
They stirred my very soul into wrathful disclaimers—fed,

perhaps, by a desire to avenge my own insult in this species
of retaliation. I did not feel the philanthropic outbreaks I
uttered. No generous pity stirred my heart for those—
unknown—so pitifully, mutely, pleading for the world's sympathy: woman rarely feels such sisterly pity, until she has
been scathed by the same fiery ordeal. If she, in her unthinking ignorance, arraigns such at her bar, and judges
without even a low call for evidence, what wonder? when
man—strong and able to *wrest* approval from the frowning
world for any deed, however unnaturally noble and helpful—
scorns, still more intensely? Words rolled from Elliot
Hume's lips, saturated in fierce opprobrium. His gesture,
his glance, spake even more. Oh! merciless, indeed, the
heart throbbing within that breast, and too common a type
of manhood. What matter indeed, for individual sufferers,
so the great whole of the world's virtuous standard be
maintained! Such atoms had *better* be crushed by the
coming car of Juggernaut, to afford freer space for purer
garments. The world recks not of such unsavory obitu-
aries.

A letter came one day for my aunt; a rare advent in the
family, and therefore scrutinized with curious glances.
"Wall," at length suggested Uncle Joel, "it strikes me that
the easiest way to find out 'bout it is to open it." So the
red wafer, bearing on its moistened surface the legible impress of a thimble, was carefully cut out, and preserved; the
missive unfolded and perused.

"It's from Hannah," observed Aunt Rhoda, "sayin' she'll
be down in June, to stay a spell. I guess you'll have to give
up teachin', Ruby; there'll be oceans to do, if they come."
Deborah gave a scornful sniff.

"If I'se *them*, I'd stay to hum," observed she; "'haint

seen hide nor hair of 'em for goin' on ten year; nor writ nuther, latterly. Jes' remember they've got connection out'n the country. Wonder what startèd 'em up so, all of a sudden? can anybody tell me?"

Dwight could. He remembered—with importance—that, "the papers were full about the cholery. I 'spose they're 'fraid o' catchin' it."

"Hum, hum," Deborah nodded her head meditatively. "If *that's* what they're aimin' at, I wish they'd stay where they be; nobody wants to wait on 'em, as I knows on. I know *one* that don't." And she looked extremely ireful.

"At any rate," said her mistress decisively, "we shan't let on but what we're glad to see 'em; so least said, soonest mended 'bout *that* ere."

I had never seen these relatives. One letter—extremely brief—came soon after my mother's death, filled with expressions of sorrow that "Car'line couldn't have lived longer," and closing by saying that in five years she should "claim us, for as long a stay. She always meant to do her duty," &c., &c. This one she failed to do, either through after prudential motives, or from utter forgetfulness of her impromptu promise, I knew not which and little cared, as I dreaded going among strangers, and my mother had never spoken very affectionately of this relative. Demis strengthened this repugnance by relating the incidents of a visit to her aunt when quite a little girl. I had no desire to repeat them.

This intelligence, together with the annual cleaning, prosecuted with unwonted ardor in anticipation of Aunt Hannah's prying eyes, put Mr. Hume to flight. He laughingly declared himself "turned away from home to make room for strangers;" though promising—if nothing happened of a calamitous nature to prevent it—to "run down and see us in August, during the long vacation." After packing his luggage, he came down with a book in either hand for "his sisters to look at when they were in danger of forgetting their brother." I took mine mechanically, with a few cold words of acknowledgment, wondering if it was—after all—a purely brotherly feeling he entertained for Demis, as he stooped to shake her hand and to smile back her gleeful thanks. Her wistful eye seemed still to detain him. The simple farewell formula had been spoken; hand-shakings successfully accomplished. Why then did he still linger! I thought that he wished a few words alone with my cousin, and taking the pitcher, I went to the well to fill it; it was the readiest excuse for gratifying their evident wish. As I opened the door I caught their lowered voices; his—tremulous with agitation, sweet, earnest, tenderly asking, "Do you doubt my faith! Remember, I have your promise." Her happy laugh answered him. I had hardly reached the well when he joined me. "How did you fathom my desire to see you alone?" he asked, with a confident laugh.

I stared in surprise. "I did not," was my cold answer.

"Well," he began, hesitatingly; "I do wish to speak of something, yet hardly know where to begin."

"I know it already," I broke in quickly; looking, as I said it, deep down in the well, that I might not meet his look of embarrassment. When I looked up—amazed at his long silence—he was scanning my face, searchingly.

"Then you *do* know my communication. Have you the gift of second-sight?" he asked.

"Why how can I help it?" I said, irritated at being forced to explain so very palpable a fact. "It is as plain as day. You wish me to take good care of your—your treasure, until you

12

return to claim it," I subjoined, quite in the approved romantic style, at which he laughed. "It is not in my line, Mr. Hume. I have no influence there now; you have driven me away."

"But I deny that I have driven you from any place. That would be, indeed, ungallant." His irony angered and perplexed me. While I meditated a fitting response, he resumed, with a light laugh, still more galling: "Then it *is* a treasure, Miss Ruby?"

"Don't you consider it such?" I asked, indignantly.

"Undoubtedly," was the cool response.

"You don't deserve it," I cried, angrily—feeling the impotency of the retort.

"No! I dare say. Will you condescend to explain its nature? Is it gold, or silver, or land? Is it invested in unsalable flesh? or, worse than all, is it buried treasure?"

"Not the latter *yet*," I said seriously. "It rests, however, with you."

"Romantic, decidedly," he laughed. "Whose life hangs on the uncertain thread of my going or coming? Yours?" His tone was too sneering to be longer borne.

"Heaven forbid!" I cried hotly. "When I throw my life away for a man's selfish thought, it will be for one I think worthy of the sacrifice."

He frowned; then answered, with startling impudence: "I really don't see why you should be piqued, Ruby, at my efforts to amuse a sick girl."

"I scorn the imputation, Mr. Hume. What is it to me, in any way?" I had lost all patience with the man. "Oh!" thought I, "for prompt aid to deal his egregious vanity a death-shock." Yet, the more I helplessly entreated, the more the requisite words receded from straining thought; and there he stood, self-poised on his cumbersome conceit, serenely smiling down on me.

"You and I will understand each other better some day, Miss Ruby," was his hopeful prophecy.

"Ah! I fancied I had attained to sufficient knowledge of that theme, now," was my curt, pointed answer.

His placidity was at last troubled. The current of truth did not mix well with the oily waters of conceit. His startled eye caught mine, then shrank from its steady gaze. "*This* is not the reception I expected for my communication, Miss Ruby," he faltered.

"I presume not! Is it your first disappointment, sir!" Very crustily I said this. I relished exceedingly this brief opportunity of paying off old scores—only it was *too* brief.

"I wonder now," he went on, "if you really feel this. I thought you liked me a little. A little, Ruby——." He paused, eagerly. I was silent. He resumed, smoothly: "What I am to your cousin, need make no difference to *you ;* you are separated in my regard as far as the poles."

"There is no need of asserting this, sir. The fact is patent to all. I have no desire to dispute it, or to will it otherwise. Now that you have at last successfully accomplished your mission—self-imposed, sir; `she never acceded to it—perhaps you will say good-by in a decently civil tone, and allow me to go in. You see," glancing at the window, "that Demis is watching us. What will she think of your conduct ?"

"It is nothing to her," he said gruffly. "You seem determined not to understand me. I have waited so long for —nothing, it seems."

"It seems so, truly, Mr. Hume."

"The fault is undoubtedly my own ?"

"Very possibly, Mr. Hume."

"Mister, Mister!" he echoed, angrily. "Why cannot you
call me Elliot, as Demis does? Will it blister your mouth
to be friendly? Even a prude may stoop thus far."

I passed over the scornful close, and answered his first
question.

"For that very reason, sir. I have regard for her rights;
but it seems you have none." He made a movement of surprise. I went on. "Elliot Hume, I heard you tell my cousin that you loved her. Your every glance, word, tone, has
long repeated the assertion."

I expected him to look confused, to falter, as I hurled on
him this home-truth, with a steady gaze. But I was mistaken. He grew bland, gentle, even tender; the waiting
sneer melted into a smile. I saw his motive clearly. It was
to wrench jealousy from its supposed stronghold. For what
purpose, I knew not. I was fortified.

"And if you did, it was only to appease the pang of parting. If it gives *her* peace, what matter? And a transient
peace is better than none at all. I pity, and seek thereby to
soothe her. It is but little, at the best. *You* know, in your
inmost heart, that *you* alone possess my every thought; that
all other affection is but chaff to fill an idle hour; the pure
grain waves and ripens there for you. Be noble, be generous, then, Ruby, in this knowledge of your power. Grudge
not the paltry civilities of a few fleeting hours; the soothing
cares bestowed on another. Trust me; trust me utterly. I
swear you shall never repent it!"

I know not which emotion predominated, as he serenely
uttered this; aversion to his sophistry, or disgust at his hypocrisy. And at the close—made eloquent by lip, and eye,
and gesture—at the appeal to my generous tolerance thereof,

my contempt for the mean, weak soul before me made me grind my teeth in rage. I eyed him scornfully—mute with passion. Words eddied up to my lips, and died in the struggle for expression. "No wonder Eve fell," thought I. "The serpent is always fair. His flattery is sweet as honey; his promises threaded with light." Sinuous his form, as he leaned gracefully over the curb. Magnetic his eye; its gaze formed for charming. Yes, the analogy was striking. I half expected to hear the quick, sharp rattle, or the dreamy charm lulling the senses to sleep, ere the fangs sent forth venom. But the venom had been sent prematurely. And the insult was too apparent. Pride, will, gave no signs of succumbing. Defiant, I met his gaze, and answered it. His eyes lowered, baffled; their eager scrutiny changed to doubt. His mouth contracted into a sneer—one not a stranger. It did not move me. Ire had been aroused ere the charm was complete. It was not to be easily lulled into forgetfulness.

I turned to go. "I will stay no longer," I said, coldly. "And so good-day and good-by, Mr. Hume; and if consistent with your past and future intentions, I sincerely hope that your journey may be a peaceful one."

"It *will* be," he said, as he extended his hand: mine met it half-way. He looked so sorrowful, that an apology rose to my lips—quickly suppressed.

I only said to him, "We need have no differences that I know of, Mr. Hume: I can freely forgive your mistaken notions."

Well! he was gone; and I was scarcely glad. Life, after all, is too sweet and brief for bickering. I had longed for his departure, as the advent of deep peace. Instead, came the silence of desolation. Then selfishness for the moment stood aside, as pride sternly accused it of grieving for a phantom;

that in which it could never have part or parcel.   Enforced comfort is but sorry comfort after all.

I thought of Demis with forgiving pity.   I longed to bind up the broken heart, sorrowing for a needful absence.   But then the past crowded up into full vision, overflowing with hateful incidents, bristling with countless stings.   I was no worm to kiss the foot that crushed me; that handed me as my portion, premeditated contempt.   Clear as the water into which I gazed, came the sequel to my mind; I was in no mood for listening to it under the sound of those retreating footsteps, knelling away into the distance with such fearful, certain precision.

There are some things incapable of analysis.   Sweet and bitter in our daily cup *will* mingle so persistently.   I leaned over the well-curb and burst into bitter tears, regardless now of prying eyes, or voices of scornful, compassionate inquiry.   Yet I was not in the least sorrowful.   They were merely tears of bitter indignation.   So spake Reason promptly, when I questioned her.   So I repeatedly assured myself, as I leisurely returned to the house.

CHAPTER XXIV.

It is June; fervid and glowing with flowery sweetness.   Sunset gilds the western skies; scarlet and golden sheets cover its broad surface, and tinge the mountain tops with beads of fire.   The blue of mid-heaven grows deeper, darker; dove-like clouds sail airily over it.   A few stars faintly open their twinkling lids, as if to sleepily watch this grand approach of a world's profound slumber.   One, more adventurous than the rest, and glowing like an eye of flame, already dips cautiously over Greybaul's summit, and sinks slowly into its gorgeous bed.

I sit in the farm-house looking at this calm loveliness of a dying day, whose hectic flush is gradually paling. Deborah, with a pail and dipper in either hand, stoops over the garden beds, sprinkling with cool moisture the drooping plants. On the upland beyond, stalks the burly form of Uncle Joel, surveying, with true farmer-like satisfaction, his promising acres. He leans occasionally on his trusty staff, not disdainful of this friendly supporter of age and weakness. Aunt Rhoda placidly knits by the open window. The roll of "blue mixed" perceptibly lessens with every round of the busy fingers, and in its stead grows the long-seamed sock for masculine wear. "Milkin' over," she can afford a clean apron, a cap, and an interval of repose. The family Bible lies in her lap—opened at St. Paul's Epistles; and as the words of the benignant Apostle fasten her attention, her lips move in a pleasant murmur. Demis comes down from her chamber, arrayed in white muslin dotted with tiny pink sprigs, looking quite too ethereal for the approved model for a country lassie; the texture scarcely whiter than her cheeks, from which the plump contour and brilliant hue have departed, with sleepless nights and aching days.

"Anny, Anny," calls Debby from the garden, "come in, now; that's a lady; and be fixed up a speck. I declare for't you look like a fright! Nobody wouldn't guess who 'twas, if they'd ever seen you afore, and knowed you *could* look like folks. Do see that are child's face!" she indignantly added, pushing Annah before her into the house. "I want you all to take a realizin' sense on't. Red's a piney! What can possess her to race round in that are medder so, in sech hot weather, is mor'n *I* can tell. For *my* part, if I hadn't nothin'

else to see to, I'd git'n the shade an' try to keep cool." She
lifted a corner of her dark blue apron and polished off her
forehead; then diverged downward, passing lightly over her
cheeks, and vigorously wiped her mouth.

Aunt Rhoda looked up from her book: "There'll be music
'nough if Har'ner's gal is sech a tomboy as that one. It
would keep two men in hard work to do nothin' but jest
keep track on 'em."

Debby dropped her apron. " No fear o' that," she retorted.
" I'll warrant ye, she's a proper well-behaved gal; sober as a
deacon. She hain't no medder to run in, you know. After
all, 'taint nat'ral to see an old head on young shoulders : I
ruther see a romp, of the two. I hear wheels, as true as fate.
They're comin' !' What a Bristo' load!" and she peered out
curiously.

Debby was right. "Har'ner's gal" *was* very "proper;"
exceedingly womanly in speech and manner, very fashionably
attired, with dainty feet encased in silk-clocked stockings,
and red morocco shoes. A broad-brimmed leghorn flat, with
a wreath of pale pink roses, crowned her yellow curls. One
arm awkwardly managed an enormous doll—manufactured
from white cotton, with very wide open eyes and the
broadest of snub noses—its figure gayly bedizened in crumpled
blue tarletan. The other hand extended a tiny parasol,
opened to display its full-frilled border or to ward off the
baleful effects of the rising moon. The little creature came
swinging into the house, imitating to perfection her mother's
gait, and, frigidly responding to her aunt's offered salute—as
an unpleasant matter of necessity—demurely slipped into a seat.

My aunt Lucas was a portly lady; florid and freckled,
with the lightest of brown hair, the thickest of thick lips—
purely Anglo-Saxon—and very faint and far away gray eyes :

merely a glimmer, and void of expression. There was an air of would-be condescension in all she said and did, intended for a mark of exclusiveness, and to betoken her *intimacy with* gentle breeding. It was too ludicrous to be offensive, as also was her perpetual reference to her "genteel neighbors"— with each name, a prefix of their rank, wealth, and notice of her own worthy self. She was possessed, also, of the imperious manners of her sisters, and seemed vastly gratified to issue orders by the score; to see people fly in all directions to execute them. Her husband must have suited her to a charm. He did her bidding with a meekness truly Mosaical. She evidently was the orbit round which he revolved, no unwilling satellite. Being of fragile dimensions, it was only natural to plant himself under the shadow of her wing, look up, and be protected, in return for his devotion. Consequently, when she told him, in the fewest possible words, to "go and look after our baggage," he obediently turned and patted away.

"Law! Har'ner, Joel'll fetch it in, bam-bye," said Aunt Rhoda, assiduously volunteering to untie a troublesome knot.

"Well! Mr. Lucas is used to it. He knows right where to take hold. I tell him when he's out of business for himself he must expect to make himself useful to home. Are these Car'line's girls?" she inquired, when fairly divested of her many wraps.

"Why, I had an idea they were small," she said, in surprise, attentively scanning us. "Well, three or four years *does* make a difference, 'specially at a certain age. I tell Milly sometimes, she grows so fast I shall have to put a stun on her head"—at which harmless threat Miss Milly simpered, and looked lovingly down on her doll—"there's no use a pulling out tacks. I'd rather make than mend, any day."

12*

"It's seven year and over sence they come here," corrected her sister.

"Why, it can't be possible!" was the answer. She appealed to me; but I confirmed the statement. "Well, time does slip away faster than we're aware of, don't it? I tell Mr. Lucas every year grows shorter and shorter; I don't know what they'll get to be finally. It used to seem an age from one Christmas to another, and from one Independence Day to another; now it don't seem no time at all. I meant to have visited you before, Rhoda," she added, apologetically, "but Mr. Lucas's business is so confining, I don't like to go without him; none of the first ladies *do*. But you might have visited *me*, I should have thought." Her sister might have retorted, with perfect truthfulness, that she never was asked, but she observed a prudent silence. "We've moved sence you was there," resumed Aunt Hannah; "we found the house getting quite too small for comfort."

"Yis, '*twas* ruther contracted, I thought," politely acceded Aunt Rhoda.

Her sister looked displeased. "I don't know as it was so *very* small," she said, tossing her head. "The *size* is no sign of gentility. Many of our first people live in smaller ones than *that*, let me tell you; and it's in an excellent neighborhood. All the Peterses and McClouds live right round there. I don't know where you'd find grander folks, *I* don't."

"Oh!" hastily interpolated her sister, "I didn't speak on that account. It looked well, but 'twas *wood*, you know, and I was afeard 'twould catch afire quicker'n the rest. I noticed them was all brick or stun, with blinds on 'em too."

"Well, yes; that *was* one reason we moved. We never had blinds put on; 'twan't wuth while, as we didn't expect to live there."

While the sisters thus exchanged confidences, Millicent had been displaying her graces for Annah's wondering eyes. Her stately parent's glance suddenly fell upon her, and thus reminded of a neglected propriety, she requested her to "go and shake hands." Very nimbly was this done, very coolly also, and she returned to her seat. Annah was essentially of a social disposition, and, after surveying with a puzzled expression the unpromising field, she drew near her cousin and tried to be friendly, opening the meeting with an inquiry as to her age.

"Seven," was the curt reply.

"So am I. Can you fish?" cried Annah.

"No! it's dirty work, ma says."

"Yes, but who cares! Dw'ght makes the cutest fish-poles out of willow. I can catch heaps of shiners, but the trout are shy." Miss Milly looked uninterested as Annah continued, and scornfully declined an invitation to "go to-morrow."

Then Annah tried school, and elicited some pithy answers. Evidently the little maid intended to waste no words upon her good-natured inquiries. "My pa's rich," said the dainty maiden, drawing her slight form up proudly, and looking hard at her discomfited cousin, who presently rallied to affirm stoutly: "So is Uncle Joel."

"But he is a farmer," replied Miss Milly.

"Well, what is your father?" inquired Annah.

"He's a-a-well, he makes money," she said, triumphantly.

"That must be nice," assented Annah. "I'm afraid Uncle Joel don't. I never saw him do it."

"Pa goes away in the morning without a cent, and comes home with a big roll; oh! as big as my fist"—holding up a small enough affair. "Our house is beau'ful. I thought Uncle was poor; the furniture is," she said, disdainfully.

Then the little heiress asked, "Who made your dress? It's as old-fashioned as the hills!"

"Cousin Demis made it. It's pretty too; and Demis is beautiful."

"Yes," observed Milly, with admirable coolness, "she *is* prettier than your sister. Ruby is a real homely old poke. I wouldn't own her," and she giggled mischievously. Annah frowned and left her. That night she declared her belief that they should not agree at all.

"Law!" said Debby, "don't you know what she's up to? She's only showing off her great gifts, that's all. I guess 'pon a pinch, you can get on your high-heeled shoes as well as she. An' she'll haul in her horns 'fore she's many months older."

Aunt Lucas seemed to think that her country relatives had no susceptibility of fatigue. She embodied in her ample proportions a compound of indolence and selfish exaction which soon grew oppressive. She managed to loll aimlessly around a portion of the domains nearly every fine day, coming in afterwards with the declaration: "I'm tired to death;" and, throwing herself on the lounge for a nap, she made no scruple of handing me a fan, with the request to "keep the flies off, as they most eat me up." She ordered things sent up to her room, as though a corps of well-trained servants were held in kitchen reserve for her especial use. She evidently thought our muscles strung with iron, for she left huge piles of soiled linen, drifting into corners of her room, to be by us cleansed and ironed for future use. She left her bed unmade and room unswept; if these offices were not performed for her at—in her estimation—a reasonably early hour, she assumed an injured look, very hard to be borne by such hospitable persons as Uncle Joel and his wife.

She thoughtlessly kept meals waiting her pleasure, regardless of the fact that, in a farmer's household, a greater necessity for punctuality exists than in a luxurious city home; regularly, just at the critical point of serving the dinner hot, after the chairs were placed and the host standing impatient, she would be missing; regularly some one would be sent in search, only to find her comfortably disposed for sleep. "I require a great deal," she was accustomed to observe, sleepily lifting her night-capped head. "Is it possible? How early you dine in the country! Well, I will try to come in a few minutes."

This meant an hour or so. For several days we politely waited, and in accordance with a hint from her husband, that the practice was a usual one, and that her dinner sent up was a pleasure to her—I volunteered to do the same ; but finding it likely to become an established ordinance, Aunt Rhoda rebelled, and one day coolly served the meal as usual. She made her appearance only to find a cold repast, which she disdainfully pushed aside, declaring a preference for "a plain diet of cream toast, poached eggs, and tea." She mortally offended Debby by calling her one day "a servant," and wondering how we allowed her a place at the family table.

"To think," muttered Debby, angrily, "how *she* was brought up: she used to scrub it as hard's ever Mis' Martin does. She allers lived on a farm. I've been by the old Lee place many's the time, up here in 'The Notch!' She *used* to know how to make butter and cheese, and to spin flax and tow, and all that are, if she *has* forgot it all now. Didn't dress very fine nuther, in them days; wore linsey-woolsey gowns and check aprons, and went barefoot allers in hot weather. Oh! I reckon I can tell her a few. I declare for't I won't put up with sech abom'nible airs. If 'twan't for John Lucas—he's a likely man—I'd pack her off, bag an' baggage. I know what I *will* do. I'll clear out. Servant!" quoth she, passionately. " I *ain't* a servant; never *was* one, an' what's more to the pint never *will* be, for Har'ner Lucas. She'd better go down South, if she wants slaves at her heels continually. She'd make a good hand to maul 'em 'round, only I'd pity the poor critturs from the bottom of my heart." Having thus vented her opinions, with no interruption, she grew calmer, and finally quite condescending " I can't, for the life o' me, see what's got into the woman," she said, contemptuously. "Car'line, now, didn't seem to feel no bigger arter she put up at the city, and I've heard tell as how York was a good sight bigger'n where Har'ner lives."

"Folks is diff'rent, I s'pose," said Uncle Joel, who came in during her harangue. "Don't you mind nothin' she says, Deborah! It's all in a lifetime, you know!"

" Well now, Mr. Martin, if 'twan't for Demis there, I *would* go 'way an' stay a spell, to make my word good, you know; as true as I live, I would. But that are child is dreadful poorly; don't know as none the rest on you see it, but I'll tell you one thing, and that is, that unless *somethin's* done, and mighty quick, too, she won't stay here long."

Poor Uncle Joel gave a start, put on his spectacles and went into the keeping-room. He came out in a few minutes, just as Aunt Rhoda came bustling in from her cheeses.

"Come now, Joel; them cheeses have got to be turned, short order. They're gittin's mildewy as the mischief, and the orter has all gin out; I squeezed the last out the pot yesterday. Now don't forgit to-night to git some more,—law! Mr. Martin, have you seen a ghost? You're as white 's a sheet." He prudently closed the door before replying.

"Why, Rhody, why on airth have'nt you spoke 'bout it
'afore? She *is* changed." (Seeming to forget that she had
not spoken of it now.)

"Spoke 'bout the orter? I did," she retorted sharply,
"last night; but you an' John Lucas was so took up with
them city papers, I s'pose it went in to one ear and out at
t'other."

"No, no," he whispered. "Speak lower, mother; do. I
'ain't deaf. I tell you it's our Demis, I meant. She looks
as thin's a rail, an' dreadful weakly. I guess I'll step up to
Dr. Torry's, an' ask him to call in, and see what ails her—
leastways, git a strength'nin' mixture."

"I guess you'll do no such thing, Joel Martin," said Aunt
Rhoda, quickly. "You'll make her think she *is* sick, and
then there'll be a nice fuss. B'tween you an' Deborah you'd
conjur' up an 'arthquake, I do believe. I can tell I guess,
as well as the next one, when anybody's sick and needs the
doctor. I'll steep up some motherwort, and she must go to
takin' *that* along; it'll give her an appetite, and she'll soon
pick up ag'in. She never did flesh up much in the summer
season."

"She never *lost* any afore though," muttered Debby, from
the closet, "but none so blind as them that won't see.'"

Uncle Joel went off to turn the cheeses, feeling hopefully
disposed towards the genial virtues of the basin of "motherwort," which his wife put at once on the stove to steep.

CHAPTER XXV.

THE scorching midsummer passed. Deborah was disabled for any service. One morning, descending the stairs ere dawn to go about the washing, she missed one step and was violently precipitated to the floor. The concussion of such a body—Debby was far from being a fairy in size—as well as her unearthly groans, brought the whole family to the spot, with dim notions of robbers and murderers—a frightened, though not a very valiant army. When assisted to rise, amid sounds of suppressed laughter at her horror-stricken face, they quickly ceased, for one leg was discovered to be broken.

"Wall," said she, amid her sobs, after it had been properly set by the doctor, and herself fairly placed in bed; "it's an old sayin', 'much haste makes waste.' You see, I thought, as we'd got sech a powerful wash to-day, I'd jess git up still, afore daylight and tackle it. One hour in the mornin's wuth two at night, I think; but I guess I missed it. 'Twas so dark I couldn't see my hand afore me. I went by the sense o' feelin' till I fell myself"—she concluded, laughingly.

This misfortune added seriously to our cares. The tortured limb swelled painfully, the severed bone being badly splintered; and it required almost constant bathing, for which we could illy spare time from pressing household duties. Poor Debby writhed mentally, at her inability to perform the slightest service.

"I feel as if I should never grumble ag'in at havin' so much to do, if I only git round ag'in," she would say repeatedly, and end with a heavy sigh. Then, begging piteously for something to do, she would bribe Annah to bring her the bowl of potatoes to peel. It was worse than useless. She worried herself. into a fever, and for days raved in delirium. I ventured one day to ask Aunt Hannah, who kept aloof from the sick-room, for some trifling attendance there. She threw down her novel, impatiently rose and followed me in. As I carefully bared the limb, and pointed to the basin of tepid water, such an ugly grimace crossed her face as I hope never again to witness. She picked up the sponge with one finger and thumb, as if she feared in its cells lurked the direst contamination.

"It isn't a very pleasant job, Miss, is it?" she said, with intense disgust.

I immediately signed her to leave—too indignant to speak. She never forgave me, deeming the request an insult.

"Poor dear!" moaned Deborah; "I shall wear you all out. I ain't fit to live. Let me alone; this old leg'll do well enough. You was a goin' to help Demis, wan't you? She needs it."

"I don't care, father," said Aunt Rhoda, thoughtfully, the next morning at breakfast, "if you do step into Dr. Torry's as you go to 'the Intervale,' and ask Cornely ef she's a mind to come down'n stay a spell, and chore it a little. It'll be a great godsend if she will, tell her; and I'll make it all even. ●You see," she added apologetically to her sister, "Demis ain't stout. She fainted clear away this mornin' while breakin' up the curd. She can't stan' what she used to. Debby says I've overworked her; but I don' know; I never meant to. I allers said I'd bring up my girls to work, and I have."

"Well, Ruby looks pretty tongh," was her sister's somewhat heartless answer, accompanied by a direct gaze at myself. "Demis *looks* delicut, to be sure; but you can't always tell by the looks of a toad how far it can jump, you know."

"For the Lord's sake," growled Debby from the bedroom, "deliver me from sech a crittur as that! Ruby's flesh and blood, Har'ner Lucus, which is mor'n I can say of you."

Cornelia Torry was well pleased to come while the "city folks" were staying. It was a rare chance to find out about the fashions and inspect their clothing to "see if t'was felled or only overcast."

She revelled in reminiscences of others' shortcomings in this line.

"But there's Mis' Deacon Sweet. She was fetched up in a city—to be sure 'twan't a city then, but 'tis now, so it's all the same in Dutch—says she don't care *how* things are made, so they only look well on and hold together. Now, I allers look at the wrong side; if that's all right, the rest'll do." She was fond of calling Deborah and herself "old cronies; 'bout the same age, and I 'spose one didn't git married 'cause the other didn't. Misery likes company, you know"—with a cheerful laugh—"not that I'm the wust off of anybody, by any means; and I must say I've never seen the man yit I'd have, no never! have you Deborah?"

"Well," said Debby slowly, "I used to think so; but I tell you it's mighty nice to have a hum and some one to take care o'you when you're flat on your back and can't lift a finger. Talkin' and doin's two different things. I might a' had one, though, as well as anybody, if I hadn't been a fool."

"Why, Debby," I said, a little hurt, "haven't you got any one to take care of you now?"

"Oh yis, child! I don't mean that, but you know jest how 'tis. A hum o' my own. Nobody can't do as they've a mint to in any other; you can't in a sister's house even. I tell you, if I'se to live my life over ag'in, I'd do different in *some* things, I promise you. I don't want anybody to be an old maid, 'cause I be. I wouldn't be ag'in; and I *needn't* a been now, if I hadn't been a mind to; but law! I never would have any thing to say t'the young men; I wouldn't go nowheres when they asked me to, and *that* ain't the way to manage."

"Well, to be sure! I never heard the beat!" said Miss Cornelia, in amazement. "I'm thankful I've got a contented heart!"

"I am, too, if you have," responded Debby, dryly.

"Speakin' o' chances," observed Miss Cornelia, rather nettled at finding herself thus set aside, "I guess there ain't no Jack but what has his Jill. If I'se a mind to, I guess I could show chances with anybody."

Debby smiled loftily. "Wall, Cornely, you mustn't lay up nothin' I say," she said, in a conciliatory tone. "I'm's as spleny as all natur', and 't does seem to me sometimes as if I should fly off the handle."

The summer passed thus. October greeted us,—a hale and hearty sire. The cholera having scourged the city and taken its mysterious departure, our guests also vanished homeward, leaving a faint invitation for a return of the long visit. Uncle John timidly took me aside one day, and cordially urged my spending the winter there, saying Annah should go to school with Milly. If she would stay through the entire course, so much the better. This came from his heart and touched me deeply. I accepted it for future thought—snugly bestowing it away in secret, that, when occasion required, it might come forth for use. However, he started quickly away, as his imperious spouse appeared at

the door to order him off on some duty—assuming an unconscious air, which led me to the truthful conclusion that
this momentous offer was made solely on his own authority,
and unknown to his conjugal mistress. He was probably
doubtful if it would meet her approbation. Poor innocent,
generous little man! I was doubtful, also, and though his
dilemma excited a smile, I liked him too well not to be content and glad to humor his scruples and preserve silence.

Debby recovered sufficiently to be wheeled to the table.

" I declare for't this feels like old times, to git my hands
in dish-water ag'in," she said, with hearty satisfaction. " I
tell you, Ruby, it's dreadful hard work layin' in bed, day in and
day out, and others a waitin' on you. I hope I shall get so's
I can stand on my pegs afore long ; its onhandy, settin' and
workin', you know."

" I miss Mis' Lucas mightily," observed Miss Cornelia,
who had come down for another week's stay—she resented
tne idea of "working out." She "only liked to oblcege a
neighbor, you know ; 'cause ev'ry one had ups and downs in
their life, and wanted favors. She was willin' to lend a
helpin' hand, for her part, for she could'nt tell but she'd
want the same in return. ' Live and let live,' *her* motter
was. If folks'd act *more* on this ere princi*pal*, they wouldn't
come out o' the little end o' the horn, as much as they now
do !"

" It's a *good* miss, I think," replied Debby, curtly, at which
Miss Cornelia indulgently winked to me to say nothing—I
had made no motion to speak—and condescendingly changed
the subject.

Mark came home this month for a week's visit. He was
shocked at the alteration in his sister, and, in much agitation,
demanded of me the cause. I endeavored to explain calmly,

but he abruptly silenced me, with " I'm going for a doctor. It's strange my mother don't perceive the necessity of doing something. It's not like *you* either," and he eyed me reproachfully.

Good old Doctor Torry came, looked serenely down on his patient, felt the pulsations in her tiny wrist, and seemed a little in doubt. " Pult regular, breathin' good, no fever," he audibly meditated. " Feel any pain ?"

" No, sir," said Demis.

" H'm, hum ; have night-sweats any, or cold chills, or fever flushes ?"

" No, sir," again said Demis, smiling.

Doctor Torry smiled, too, and looked at her quite patronizingly.

" Guess don't much ail you, does there ? ain't playin' possum, are you, to scare these good folks into fits ? Some little gals do it, and seem to think it rare fun."

" No, indeed," said Demis, laughing.

" That puts the pink into your cheeks a little, I see. How's her appetite ?" he asked, turning to her mother.

" Not much to speak of," she placidly said. " Can't tempt it none."

" Ah! just so! Well, she won't crave any thing right away. I should recommend now," he resumed, slapping his knees thoughtfully, " a good stiff cup of yarrow tea ; a little mandrake would be beneficial too, which I will leave you." He opened his saddle-bags, fumbled awhile, and held up a tiny vial to the light, full of a dark liquid. " And this you will take a teaspoonful of every hour; shake the bottle well before using. I will read up your case, and call again," he said, preparing to leave. I made the tea; she refused it, declaring it bitter and needless.

" It's bitter and wholesome," I urged, approaching the cup to her lips.

". Perhaps so; but not for heart-ache," she said pitifully. " Ruby, will he ' read up' that name for my disease, I wonder ?"

" Dear Demis, don't talk so." I bit my lips, to keep in the tears. " You have no heart-ache. That is pure nonsense."

" Yes! That is what they call it, and they laugh at people for having it. I could tell no one but you this, Ruby. You are my best friend after all. I know it *now*. Don't let them sneer at me."

" Oh, Demis," I sobbed, " I was to blame then, more——"

" There, there, stop crying, dear; you hurt me;" and the little hand came patronizingly down on mine, as in the old long ago.

" Shake it off, Demis," I urged; " you are so strong. It is only the weak who should sink under it. You have so many to live for who love you."

" Yes," she answered sadly. " And I am dying for one who does not care for me one thought. I have been so deceived. It's my fate, I suppose, as Debby would say."

" Not at all," I said. " Mine was the fate centring all life's dreary possibilities. I was to experience bitter disappointments, and lonely—perhaps sinful—hours. She never predicted such a future for you—' her bright darling,' she calls you; and Mark ' his Gipsy Queen.'"

She shook her head. " Better die young, than live old, soured, peevish, and rebellious. Don't look so sad, Ruby. I want to die. I've had hours, when, if I could have got it, I should have poisoned myself, to escape dragging out that one weary day. To look forward to years of such days! Oh, it's dreadful," she added, shuddering, " this trying so hard *not* to think; *not* to regret; *not* to feel."

I turned away to hide my tears. *I*, poor worm, had so misjudged her.

"I don't care *now*, Ruby. Come back! You must hear me. It's such a relief to talk it all over. I've walked the house for hours and hours, and gone to the garret when I heard you coming; and down in the cellar in the cold, damp darkness I have lain, till I felt turned to stone. And I couldn't die. I couldn't even take a common cold. , I've felt the spiders crawling over me, and earthworms, so horribly slimy and cold, and I lay still and let them crawl, to get used to the grave-worms, you know, Ruby ——. Don't turn your face away; I like to look at it now, but I've almost hated the sight of it this past year. It seemed, some days, as if I must kill you when you put your arms around my neck or kissed me. Once, I carried the carving-knife to bed with me, and got up in the night, and stood over you with it—just to see how it would seem. I believe in my heart I was a murderer; for I got wild at last, brandishing it over your head, and I almost touched your throat with the sharp edge. You slept through it all, little dreaming how wicked your dearest friend was. I confess I wanted to try it on you; but you smiled in your sleep, and drew Annah's head to your bosom, and that broke the spell. I was terribly frightened to find how near I had been to an awful deed. I tossed the knife out of the window, lest I should be again tempted. Ruby, the devil put it into my heart; he was with me that night; he is with me continually, and I shall go to him I'm fearful, for I am so wicked."

"Hush, hush!" I whispered. "You are getting excited. You dreamed all this you mean, my darling. Stay; I remember Dwight's bringing in the knife one morning, and wondering how it came there in the nasturtium-bed."

" You perceive then it wasn't a dream," she said quickly.
" No ; I have such wild, selfish thoughts. I used to pray,
when a little girl, to God to let me die before my friends. It
seemed to me I could never see one of them buried. Well,
Ruby ; it's awful, but I have felt lately, as if I could re-
joice to see every one in the house in a coffin at the same
time ; and I have thought how nice it would be to have a
dance at the great funeral. I don't want to have such thoughts,
Ruby ; I try not to let them in. I commence thinking resolutely of something else, and before I know it, there it is
again ; I am imagining it all over. Then I say over and
over, aloud, ' no, I *don't* mean it ; as true as I live and breathe,'
—just as we used to, Ruby, when little girls ; but the wild
things come into my head again. I wanted to tell you all
this, that you may not think me better than I really am ;
and that you may forgive me for all my thoughts towards
you, and for brandishing that knife over you. *Can* you forgive me, Ruby, for *that?*" she asked, wistfully.

" Yes! readily. That was nothing. You were not quite
yourself. But why have you kept all this so long? You
are not afraid of me, are you?"

" Oh no ! but I was *so* miserable, and you were not. How
could you understand me? You cannot, Ruby, unless you
ever feel as I have, which God forbid ! I know how the
poor lost wretches feel, flinging themselves over bridges into
dark, cool waters below. Any thing quiet and cool they
seek, as I sought the cellar. I used to fear it, mortally, but
it seemed my home, my place of refuge at that dreadful
time. Of course, I couldn't tell you this now, Ruby, if I
any longer felt so. I do not ; that is all passed away.
Don't cry for me. I don't for myself any more. I feel
beyond tears or any earthly longing. Nothing now could

tempt me to live for long years, and endure this all over again—for I should, when health, and strength, and. ambitious dreams of the future came back." She wearily closed her eyes as if going to sleep, but soon opened them to say : " August is long since past ; the ' long vacation' is over. How easily *some* forget their promises."

" He may have other engagements," I endeavored to say cheerfully. " You remember, he had received an urgent invitation to go West with a party of college friends." She shook her head.

" Can it be that he reads my secret, Ruby !" her face crimsoned. " He does; and he will never come again. Oh ! I have seen——"

" Nothing worth telling," I interrupted. " Now, don't be unreasonable. He is not worthy to untie your shoe. Here; drink this, and go to sleep."

" Why, how hot you look, my sister," she said, with a touch of her old gayety ; and she pushed aside my hair, and patted my flushed cheek, as I stooped over her.

" I like this, Demis. Go on. It sounds like your old self—or your young self, which you will. It reminds me of the evening I came here. I thought you the happiest being in the world. You are dearer now than all !"

" All !" she murmured, incredulously. " I am generous enough not to invade the sanctum filled by another."

" My darling, no one fills it save yourself,"—she brightened—" be convinced and go to sleep; you have said enough for once. Besides, this tea is cooling ; this famous dish of yarrow, which, it is to be hoped, will give you strength, and —spite of Dr. Torry's prediction—'a craving appetite.' "

" No," she said, with a determined start. " The tea can wait, while we talk further of this matter."

13

"To-morrow!" I pleaded.

"There are no to-morrows in heaven, Ruby, and no reserves; there should be none on earth. I used to have the queerest notions in my childish brain," she resumed, after a long pause; "I often wondered if I was not an adopted child—no wonder you laugh; I do now, when I think of it —I remember, full well, sitting hours in my little room, reasoning myself into that conviction. I believe I usually put forth for plaintiff the shrewd plea, that, if I was in reality her daughter, my mother would show forth more love for me. I ardently longed for it, and I have shed many bitter tears after witnessing how my playmates were caressed in their homes. Debby, to be sure, was always affectionate, but, like my mother, the boys were her especial pets. Dear Mark was such a teaze; but I know in his heart he liked me. Yet, that was not sufficient. I wanted some one to tell me so. My father would have been more demonstrative; it is his nature. But whenever he drew me to his side, or on his knee, and kissed me, my mother was always sure to start suddenly in sight, and say something sharply sarcastic—'she didn't like to see old folks make fools of themselves,' or something to the same effect—and he would put me down as if he had been shot. I believe he is afraid of her; she has such sudden ways. *She* never kissed me in her life. I never saw her kiss the others: consequently, the defendant's view of the case, including the customary maternal care of clothing and nursing in sickness, I always ignored, and rendered the same unlawful verdict. Even now, I have my doubts if she would have rendered those cares for love—set aside custom."

"What a silly idea, dear Demis!" I said, smiling at her fervor.

"After you came," she resumed, gravely, "all was so different. It seemed as though Providence sent you in answer to my wants; a blessed gift. What was your sorrow became to me, by some mysterious transmutation, my greatest joy; and when you sobbed through those long hours, that first night, my utmost efforts would not summon sadness. I felt only a thrill of satisfaction that you were even more miserable than myself, so that I might win your heart by feeding it with comfort. You didn't draw back when I threw my arms around your neck; you didn't say coolly, ' There, that will do : you muss my collar,' when I pulled down your head to kiss you—as Amanda usually did. You returned the caress with interest."

" Well, that was because it was pleasant," I interrupted, laughing. "I never cared to kiss your sister. To please myself, I will give you one—two—yes, a dozen, and leave you. You won't let me say a word."

" That's a pity—you are such a talker ;" she spoke quite gayly. " Go, if you will, but I want first to tell you—I may never have another chance—that perhaps there is an unsuspected design in all afflictions; that one may be taken to make room for another's happiness, and then they in their turn, removed for the same cause : that your mother—don't think me irreverent or unfeeling—died to make *my* happiness, and I may——" I put my hand over her mouth.

" Don't say it, Demis. It is a terrible thought. If you go thus far, whose happiness am *I* preventing, and when shall *1* be taken from earth, for no other purpose than that another sinful soul may wax fat in the fulness of a brief joy, and then give room to its heir? No! we are not mere puppets of an unseen intelligence, I feel sure. We have our mission; we move in our appointed course,—Divinity thus reproduced."

"Ruby, it is a grand idea to me: this making death—usually so repulsive—a sacrificial offering. I would far rather die that an object might be attained, the which my living rendered impossible, than to go out like the exhausted wick of a candle, simply because there is no further supply of vitality. At least, if one's life is shorn of good deeds, its close makes some amends, if it bequeath to one soul the priceless legacy of happiness."

"What an admirable martyr you would make, Demis!" I said. She did not return my smile. She gazed at me earnestly, and resumed, unheeding it:

"But Ruby, it is hard for the living to view the great change in its beneficent aspect. The mystery of that future is shrouded with dread. We gaze aghast at the spectacle of the beautiful spirit seeking to be delivered from the thraldom of the body. Human love is always proven stronger —in its hour of trial—for the decaying case, than for the fleeing, imperishable portion. It appeals so vividly to every sense—the pale, lifeless lump, oh! so familiar—and it is hard to believe that all which once constituted it our own is not there still, though dormant from the reaction of physical pain."

She was silent now, and seemed dreaming, while a triumphant smile wreathed her lips. I noiselessly left her.

CHAPTER XXVI.

The Doctor came again. He announced, with solemn satisfaction, as the result of his researches, that "Demis had the consumption."

"But she don't cough none," remonstrated her mother.

"Can't help that. Some never do," he responded, sententiously; "but for all that, they die of consumption."

He immediately commenced an application of pills, powders, and plasters, after the good old rule. His unresisting patient must also be "cupped," and suffer leeches to be fastened to her white throat, and blisters to be raised, until she summoned courage to decline further torture. Dr. Torry, offended and at fault, left her.

"I shall send Doctor Luther to see her," said Mark, the morning of his departure. He had lingered a month to see if his sister rallied under her vigorous treatment. "I don't testify personally to his skill, but all Chispa sounds his praises."

"Dear me," said Demis, with a dismayed face, "I have had enough."

"Of blue pills and powders," cut in Debby, quickly. "I should think so. She's had a cal'mel sore mouth ever sence that fust dose. I knew how 'twould be in the time on't. Dr. Torry's a proper clever man, but he don't know ev'ry thing, no mor'n I do;" and she rocked, indignantly. "I never could abide merc'ry; it stays forever in the system, jest where you put it: nothin' less'n Gabriel's trump'll ever start it a peg. It'll have to come then, if we expect to take these poor old bodies up t'the New Jerusalem—though what on earth we want 'em there for, is mor'n I know. I know one thing, if I's to take my pick, after I'd once got fairly out of it, I'd bet I wouldn't be sech a fool as to take my own ag'in."

"Dr. Luther is called all sorts of names," said Mark. "Debby can find out all about him when he comes;" he laughed; "she has a genius for putting people through the catechism."

He came the third day from Mark's departure. He did not impress us very favorably, for he entered the house without the usual ceremony of a rap, inquiring abruptly for his patient. He looked coarse and ignorant; vulgarly presumptuous in manner, and inelegantly careless in attire. He was perseveringly obtuse to all repellent movements on his patient's part, and drew his chair to hers, looking in her face with decidedly non-professional disrespect and indelicacy. Demis intuitively shrank from him, yet she could not avoid a smile at his round, ruddy face—not unlike a full moon—encased in an atmosphere of short red curls. His little black eyes roved restlessly around the room; up at the ceiling, then seeking the faces present, as he talked. He looked as if he might be bound upon some treasonable errand, or a burglar in disguise, seeking out the vulnerable points for a midnight attack; alternately throwing Demis bayoneted glances as she sat before him, as though he were thus probing her disease by means of their lance-like efficacy. He deigned to ask her no questions: they would have been a virtual admission of the fact that his medical knowledge was not quite omniscient. Then he cleared his throat and gave us the result of his analysis:

"I see, Missis, that you have the induration of the circulation of the whole corporeal system. The liver is the seat of life. It lies to the right, and projects to the left. It is out of its orbit, and must be restored. Hem! The several vestments which encase each several offices of all that constitute the human frame are highly inflammatory; they must be subdued. Hem! Fever is certain; your rapid pult tells *that* story. Hem! The blood mounts to the brain, causing red cheeks; that's hectic. Fits sometimes ensue; I see 'em in prospect. Hem! You must stop drinking coffee and tea, and eating pork. Tea contracts the nerves, and coffee thickens the blood : I know you eat pork, because your face shines. Hem!" ("So does yours," I subjoined, mentally.) "You musn't sleep with your winder open; night air's very injurus. Yes, Missis, I see your system is in a very complicated state of internal disarrangement; more so than nsual, although one constitution differeth from another, as one star differeth from another in glory. The prophet never said a truer thing than this—'all flesh is grass.' So it is, Missis; so it is: but we can cure the grass, Missis, and make it grow again. Hem!"

He chuckled at his own conceit. How long this florid style would have prevailed, it is quite impossible to say; for Debby, in misguided curiosity—no longer to be restrained—interrupted him with—

"Wall, now, Mister Luther, do tell us what you're drivin' at. What be you? I never heard no sech talk afore: it's part scriptur and part somethin' else—a new-fashioned doctrine, ain't it? I heerd John Lucas a talkin' one day—ever hear of him? He lives in Shiler, and's a broker by trade. He married Mis' Martin's sister; they've been out here this season—'bout there bein' a new kind o' medicine comin' into vogue; nothin' under the sun but leetle teeny pills o' sugar, as big's a pin-head. Dr. Torry makes his'n out o' brown bread crumbs, and they're as diffikilt to swaller as bullets, but't does seem kinder curus to take nothin' but sugar instid. I 'spect though it's mostly for children, but when sugar's high, seems to me bread'd do as well. He says they cure folks astonishin'.; make 'em sweat like the mischief. I forgit what he called 'em, but be *you* one o' them sort?"

"I am a dissectionist, Missis. I tell just by looking in folks's faces, whether any thing ails them. I learned it by seeing the different expressions on dead people's faces. You can't hide an ailment from *me*. I see it in a twinkling, Missis. Hem!"

"Law! Then you've got second-sight. Born with a veil over your face, most likely; and sees strange things, now don't you?" she queried eagerly.

His face clouded. "No, Missis. I don't have nothing to do with the devil nor his works. I'm a plain man, Missis; and if I do say it as shouldn't say it, an honest one too. Hem!"

He now produced, from a bundle, tied up in a red silk handkerchief, all manner of pulverized herbs, and strange-scented drugs, which went through the usual professional formula of smelling, tasting, and pinching. Then he called for a quart bottle, with molasses, gin, sulphur, cream of tartar; with which, formidably arranged in a row on the table before him, he proceeded leisurely to compound an infallible cure for the above-named frightful combinations of disorders: his keen bead-like eyes keeping up their intermittent survey around the ceiling, and occasionally darting aside to watch the effect on our faces of his mysterious proceedings. Over some of the drugs he lingered doubtfully—shaking his tawny curls as if fearful of consequences, should they leap into the quart bottle; but stealthily gathering our impressions by a quick glance, he invariably dropped them in. Finally, it was filled to the brim, corked and handed to Demis, who looked at it rather ruefully. "Have I got to take all that?" she asked, demurely, holding it up to the light.

"Certain, Missis; and more too when that's gone. We must make an outlet for the system: such a case as yours ain't cured by one dose, nor for nothin'. To be well shaken before taken, Missis. Eight teaspoonfuls, mornin', noon, and night. When this is gone I shall compound more. That induration must be cured, Missis; must be cured. Hem! Hem!"

Demis laughed as he departed ; his little black eyes giving a farewell roll around the room, with his accompanying, " Good-day, good-day, Missis. Hem !"

This visit of the learned man of science—the pride and oracle of Chispa—had, at least, one beneficial result : it afforded food for mirth, and in laughing at the recollection of his oddities, Demis temporarily got the better of that frightful " induration," which, after all the renovating virtues in the huge black bottle had been exhausted, refilled, and again emptied, obstinately lingered unscared.

CHAPTER XXVII.

RAP, rap, rap on the doors of the kitchen. Demis started suddenly into an upright posture, but quickly sank back again, on hearing a strong nasal voice answer the opening. During the past month a bed had been brought down into the keeping-room ; for she grew quite too weak to climb the stairs to our little room. There were days when she scarcely left it ; and others, when the flattering side of the disease came uppermost. She seemed so strong then, so well and cheery, that her father's face brightened into renewed hope, and we all looked upon her speedy recovery as certain.

I opened the door softly, and peeped out. "It's a peddler," I said, leaving it a trifle ajar.

Deborah was preparing pies for the oven, sitting at the table, with Annah standing ready to help her to articles beyond her reach. " I kinder guess now, I've happened along

13*

in the nick o' time," he observed, depositing his hat and bundle on the floor; deliberately crossing his short fat legs, and keeping up a quick rocking motion of the elevated foot. "Now I've got an article here, that the old Harry himself can't beat, if he tries till doomsday. It's jes' what you *want* precisely. I sell 'em in ev'ry single house I come to—and double ones too, for that matter; it makes no odds if they've got one or a dozen a'ready; they allers buy one o' me. I'm so pop'lar, you know"—with a succession of winks to Annah, who looked much astonished thereat—" and, I take it, *this* is a leetle super extry to any thing of the kind that's ever been round before."

" Humph! What is it?" asked Debby, curtly.

" Can't you guess now, marm? Give you three, and out. You won't? well then I 'spose I'll have to tell you. It's a patent pie-crimper, and a leetle the cutest thing you ever did see. I sold Mrs. Pierce up here, on Sampson's Hill there, one for herself and each of her gals 'gainst they step off—as they're sure to do. Likely young wimmen they be! If I'se richer, I ain't sure but I'd take one on'em myself at a ventur'—some takes one; some two (these crimpers I mean, marm), jest's they feel 'bout it. Don't want to urge nothin'. Have one for fifteen cents—two for twenty-five; so, you see, it's a sight cheaper to take two, after all."

" I don't want any," said Debby, grimly.

" But *ev'ry*body takes one," he stoutly maintained, " and some takes more. Now it's nothin' to me, I don't make 'em; I git 'em down to York, and don't have a plaguey sight o' profit. Wait till you see one operate, marm. I carry a block round with me, 'bout the size of a pie, you know—only not quite so'temptin',"—he interrupted himself to indulge in a hearty chuckle, and a few more winks to Annah,—"to show folks how it works." He whipped out of his bundle a round piece of wood and a small roller. "There! you rest the pie so fashion, on this hand; then, with the other, take the crimper and go half way round, so fashion; then turn the pie, and go the other half. Don't no juice run out then. Can't if it's ever so much disposed to, to say nothin' of looks. I don't wonder there's so many cross women bakin' days!"— Debby turned on the chair and gave him a withering look, which he did'nt heed, but rocked his foot and proceeded coolly, "have to stand pinchin' the crust down so long with their thumb and forefinger, it's 'nough to make 'em tired and cross. Now, with this little concern, you can do it in no time, and save your temper int' the bargain. Jes' try one on them pies!" he entreated. "Only try it once, and you wouldn't do without it on no consideration. Come! that's fair, ain't it? I wouldn't offer it to ev'ry body. You'll need it too for your little gal, 'gainst she goes to housekeepin'. Pretty little thing she is too; looks jes' like her mother! Your'n, ain't she?"

"No," answered Debby, wrathfully. "I ain't come to that yit, I hope. I never expect to, nuther."

"Never mind, marm. Plenty o' time yit," said the undaunted peddler, facetiously, rubbing his knee. "Come to think on't, you do look too young to own sech a strappin' gal as that. How old might you be, sis?" he inquired patronizingly.

Deborah gave her a look not to answer; accordingly Annah observed silence and shoved her the all-spice box, with officious zeal.

"Now! I want to know if you print 'em that way?" inquired the peddler, rising and going to the table. "With an old back-comb! I never!"

"It's a clean one, if it *is* an old one," said Annah, indignantly.

"Certain, sis. But a few coppers ain't much to pay out for a nice one ; real patent too. I'll warrent 'em or refund the money. I ain't in the cheating line : mean to do the fair thing by my customers. One'll last a lifetime, but it's better to take two, in case one gets lost or stolen. Then a large fam'ly takes a good many pies, you know."

"Yes, I know that ; I don't want to hear no more talk about it," sputtered Debby.

"Wall, don't want to urge nothin', but I think you miss it ; to-morrow'll be too late. I expect to sell 'em all out before then. I've got over seventy here"—slapping his bundle. "Had a cool hundred to start with ; go like lightning, you see. Some takes one or two, jes' as they can afford ; 'taint much, any way, for a convenience."

Demis laughed. Just then he turned his face, and commenced to pack his bundle. "Why, it's Andrew Jackson," I cried, in surprise.

"Mercy ! how do you know ?" said she, with a start.

"Oh ! not the General, Demis. Only one of my pupils. I must speak to him."

"Oh, I'm well as common, Miss Brooks," he said, in answer to my greeting ; "though I've had a pritty tough cold 'long back ; feel yit 'bout half and half, or betwixt hay and grass —as the farmers say. Glad to see you, Miss Brooks. Been meanin' to give you a call this long while."

"And how long have you been a peddler, Andrew ?"

"Oh, all summer, off and on. Most sold out though. Yis, I've got the cutest invention, Miss Brooks ; a powerful labor-saver," and he volubly repeated the preceding round of arguments in favor of buying. "Can't git marm there to take one even on trial. Don't *you* want one, Miss Brooks? It'll keep, you know; won't eat nor drink nothin', nor take up much room. Cheap as dirt too. I don't make no profit on 'em scursely. Now this is all talk and no cider. I'm bound to trade; always do, you know."

" I'd kick it out of the house," said Debby, hotly.

" Just so," said Andrew, coolly. " Don't want to urge nothin'. You know your own feelin's best, I 'spose, but I really think you miss it; never'll have such another chance, see if ye do. Sell 'em ev'rywhere I go." He slung his bundle over his shoulder, and departed, still chanting the merits of his neglected wares.

" Thank my stars ! He's gone at last," said Debby, angrily. " Impudent young rascal as ever I see ! If he don't come to the gallers some day, it'll be 'cause the rope ain't long enough to hang him. One o' your scholars, hey ! A pretty lot they must have been, if that's a specimen."

CHAPTER XXVIII.

FAST and faster fell the first snow-flakes. The mountains were wreathed in haze; only their broad bases visible, crowned with firs, pines, hemlocks, and hosts of skeleton elms and beeches. Here and there a fluttering leaf—withered and sapless as a forlorn human heart—rustled wearily by the window to rejoin its fellows. Heaps of these lay crushed and sodden in their annual graves; their bright hues faded with long, lonesome autumnal drenchings. Demis lay mute for hours—often for days—comparatively painless; her thoughts apparently wandering in some fondly remembered past, of which she never spoke. Then a holy calm would settle on her face, and I knew that she was meditating of coming mysteries. At such hours. her mother often endeavored to draw her into conversation upon solemn themes, but the effort was always futile. The antagonism between the two natures could not be thus easily dispelled by confidence. Aunt Rhoda's voice never failed, indeed, to rouse her, but she answered her questionings at random, and sighed with relief when she left the room. Her father sat for hours on the bed's foot, watching her every motion with serious, misgiving eyes. He anticipated every want, and talked confidently of her recovery when winter should have melted into spring; but it was evident that fear mingled largely in the hopeful compound, daily mixed by him and held for her pale lips to swallow. None however seemed to think that she was really treading the very verge of the sunless path we all must enter upon sooner or later, either willing or reluctant voyagers, but Deborah. She shook her head ominously when she heard Uncle Joel's cheering prophecies, muttered unintelligible forebodings, or set up a dismal strain of some ancient hymn—her usual resource when her emotions overpowered words.

One day, after hours of silence, broken only by the coming in and going out of the household, she roused herself to say : "Did I not prophesy rightly ? I knew he would not come !"

"Do you wish to see him, Demis? He is easily sent for, you know."

A radiant smile answered me. "No ! That is all past. I have thought, sometimes, that I must see him once more ; but I do not desire it now. I wonder I ever did. I shall look down upon him from Heaven, as calmly as upon a stranger—only, there will be no strangers there : all will be to me as brothers and sisters, welded to my heart with a spark of the Divine love. Ruby, I have also wondered at the smallness of earthly love. It is all full of self—with occasional pure sparkles in it perhaps, but still gross and calculating. Divine love is purity itself. Judas's gold cannot buy it. The tempter cannot seduce it. Humanity, in its worst form, cannot weary out its long-suffering patience. It is incorrupt and incorruptible. I have felt, sometimes, a brief taste of it. I believe I now love the whole world; at least I desire to; only ignorance will so crowd us into retaliation. Ruby, I used to be a passionate girl. I have hated intensely. I am sorry for it; do you think it will be remembered against me?"

"I have been thinking of Heaven," she said presently. "Oh, Ruby, I have such glorious glimpses of what was once so dark to me. I see the dividing shores between Time and Eternity, and they are not gloomy. My precious sister, it is our blindness that makes them gloomy to us; but we shall slip that off like a garment, as we draw near and nearer. Time fades to a mere speck in the distance. I often fancy that I have left it forever behind, till I open my eyes and see your dear familiar faces still around me."

"My darling, you are talking too much," I said softly.

"No! I do not talk enough. I cannot talk to the ministers, and I rarely see you alone. I love best to *think*, but God gave us our faith to tell to men; not to keep it unused and palsied. Oh! Ruby, I see revealed other mysteries, but a seal is on my lips; I cannot tell you. Oh! it is not a silent country. It is not music which I hear; it is not harps or angelic praises. It is far, far more wonderful, more glorious, more satisfying. It is Divine Harmony." She closed her eyes in a sort of blissful trance, and clasped her wasted palms together; she neither spoke nor moved for several minutes. Annah looked in at the door, but I motioned her away in silence. Presently she said, slowly:

"You think your vision good, Ruby. Imagine it infinitely increasing. Conceive each faculty expanding with never-ending power. Conceive all earthly annoyances, and irritating hindrances, forever abandoned with this frail, ignorant body. Conceive the temporary reign of matter ended, and the immortal reign of mind begun. Then, can you imagine Heaven? No. Do you remember the evening when Natty was brought home? and our talk, that sad, watchful night?"

"I remember many things which were said, dear Demis. We spoke of the future life."

"Yes! Mark thought it a permanent location of the blessed abode of the saints above, and a dread abyss of woe below. He thought one abode ringing with hallelujahs of praise; the other, reeking with fearful curses and endless wailings of the lost. Ruby, every heart that overcomes, and purges itself of a great temptation, a great sin, is a saint—if uncanonized by doctors of divinity upon earth. Notwithstanding *their* limited number of 'The Elect,' I believe there will more saints than sinners stand before the 'judgment-seat.' How can we judge of every soul, every life; encumbered, as we are, with a still greater proportion of fleshly lusts and vain-glorious conceit?

"The schoolmaster thought that heaven was not a country rather one state of mind which made heaven and hell; yet he, too, believed repentance, pardon, impossible beyond the tomb. Reward, certain for the good; and punishment, never remitted, toward the wicked."

"Yes, Demis;" I interrupted. "I remember your startling

them by observing, 'the Bible tells us that heaven is where God is; and it also says, that God is everywhere, even in the depths of hell. Then, of course, that must be a blissful state, call it by what name you will.' I recall, perfectly, their amazement, and Mark's saying quickly, 'Where can she have got such doctrine?' The schoolmaster said, thoughtfully: 'I have some old pamphlets of Parker's works; Miss Demis, have you been dipping into them? They are in my room, I believe.'"

"Yes," assented Demis. "But, Ruby, I had not read his books; I never knew of their existence. That remark came uppermost in my mind, and I made it. It seemed to me the only reasonable conclusion."

"Poor Mark was frightened," I went on. "'Are you a disciple of Theodore Parker?' he asked of the schoolmaster. 'No,' said Mr. Hume. 'But I like to read his works. I do not believe his reasoning. He so glorifies and ennobles nature. There is no God in nature. It is so futile, so earthly, that it falls apart with picking; a will o' th' wisp, it leads the unwary into miry bondage—a bondage unchastened by Divine sovereignty.'"

"I remember, I thought it very fine talk *then*," laughed Demis; "and Olive's question pertinent: 'Why do you read them, then?'"

"Well, Demis, his answer was a good one. 'To profit by their false philosophy. I expect some day—God willing—to be a minister. I must know what arguments to refute, or my preaching will fall to the ground.' I remember that Mark rather solemnly rose and offered his hand to the schoolmaster, saying, 'We are then brothers in Christ Jesus our Lord;' and how heartily Mr. Hume grasped it, responding earnestly, 'I am glad indeed to hear it.'"

"I see," said Demis, smiling, "that you have a good memory; but," she added, doubtfully, "Mark will never be a successful minister; he has no taste or talent for the office," —she hesitated,—"nor Mr. Hume either."

"Mark should be an artist, Demis. What a pity he burned his things!"

"No, I think his passion is for the sea," she returned decisively. "He took to drawing as the next thing to that; but, if you ever noticed, nearly all his sketches were of the sea—purely imaginary of course, yet showing whither his thought tended. He ran away when a little boy, 'to go to Boston,' he said, when father followed and brought him back."

"Why you never told me of that before," I said, in surprise.

"No; I thought it best not; and, in fact, I had nearly forgotten it. I have a faint recollection of the whole scene. Mother was opposed to any mention of it, but Amanda would maliciously speak of it when Mark teazed her too much. Mother has a delusive idea, that the word sailor is synonymous with every thing wicked: profanity, drunkenness, Sabbath-breaking, and so on, through the list of stereotyped vices."

"Stereotyped vices, Demis?"

"Yes. For there are vices just as bad as these, which no one ever thinks of accounting as such, because they affect less strongly our physical well-being. To a sensitive soul they are infinitely worse. Well, Ruby, there is no such thing as persuading mother out of a prejudice, and she labored so zealously to wean Mark's thoughts from a seafaring life, that of course she succeeded; she always does. But he did not forget. Yes," she laughed softly, "Mr. Lee asked him,

a year or two after, what book he should give him for com-
mitting so perfectly to memory the Gospel of St. Luke!
Mark forgot that he should nominate one of a pious character,
and promptly put forward, 'Captain Marryatt's Tales of Ship-
wrecks, if you please, sir,' much to the good Elder's horror.
However, he wisely said nothing, but forwarded next day
by Bessy, 'Doddridge's Saint's Rest,' that exceedingly good
book, which everybody respects and values, but nobody likes
to read. I used to think if I ever had a library, I should have
—for respectability's sake—to put it on one of the shelves;
but I shrank in despair from the thought of its perusal."

"But your mother is equally opposed to his painting."

"Yes; she wants her own way. She is determined that
he shall be a minister, so one he will have to be. That is
the reason of her bitterness toward art. Olive now——"

"Why there she is, coming through the gate," I cried,
springing up.

"Bless her sweet face. It seems an age since we have
seen it."

I met her at the door. "How is she?" nodding her head
in the direction of the keeping-room. I thought her unusually pale and anxious.

"Gradually passing away. Don't start, or look shocked,
when you see how she has changed. It annoys her exces-
sively. And where have you kept yourself, Olive, during
all these weary weeks?"

"Oh!" she said, painfully, "do you not know! I thought
you would have heard."

"I have heard nothing. I have been nowhere to gather
information."

"Well, we are hoping that it.is only a temporary ailment,
that will soon yield to careful treatment and absence from

exciting causes. "It is Avis," she whispered huskily; "her reason is gone completely. She is quite gentle most of the time, but at times she raves fearfully." She removed her bonnet and shawl. "I can stay until evening," she said sadly. "She is quite herself to-day."

I was shocked. "Is it hereditary in your family, Olive?"

"Indeed no," she answered quickly; "we are at a loss to account for it in any other way than these late revival meetings. She is naturally shy, and deeply imaginative. She was one of the first who were convicted, and her anxiety to get relief was intense. We all prayed with her, and for her; we held special prayer-circles on her account, but still she was tormented by her overpowering sinfulness, and could not feel that she was pardoned. She saw others received into the Church, and it made her more earnest in her endeavors. I have frequently heard her up all night, reading aloud from the Bible; walking her room and making such pleading prayers. Ruby, it was enough to move a heart of stone. She fairly wrestled for the blessing, but still it was of no avail. The ministers encouraged these unnatural strivings, and all *we* could say was thrown to the winds. Mother tried to convince her that she *was* accepted, but she said that she knew better. She looked for the sudden peace to fall on her bruised heart,—the great blissful calm of which other converts tell,—and she would have nothing else. Elder Fuller exhorted her to strive until she obtained it, or she would be condemned forever. It haunted her; and oh, Ruby! she at times thinks she *is* damned, when her oaths and revilings are terrible to hear. When in a quiet mood, she abhors all mention or sight of Elder Fuller. If he passes the window, it makes her rave immediately; she thinks him coming to conduct her to torment, and we have been obliged to request him to stay away. We locked up the Bibles from her—for she will read constantly, and dwell upon the denunciatory passages, as particularly applicable to her own case. It was of no use, however. She ran off one day to Mr. Wright's, and told them that we were such heathen that we had not a Bible in the house; begging so piteously for one, that they had not the heart to deny her. She keeps it hidden from us at night."

"It is all because of those exciting meetings," I cried, indignantly; "I wonder there are not *more* made insane by them. It's shameful; it's abominable; it's——"

"Hush! oh, hush!" she entreated, wringing her hands and crying softly. "It's hard enough to bear, Ruby, but I don't feel as *you* do about it. It's the will of Providence, doubtless, for some wise purpose. 'Whom the Lord loveth, he chasteneth,' you know. I need this trial, doubtless; yea, I welcome it gladly, for it sets to rest all my doubts; I know by this scourging, that I am received into the heavenly fold."

"Well," I said, nowise convinced, ".don't mention it to Demis; she is too weak to bear the shock. Oh, Olive! you should hear *her* triumphant creed. You should see how calmly she is treading eternity's marge. Not one anxious thought to distress her: not one sweep of the wind of empty doctrine can overturn the firm, sure foundations of her dying faith."

"Don't the ministers come to talk with her?" she inquired, anxiously.

"Oh, dear! Yes. Every week; and I am weary of their trite exhortations and meaningless prayers. Excuse me, Olive,—but when they roam so over the old monotonous round, seeming never to know how or when to conduct a prudent retreat, I always feel a reckless desire to clip the tangled thread somewhere, anywhere, so it but bring the relief of silence. Now, put on your company face, for here we are at the door, and that sorrowful visage tells its own story."

Demis greeted her friend warmly. She grew cheerful, animated, and all at once, declared her intention of "sitting up." I remonstrated; she had not risen for a week; but she showed me a flash of her old wilful ways, and peremptorily told me "she knew best." So we soon had her snugly ensconced in a soft, warm rocking-chair by the window.

"Now, this is nice!" she cried, delightedly. "You two are my world, and this is our haven of refuge. The sky looks wintry and sullen. The wind moans drearily; but what matter? Inside, all is peacefully secure. Why, it's a step toward the perfect realization of our day-dreams, Ruby," she said gayly. "Ah! those were too extravagant to last."

"And what might they have been?" laughed Olive.

"Oh, the sweetest ones," I interrupted. "Demis, be quiet, pray! You are beside yourself."

"No, you mean I am beside Olive," she laughed, gesticulating absurdly.

"We were to have a nice little nest to ourselves—Demis, Annah, and I—on the whole, my pet, we will admit Olive, I think?"

"Of course," said Demis.

"Thank you," rejoined Olive, demurely. "A compliment from your exclusiveness, certainly; but I will first hear where this miniature Eden is to be located. I reserve my acceptance."

"A lodge in some vast wilderness," sung Demis, saucily.

"Nonsense! Fancy three rooms, neither large nor small in some populous city," I began.

"Of course. · It's a stretch of the imagination; but I can do it," said Olive.

"One, containing a bureau, a wardrobe, two cots, and a rocking-chair; a pretty wall-paper, and a print of · the 'Holy Family.'" Olive laughed provokingly. "Another, contains more chairs; a sofa, an open piano, a round table, thickly strewn with books, magazines, and papers; a well-filled work-basket also stands on it, never lessening, as it ought, the size of its piled up contents. Pure harmoniously tinted landscapes hang on the white walls"—Demis stoutly petitioned for a gorgeously gilded wall-paper; but I for once was invulnerable—"a tiny clock ticks on the mantel, a pretty lamp sheds over the scene a mellow radiance."

"Is it occupied?" inquired Olive, with interest.

"By all means. A dark-eyed lassie with rosy cheeks bends by the pleasant fire-light copying musical score ; humming softly to herself the magical notes which the ready hand transfixes on the paper. Anon, she shakes her head merrily and breaks into a louder warble. Shall I whisper to you of triumphal nights, when, flushed with victory over effort, and her love *for art*, the sweet intoxicating applause of listening thousands ringing in her ears—"

"There, that will do," broke in Demis, with a wistful laugh. "I didn't know that your fancy was so unmercifully vivid."

."Very well, then. Another girl, with disordered attire, and an ink-spot on each finger—pale, haggard, and woe-be-gone—wrinkles her brow convulsively with fruitless effort to embody the embryo thoughts in her brain. She frowns horribly, having a capacity therefor, and casts appealing glances at the fair, lovely landscapes; they smile back on her a calm disdain, and seem to nestle more lovingly together, in their serener intelligence. The sweet voice warbles still; the tiny clock ticks still louder. Then the paper impatiently rustles: 'I cannot do it,' she cries; 'do what I can, the clothed thought in no respect resembles its naked progenitor. It is a weak, miserable, conventional worldling. My book will be a failure.' 'No, indeed, sister!'—a young girl starts from the piano, whence wonderful vibrations have been floating out on the confined atmosphere; and, approaching, drops a kiss on the tired brow;—'there's no such thing as fail to a determined spirit. I have heard you say that, sister, a score of times.' 'Ah, yes! but I may be mistaken,' says the other, wearily. 'It is a rugged path to tread, when not even the anticipation of success waits for one at the end. I abjure literature, and go straightway to shirt-making.' 'At your peril! Put down your work awhile and listen,' and she darts, like a humming-bird, back to her stool; the tiny hands sweep a flood of harmony from the snowy keys. 'Ah! Von Weber is divine!' she murmurs passionately; 'is there any thing like it?' Demis, come and add emphasis to my paltry rendering, with your wonderful voice.' "

"When am I to come into the scene?" inquired Olive, rather ruefully.

"Ma belle, *you* are general superintendent and comptroller of the customs of this fairy household," I returned.

"Do you mean—the housemaid?" she exclaimed, in mock indignation. "Am I to stay in the kitchen?"

"Ah! we forget the kitchen; for we boast one—a mimic affair, but containing, within itself, all essentials for comfort. A little table, spread with the snowiest of damask, the lightest of rolls, the most golden-hued butter—with the usual oak-leaf stamp ; pure, transparent honey, oozing from its perfect cells ; young hyson, steaming fragrantly from the silver urn, also waits to greet us. Then. the long evenings, gliding away into yesterdays, on a pleasurable stream of reading, talking, planning, hoping, singing : very little work—the days are for that. Do you like my picture, Olive !"

"Yes," observed Demis, dreamily ; closing her eyes to imagine it all the more perfectly. "We have passed many wakeful nights in building such unsubstantial domiciles. A piano? I wish I indeed had one," she murmured wistfully. "I never saw one, but it seems as if I could play. I know I could breathe it all out ; all, which, pent up here, threatens to strangle me." She smote her breast softly, then, as if suddenly remembering, opened her eyes with a start. "I feel absolutely strong to-day, girls. I should like to sing a little, if you will choose what you would like to hear."

"Oh," I said quickly, "the first ballad you ever sang to me, 'Barbara Allen.' "

She laughed softly. "I caught it from Deborah. It is one of her old songs." She sang it with tremulous sweetness. At the first strain, Debby opened the door, came in softly ; and as the sad refrain floated away, the tears rolled down her withered cheeks ; she wiped them away with a corner of her apron.

"I know it's foolish, but I can't help it," she said at last, as Demis feebly laughed at her. "It's as true as the grave ; that story is. I heard all about it in the time on't ; long 'afore 'twas set to music."

"Dear me !" whispered Demis, in dismay, glancing out of the window. "Here is Elder Love coming again. It's worse than the inquisition !"

14

"I knew *some*body'd come," said Debby; "for I put two chair-backs together, and dropped my dishcloth, in't the bargain. I never knew 'em to fail."

"He shall not see you if you say so, Demis," I said, with something of a martial air, I suppose, for they all laughed.

"I don't *want* to see him, but I *will*," said Demis, sweetly. "My mother would be displeased, if I made éven a show of objection, and he would never forgive it. Besides, it will soon be over." I could not divine if she referred to the visit, or to her own stay upon earth.

"Good-day, young wimmen!" was Elder Love's solemn greeting, as he entered the room, followed by Aunt Rhoda, and deposited his ungainly bulk on the side of the bed, close to Demis's chair. He ignored our presence further, and immediately opened a conversation with her.

"Has the Lord been graciously pleased to incline your heart unto his testimonies yet, my young friend?" A silence followed. "Do you feel the need of his merciful intercession by this time? or, is your heart utterly given over to the lying and deceitful vanities of the world?" No answer: I was mentally speculating, whether it would not be well enough, if he had an appreciative sense of these vanities, in the shape of clean wristbands—his own were unwholesomely dirty—and I resolved to give him a hint to this effect, if he continued his persecutions to an unwarrantable length.

"What do you consider vanities, Mr. Love?" asked Demis, placidly. Now, he liked to be called Elder; and this plain title by no means suited him. He looked angry, and irefully retorted:

"Irreverence does not become the young; it is unseemly."

Demis looked astonished, but forbore to ask him his

meaning, and after a moment's pause, he proceeded to define vanity. "It springeth from an unregenerate heart, my friend. All carnal wishes and desires for the pleasures of this poor world—singing, dancing, and all manner of like sinful amusements; they are full of abomination in the sight of the Lord."

"Is singing wicked?" I asked, demurely.

"Not singing praises to Him with psalms, and hymns, and sperritual songs, young woman; but from frivolous songs turn thou away. They are a deceitful snare; one of the pits of the Evil One."

"I like them," I said, mischievously, "although I cannot sing them; the more's the pity." He turned on me a wrathful glance.

"Better be thankful, young woman, that you have escaped *one* temptation," he said, severely. He thus continued prodigally sowing good counsel, but in his estimation it was wheat dropped in stony places: not one wayside flower of promise to decorate his spiritual hatband, when he should exultantly appear before his King. All around ran rills of living water, but in our blindness we saw them not; in our ignorant obstinacy we would not sip when offered. We rebuffed the generous donor, and spilled recklessly the priceless drops. We spurned the glad tidings of free grace, and slaked our burning thirst with the briny vintage of death—quaffed with unbelievers. He saw only one road to Paradise; the way *he* trod. "Come with me, or you will be lost," he cried; "those other paths are flowery, and *look* pleasant: but deadly miasma lurks beneath the shade, and they lead to a great gulf called Ruin;"—never heeding the fact that all these diverse paths of our human pilgrimage must be submerged in the intervening river of Death; and that, perchance, *all*

sects, and creeds, and dogmas, will be stripped by the rushing torrent of their earthly significance, their carefully decked apparel of words, and our souls enter the pearly gates beyond, naked in the beautiful simplicity of the religion of Jesus.

Let me do him justice. He was sincere in his appeals.
He labored faithfully, in his convictions of duty. His skirts
were cleared from the blood of the perishing; for wherever
he was—in season and out of season—he broached to them
this subject. It was uppermost in his thoughts, but alas!
pervaded not his life, after the true Christ-like pattern. He
might have preached effectual sermons, simply in living daily
the life of the saints; in wearing around his self-righteous-
ness the mantle of charitable oblivion to others' defects; the
abundant vestments of Christ-like forgiveness.

He remained until over the blue-gray sky slowly dawned a
starless night, and never once was he silent. He reminded
Demis that she was dying, and asked her if she was not appalled at the prospect beyond. With a radiant smile, she
answered " no."

" What blind levity !" exclaimed the zealot. " How can
you face your God ?" She turned towards him as if she
would speak, but remained silent. His cold eyes lighted
with a vengeful gleam. "Go! then," he exclaimed, "and
find out, when too late, that there exists both a heaven
and a hell." He rose and shook himself. What insane fury
prompted him to advance close, close to her side, and shout,
with uplifted hand, as if venting a malediction : "Before the
Most High I swear I am clear of your blood. I have done
my duty. Be it upon thine own head." Then, without even
a farewell look, he seized his hat and departed. As his
slouched hat vanished through the door-way, I turned to look
at Demis : she had fainted.

" It's a burnin' shame and disgrace," said Deborah, as we laid her in bed, and applied restoratives to her white lips; " a keepin' this sick child up three mortal hours a list'nin' to sech truck as *that*. If he darkens the door ag'in, I'll give him a piece o' my mind that he'll remember one spell; that's what I will. I ain't afraid o' the whole boodle on 'em. Got his high-heeled shoes on. Humph! He ought to have a guardeen put over him." She dropped into a chair and folded up her knitting with an angry jerk that made the needles fly out, and the ravelling stitches form a closer acquaintance. " There now!" she said spitefully, surveying it in some dismay, " see *that*, don't ye? That's all b'cause he come here and got me so riled up. It'll take the whole blessed evenin' to pick 'em up; and my sight ain't so good as 'twas once, nuther. I hain't no patience with none on 'em," she exclaimed, wrathfully.

Either the unusual mental excitement of the afternoon's talk, or the prolonged physical exertion of keeping up, proved too much for our dear invalid. A ghastly pallor succeeded the hectic glow, and she lay completely exhausted. But nature might revive. Uncle Joel's distressed look and anxious inquiries were not to be borne; at tea I sent them all away, and remained alone with her. Tears rose involuntarily, as I surveyed the change a few hours had wrought. As if she read my thought, she opened her deep, dark eyes, and looked at me, pityingly. " Dear Ruby," she faintly whispered, " don't weep for me. He does not share my belief, but that is of no consequence; I shall meet him in heaven yet. What will make his happiness there, may not make mine; but we shall all be gathered into the same fold, close to the Infinite heart. One pattern of the robe of righteousness will not fit every soul, but all shall be equally

clothed and satisfied." Olive here came in to say good-night.
Her bonnet tied, she was slowly fitting on her gloves, as she
stood by the bedside. Demis motioned her to stoop. "Don't
go," she whispered faintly, her eye brightening into a contented smile as Olive removed her bonnet. Then she lay motionless, except her eyes, which roved wistfully from Olive's
face to mine, and one small hand nervously clutching the bed-
clothes. Then they turned lingeringly to every object in the
room, as if seeking to faithfully impress their familiar outlines on her failing memory . . . . Through the open
door to the kitchen came the familiar household sounds:
the rustle of the newspaper and the jingle of the snuffer-
tray, as Uncle Joel drew out the little light-stand, and settled
comfortably for the evening's reading; the brisk patter of
Aunt Rhoda's feet—never hushed by sympathy with suffering—bustling around the room, intent on her usual cares of
"setting to rights" the disturbed elements of housewifery
for the night; Dwight's heavy tread, as he tied on his comforter and searched fruitlessly for his missing hat, preparatory
to a walk to "the village;" and Debby who, as she briskly
washed the dishes, sang to their pleasant clatter a solemn
accompaniment:

> "Judge not the Lord by feeble sense,
>   But trust him for his grace;
> Behind a frowning Providence,
>   He hides a smiling face."

Divine words which have soothed many a sorrow! Demis's eyes lighted with serene joy, as the solemn measure
rolled through the room. She put forth her hand and essayed to rise. I bent over and partially lifted her. "Why, when
did Natty come home, Ruby? He is here!" she whispered,
exultantly; and fell back suddenly upon the pillow—the

crimson life-tide surging in a torrent from her pale, parted
lips. She looked in my face with beseeching eyes. I could
not comprehend the glance, but as I held the napkins to her
mouth I pointed to the door. "Should I summon the household?" She feebly shook her head. Then I flung my arms
around her and buried my face by hers in the pillow. Oh,
precious moments, wasting fast! life ebbing from our loved
one's only strand; our remaining selves fast on the shores of
vain regret and longing! In that fast embrace I sought still
to bind her life to its earthly tenement. The vista of separation had seemed immeasurably removed before : this sudden shortening of the distance was cruel, cruel ; and the sobs,
so long repressed for her dear sake, burst forth loud, long,
and vehement.

The rest is borne in upon my mind like a lightning flash.
It was so swift, so sudden—she turned her cheek to mine
with a fond movement, and held forth her hand to Olive, who
knelt sobbing by the bedside. Then Olive hastily rose and
forced me away; for the hand had grown icy in her clasp.
This, this was death.

Olive stole gently to the kitchen and informed the family.
A pause of several minutes followed; to me it seemed
an age. Deborah then burst into a flood of tears, and set
up an agonized moaning. Aunt Rhoda remained calm as
marble, and began speaking at once of the necessary last sad
preparations, which brought to my recollections, as if it were
but yesterday, the scene of my early orphanage. She dispatched poor Dwight—who stood rooted to the door with
awe—for assistance. He came to me, and in a faint tremulous whisper, inquired " who he should get?"

" If you don't mind the long ride, I wish Miss Sinai would
come," I answered ; and he turned away, treading on tiptoe,

as if to avoid waking the silent form, never, alas! to rouse
from this dreamless slumber. Dear Uncle Joel was almost
paralyzed. He had not realized how near the shadow had
so long lingered: its descent found him unprepared.

"Her life was brief," murmured Sinai, as we stood alone,
late in that night-watch by the shrouded form. "She was
young to die!"

"Oh, dear, dear Sinai, it will kill me!" I sobbed and panted
hopelessly. "Why can I not die too, and go with her?
This life is so long;—so long to live without her!"

"Be comforted, dear child," she rejoined, soothingly.
"This life is brief at the longest. Ah! Ruby, by such
tender cords of looking and longing for our lost treasures,
our Father seeks to draw us into the path of holy effort.
You shall go to her—she will wait for you there—in *His* own
good time. You, who were inseparable in your lives, shall
not be divided in death. See how peacefully she slumbers,
with the seal of the Divine covenant resting lightly on her
brow."

Standing face to face with a dying or dead friend, how
vividly all their beliefs, maxims, advice, and tenderness—
manifested in a thousand ways, and before unappreciated—
crowd upon our consciousness! They seem more individualized, as it were, by this approach to the Eternal: photo-
graphing, in those few moments of intensity, their moral
shape upon our memories, to remain with us forever. Now,
Demis's bright faith flashed into my comprehension, as something altogether new; and as something strangely real, true,
comforting. And, as if a similar intuition—too vague to be
called a thought—entered into Miss Sinai's mind, she said—
and with ear and mind tuned akin to this suddenly developed
relation, her voice sounded like a musical echo of Demis's

own—"Oh! my dearest Ruby, let us cease to mourn, and give joy; joy, that the life-struggle *is* brief, else would our footsteps falter, and the crown of thorns press too heavily, ofttimes, on our bleeding brows. One truth glows in the moral firmament with a quenchless fire. Not all the cold, dry dogmas which clumsily stalk earth's highways, can abate one whit its genial heat, or dim its eternal shine. 'God is love!'"

CHAPTER XXIX.

THE little white church, with its quaint diamond-paned windows and square high-backed pews, was crowded with sympathizing friends and neighbors, the afternoon of the third day following; for Demis had been a universal favorite. All loved her frank cheery face and truthful ways, and all mourned her sincerely. Groups of young girls had filled the house, after hearing the sad tidings, bringing buds and flowers from cherished house-plants, to lay on the pulseless breast. Mark arrived from Chispa, almost broken-hearted that he had not been summoned before. Amanda, who came down to stay, broke out of her usual lethargy, and wept spasmodically, whenever a fresh band of neighbors arrived—calming into a resigned expression immediately after their departure. Annah, poor child, refused all comfort: she would climb upon the bed, and wind her small arms around the cold form, while she poured forth the most heart-rending cries. She fretted herself quite ill, and on the day of the funeral looked so weak and pallid that I left her at home, Miss Sinai volunteering to remain and keep her company.

14*

I was surprised to see Elder Love in the pulpit; it was an unusual custom for the minister of one denomination, to preach from the desk of another. Elder Fuller chose a seat below, after reading a beautiful Psalm from David. Mr. Love then rose, and solemnly announced, as his text, Psalm vii., 12. "If he turn not, He will whet His sword: he hath bent his bow, and made it ready." Strange, stern resolve slept in his eye, and twitched the muscles of his mouth, as he proceeded. He pictured, in emphatic language and terrific tones, the awful meaning lurking in these words. He held up before us the merciful long-suffering of the Judge of all the earth, and endeavored to define its limit; then, in graphic tones, the whetting of His anger and the extinction of its object. Then he applied this text to the case of the deceased. She had been unusually favored with counsel, with timely warnings of her dangerous course; but she gave them no heed. Instead, she had laughed and exulted with thoughtless gayety on the very brink of death. The child of many prayers, she yet scorned prayer, and clung madly to the rotten plank of good works for finding acceptance with her Saviour. Of the existence of faith— without which, we cannot be saved—she had no practical knowledge. She sat in the seat of the scorner, and walked in the ways of the ungodly. "My friends," he uttered, in a hoarse whisper, "do you know her fate?" Not a soul stirred among the throng but Mark, who half rose, his face of ashen hue; but remembering himself, sank back again in his seat. "Do you know her fate?" he impressively repeated, rolling those cold orbs above, as though he saw there, in terrible reality, her doom. "Much as I would like to say something consoling to this stricken group; much as I would like to pronounce a eulogy on the dead, yet, for the sake of the

living impenitent young, I must speak the truth. I do
know her fate. I see her knocking at the gates of the New
Jerusalem, in vain, in vain! My friends, her virtues carry
her there; she had many; you all loved her. These sobs,
now convulsing you, all attest that fact. Weep then for her
freely; weep for her sad end, for she has no passport with
which to enter the Father's mansions, and the angel at the
gate admits no soul without one. You will ask, What then,
is a passport to future bliss? I answer, to be baptized and
believe on the Lord Jesus Christ. There is none other.
Nay, ere she can even petition for entrance, the demons
seize her, with shrieks of delight. Just like this,"—he lowered his eyes, and turned to the doors of entrance, on either
side of the pulpit,—"one door is heaven; the other, hell.
She is at the gate of heaven, but the infernal host are not
to be baulked of their prey. One demon seizes her; the
clutch is eternal; then another. She is surrounded by the
satanic army, amid unavailing repentance and cries for help.
My hearers, do you now ask where she is? I will tell you;"
—slowly and with emphasis—"there is no intermediate state
between the abode of the saints in glory, and the regions of the
lost. She disappears through the other door, where, from
the awful, unsounded depths arises weeping, wailing, and
gnashing of teeth, forever and forever! Oh! the agony, the
fearful agony of 'the second death!' Souls that are immortal,
pause ere it be too late! Reflect, or a like doom awaits
you!"

There followed more, in the self-same style, I suppose, for
of it I heard not one word. My eyeballs seemed flame; my
mind in a helpless chaos of apathetic, revengeful fury. Had I
possessed the requisite physical power, I believe I should
have deliberately risen, walked up the narrow pulpit stairs,

and with one blow hurled him from the sacred height, defiled
by his presence.   Then, smitten by this thought of inability,
I looked round icily on the tear-stained pallid faces, and for
a moment hated them for their quiescence.   Never before
had I experienced in such dread intensity, the fell passions
of eternal hatred and revenge; but they burned into my heart's
core, there searing a ghastly wound, easy enough since to re-
open. "This, then," I bitterly reflected, while his unholy tirade
went on triumphantly, " is your mean retaliation for her calm
indifference to your proselyting zeal.   A spiteful tincture of
the pit you so strongly anathematize, could alone give it
birth.   Elder Fuller, though zealous for additions to the
Church, could never feel it!   Ah! sanctified clothing will
not prevent Satan's claiming his own in due season."   As the
reading of the last hymn proceeded, a violent trembling of the
seat roused me from my revery.   I turned to look.   Uncle
Joel's face was crimson from suppressed emotion; but he
grasped the seat firmly and restrained himself.   Would you
have the hymn?   It was this: incredible as it may seem to
your more Christian ears.   With slow, deliberate earnestness
he gave it out: " Hymn 50.   To the old proper tune.   Pause
the First:

> " 'I am the Saviour!   I, th' Almighty God!
>   I am the Judge! ye heavens proclaim abroad
>   My just, eternal sentence, and declare
>   Those awful truths that sinners dread to hear!'
>   When God appears, all nature shall adore him!
>   While sinners tremble, saints rejoice before him.
>
>   'Stand forth thou bold blasphemer, and profane,
>   Now feel my wrath, nor call my threatenings vain.
>   Thou hypocrite! once dressed in saints' attire;
>   I doom thee, painted hypocrite, to fire!'

Judgment proceeds : hell trembles ! heaven rejoices !
Lift up your heads, ye saints, with cheerful voices.

'Behold my terrors now ; my thunders roll,
And thy own crimes affright thy guilty soul !
Now, like a lion shall my vengeance tear
Thy bleeding heart, and no deliverer near.'
Judgment concludes · hell trembles ! heaven rejoices !
Lift up your heads, ye saints, with cheerful voices."

Profound silence followed. To the credit of the choir be it spoken, they unanimously refused to sing it. Demis had been the leading singer there for years ; her sweet voice waking vibrations of harmony, which they caught and repeated. Not one among them but was weeping for the vacant place, draped in crape. The viol leaned mournfully by the side of its bass fellow ; their strings mute and indignant. Elder Fuller broke the pause—dreadful in its intensified misery—by reading calmly a more appropriate hymn, and the services concluded by lowering the cold form into the colder earth.

"Dear me," exclaimed Miss Sinai, in dismay, as we re-entered the shadowed dwelling, "what is the matter? You all look strangely."

No one replied. Deborah beckoned her aside, and a low whispering succeeded, broken occasionally by angry interjectional phrases. In truth, we looked a stern band of mourners ; not an eye closed in slumber that night in the old farm-house. Uncle Joel sobbed, and wrung his old withered hands nervously. "I never would a thought it," he said again and again ; "I can't walk with such a church no longer." Strange to say, Aunt Rhoda alone maintained its truth. "I believe it," she-said, firmly ; "it's good orthodox doctrine. it's only because it comes hum so plain, that you don't like it, Joel. If it had been one of our neighbor's children now, you *know* you'd a said nothin' agin' it."

"Yes, I should, too," he rejoined, mildly; "common humanity'd set me' agin' sech talk." Aunt Rhoda pursed up her mouth into a most decided expression, and shook her head slowly, to intimate that she was not disposed to argue the point; but she should hold positively to her first opinions. "Wall," sobbed her softer-hearted husband, "I want to go where our children go, Rhody. I shouldn't take a mite o' comfort singing praises onless they was all round me too. Should you, Rhody?"

"Yes," she declared, unwaveringly; "I don't think 'twill make a bit of difference to *our* happiness. We shall overcome earthly feelings when we leave the body. I'm afraid, Mr. Martin," she added, severely, "you hain't experienced the right kind o' religion after all, or else you're backslidin'. It's high time you'se up and workin' in the Lord's vin'yard, lest the enemy of unbelief git in and spile the good crops. I hope these girls'll reflect on' t too. It's a lesson to *them*," she added, turning to me.

Mark paced the kitchen through the live-long night, never pausing to heed the fragments of controversy floating around. However, he heard this conjugal debate; and, as if his mind had suddenly decided a vexed question, with a look of relief and angry scorn, he wheeled in front of his mother. "Is *that* your belief, and the creed of your church? By heavens, I abjure it utterly! I wonder the judgments you are so fond of talking about don't fall and destroy such scandalous mockery!" he cried, passionately. "I tell you that I denounce it, and renounce it utterly. If there is a heaven and saints in it, my sister is there! Sweet soul! She never wronged a worm. I say with my father, I go with her hand

in hand, wherever that may be. Now, hear my deliberate
conclusion : for *your* sake, my mother, I have renounced
my own wishes ; suppressed every rising inclination, and
adopted your own. I would have labored cheerfully on that
account for the conversion of souls, but you say *this* is the infernal doctrine I must preach, for I have sworn assent to it in
the creed of the church. I tell you no !"—here Debby interposed to stop him, but he roughly pushed her away, and resumed with gathering wrath : " I renounce such assent forever.
I renounce the ministry forever. I renounce home forever.
I renounce *your* heaven forever and ever and ever." His
mother grew pale as death. Never had I seen her so shaken.

" What do you mean, sir ?" she demanded, hoarsely.

" I mean, madam, that in a week from to-night I hope to
be beyond the reach of these detestable influences. I hope
to be my own master. I will not again change my mind," he
said, firmly.

" And Olive ?" I timidly questioned.

" My cousin," he answered, " she doubtless believes this infernal sermon It will break our engagement. I cannot help
it. I shall be sorry, but there are things even worse than
that," he cried, desperately. " Oh ! is there no sanctity, no
rest for the dead, that they must be jostled so roughly ! How
many themes for warning discourses will this one affliction
furnish to your ministers, mother ?" He laughed hysterically,
and resumed his walk. Aunt Rhoda leaned her head thoughtfully on her hand and made no reply. Uncle Joel groaned
heavily. Mark went up to him, looking almost penitent :

" I forgot *you*, father. Can you forgive me for disappoint-
ing your hopes ?"

" My son ; my well-beloved son. You're all leaving me,"
he whispered brokenly. " But, ' go thy way in peace.' It

would have rejoiced my old heart to have heard you preach-in' the word; but not such doctrine as that. No, no!"

The succeeding day was irksome in the extreme. The dull hours crept lifelessly away, in our vain attempts to quicken their flight. Mark went up to Mr. Pierce's in the afternoon, and did not return until dark. Deborah went about her work much as usual, ever and anon humming in a mournful tone, some chance fragment of a funeral hymn. As the early twilight of winter fell, I crept into the keeping-room—deserted now, and silent: the useless bed removed; the odor of medicine vanished. The room had been thoroughly fumigated that day; put into cleanly primness, and shut up, as though haunted. As I sat in the darkness, by the newly kindled fire, Mark entered.

" Ah !" he said, gloomily dropping into a chair, " I thought I should find you here. *You* are not afraid of sitting in this dear room ; *you* don't shun it."

"Well! and how fared your visit?" I tried to speak cheerfully.

He sighed. "Oh, just as I expected. I was received cordially enough at *first*," laughing sarcastically, " but the tune changed quickly, when I broached my change of pur-pose. So be it, Ruby. I have got over caring much for any thing."

" I hope not, Mark! But tell me about it. Did they up-braid you ?"

" No. I was prepared for a pretty stormy scene, but not for cold indifference. Ruby, it cut me to the heart; then I got angry." We hate people for cutting us, albeit the thrust is unconsciously given. " I wanted to see Olive alone, but her mother vetoed that measure ; I suppose she thought I should try to make her run away with me. Well, it is all ended. .That crazy girl shook her fist in my face, and called me 'one of the ungodly,' and the rest, 'hoped I would do well.' Won't I, though?" he rejoined, enthusiastically, straightening his manly form, and tossing back the clustering locks from his noble forehead. The face. always frank and truthful, looked the better for its new shade of sad, thoughtful serenity. "I love the sea," he murmured. "I have lain many a night, dreaming of its music. I like stories of sailors too, bluff and hearty; I tell you, Ruby, there is nothing like it."

I shook my head. "I don't know. There are many things I should like better."

"Oh!" he started, as if suddenly recollecting. "What are your plans for the future, Ruby? or have you none, as yet?"

"No plans, Mark; only crude cogitations, and, they may develop into nothing more. I wish I could leave Northfield!" Spite of my effort, this burst forth fretfully.

"Where would you go, Ruby?" he said, in surprise.

"Where? I don't know. The world is large enough. I must *see* before I can tell. Fate and I must have a hand-to-hand conflict. Why not begin?" He did not understand me. How could he? I forced back the rising flood—was.it destined to forever lie dormant?—with a keen sense of pain. At what? Why, I could never have told you, had sympathy's key been lacking in your hands. I felt; I did not reason. Then I managed to calmly return to the broken theme. "When do you go, Mark?" I said.

"I have sent in to the conference, at Chispa, a brief account of my altered purposes, and I expect a reply to-morrow, probably a stern decree of banishment. Then I shall leave immediately."

He did not receive the expected missive the next day;

nor yet the next. On the morning of the third, he told me that it was all as he had predicted.

. "I have no idea of stealing off without bidding *you* good-by," he said; "but it is better that my parents should not know; and Debby too. Poor soul! she would go frantic, and might break my good resolves. I shall go, this very night, to the next station, and from there take the early stage for the East. I will knock at your door before I start."

I was a sound sleeper in those days, and I resolved to sit up. Ere midnight, his low rap sounded. I opened quickly. He entered, bent over and kissed Annah softly.

"Dear little Annah! She looks pale, Ruby; take care of her." Brave heart, that, in the bitterness of the first real home-parting, found tender words of care for others! He talked on fast, to appease the treacherous desire to weep, shown in the trembling mouth. "I wish, Ruby, you would see that my trunk is sent to this destination," handing me a slip of paper. "It is quite ready."

"Yes, dear Mark. Is there nothing else?" How I wished that he would overwhelm me with orders! Memory, thus occupied, might let slip the coming pain.

"No, I think not," he answered slowly. "You see I am cautious," he held up his boots. "I shall wait until I get outside, before I put them on. Don't think of coming down with me; you might wake Debby." He dropped his bundle, opened his arms, and gathered me to his heart, sobbing, in a close embrace: "God bless, and forever keep you from all harm," he murmured, "for *she* loved you!" Sweet benediction, succeeded by a kiss.

"Oh, Mark, is it right to go, after all? Stay with us; we shall be so lonely!" I pleaded.

. "It is harder to go than I thought for, Ruby; but I will

not change my resolve. Good-by." As if fearful of a
longer tarry, he glided down the dark staircase. Bending
over the banisters, I saw him tread softly the creaking
boards of the kitchen in his bootless feet; I heard the outer
door softly unlatched, closed,—and out into the wintry midnight went forth our wanderer.

There was a storm of questions and reproaches, the next
morning, when I told them of Mark's departure. Aunt
Rhoda called him "an ungrateful brat," declaring, that her
"children were turning out jest as she allers expected. She
s'posed 'twas too strict to hum to suit." She was too
angry to feel grieved, and tossed her head in scorn, at every
mention of his name. Then Deborah, with quivering lips,
took her up irefully, telling her decidedly, that "she had
driven him away herself. She might blame her own blessed
self for what had happened; no one else under the sun,
would a talked as *she* did, that night; 'twas enough to rile a
saint's disposition, to set an' hear it. For her part, she
thought 'twas a judgment *on* her."

Aunt Rhoda responded bitterly, and an angry scene ensued between the two. "I've borne with your insolence
long enough," she said, with pale lips. "You'd make an
underlin' of me in my own house; or, p'raps you think I
ain't mistress. You're allers a talkin' 'bout your children.
I've said it now, and I *mean* it."

"I'm sure I'm only too thankful to go," retorted Debby.
"There's not much to stay for, and ev'ry thin's gittin' wuss
and wuss. There's plenty that'd jump at the chance o'
gittin' me to work for 'em. To think a *mother* should have
no more feelin' for her own flesh an' blood—" Debby
broke short off, in piteous tears. "To think you should be
jealous of *me* too!"

Aunt Rhoda replied; but, in the middle of her harangue, her meek husband for once interposed: "I wish you'd stop. This ain't suitable talk for children to hear. Dwight, if you've finished your breakfast, you'd better go and *see after* the cows. Ruby, *you'd* better take Anny up stairs." I obeyed; but, as I crossed the room, I heard him say, decisively, "Deb'rah ain't goin' away. Say no more 'bout *that.*" What more was said I know not; but for a full hour the sound of mingled voices reached me; now sunk to a murmuring key, anon raised in sharp, sudden tones of contradiction.

Mark's trunk was sent according to directions. Debby unstrapped it; privately hunting the house over for a key to fit its lock. Then she repaired to the neighbors; finally successful, she opened it, and after indulging in a hearty cry over the vision it revealed—a scant wardrobe and his books—she dexterously set to work, filling every vacant corner with cakes—crowding down and pressing together with her broad palms—so that, when her labor was fairly ended, the trunk's surface revealed a curious mosaic of clothes, books, cakes, and pastry. "There! that'll do his eyes good, I guess, when he sees it," she pronounced, in a tone of gratification. "He'll know who had a hand in it, right off; but won't he wonder how I got into it. I'll bet a copper he'll have a crying spell over it!" And, fairly overcome by this probability, she sat herself down with considerable effort on the floor beside it, and recommenced sobbing.

"Don't you tell Mis' Martin 'bout this ere business, Ruby. She'd take my head off for'zi know; but Mr. Martin provides, so I don't feel as if I's doin' anythin' out the way." She wiped her eyes, with a resigned expression of duty, and briskly shut down the lid. "Oh! Ruby," she began, dole-

fully, "I haint no gift nor nothin' these days. I don't git
cast down once in a dog's age, but somehow latterly—."
She broke off, as a sudden thought crossed this train, to say,
"I guess Jesse Warner's goin' to hire you this season to
keep school ag'in. Miss Charity ain't rugged 'nough yit.
What a sight o' trouble that fam'ly sees. If there ever *was*
a saint on earth it's that Miss Siny. She's a proper hand
when one's in trouble to make 'em feel contented. I b'lieve
she'd say 'twas the Lord's will, and marvellous in our sight,
if ev'ry friend she had should up and die, and the house be
burnt over her head, int'the bargain. I don' know but it's
wicked, but I've often thought, what a good wife she'd a
made for Job. 'Taint often two such patient souls git
together."

"I wish I could board with them," I remarked, thoughtfully.

"Who? Job and Siny?"—she shook with laughter—
"Law, Ruby. I ain't a fool. I know what you *meant*, and
I'll speak to Jess 'bout it. He said you could have a
stiddy boardin' place. I heerd him."

CHAPTER XXX.

THERE are moments in our lives of dreary suspense; of
uncertain ignorance of our future—a crisis, as it were—
ready, yet reluctant, to break the hateful cords of monotony
binding us to a seeming present necessity. I trudged home
from Mr. Warner's one night, only to feel a vague sense of
this, instead of the anticipated joyous welcome. Desolate
looked the wintry landscape under the gray enveloping sky.

Greybaul towered stern and gloomy, in a thick shroud, above
the low farm-house. No signs of life were visible; not even
a cat ran across the yard, or a discontented hen showed
itself at the open barn-door; only a faint wreath of blue
smoke exhaled from the mammoth chimneys, and a light in
the kitchen, like a beacon star, guided me to its door. Yet
it seemed cheerful, compared with the atmosphere within.

"Yes," said Debby, when we were alone together, " Anny
can't stir but what it's : 'Make less noise, can't you ? You're
enough to craze a nation.' She's tied right down to work the
whole livelong time—what for ? massy only knows; I don't.
Between you and me, Ruby, it seems as though Mis' Martin
grew peakeder and peakeder ev'ry day. She can't put up
with nothin'; and Anny breaks out a singin' 'fore she thinks.
I can see it don't set the best kind on her stomach. Then
she don't like stents over 'n above board (I don't blame
her, nuther); and *that* puts your aunt terrible out o' sorts,
if you only knew it. 'Twas only the other day she said
to me, ' This comes of keeping folks from goin' to the poor-
house.' I d'clare for't *that* riled me; I flared right up then.
'How'd you like to have *your'n* treated so ?' si; ' mabbe
they will be some day. You can't expect to live fo'ever !' It
was sarcy, I knew ; but how could I help it, I'd like to know ?
If she don't haul in her horns, I'll light on her again."

" No, Debby," I said, rather bitterly, " she shall not have
occasion to say so much longer."

" Wall, I won't stan' by and see her 'bused. She never
whips her when Mr. Martin's round; I know the reason too ;
she can't pull wool over my eyes," declared Debby. " I
don' know as she *means* it r'ally. She'll put some salve on,
when it's likely to be a witness aginst her—that salve though's
as hard as Pharo's heart; jest about—she allers *was* a 'mazin'

hand to whip an' pound: for my part, I don't b'lieve in't. Wall, then, she won't let her sleep with me; she'll make her go off in the dark, for fear she'll set the house afire if she has a candle. I don' know how she's the heart to do it. *I* couldn't, if I hated a body the wust way."

Sleep did not visit my eyelids that night. I zealously fed anger by pondering these unexpected events—trying to bring to light the hidden remedy. Vain effort! The path before me looked shorter and narrower than ever. I felt that I must quickly traverse it; but my eager glance saw no way-side outlet to highways beyond: only the same dead mono-tony, bounded by impenetrable thickets which I might not hope to scale. I look back now to those restless plans, pro-ductive of naught but chill discomfort, with a vague feeling of pity for the ignorance which entailed them. For it is not amid the tumult of conflicting passions that the mind wakes to clear life, and shapes its course of action; only the dregs of ambition are stirred thereby, and the muddy waters must settle calmly, ere Reason, stern and pale, can effectively counsel.

It was evident that my aunt's injudicious harshness was producing the result of a nervous derangement in the child, that in after years might be difficult to check. She did not consider that sending her solitary to bed, in a cold silent room, from which death had so recently snatched one occu-pant, while it would not in the least affect her own nerves, might affect Annah's more sensitive ones fatally. I think my aunt's bereavements, following each other so suddenly, had rendered her naturally harsh nature morose. Perhaps she grudged that the two orphans should be spared, and her own offspring taken. I did not wonder at it. I had, I trust, sufficient charity for the doer, while condemning the deed itself. Sturdily vindictive I assuredly was; but only to persistent, ungenerous unkindness.

The two graves in the churchyard grew green in the summer showers. I planted wild roses around them, and studded their tops with violets. In the long dreamy afternoons, it was a sad pleasure to visit them; clearing away the rank mullein and dandelions which perseveringly threatened usurpation. Uncle Joel often followed, and watched my work in silence. Dear loving old man! If I sought his face with a questioning glance, he smiled approvingly, and turned away. His staff had worn a series of indentations in the soil round them, for his visits were daily. Aunt Rhoda never accompanied him. It was her custom to stop there, on her way home from Sunday services, for a brief inspection. Her meditations amid these crumbling relics of mortality were characteristic. She wandered carelessly among the narrow grassy paths, taking a critical survey of each tenement—audibly recalling incidents in the lives of the deceased incumbents, not always of the most appropriate nature for discussion. "I allers told Joel," she was accustomed to say, "that, if I should go first, I was perfectly willin' he should marry agin'; only I want he should wait long enough to be decent. I want my shoes to have a chance to cool 'fore another woman steps into 'em. He allers declares, right up an' down, he never'd marry ag'in; but, law me! he *would*. They all act like possessed, and make perfect fools o'themselves over ev'ry young gal that comes along, I allers said, if I had my life to live over ag'in, I'd marry a widower; they know how to 'preciate a wife after they've lost one."

This summer's placidity was broken by a visit from Mr. Hume. I felt no desire to see him. Deep down in my heart rankled unforgiving bitterness; for I could not forget that but for him my cousin Demis might have been flitting, blithe and merry as of old, around the old homestead. And why could he not have returned her pure affection!—won too openly for his own vindication. "Man's love," thought I, bitterly, "is but a caprice; retained best by repulses, coyness, distrust—often by positive dislike. It likes shady nooks and cold surfaces, and treats with unappreciative disdain rich, fertile prairies of feeling; the sunny, open glade, where grow spontaneous clusters of the fairest flowers. Well," I thought, as I stealthily surveyed him, "I want none of your love. I feel no thrill of tenderness for you. Even your virtues depreciate, in my sight, below redemption. Your defects stand forth more prominently than of old: that creeping smile has hardened to a sneer; its benevolent life warped into surface coldness. The longer I gaze, the more it seems as if I knew you not. Some friendly film has dropped from my eyes, rendering their vision keener. Distrust—the guardian-angel of the inexperienced—has uncovered her talons, and planted one in my heart."

He remained several days in Northfield, meeting warm greetings in the farm-house; but they could not feel as I did, because they were ignorant of what I knew. Debby, it is true, sometimes hinted of her foresight, evidently desiring to enlarge at length, and, if possible, draw from me confirmation of her suspicions. She reported significant dreams and marvellous signs; but I steadfastly discouraged such disclosures, shortened such conversations, and faithfully kept my dead cousin's secret. I avoided meeting Mr. Hume alone, and on all occasions, treated him with coldness; if it piqued him, he discovered no evidence thereof in his manner.

One day—a bright, cool afternoon—he came down sud-

15

denly, with an urgent request for a walk. I gave him a curt
negative.

"Sartain," cut in Debby, quickly, "you can go as well's
not, Ruby. There ain't no chores to do up, but to mend the
stockin's, and them I allers do myself. I allers darn with a
double 'thread, but Mis' Martin don't; I can beat her a
darnin', any day."

I repeated my answer; he turned away, looking cut to
the heart. "Very good," I thought, grimly surveying his
crimsoned visage; "that don't suit, does it, my master?
You gave poor Demis many such thrusts; now I intend to
return them with interest." As he turned away silently, a
flash of repentance smote me, almost retracting the uncivil
words and the bitter after-thoughts : I suppressed it speedily.
My conscience, however, once pricked with remorse, would
not let me rest. I could not help thinking that Demis would
not thus have acted. Could her pure spirit look from celestial heights, and penetrate the earthly vapor enveloping my
soul, she would be immeasurably grieved at my perversity.
Surely, the civil request merited equal civility; a walk would
not have harmed me, much as I despised him. The thought,
once started, pressed harder over the ground, and fairly ran
down my unusual haughtiness. After trying in vain to sew
calmly, I gave it up, and tried reading, with no better success. My own reflections crowded on the page thick and
fast; very confused and hideous looked their ranks as I surveyed them, and, captain over the throng, brooded sullen revenge. I could not absolutely detest him: the past was too
rich in reminiscences for that; but I flattered myself that I
had arrived at the climax of contempt, which breeds hate
readily enough. The book, too, was one he had brought
me—long coveted, but the donor hardly thanked for making

the desire a possession. I turned the leaves slowly, passing, I suppose, an hour or two in this employment; then I closed the book, and leaning my elbow on the window-sill, and my head on my hand, I listened willingly to the still small voice of repentance. The surroundings were favorable for such reflection. I was alone. Aunt Rhoda had taken her knitting and departed for an afternoon visit. Annah had early petitioned to be permitted to "go and see Olive." Debby had taken her basket of yarns and the pile of mutilated hose, out on the piazza, where, as she slowly passed the long needle in and out of the huge rents, she sang to herself in a dreamy monotone. Occasionally she paused to remove her spectacles and wipe their dimmed glasses, as some sad recollection surged up with the mournful cadence and moistened her eyes. It was too dreary to be longer borne. Strong in my desire to do justice where I had deeply wounded—ah, reader, reluctant, after all, to admit one tenderer plea—I started, and, seizing my sun-bonnet, walked slowly to the gate. Debby ceased her humming, and gazed after me with a questioning glance. I opened, went out, and shut it deliberately, pausing a moment in fastening down the latch, to ask myself if it were best to retreat ere a single battle had been fought. I half opened it again, to re-enter the house; but, glancing up, I caught Debby's look of intense curiosity—she had stolen to the front windows, to watch my proceedings— and I resolutely turned, walking with a rapid step to the village. I entered the humble gateway of the churchyard. As I expected, Mr. Hume was standing, with uncovered head, by a well-known grave. My dress rustled over the long grass. He turned quickly. "Ah, Ruby," he exclaimed, sorrowfully, "you scorn my very presence; you utterly despise me; but is love so cheap, that you can thus recklessly fling it to the winds? At least, be a just judge before you pronounce sentence. Hear me!"

Strange place for such a declaration. I can no more remember what next he said, than I can recall the events of the first unimpressive year of my life. The comparison is ill-chosen: the very rush of the wordy torrent smote memory into helplessness. I have a dim idea of a succeeding stormy burst of passion, reeking with vehement protestations, entreaties, and pleadings, as he knelt in the rank grave foliage, and with trembling eagerness sought my hand. His look, more than his words, rolled in upon my questioning consciousness, bringing in its wake a long train of assents. The mist was clearing from my heart: its motives, so long flattered into a belief of their generous self-sacrifice, looked more terrestrial. I looked eagerly inward during that brief space, only to behold, with a volition not of my approval, his image firmly stamping itself there. Love came to me, not a mere feeble child to be fostered into ardent maturity ; he sprang, vigorous and of full stature, at once to his throne in my heart. Thus, though I battled bravely against one spark of truant tenderness, thinking it a wrong to the sleeper at our feet, I could not resist the flood from rolling over the thirsty desert. It carried with it all sign of opposition, but under its waves distrust still lingered. Then I heard his voice stealing in upon returning attention, softly, like a dream of music saying, "Let us court happiness while yet we may. Let us be all the world to each other," and my heart silently answered, "Oh! if I could efface the memory of wrong, love would be so easy." Borne down I was by his strong asseverations, but not convinced.

" Life is but short at best ; and who can tell what dark clouds may linger over our future horizon?" again I heard him saying.

What ill-omened words were these, after such a confession? What mystery was this man, who one moment woke responsive echoes to his own wild pleading—almost a murmur of assent—the next, as with a sudden after-thought, frowne l back to the farther shores the full-freighted, coming wave? I was mortified to perceive the incongruity between this speech and the preceding; the truly selfish reason' for indulging in happiness—fragile thing—to be shattered by a wave of adversity. I thrust back the skeptical thought defiantly.

" Why seek for dark probabilities, when bright ones are just as cheap, and far more agreeable?" He smiled indulgently; and I felt a damp cloud settling gradually over my springing hopefulness. We walked around to the church steps and sat down. Then followed long consultations—all on *his* part; *I* was only expected to quietly accede—in the gathering evening shadows. The scene rises before me now like a once seen, dimly remembered picture. The glimmering walls of the church for a ' background; before, and at the sides, the serried ranks of the dead, with their ghastly tablets; while far, far above, rose a deep blue vault, hung, here and there, with a stray evening lamp, the faint disc of a crescent moon illuming its centre. Life seemed to eddy away farther and farther, in the solemn stillness; and all talk of material hopes, fears, happiness, sheer impracticability, mere idle tattle. Old mother Nature is a grand confidante. Into her sympathizing ears are poured, what wondrous secrets! She listens in silence, hiding them deep down in her inmost heart. But think her not neglectful of responses. She twinkles approval or doubtfulness from the stars. She sends warning messages in the breezes; and for the sorrowing, she infuses the oil of consolation by her mere presence.

For every unveiling of your heart, she returns an answer, hidden from you only by your own dullness. I felt, and was soothed by this strange confidential charm, as I sat there, mechanically making the desired responses. The school-master seemed unconscious that I had given him no promise. Very confident his tone; very emphatic his phrases.

"Where will you be when I come for you? In the peaceful seclusion of these grand old mountains, I hope. I shall see you in imagination, flitting among your old haunts, going soberly to church, and fulfilling your duty in every righteous way."

I laughed involuntarily. "A pleasant little picture; but I do not mean to live up to it. I am going *somewhere*"—my ideas were vague, you see, reader—anywhere. He stared in surprise: then he began to protest vehemently. "It was madness, folly, to abandon home. What did I expect to do in the world? What special vocation had I? My duty clearly lay among my uncle's family. I must abandon it at once. My schemes were wild."

Exhibition of will in another, always roused mine. I lost my passiveness. "I do not agree with you," I said coolly. "Mark said the same thing, but he failed to convince me."

"What a pity," said Mr. Hume, "that your cousin abandoned his noble calling, for a vagrant's life on the wide waste of waters. I was astounded when the news reached me."

Again the old feeling of repulsion crossed me, as the schoolmaster pronounced these words in a tone of cold, hard disapproval. The wild excitement of the scene amid those same church walls rushed vividly over me. I drew a little away from him as I answered. "I could not blame him. I would have done the same. I should have despised him if he had thought it just. Even at the mere recollection, my carefully cultivated amiability vanishes like a sprite of air. I cannot yet; I never *shall* be able to treat the ministers civilly."

" That is all wrong," said he coldly, and I drew quite away from him as he said it: he noticed it, and smiled ironically. "I heard all about it. It was indeed awful, but I must admit its justice," he added, looking away towards the western horizon.

" Then do *you* say amen to such a heathenish code?" I cried in dismay.

" I believe we cannot limit the Divine forgiveness; neither his avenging justice. Of their conflicts, and the final sentence, we must be content to draw our knowledge from revelation. It is terrible to the wicked—sublime to the good."

I rose abruptly. " Where are you going, Ruby?" said he

" Anywhere. I can sit here no longer. Down these steps they carried her, out to that narrow home, religiously fancying they had consigned her to eternal torment. Oh!" I said more softly, as I stooped over the blooming mound. " Hers was such a beautiful faith! Demis, dear Demis!" I uttered, as if she could hear me. " I receive it into my heart, my life; I believe with you, that for *all* of earth's desolate ones there is at last a rest, a hope, an immortal soul-life, pure, beautiful and true, from which all earthiness is forever purged, and which rises and expands progressively, until at last it shall bloom in divine beauty." It might have been fancy; it might have been the rustling assent of the wind-swept foliage near me; but I thought a presence, a living form, drew to my side in close communion, spirit with spirit, passed swiftly by, and floated away on the returning breeze. I listened intently, as if for the sound of retreating footsteps. I glanced upward at the stars, now thickly studding the dark-blue arch; they seemed imbued with a holier radiance; they seemed tranquilly smiling with a tenderer light. The schoolmaster broke the spell.

"You are sadly heterodox," said he, smiling, in spite of his efforts to look grave: "an obstinate little piece of humanity, as ever I had to deal with. How you *do* retain an idea, when once thoroughly imbibed!"

"It will prove so in my love for you," I said thoughtfully. "So beware how you foster it, unless you care for it!"

"I do care for it," he returned seriously. "I mean to be a faithful gardener; I mean to prune sorely at times, but only for our mutual good. I may as well tell you that I intend to make your newly expressed religious views conform to mine. Ah!"—and he patted my head forbearingly—"you will be as orthodox a minister's wife as I can possibly desire."

"Humph!" was my sole reply. He looked annoyed, and dropped my hand. "I hardly know whether you love me or not," said he, after a pause. "You won't bear with me one whit."

"No, indeed," I cried quickly. "Why should I, pray? Better wait, ere you attempt any renovations, for the period when your slightest wish becomes my law, after the praiseworthy fashion of story-books. I don't anticipate such a masculine millennium. Women are fools to sink their individuality, and become weak, soulless pieces of mechanism, merely because their self-styled lord and master disapproves of *this* expression, or prefers that they should entertain *that* opinion; looking up to him on all occasions as their embodied source of inspiration. I tell you they know as much as their masters, if they choose to think so."

"I suppose *you* intend to think so, at all events, and set

the poor misguided sisterhood an example," he returned, sarcastically.

"Yes! I have a mind of my own, and I will use it. I have opinions of my own, and I shall not borrow yours. Out of the future I will shape a destiny, which, if not brilliant or famous, will yet suit my inborn originality. I can never be your echo. If you want some one to surfeit you with flattery and laud you to the skies to others, go seek her elsewhere. I am my own mistress."

"Fool!" he ejaculated wrathfully. "I *will* go," and his lips grew white with anger; "but," he added, turning away with a laugh, short and spiteful, "you will then be running after me. I will make you love me yet, Ruby Brooks, and then we will see."

"See what?" I said abruptly, and half angrily.

"See what becomes of that declaration of independence. All women are remarkably self-sustained until they really love"—he threw me an insulting laugh. A long silence followed.

"You and I will never suit, my master; I always felt and knew it," thought I bitterly—all the *more* bitterly for suffering the advent of a few precious moments of happy hope. "Each fountain may gush profusely, yet their waters will never mingle." Aloud, I felt impelled to say : " I love the qualities embodied in manhood, Mr. Hume, not the man himself. If you showed forth great courage, I should love the courage, and *you*, simply because you represented it."

"Your idea, Ruby, is silly and weak. Your notions are too vague ever to develop themselves into substance."

My mentor, as he said this, glanced down with very proper scorn, as if from an immeasurably superior elevation. "Let us go home," I said, coldly, at the same time turning away.

15*

"Very well," was his brief rejoinder; "and tell me, if you please, as we go, about your dreams of this wonderful destiny of yours."

I smiled disdainfully. "It is swathed as yet in swaddling-clothes; but I dare attempt to lift it from a visionary infancy, to a bright realizing maturity."

"But how?" he questioned. "Your ideas are so vague. One never can understand you."

"It is not necessary that one should," I replied, perversely. "I understand myself, and that is sufficient."

"I suppose so," he said, with another laugh; and he crossed the road, walking on alone. He was angry, but I did not care. An hour since I had almost loved him. Fond words and caresses had passed between us as he bent over me with tenderness, and talked of *our* future. Now, it seemed as though it had never been. In its room came back the recent dislike and distrust. I watched him scornfully, as he strode on with angry unconcern, and I gradually slackened my pace, and fell behind. At the foot of the hill he stopped, as if struck with a sudden thought, and looked around. I came on still more leisurely. He chose to seat himself on a log by the roadside and wait for me: his face wore a look of experimentive raillery.

"Suppose you preach instead of me, Miss Ruby!"—a little while since it had been dear Ruby, and darling—"You claim such equal rights. I assure you I shall be charmed to be one of your listeners. What will you advocate? You must have a platform of *some* kind."

"Yes, I would. The platform of help to world-weary, suffering humanity."

His smile stung me. I felt bound to retort in some manner, but severe words failed me. Instead, he, poor miserable stripling, sitting on the blackened log and smiling so superciliously in my face—faded. The road, a winding, prostrate column of dust, vanished. I was again in the churchyard, kneeling among the grassy ridges; and the coming years stretched out before me. I was not dismayed at the revelation. I shouldered my pack, and traversed them. I felt solitary, but not disheartened; weary, but I sat not down to rest. Sloth lurked under the thickets by the wayside; but I pointed my finger in scorn, and it disappeared. I fainted often under grievous burdens, but my failing strength as constantly renewed itself. Illusions faded as I advanced, and stern reality showed me its bitterness, its gloom. Then, when the end had been reached—the end of youth—and I saw still the same unvarying road before me; felt the load still clinging to my back—felt my feet falter, and my tongue grow parched with unquenched thirst, I cried, almost despairingly: "Let it come! let it come quickly. Since it *must* be so, let me drain the very dregs. In them assuredly lies strength."

Oh! a fairy-land is the future to the novice. Fair skies and soft breezes fan the still perfumed air into choruses of song. Fools! The aged pilgrim will tell you that it is but the sirocco's dreadful breath; a deadly whirlwind sweeping over each cherished hope, and crushing them to atoms. The promises shine golden in the west: ripe, tempting from the green boughs, hangs the cooling fruit with which we hope to slake our fevered lips. The fruit, when plucked and eaten, turns to ashes in our mouths, choking down complaint. "Oh!" exclaim we, "for a stronger arm, and faster feet, that we may reach the goal the sooner; where sweeter possibilities cluster;" and onward, more and more eagerly, we plunge as it recedes from view, or glows fainter through

the mists of dimmed eyes (for, alas! our eyes do grow dim
with sorrow, age, and much weary, lonely weeping. Hopeless griefs, unredressed miseries, fruitless watchings and wait-
ings for deserting blessings and alienating friends, each
draw a pall over them, and death adds the last with the bier);
and so blind are we that we heed not the real truth, that
though our sorrowful pilgrimages apparently estrange us from
the happy country, they are in reality but the stepping-stones
to hasten our progress thither. "Yes!" I added, triumphantly,
"it is all right after all. It is best that illusions should die,
having served their purpose. We cannot grasp heaven with a
wish, however fervent; but, like all earthly good, it must be
toiled for. In doubt, darkness, through this weary lapse of
time; with groanings that cannot be uttered; with tears
wrung from slowly oozing life-forces; with wasting form and
feature; with spiritual eagerness, which cannot, *will* not take
denial; with faith the most exalted, love and hope the most
humble and ardent. The soul thus purified *shall* attain it,
and its pack roll after poor 'Christian's' pack—to be seen
no more forever." I stopped abruptly, and found myself
flushed and trembling before the schoolmaster. He looked
astonished first; then he smiled ironically.

"Not quite a sermon yet; but pretty well for a beginner—
only your hearers may not all like such a flowery burst of
eloquence. Try again, Mistress Ruby. You will soon be
able to preach for *even* me."

"Yes, I *will* preach to you, Mr. Hume. Every soul is
created a preacher, sneer as you will at so democratic an
idea. You ministers are would-be aristocrats in heaven's
courts; you would hem yourselves in—a class by no means
to be approached, save with full, unquestioning acceptance of
any doctrine you choose to promulgate. I don't like to see

God's truth—eternal, infinite truth, so glorious in its severe simplicity—obscured; its white disc even temporarily sullied by the merest speck of manhood claiming to be its representative; cradling the pure image in his own shallow nature, only to turn it forth to the world as—a lie."

" But why can you not, Miss Self-confidence, be equally deluded—be equally the champion of falsehood?" asked the schoolmaster, his eyes ablaze with angry glare.

"I? Because I honor truth too highly. Because my occupation would not be gone if I dared to proclaim from the house tops what you ministers—falsely so called—hide under a bushel. Ah! vainly. The light *will* glow, and stray gleams *will* penetrate its living prison, and weary, hungry souls *will* some time bathe in its full effulgence, radiant in a newly-born humanity."

" So the poor minister's office is a sinecure in your estimation; to be done away with from earth. What shall I do?" in a mocking tone of inquiry.

"Better break stones on the highway, say I, with a noble soul, than to blindly attempt to guide the blind into ignoble ditches."

A scornful laugh answered me. Undaunted, I continued : "Strike the broad surface of truth upon the anvil of calm, intelligent reason, and listen to its resonant ring. Approach a finger to its sharp edge, and no wonder you shrink back wounded. Nature deals not in evasions—she mates not with hypocrisy. Face her honestly, and you gain a noble answer, a mighty helper, a generous friend."

" Indeed?" slowly, and with bitter emphasis.

" You are angry with me, Mr. Hume, but remember it was you who provoked retort. I cannot clip the wings of a truth, because it flies straight home from my lips to your heart."

"Truth! You do not even perceive truth, Miss Brooks," he sneered.

"Oh!" exclaimed I, passionately, "we may as well part now, and forever. I do not love you. I wonder I ever did."

"Nay!" he broke in, triumphantly, "I shall hold you to your promise. You need not begin to deny it; a tacit promise is as binding as any. And we need not quarrel if you would but be more placable; if you would but hear to me; trust me. Can you not trust me, dear Ruby?" Again his coldness melted, and he bent over me, all fire and tenderness. I felt the charm, the magnetism of his slightest caress. I felt contrition for what I had said. I almost yielded to the strange attraction which his mere presence had for me. Will again slumbered. Reason retired. Only caution, of all faculties the most prominent, remained to guard her rightful heritage.

"No!" said I, gently, "I cannot trust you utterly. I do not appreciate coldness, raillery, sarcasm. Why do you not hear to me—trust me? It is a poor rule, you know, Mr. Hume, that won't work both ways." I surveyed him calmly.

"You are such a strange girl!" he said, in surprise. "But you will have to submit at last; it is woman's destiny."

"Submit!" I echoed. "For shame, sir! It is an insult to speak so to me. I will never marry you. I annihilate my promise, if any such existed."

"You cannot," he replied. "God and the angels witnessed it; and it is not so easily annulled. But here we are at the gate, and we will finish our talk in the house, for to-morrow I must leave Northfield." He placed his hand on the latch; but I removed it.

"No! you need not go in," I said, coldly. "We have no more to say. I can here bid you farewell, and all prosperity."

His late anger appeared vanished; he looked at me long

and seriously — like an indulgent parent, pitying, yet despondent of a cure for perversity.

"Does such conduct make you happy?" he at length asked.

"I don't know. I can't quite determine, Mr. Hume. Sometimes I wouldn't give a copper coin for my whole life—past, present, or future; then, again, I feel like singing *Gloria in Excelsis* over it. I am so blissfully contented, that common cares, common griefs, move me not a grain. I swing high above them all, and rock myself to sleep with my own imaginings. *You* couldn't call me miserable *then*. If you did I would laugh in your face, and bid you, you old prosaic growler, try to attain to the same elevation."

"Those moods don't last long," said he, confidently.

"Nay, there is their greatest charm. They are only the natural reaction of as many hours of misery; the inevitable balancing of Nature, to keep our moral and mental well being nicely poised."

"What strange talk!" he exclaimed; "what strange phrases you use! Which state are you in at present?" He eyed me curiously.

Again the unwelcome conviction would recross my mind, would resume its accustomed arguments, that his sudden, ardent passion was a myth. That he was merely revelling in his former habits of artful experimenting with human hearts; carefully testing each chord, to wake its accordant or discordant chime for his own selfish pleasure. I replied, demurely:

"If I should tell you, you would gain little credit for discernment. You might make that out for yourself, sir, I should think."

"I'll be blamed if I can make you, or any thing you do or say, out," he half growled. Lifting his eyes, he caught my mocking smile, I suppose, for his swarthy cheeks flushed deeply red. "Are you a devil or an angel, madam?" he asked, with a ridiculously earnest air; "for the life of me I cannot tell."

"I begin to suspect, Mr. Hume, that I have a composition of both specifics ready and willing to be used."

"Specifics for what?" He clutched irritably at the nearest rose-bush; starting back the next instant, as the tiny thorns struck into the quivering flesh.

"Sweet oil is a specific for that piece of hardihood," I suggested, holding out my hand for the suffering member. Half-doubtfully he gave it.

"One moment," said he, eyeing me, "you are as cold as an iceberg; the next, fiery as Vesuvius. Every gesture is scornful contempt; every word is scorching lava. I cannot come anywhere near you. Then, when I don't ask, don't look for kindlier favors, lo! you show a sweeter, sunnier side, and there in a shady nook stands my angel, smiling and beckoning me on to happiness." He uttered this in a dreamy tone of soliloquy—then, a little louder: "Are our quarrels forever past, Ruby?"

Why did not some spirit whisper away the impulse which seized me? I was happy, but I would not show it; I felt very gently disposed towards him, but I twisted it awry with a glance at the previous hour. I think it was the recollection of those bitter words, and the shadow of a sneer still hovering round the mouth—not to be utterly routed by more genial feelings—which prompted me to answer coldly: "They are but just begun, sir."

He suddenly released me. "Perhaps it is better as it is," he coolly mused—a moment since he would submit to no repulse—"I shall not blame myself if I leave you, never to return again. You have brought it on yourself," was his indifferent soliloquy.

" Oh !" I cried, from the depths of my heart, " you might have made me what you would, but not by tyranny. It would have been a pleasure to crucify any plan or pleasure interfering with your will, but you throw me scorn, and expect me to greedily swallow it."

He steadfastly persisted in misinterpreting my words. " Remember what I tell you, Ruby Brooks; when too late you will regret your course. You *must* give up your will to be any thing to me : I shall reign in no divided heart. And what does it matter to *you ?* a woman; incapable—whether you will own it or not—of guiding yourself or others. Now think, and choose not hastily. I shall come to-morrow for your answer."

" I have chosen now, sir."

" No : you are angry now. I do not release you from your promise in any case. It is only to absolve myself from blame in your eyes, if—as is not unlikely—you should ever feel disposed to blame me."

" Do you mean to say, Mr. Hume, that you hold me to my promise—so called—and consider yourself at liberty to discard your own ?"

" Why, yes. Though I do not look at it so," he answered. " In my case I am incapable of breaking mine ; but, for you, I require some security."

Cool insult, not to be tamely borne. Unmanly way of extrication from a sorely-repented-of proposal. I read his motive well. To test it further I said no more, but bade him a quiet good-night, and went in. It was as I thought. He did not come down " for my answer"—final as fate—but early the next day left Northfield.

Was I sorry? Did I feel humiliated by the intentional slight? I hardly can tell. When one's whole life is a spasm of pain, one scarcely notes and analyzes each individual pang.

CHAPTER XXXI.

ERE autumn set in I dispatched a letter to my Uncle Lucas, briefly reminding him of his kindly offer, and as briefly intimating—I did not like the task—my readiness to avail myself of his offer to Annah. It is well, perhaps, that we have to subdue pride occasionally, else it would run over and smother all gentler feelings. It cost me several weeks of thoughtful revolvings as to other practicable plans, and a few sleepless nights—those few lines to my uncle—but write and send them I did at last; and urged, in a postscript, an immediate answer. Not that there was any need of haste in going, but I dreaded being impaled on the thorn of suspense longer than was absolutely necessary. I also hinted in my letter that for myself I asked nothing: I should look out for work to do immediately—that he might not think his foolhardy invitation had turned on him *two* burdens. I felt constrained to make some change, and I resolved that it should be a move forward. Several reasons prompted this. I felt, at times, that in some sort my aunt considered us a grievous burden. She discussed the family prospects with so gloomy a countenance, and prophesied—that last dreadful calamity to a thrifty New Englander—a speedy approach to the poor-house. I thought, too—it may have been a mistake—that she repented taking us from that, our inevitable home, had we been left on charity, and she grew into a habit of dropping significant phrases into Annah's ears; she, of course, repeated them to me, as our

aunt intended. If she skipped round the room in the exuber-
ance of youthful gayety, or warbled a cheerful strain, Aunt
Rhoda seldom failed to bring her soberly down to silence, by
hoping " she wasn't gittin' to feel above-board," or wondering " how she had the heart to, when there'd been a death
in the family." Often I heard these cold, curt observations.
The scant wages earned by teaching were not quite sufficient
to clothe us, though we had nothing but the barest necessa-
ries. If Uncle Joel purchased any thing, however trifling,
Aunt Rhoda's mouth pursed up into a still more forbidding
expression than it ordinarily wore; and she never failed to
leave the impression that she must do without in consequence. My services at home, of the most laborious nature,
she counted as nothing—in no way an equivalent for the food
we consumed. I was not surprised at this. She was so habit-
uated to unceasing work, that she could not fully appreciate
another's labor. Work was the element she lived in, delighted
in : she judged all by the same standard. Then the charm
of the old life was gone for me. Sweet had been the long
summer days, when Demis shared my tasks; the busy morning hours ; the calm afternoons of sisterly communion. Now
in every room lurked memories, saddened by the thought
perpetually haunting me, they are no more; they are gone
forever.

Something unceasingly whispered to me, saying: " You
are eighteen ; old enough to judge for yourself. Go out
into the world ; not hive yourself in grudged precincts any
longer. Shake off lethargic dependence, and enroll your
name with other workers."

An answer came from Uncle John in due season, cordially
approving of my resolve. " The sooner I came the better, as
the fall term opened in a fortnight." He added, also, a kind

message from Millicent—self-suggestive, I afterwards found.
Nothing remained to be done but to announce my speedy
departure to the family.   I am sure Uncle Joel really grieved
over the news.   When away from his wife's sharp eyes, sharper
ears, and sharpest tongue, he gave expression to this regret in
his own quaint language, with tears in his dark, soft eyes.
Debby, too, frequently interrupted herself in some heavy
household labor to declare, with a despondent droop of the
piteous eyes, that she felt " ruther down at the heel 'bout our
goin'.   I don' know what's got into me, Ruby, but I haint
no faculty to work ;" and the tears would start afresh as she
mournfully looked up at me.   " All you'll git out o' Har'ner
Lucas," said she, with emphasis, " you can put in a chippin'-
bird's eye, and not put it out.   A closer critter never drew
the breath of life.   She's as tight as the bark to a tree."   She
seemed to consider it foolish in the extreme, and one day,
after a profound cogitation over the ironing-table, she lifted
her head and remarked to Aunt Rhoda : " Young folks are
desp'rate flighty now-days ; don't know when they're well
off ; t'want so in *my* day.   And I should think *you* might
reason her out o' her projicts, Mis' Martin.   You can carry
through most any thin' you undertake, you know ; but law
sakes alive ! she won't hear to me one grain.   I'm nothin'
but a passenger."   No perceptible effect followed this bit of
flattery, and she once more bent in disappointed energy over
her work.

I was glad Aunt Rhoda said nothing.   I was spared the
pain of hearing myself announced as " in the way," for she
was no hypocrite to dissemble : if she said any thing, it
would be the truth.   However, I did not hurry needlessly.
I paid dear Sinai a visit, and during those delightful days we
discussed the probable future, twisted, turned, and endeavored

to lift the inscrutable curtain hiding it from our view. Fruit-less endeavors, but they begat hours of pleasant chat, and a stock of hope—abundant enough to feed upon in the coming separation. Not alone of the years to come did we talk; we sent a backward glance now and then down the halls of vanished time, freshly embalming each withered flower in its niche of memory; lingering over them lovingly, as we trod with hushed breath the sacred portal. "Ah," murmur-ed Sinai, "if we could go out of this form, and leave no gap! If the disintegrated elements of the affections would reunite and flow onward as easily as the divided ocean-waves! But that is impossible. Our heart-strings once cruelly wrenched asunder, never again quiver with just the same vibrations to the old familiar melody. The chords may be firmer strung, and send forth sweeter airs; I do not deny it," she resumed, plaintively, "but oh! they're not the same. Ruby, my child, do you not know and feel it?"

"Yes, Sinai. It seems sacrilege to me to even think of supplying the places of the dead with other friends; they may be good, but they cannot bring the same sense of kin-ship. No, they should live and reign in our hearts forever. Alas! that one human life cannot be torn from time, but it leaves some root bleeding. All unconsciously it may be to ourselves, we twine round each kindred heart-beat in our neighbors, and when the separation takes place, how we groan and suffer, and cast our mangled tendrils of love de-spairingly on the ground! They can never flourish again; never bloom with the same flowers as of old."

"That is true," said Sinai; "we are each—however poor, and weak, and ignorant—a prop to some weaker soul; a teacher to some one more ignorant; a guide to some one more blinded. There is comfort in that, Ruby. Who shall say, then, in a vain spirit of bitter complaining, 'Nature made me in a lowlier mood than she did my neighbor: I am good for nothing—useless?' Let his tongue cleave to the roof of his mouth in horrified refutation of the base calumny. Heaven would not tolerate idle dependences. We are all workers, voluntary and compulsory, in the divine vineyards. Know, O repiners, that you serve an important purpose in the economy of nature, if you but teach one fainter heart than your own the brave, grand lesson of endurance."

"Yes, *that* is it, Sinai; the lesson of endurance! Ah! it toughens one merely to *imagine* the scenes of temptations and trials, and bitter strivings with the world and the evil within us; and the coming off victorious over all; and the renewal of strength after each bloody combat; and the robes of the victor at the end." I paused, and laughed exultantly.

"You look very much as if you liked it," said Sinai, gravely.

"So I shall! so I shall!" I repeated, clinching my fist and shaking it in the unseen faces of my imaginary foes. "I long to be at it, Sinai. The world! I but laugh at you. I will ride on your topmost crest some day, and think it but a paltry triumph. I know—I see your sneers, and frowns, and angry dodges; your slights and freezing smiles, and decided cuts; I don't feel abashed. I feel your pricks, and indignant thrusts, and violent kicks, and the spurs quivering in the warm flesh. They will not kill me; the armor of pride is invincible. What are you but a menial, ministering to immortals? You shall bend the knee to me. As for devils, both great and small, in knotted legions, I defy you all. I feel superior to all such demoniac affinities to-day, Sinai," I continued, laughing at her astonished face. "Though, for any thing I know to the contrary, it may be the charm of your presence out-battling, out-riding the malignant spirits. They are often more potent for evil than to-day."

" I am but a sinful mortal, like yourself," she murmured, gathering up her work.

" Nay. Debby declares you to be an angel, and I don't feel tempted to contradict her," I retorted, smiling at the grieved, horrified air with which she disclaimed all celestial attributes, and shaking my head in gentle denial at her argument's close.

However sad the beginning of our chat might be, we rarely left it so. Some sudden turn of the conversational road showed us a broad sunny field of mirthfulness, in which we sported, relieved and refreshed. Or her sisters would break in upon our seclusion with a quaint observation, completely sundering gloom, and sending a rift of cheerful laughter to end it. On the whole, happy, hopeful plans predominated over evil forebodings, and I bade them all good-by with a doughty heart.

There remained only one more friend to visit; so one sunny afternoon I gathered my work, and went up to see her. There had been a falling off in cordial visits since Mark's departure—not an acknowledged mode of declaring warfare, since each matron spoke when they chanced to meet in prayer-meeting, sewing-circle, and conference, and the two sires clasped hands as of old, and sent forth as hearty an " How are you?"—there was a restraint plainly felt, though unexpressed in words; and gradually the intercourse came to be limited to very few and far between visits.

Olive, indeed, rarely went anywhere in these days. Her sister's infirmity increased, and she wrapped herself in an atmosphere of love and duty, seldom stirring from the poor

maniac's presence. They admitted few visitors. Their
presence usually inflamed Avis to such an extent, that she
forgot herself—lost all trace of her pure, shy womanhood,
and broke into fearful, blasphemous revilings and foul-
mouthed obscenity. These spasms were in her wildest days.
Often weeks would slip by, when, if nothing occurred to ruffle
her, she was pliant and gentle as a lamb—distinguished from
her right-minded former self by nothing save an idiotic va-
cancy of look in her deep dreamy eyes, and an entire unob-
servance of family movements. I usually saw Olive by
stealth, a few moments at the gate, or in a walk down the
long hill homeward. Now I knocked at the door, rather
doubtful, it must be confessed, if I might not be denied admittance. A rustle and a scamper of feet followed; then a
pause, when the door opened, and Olive stood there somewhat flushed, but smiling a cordial welcome. " Come in,"
she cried, seizing my hand, "don't be afraid; Avis ran
when you knocked, but *that* is nothing."

" Is she worse than usual ?" I inquired, as I tugged at the
knot in my bonnet-string.

" We can scarcely call her better; much the same. She
was very wild this morning. Eliel brought home one of his
young friends to dinner, and she went into a paroxysm directly. She has been quietly expounding Scripture to us all
the afternoon, until you came : then she shuffled away, and
mother went after her."

Mrs. Peirce here returned, shook my hand with brief kindness, and soon after slipped from the room, pausing a moment in the doorway to say :

" I hear you are going away, Ruby; is it so ?"

" Yes," I tranquilly replied. Olive looked up in surprise.

" Where are you going ?"

"I don't quite know myself," I said, smiling in her wide-open eyes.

"Better let well enough alone," said her mother, seriously. "I don't believe you'll better yourself."

"I shall be sorrier than I can tell, to have you leave," observed Olive, after a long, thoughtful pause. "I suppose you will do better to go, however; and sometimes I almost wish I could go where I could never set eyes on Northfield again. But that's a selfish wish, and I blame myself for it, and strike my breast hard—so—to keep such hateful thoughts in their places."

"Are they any worse out than in?" I questioned, abruptly.

"Decidedly," was her cool, calm answer. "My duty plainly lies at home. I shall never leave it," she added, firmly. "I sometimes seem to be walking in a dream," she proceeded. "I can scarcely realize how, when, or where my future has become so changed. I never looked forward to the possibility of its coming in this shape. If it had been but a *gradual* approach, I think I could have borne it better. Oh, Ruby!" she let fall her work, and eyed me wistfully, "I am quite discouraged at times."

I bent a searching glance at her. The poor girl had changed, as well as her prospects. She looked thin, sad-eyed, and pale; her figure had lost its buoyant erectness, and gained a desponding droop—a weakness, showing itself in every motion of the wasting arms and trembling fingers; an unwonted nervousness, which started at every sudden sound, even to the dropping of her thimble, or the sharp click of her scissors striking the bare floor. Her innocent, coquettish love of dress seemed also to have fled. In place of the trimly-fitting delaine, the narrow wrought ruffle, and

16

the black silk apron, she wore a slovenly, bedaggled calico, a wide, long woollen apron, and a blue gingham 'kerchief tied around her white throat. She caught the disapproving glance I cast upon these articles, and half-laughingly attempted an apology.

"No one comes to see us now, so I don't mind about being particular. What is the use?" she sighed, as she resumed her needle.

I—rather heartlessly—said something regarding Mark's tastes in these appointments. She lifted a pair of reproachful eyes to my face. "Ruby, you don't know *every* thing. Let his name alone. He will come back some day, and all will be explained. I can wait," she said, sadly.

"Yea, verily. Be not cast down nor dismayed, oh! daughter of Zion!" now pronounced a deep, strong voice from a corner of the room. I turned at the sound, to see Avis composedly sitting on the floor, Bible in hand—partly closed—while her great eyes regarded us with flickering light.

"Avis, come and speak to Ruby, won't you?" asked Olive, coaxingly.

Still she stared at us, moving not an inch. "How do you do, Avis? I am very glad to see you!" I exclaimed, rising and going over to her. I stooped and offered my hand; she glared at it a moment, and snorted an impatient "Humph!" ere she reached forth her gaunt arm, and struck it from her contemptuously. "Humph!" she again muttered: "You're a messenger of evil, and I don't know you—begone! Get thee behind me, Satan." She shrank farther into the corner.

"Why, Avis," said Olive, soothingly, "don't you remember Ruby, whom you used to go to school with, and whom you liked so well? I'm sure you do."

"Ah! you can't deceive me," she chuckled, with a hideous grimace. "Ruby was well enough once, but she belongs to the devil now—soul and body!" she added, aside to her sister. I got up and walked away. Olive followed, and we resumed our sewing. Presently some one nudged my elbow; I looked, and beheld Avis.

"Poor chick! why don't you try this?" she exclaimed, in a tone full of pity, and rapping her ·Bible with a forefinger. "Didn't you ever try it? I have. It's all that does any good. You don't know how the little imps fly when I take this out and shake it in their faces. They can't stand; so they give a yell and pitch head-foremost into the brimstone again, and I get a little peace. Did you ever see hell-fire?" she asked, in a whisper. "No! Well, *I* have, times without number. I tell you it's awful; there's so much of it, and it keeps burning year after year; never dies down a moment; rain don't put it out—only makes it blaze the fiercer. Then the worst of it all is, that away up above the skies I can see the elect, with the holy angels keeping company together, with songs and laughter, and every once in a while they get up and play on their harps—real shining gold ones, too—and dance before the throne. You remember the hymn, don't you? 'And sing, and dance, and shout, and fall o'erwhelmed before Thy throne.' Just like this;" and Avis commenced capering around the room with extraordinary gestures; every now and then bobbing her head almost to the floor.

"Hush! oh! hush!" whispered Olive, soothingly. "Ruby knows all that. Sit down, now, and tell her about your schools."

"I tell you I *won't* hush. She *don't* know all about it!" roared Avis. "If you do, come and show me how they do it," she cried, turning and seizing my hand. "There! she can't take one single step," she added, triumphantly. "Well, they sing and shout, and take off their crowns to throw at the foot of the throne, and all sorts of things; only I wonder if they pick 'em up again, or do they get new ones every time? Say, do *you* know? Tell me."

"Don't they pluck them from the tree of life?" I faintly suggested, feeling rather frightened at her strange looks and tones.

"Yes; that's it," she cried, delighted. "I never thought of *that;* and I've wondered and wondered, and read and read, and never could make out where their flowers and things came from. Well, why do they look over and laugh at *us*, away down, down in the darkness below? Tell me; you know."

"They do not," I said, calmly as I could; "they are sorry for and pity us."

"That's false!'" she returned, decidedly. "I've seen them shouting and pointing their fingers at us—just as we used to shame the little girls in school to make them cry. Now it strikes me that, if they were good, they'd be in better business. They are *not* good; only they are the elect, you see, so they are up there all safe and sound, without hardly trying for it. Oh! they don't know how the fire burns us, right in through the flesh, dries up the blood and scorches the bones; how they crackle! It's fun to hear, only it's awful to feel. I'd like to get 'hold of some, and pull 'em over the battlements into the flames! Then, I guess, they'd sing a different tune. But, no; that I never can do. That's part of our punishment, you know; to be spit upon and reviled, and to wear the thorny crown."

"Never mind her," whispered Olive; "don't answer, and, perhaps, she will stop."

"Well, we are alone to blame," proceeded Avis; "for we made a pit, and digged it, and have fallen into the ditch we ourselves have made. Poor child!"—to me—"you don't carry this book around with you, so you don't know what is in store for such as you. Listen, now!" She proceeded to pick out denunciatory passages in the Old Testament with ready zeal.

"Read right along," I suggested.

"No. The next are angels' verses; we have nothing to do with them," she muttered, as she turned hastily to Malachi. "Here, now, this is directly to the point: ' For behold, the day cometh that shall burn as an oven ; and all the proud, yea, all that do wickedly, shall be stubble; and the day that cometh shall burn them up, saith the Lord of hosts, that it shall leave them neither root nor branch.' That's it," she chuckled—"neither root nor branch. But how long it will be before *that* happens! such slow burning for ages and ages. That's what Elder Fuller says all the proud and ungodly shall come to. Yes, he says I shall come to it if I don't watch and pray. I laughed in his weasen face, for I *have* come to it, and he didn't know it."

"Read the next verse," said I.

" 'But unto you that fear my name, shall the sun of righteousness arise, with healing in his wings; and ye shall go forth and grow up as calves of the stall. And ye shall tread down the wicked; for they shall be ashes under the soles of your feet in the day that I shall do this, saith the Lord of hosts.' Pretty good authority," she paused to suggest. She was going on, when some word in the last verse caught and riveted her eye.

"What next doom will be ours, I wonder?" she remarked, thoughtfully. "Trodden into ashes—burnt up root and branch! Doubtless, after every such extinction, we come to life again, in greater bodily perfection; with greater capacity to suffer than before, and are immediately assigned a new torment." She stopped to ponder a new thought, and suddenly exclaimed:

"They say Demis Martin is dead and gone to hell. I didn't believe it, and I asked Elder Fuller, and he said it was so. Now what do you suppose she is doing? *I* shall find her out. Oh! it's nice to have some one you know there. It seems strange; I thought her good; but it must be so; you know ministers can't lie. It must be her pride, I think; for she *was* as proud as Lucifer. Oh! a rare match they would make in that respect." The maniac paused, and putting both grimy hands over her mouth, laughed demoniacally.

I felt suffocated; and rising, I went to the further end of the room, away from her, and looked out of the window. While I mused there of Olive's sad fate, in daily living this life, Avis stole nearer. Awhile she eyed me askance, then came boldly to my side. I would not exhibit fear; she was brawny, and, if excited, had strength enough to throttle one. I made room for her in the window. Olive left the room to prepare tea.

"Have you ever been dead?" whispered Avis, confidentially. I shook my head. "I have," she responded, with gratification. "I went there last night; into the land of the departed—those vast unknown regions. I'll tell you about it. The living think that silence reigns there; they lay their beloved in the cool, damp earth, say a prayer over them, and think that they sleep well. Sleep! There is no sleep for the dead—unquiet rest prevails. Insects in countless swarms sing your eyes wide open. I lay still, in a half trance, soon succeeded by a species of apathetic wonder, as I began to take in the strangeness of every thing around me. Humanity had certainly vanished. I listened. Concussions of the millions who walk earth's surface shook the very foundations of my new abode. I knew that they were alive up there, walking, riding, working as usual. I knew that some were rejoicing, some sorrowing; I thought and reasoned about this, and yet—I was wearing the garments of the dead, inhabiting the last dwelling. Earth had become a memory— heaven a speculative wonder. Was this the entrance? I put all sorts of questions to my mental consciousness; I posed it with arguments. Myriad thoughts; strange, impossible solutions of this enigma revolved themselves in my brain. Vain human longings awoke in my heart, ravenous for sustenance. I gorged them with promises full of misgivings, and upon their repose other desires seized me. I tried to move, to turn over; to my joy, I found that I was not stationary. Ah! thought I, a coffin shall only be my couch at night; the day is for amusement. One leap, and I rolled out of it as easily as I might have done above ground. I said day and night. Well; although the sun does not warm or light the grave, in one sense two periods do exist— periods of eternity—for, you see, I had done with time forever. Ha! ha! ha! You see, do you? I set out to find other inhabitants, and I did not have far to journey. There are countless caves under ground where they loiter. I came upon them suddenly. I attended, without ceremony or question, one of their levees. They made room for me, as a matter of course. 'Oh!' I whispered to my nearest neighbor, a tall skeleton, whose rattling bones produced a sound like castanets, 'it isn't exactly polite to come to a party without an invitation, but I got lonely out there. Who gives it? You must introduce me; my name is ——.'

" ' Never mind!' interrupted the old skeleton. ' You left your name behind you when you came here.'

" ' Very good,' I responded, politely. ' I'm glad enough, for I never thought 'twas a pretty one. But I don't see how you distinguish one from another.'

" ' There is no need,' he said, solemnly. ' We are all alike here. This is my home.' I looked around anxiously. ' Oh!' said he, ' and every one's likewise. You can go where you like, only when the gun sounds you must hasten to your bed without delay. We all have to do that.'

" ' What gun?' I inquired.

" ' I don't know,' he answered. ' Some call it the great sound of vanishing time, calling us back to eternity. I call it a gun.' He laughed convulsively, and walked away. I began to improve my newly-discovered privileges. I was glad, after all, that it was not an unconscious slumber. I went up to a jolly, fat man, who was jumping up and down for sheer amusement.

" ' Come,' he cried, seizing my hands, ' I want a partner. Those old maids won't dance; 'fraid their false curls will tumble off,' he whispered, facetiously. ' One of 'em tried a jig with me, a spell ago; fact. One set of teeth tumbled out her mouth—couldn't stop to tuck it in again, you know, so she lost 'em completely—won't even smile at me now. Breaking her old cracked peanut shell of a heart for those teeth; blamed good dancer, too—ain't much on the new-fangled curlykews, but can't be beat on a good old cotillon, or the Highland fling. Don't dare to ask her to take another round, for fear her eyes 'll fall out, and then she would be madder still. Now, off we go,' and,

with a vain attempt to twine his little fat arm around my
waist, he whirled me in a giddy waltz, till my head swam;
my eyes grew fixed, and almost started from their sockets;
and the blood seemed bursting from my cheeks. Coffin-lids
burst off, and their amazed occupants popped out their
sleepy heads to look at us. Some turned on end, and the
inmates looked and cheered uproariously. Skeletons, sitting
cross-legged on the ground, gathered up their rattling limbs
as we wheeled and glided near them, shaking themselves
for an accompaniment.

"'Oh, can't we stop?' I gasped at length.

"'To be sure,' and my jolly fat neighbor paused, panting.

"'You see,' said he, 'I am slowly getting rid of it. This
has been a pretty fair stretch. I must dance with you again;
you're so young and lively, you hop like a cricket. I must
have lost a pound at least.'

"'Of what?' I asked.

"'Flesh, of course;' he pinched himself in sundry places,
as if to test the truth of his assertion. 'It is such an en-
cumbrance! I shall be thankful to be rid of it, but it will
take *so* long ere I can dance well.' He sighed despairingly. 'Now, there's a partner yonder,' and away he
danced towards her, as fresh as ever. Near me was an
exciting game of leap-frog. I watched it a while, but finally
turned away in disgust; for two long-limbed skeletons
took unfair advantage of their shorter neighbors. What
are you looking out of that window for? Attend to me
when I am telling you all of these secrets."

Avis paused, to treat me to a very angry frown. I complied, and she resumed, as she paced up and down before me.

"I'll tell you *one* thing, and you'll find it true some day: they
cheat in the grave as much as they do here. All professions

16*

stalked there. Ministers read sermons; lawyers stirred up
contention, followed by suits, held courts; jurors brought
in verdicts; and judges pronounced sentence. It seemed as
though the long-continued habits of earth-life formed a chain
too powerful to be at once severed. All at once, they began
to gather themselves up ; to move, as strokes of some distant
bell clanged, peal after peal, like musical thunder, through the
vast charnel-house. We hastened back to our coffins, and
then began repose till another awakening. All believed in a
resurrection. We discussed it often, the sole point of entire
agreement among the army of the dead. Our departed
spirits now roaming space, unconscious of our whereabouts,
should in some happy age resume their relations to our
bodies : every particle of matter be resuscitated in new and
divine glory, and the twain—body and spirit bound indissolubly in freshened holiness, should enter upon a heavenly
inheritance. Meanwhile all vileness must crumble away
from us, ere the august era could commence. I believe *that*,
don't you?" cried Avis, suddenly facing me.

"To be sure ! But look at that lovely maple." I pointed
to a gorgeous cone-like height of scarlet leaves. I wished to
divert her mind from her gloomy theme. She came to the
window and looked out.

"That's a soft maple," she observed, with a sidelong
glance, to see how I took this wonderful intelligence. I
assumed a look of surprise, and began to ply her with
questions. She was accomplished in that lore; a thorough
botanist. She warmed with the thoughts thus carelessly
suggested, pursuing them with the same impetuosity char-
acterizing her subterranean revelations. I listened now,
delighted. What a fine mind she possessed! What a
wonderfully retentive memory ! She appeared not to forget

the merest scrap of information—no matter how, when, or where received. Fact after fact came sifting through her mind—then dropped from her eager tongue, to illustrate some botanical mystery. No wandering speech. No lurid glare in the dark, thoughtful eyes. No fierce, impatient gesture. Quiet her posture, intelligent her speech, with an occasional pause, and a look into my face of inquiry. I could hardly believe her the same creature, who a half-hour since railed at all human kind; shook her fist fiercely in my face, and called me a devil. I assented to all of her propositions, nodding my head spasmodically if she but faltered in a sentence, for fear this sane interval would vanish as speedily as it came. How long we stood thus, I know not; but until my limbs seemed ready to drop to the floor with fatigue, and until the shadows grew broader and broader over the mountains, and the flaming foliage of the maples grew colorless with the loss of daylight, and the young moon rose up from her eastern bed, a silver-white crescent, and poised herself high over the dark line of distant mountains. Olive re-entered the room, and summoned us to tea. I twined an arm around Avis's waist to draw her away with us, but she darted a look of jealous rage at Olive for interrupting her, writhed herself fiercely out of my embrace, and hastily opening a door, disappeared. I heard her stealthy steps pacing to and fro the narrow entry. I heard her unintelligible mutterings, emphasized startlingly by sudden blows of her fist upon the intervening door. My last view of her that night was from a knoll commanding the house, as I wended my way homeward through the dewy meadows. I heard screams, with the sound of voices in expostulation, and hastily turning to discover the cause, I saw a tall female form flinging from one of the upper windows. She landed in the garden below. The height was inconsiderable. Apparently she was not injured, for, straining eyes and ears to their utmost tension, I presently observed her slowly rise, and, assisted by two other forms, slowly hobble into the house, while one—the sweet, sad tones of Olive—remarked, " Avis, Avis, you *must* not do so. You will break your neck some day ;" and was answered by an ironical, sardonic roar.

CHAPTER XXXII.

I ARRIVED in —— late in the evening, after a tiresome journey. The morning was dark and uncomfortable. In the afternoon rain began to fall, gently at first, but increasing in force, and ending in a downright pour. This I did not mind. The changes were few ; the stoppages at stations brief. At every one I peered through the splashed windows, only to encounter strange faces, wearing anxious, disappointed expressions, thrusting eager glances down the line of seats, then retreating hastily to make way for new searchers. But our time came at last to leave, and we stepped from the platform into a noisy throng of hackmen. There were crowds, too, of waiting friends for the swarms of passengers. On every side glad greetings arose, with smothered kisses and joyful exclamations. I stood irresolute. I had written Uncle John notice of the day of our arrival, and I—perhaps unreasonably—expected some one to meet us. The crowd of drivers surrounded, jostled us. On all sides arose angry altercation. Annah pressed close to my side, whispering her fear. I roused my scattering wits sufficiently to select one of the gang, and to tell him my destination. The name seemed potent to command respect; for he at once grew respectful, and shouldering my scanty luggage, he plunged through the giggling ranks, and signed me to follow. There were two other passengers—a gentleman and a lady. It seemed that my destination was reached first. The rain poured in torrents, so I kept my seat as I demanded the fare. He named an exorbitant sum; I drew out my purse to pay him. Not so the gentleman opposite; he stopped me. "Driver!" he called sternly. The driver thrust in his dripping head. "Name the regular rate. You remember Hattuck, don't you?"

"Yes, sir," meekly replied the jehu. "I forgot, mum"— with a wrathful, discomforted glimmer in his hungry eye as he received the lower rate. Good and timely service from an unknown friend; a true gentleman.

I alighted before a large brick mansion. Lights glowed through crimson curtains in the drawing-room windows: over these massive folds, looped back on either side, I caught a snowy glimmer of rich lace, veiling, not concealing, the attractive interior. Over the massive door, through rows of tiny stained panes, the brilliant light streamed, making pleasant pictures. It was but a glance, as the driver slid my trunk up the marble steps and rang the bell. A neat housemaid answered it. She opened the door just enough to peep from the aperture a pert, pretty face, and to inquire in as pert a tone, "Who is it?" Jehu replied by roughly pushing the door, and shoving the trunk inside. Then he shuffled down the steps, mounted his box, pulled down his oil-cloth cape, and rattled away as furiously as the storm and the consequent soft nature of the streets would allow. "Come," said the pert face, "don't keep a body here all night, if you please." She swung it open wide.

I stepped into the hall. " Is my uncle in ?" I managed to ask. She gave a prompt negative, and plunged her small brown hands in the shallow depth of her apron-pockets. I then asked for my aunt. "She has gone to the synod of ministers, at the Church of the Apostles," she replied, glibly.

" Why, who *can* it be ?" now exclaimed a voice from the open drawing-room door. A silk dress rustled into view, and my Cousin Milly filled that space. She put up both hands in affected surprise. " Why, I declare it's Ruby and Annah. Where in this world did you come from ?" she inquired, with a pretty lisp. She withheld her hand from my offered clasp.

" Where, indeed, but from Northfield ?" I retorted curtly, for her manner angered me. I suspected her ignorance of our arrival to be assumed. " Were you not expecting us ?" I asked, quickly.

She simpered and dropped her eyelids as she answered : " Really, now, I dare say he quite forgot it ; he is so full of business now-a-days, and has so many *important* matters on his mind. He says the times are really dreadful, and I dare say he is right ; but, mercy ! what's that to me ? as if I cared. We don't have to screw and pinch to get along ; we don't feel them any. Celia"—she turned to the girl, who stood listening—"tell John to take this trunk up the back stairs."

" Into the green-room, Miss Milly ?" inquired Celia, with a giggle and a sidelong glance at my despised possession. Milly laughed also, but said coarsely: "Get along, stupid ! of course not ; nor in the-oak-room either ; but the one at the end of the entry." A wink finished the sentence. "And kindle a fire in the dining-room," called Milly after the retreating Celia.

Servants take their cue from their mistresses. I considered

this, and felt no anger at Celia's insolence. I turned and surveyed my cousin calmly. She looked taller than of old; but no better. Her thin, bloodless lips had the same scornful curve. She assumed *hauteur*, and thought herself on that score eminently aristocratic. Pride—of some species —is quite endurable, and even to be commended; but insolent airs of superiority always gall to the quick: unless the receiver has arrived at the stage of viewing them as merely amusing acting, and can treat them in a *nonchalant* way. I had not arrived at this desirable point; therefore Milly's airs nettled me. I looked at her again. A skilful *modiste* had fitted her well: her robe of dark-blue silk was unexceptionable; so were the tiny muslin collar and cuffs, and the gay little silk apron, with heavy silken tassels.

"Are you tired?" she presently asked, in the cold tone of one who had neither anxiety nor interest in the answer.

"Somewhat," I as briefly said. The drawing-room door stood open, but she said nothing about our entering, nor even invited us to be seated in the hall. I smiled at this. The extremity of insolence is always a ludicrous point. Braving her look of astonishment at my ignorant presumption, I advanced, and settled myself on the sofa. "How long before your father may be expected?" I now asked. "Oh, I don't know; not until late," she answered, coolly; and probably considering the duties of hospitality amply discharged towards such unwelcome strangers, she wheeled around and walked into the drawing-room, carelessly humming a tune. "Never mind," I whispered to Annah's look of dismay; she leaned wearily back on the sofa. "The *source* of bad manners is to be taken into account, ere the poor, faulty things are to be judged; so don't honor her with your notice, my dear."

The bell again rang. Celia again tripped up the stairway, and Milly again appeared at the door. "It must be Edward," she whispered nervously. "You don't want to be found sitting here, I suppose?" she added, turning to me. "Do you mind stepping in here a minute?" opening, as she spoke, the door of the cold, dark "tea-room," on the opposite side of the hall. I rose, and silently complied. Annah followed. The room was damp with December chilliness, and dark as midnight, but for one ray penetrating through the keyhole—a kindly gleam from the hall lamp. I opened the door on a crack, and looked out. A tall, thin young man entered, fashionably apparelled, who, I suppose, was "Edward," as he got a very cordial greeting. I think I must be truthful, and record, in addition to sundry favors, a kiss given and taken, while Celia discreetly averted her gaze.

"Have you company?" he asked, while arranging his shining beaver on the rack. "I won't detain you from your friends."

She lowered her voice, but I caught the reply distinctly:

"Only some of our backwood cousins, who have quartered themselves on paw, just after the usual fashion of such folks, you know."

"Verdant, of course?" laughed Edward, twining his arm about her waist, and bestowing upon the upturned, expectant lips another delicately-dropped kiss.

"Oh, you can't ever imagine! I promise you some rare fun, only paw must not see us—they call him Uncle John! only think of it. Paw is completely taken up with them, calls them wild flowers, and all that. Well, they're dandelions, if any thing, I guess; homely stuff as can be!"

Edward simpered: "I thought your friends didn't usually carry a brown hair trunk. I never saw but one before. My grandmother has one in the attic, full of old relics. She keeps it religiously secure, for the sake of old times, I suppose. Queer old girl she is. But where are *they?*" He looked curiously in at the vacant drawing-room.

" Well," she replied, hesitatingly, " I put them in the tea-room; it's rather coldish, I expect, but I shan't have them in here, that's certain. One hardly knows what to do with them. It won't do to stow them in the basement among the servants. You see, paw left strict orders to send the carriage for them, but I forgot, you know; and *they* think that *he* forgot to tell us of their coming. I hope they feel comfortably over it. I told maw *I'd* fix 'em. Serves 'em right, too, if such folks *will* poke themselves where they ain't wanted."

At this juncture they got out of my sight and hearing; and the heavy door crashed to, and shut them in the draw-ing-room. I went into the hall, meeting Celia coming to call us to supper. She led the way down stairs, through a narrow entry lit by a hanging camphene lamp, to a pleasant dining-room beyond. A fire burned in a large box stove. A gay oil-cloth carpet covered the floor; a white linen crumb-cloth was spread beneath the square cherry table. Gayly painted shades hung at the windows. The broad sill of one was filled with plants, stunted and sickly looking. A strag-gling, neglected cactus—its pot labelled " case-knife variety" —and a thriftless " Jerusalem cherry-tree," kept company with a tall, spindling " lemon-tree," which Celia, officiously compassionating my ignorance, informed me had " never borne, though it had been noc'lated twice." In a corner, on the floor, uprose a trim shaft of " oleander," its top spread-ing out in a circle of drooping, glossy leaves, crowned by fragrant, rose-tipped buds. The other window-sill held two canaries, in separate cages—tuneless, now, on their perches; each yellow head tucked from sight, but emerging quickly at our approach. Four black bead-like orbs scanned us. I noted these things as I took a seat at the table. This was spread with hospitable abundance. I was both hungry and thirsty, and I did the meal full justice, in spite of the pert Celia's constant gaze. Her sentinel aspect operated with a different effect on Annah, who tasted every thing in the tiniest imaginable bits, looking the while heartily home-sick. After this cheerless meal was ended, I drew a chair to the stove, and she drew a stool beside it, resting her tired head in my lap. I stroked her beautiful hair fondly. "Don't," she whispered, convulsively, "don't touch me, or speak to me, for I shall cry." I peeped into her eyes smilingly; but finding them already filled with tears, and the sweet mouth quivering with a strong desire to shed them down, I averted my head, and folded my arms in silence.

My aunt came soon after. I recognized her voice in the hall, confirming Milly's direction about our ridiculed baggage. She did not come down to see us; she entered the drawing-room.

"Not a very flattering reception," whispered pride, bitterly.

"But you must make the best of it. It is too late to go back; besides, that would be cowardice. If you cannot do as you would like, you must do as you can," subjoined prudence.

I listened to her worldly maxims, and put pride resolutely down. It seemed as though hours passed over our heads while we sat there. I had no means for ascertaining, but probably not more than one hour elapsed. The servants chatted and laughed boisterously with their "followers" in the kitchen. Occasionally Celia came in and replenished the fire. I was grateful for this solitary attention, and I pre-

same *looked* so; for her insolent airs melted a little, and an expression of shame grew upon her face. During one of the pauses which greeted her return to the kitchen, I heard her exclaim:

"It's a downright shame, after all. *I* wouldn't like to be treated so, an' it wouldn't set very well on *their* stomachs' either, I reckon."

I lost the rest, and again chewed the cud of silence. I had thoroughly masticated it; abstracted all the nutriment it may be supposed to contain, and was yawning wearily, when the bell again rang, and this peal sounded joyous to me, for my uncle arrived. He came down directly, and gave us a cordial welcome—more cordial, I suspect, that his wife's sharp eyes did not scan it.

"I intended to meet you at the dépôt, but an engagement called me away. You came just as well under John's guidance, I trust," said he, inquiringly. "You met with no trouble?"

"Not the least, uncle."

"I'm glad of it. It rather worried me after I had gone, for fear you might not see John, or he might not find you. But why do you sit down here in the cold? Come up where you belong. Come!" He took Annah's hands, drew one under his arm, and marched away. I followed. "My dear"—to his wife—"we must try to make the girls feel at home—" he broke short off, when her greeting revealed that she had not before seen us. She frigidly extended the tips of her cold fingers. "Is your aunt quite well?" she asked, carelessly.

"Very well, ma'am. She sent you her best regards," I answered.

"Thank you," she replied, unconcernedly. "We heard

of her daughter's death; it was very sudden, and very sad: so young, so unprepared."

I said nothing. A pause followed, during which Uncle Lucas looked uncomfortable. Edward and Milly snickered, and exchanged foolish glances. At last, ventured Uncle Lucas in this wise:

"Really, Annah is getting to be a young lady."

Edward at this nudged Milly, and she smothered an affected grin in her handkerchief. Her father did not notice her; his gaze was fixed on Annah. He went on briskly:

"Not a bad-looking one, by any means. Is she, Hannah? Now own up fair and square."

"Mr. Lucas, you forget yourself," she replied, with a withering look.

"Well, Mrs. Lucas, then. You see it comes more natural to call you Hannah. I used to, and I've no objections to the name now," he said.

"It's dreadful old-fashioned," lisped Milly.

"I was named for you, aunt. Sister says so," rather unluckily informed Annah, delighted at any notice being taken of her.

"Sister don't know every thing," said her aunt, coolly. "I don't consider it so. The first letter omitted, makes a different sound entirely. I presume your mother was ashamed of the ancient name, and tried to modernize it. At any rate, you needn't look for a present: I didn't get one for my own, and I never give any."

"I don't expect—I never thought of that!" said Annah, hastily, her blue eyes filling immediately.

"Who was Miss Ruby named for, I wonder?" said Miss Milly, mockingly.

"I can tell you," I returned: "I was named for my grandmother." I gave her a defiant glance, which she treated to a cool, insipid smile.

"My mother's name was Rubina," interposed Aunt Hannah, triumphantly. "Such naming don't amount to much, Car'line was great on pet names, I see."

"At least, it was all the petting I ever got. You need not grudge it," I said.

"Pah! she don't," returned Uncle John, cheerfully.

"No. Thank fortune, I'm above *that* low business," she returned, with emphasis. Lest she add something decidedly unpleasant, her husband interposed quickly, with:

"How tall Annah is getting!" A most unfortunate observation, especially when he added, "Millicent, you will have to look out now, or you will be quite eclipsed. I'm afraid you're done growing."

She tossed her flaxen ringlets scornfully. "I don't want to be any taller. I wouldn't be for the world. I think Ruby is too tall for a woman; and she's got such a horrid stoop. I've noticed all tall women *do* stoop. Annah will in time," she finished maliciously. Her mother smiled approvingly, and cast a look at her meek little spouse—who sat quite disconcerted—implying that he had got it now: he had better be careful.

"Oh, Uncle John," I thought, "you are but a poor little dove between two hawks. Why will you rustle your sober plumage right into their outstretched talons?" He could not avoid putting in a sort of an apology for my infirmity:

"Poor Ruby's stoop is occasioned by overmuch work and study, and at all events is praiseworthy," said he.

"Do let my round shoulders alone, Uncle," I put in, impatiently. "They matter to none but their owner."

Millicent resumed, perversely: "Now I don't want to look

down on my husband, as Ruby will have to do; she never will marry a man as tall as herself. Little men always pick for tall wives."

"Perhaps she won't marry at all," murmured Edward; "old maids are not yet a defunct species."

I was now exasperated. "Don't be in the least' alarmed, Millicent," I retorted, sarcastically, eying her leisurely from top to toe—a look I have found especially irritating, when levelled at myself—"*you*, at all events, never will look down on your future husband, either physically or mentally. That towering advantage must assuredly be his. Rest in peace on that score."

"Good!" chuckled Edward, rubbing his little white palms together; then murmuring softly aside, "you have found your match there." She turned on him an ireful glance, and biting her bloodless lips, meditated a cutting retort, which he averted by rising and bowing his adieu.

After this unexpected rejoinder from the country cousin, constraint fell on the inharmonious circle.

"Are you sleepy?" asked my uncle, presently, of Annah.

"I should like to go to bed," she answered, timidly.

"You shall," he responded, in his kindest tone.

"Yes," said Aunt Hannah, pointedly, "you can *retire*."

"Certainly," echoed Millicent—rising and ringing the bell. "Celia"—to the advancing servant, "show these *ladies* to their apartment."

"I wish I could go with you, Ruby," observed Annah, disconsolately, as we stood alone in our room; "I can see they don't want me here. Milly never shook hands."

"That's nothing," I said, decisively.

"I think it's a great deal," she returned, naively.

"I wish I could take you," I said. "I quite repent bring-

ing you here. You evidently will have many trials, taking
this night for a specimen. Now, when you feel desponding
and impatient, and almost forsaken, you will turn right about
and think how hard your sister is working to earn us a home.
You feel that, don't you, darling? and know that as soon as
I can I shall claim you?"

" Yes," she said, mournfully.

" I won't deceive you," I continued. " It will not be very
soon; perhaps not for years; but you have a friend in Uncle
John, who offers you advantages not to be lightly rejected.
They are worth a little endurance," I said, cheerfully.

" Yes, indeed, Ruby. I don't mean to complain. We
cannot have our own way in every thing. You shall see how
I can study, and then we can some time teach and live
together." She bravely choked down the rising home-sickness. I steadfastly encouraged her philosophy, as I busily
put the room in order.

" To think that they should laugh at our mother's
trunk," said she, an indignant flush mounting to her fair
cheek.

" Never mind. I shall take it. You will need none. See!
here is a tiny drawer, just large enough, and your books will
do very well on top. Oh! I shall see you many a time here
in my thought, and waft you a kiss at the sight. I'm afraid
I shall get none back."

" No, for I shan't know where to send them," she answered, thoughtfully.

" I shall write you every week, my pet, and you will do
the same. Oh! we shall have rare letters. You will tell me
every thing that happens, and you don't know how I shall
watch and long for them."

" I see one drawback," she said, anxiously."

"Do you? What is it? We will fight the monster," I returned.

"I write so very, very poorly!" with a deep-drawn sigh.

"That's true enough," I laughed. "Never fear but that I shall decipher them, and in the mean time you must give attention to that branch of your education."

"What shall we do to-day?" asked Annah, sleepily opening her blue eyes the next morning.

"'Pears to me, Ann, if I'se *you*, I'd git up the fust onset; but I don't know. I'm only a passenger," I answered, bending over her.

"Oh! that's Debby," she cried: "dear old Debby, I want to see her."

"And," I continued, more soberly, "I am going to write; then we shall go down to breakfast, and then we may venture on a walk." I was answering an advertisement in the morning paper for "a governess for small children; one of prepossessing appearance preferred. Address Mrs. Selwyn, No. —, —— street, New York."

At breakfast I showed it to Uncle John. He read it slowly. "I don't know about it. It don't specify terms, or say how many children," he remarked, in a doubtful tone.

"What of that?" cried his wife, quickly. "I'm sure I see nothing amiss in it, Mr. Lucas. You don't expect every one to write an advertisement as *you* would, do you?"

I smiled haughtily at her clumsily masked desire to get rid of me. I was determined to send my letter, at all events, and await the result.

A week elapsed before an answer came; a week full of the same petty annoyances, petty slights, and visible sneers. I did not appear to notice them. This plan succeeded well. I overheard Miss Milly and her mother wondering at, and regaling themselves with laughter at my simplicity. Very unflattering epithets they bestowed also; Edward joining in the fun—if fun it was—of running down two defenceless strangers. His silly-sally angered me more than all the rest. I quivered sometimes in impotent rage, and it was only then, when striking against the bars and bolts of my prison, that I felt how really helpless I was to retort—to fling back a thunderbolt which would stun him into silence. This, I felt, was what they ached to have me do—lose my temper, only to find it again when pitilessly thrust from their door. For Annah's sake, and for Uncle John's peace of mind, I forbore, and I think my resolute silence and unheeding ways tormented them beyond any retort. In the mean time I bathed my wounded pride in the consolatory reflection of my speedy absence; but I shivered anew for Annah. "I must work the harder," I thought; and each taunt acted as a spur—painful, but necessary to goad me on to greater effort.

Mrs. Selwyn wished me to come immediately, but said nothing of terms or the number of my pupils. I did not think it strange.

"I wish I could go down with you," said Uncle John, thoughtfully.

Aunt Hannah gave him a look of astonishment. "Well, why don't you?" she asked, icily.

"I—I don't see how I can, just at present. If Ruby would be content to wait a little, I would try——."

I broke in: "I shall write for them to meet me on Saturday. I shall get along well enough, Uncle John."

Aunt Hannah sipped her coffee in silence. She did not think it politic to precipitate a longer stay by too open repugnance therefor. I have a strong spice of the contrary in my disposition.

17

Saturday came all too soon. I dreaded unspeakably taking this solitary step—fraught with unknown combinations of good or evil. Hitherto I had been trying my self-reliant wings in the shadow of some friendly nest. There yet remained for them the eddying circles in mid-air, and the—hoped-for—long flight onward. The parting with Annah was a trial unavoidable. She clung frantically to me, rejecting solace. My aunt gave me her hand, wishing me "success in my undertaking," as coolly as if I were a total stranger—whom by chance she met—bound on a mission to Liberia. She had no emotion to waste; for which I was devoutly thankful, as I thereby husbanded my store—not destined certainly, *as yet*, to poverty. Milly, seated in the window on a divan, just lifted her eyes from a fascinating novel, and bade me a decently civil "good-day," which I returned in coin of the same stamp.

Thus I passed from the portal of this stately mansion, and, mentally, shook off the dust from my feet.

Uncle John was to go with me to the station; a kindly offer—its value enhanced by the fact that it was made in spite of his wife's sneering, steady gaze. The effort which it cost him was, however, fully rewarded by the conscious sundering of the first powerful coil around his manhood. His meek demeanor straightened into a near approach to dignity, as he followed me into the carriage. The driver cracked his whip. The horses started. I leaned forward to nod gayly to Annah, who stood in one deep crimson embrasure in the gorgeous drawing-room, one hand clutching unconsciously the rifted cloud of snowy lace, the other shading her tearful eyes. I glanced at the other window, where Milly and her mother stood, pointing to my little hair trunk strapped on the outside, both heartily laughing. Suddenly Milly

pointed to Annah. In a flash I saw Aunt Hannah dart
forward and strike her hand from its grasp on her elegant
curtains, just as the carriage wheeled around the curb and
rolled heavily away.

"Uncle John—you don't object to my calling you so?" I
said, with a questioning glance. He colored visibly.

"No, indeed; I like it," he answered, warmly. "But we
all have our little peculiarities, you know. It always comes
natural to me to say Hannah. The minister called us John
and Hannah when he married us; may be that's the reason,"
he finished, apologetically.

"I was merely going to request you to let me know immediately, if it should be best to take Annah away," I said,
sadly.

"I will—I promise," he said, earnestly. Again he colored,
fidgeted a while on the seat, and finally stammered, "How
well off are you, my good little niece?"

"Oh! I have a little fortune in prospect," I said.

"I'm glad of that," he responded heartily, "but it won't
supply present wants. Let me add to it a trifle." He drew
out a plethoric pocket-book. "The richer should always
divide with the poorer," he added, laughing; "so if you can
prove yourself that, why I'll take my share."

He shut his eyes, and held out his hand. I dropped my
little green silk, ivory-ringed purse therein. "What a genial
little man you are," thought I, "when away from your wife's
eyes!" He counted my purse's contents. All told, to every
stray copper coin, they reached the overwhelming magnitude
of seven dollars. Uncle John laughed.

"Just about half what Milly asks for a new bonnet," quoth
he, "and *you* begin life with it. Well, capital will grow if
properly managed."

He crumpled a bill into one end of the shrunken silk; a bright gold piece balanced the other. His kindness ended not here. He discharged the hack, procured my ticket, placed me comfortably in the car, and handed me a silver coin.

"If Mrs. What's-her-name don't meet you, give a driver this, and tell him her direction. I hope you will find it all right. I'll see after your baggage."

"Uncle, how can I ever thank you?" I murmured, clumsily.

"Pooh! don't make me feel ashamed," he interrupted, laughing. "Good-by, and Heaven bless you! Come back to us if any thing is the matter, my child," he added, earnestly, and, wringing my hand, he was gone.

CHAPTER XXXIIL

MRS. SELWYN *did* meet me. I overheard a gayly-dressed little lady inquiring for me among all the solitary lady passengers. My turn procured her an affirmative answer.

"Come this way," she cried, quickly. "Thank Heaven, I've got the right one at last. I believe I asked three-score and ten, and angered most of them, of course; every woman, be she named Jones, thinks her name a beauty, and all others horrid," she laughed.

She was a suave little body; she put me politely into a handsome carriage, entertaining me all the way to her residence with a smooth string of easily-spoken phrases; in anybody else, they would have sounded uncouth and abruptly delivered.

"I declare this carriage seems like a hearse, Max"—to the footman—"let down the windows. Ever been to New York before?"—to myself. I informed her of those early years with a precision which must have amused her; but she gave no sign.

"Possible? Did you, indeed? I'm sure you'll like it—so much to be seen—such a gay city—perfect panorama all the time. We shall have charming times. Dear old Broadway!—as we drove slowly through the brilliant thoroughfare —none like it in any other city. Such shops, such theatres, and operas, and the like! Oh! in an exceeding short time you will be enchanted."

I wondered if she forgot, or only for the present politely ignored, the fact that she was addressing a governess—a miserable, obscure creature, who had neither part nor parcel in such pleasures, or heart to appreciate and enjoy them; who had been hired for the express purpose of staying at home in some upper chimney-corner, secluded from the gay area of the grand mansion with the children, while their lady mother sported her bright plumage in the light of these and similar attractions. According to story-tellers, governesses were not accustomed to much attention; did not receive much sympathy; led a slavish life, in short. Contempt from every quarter greeted them oftener than civility, and gratitude from either parent or child, after devoted service, was an unlooked-for payment. "It appears I am to be an exception," thought I. "The rigid rule is reversed; or my ignorant rusticity has founded too much faith on the veracity of these complainants: their woes are imaginary, extorting no sympathy from the experienced gazer, or the transient shade is effectively deepened into gloomy vistas by exaggerating fingers."

As Madame's conversation neither required nor seemed to

expect any answers—my responses being treated with good-
natured indifference—I soon amused myself by comparing
the lively lady with her grave companion. Never was there
a greater contrast. The first-named figure wore a crimson
dress, long, voluminous, with a black velvet bodice, exqui-
sitely shaped, and profusely decorated with lace and buttons.
Over her sloping shoulders draped gracefully an India shawl;
the colors warm and glowing. A jaunty velvet bonnet tossed
its sweeping plumes with her head's incessant motion. Kid
gloves, rounded smoothly over her taper fingers—these latter
swung to and fro with a graceful motion; an embroidered
silken bag—a fine cambric handkerchief peeping from between
its strings.

The other figure—I remember it well, and, with the usual
inconsistency to our earlier selves, I laugh at it now remorselessly—was attired in a coarse plaided gown, of country
manufacture. A village mantuamaker had exhausted her
skill thereon, " to get a fit," and signally failed—quite unconsciously, of course, to the artiste. The gored skirts looked
prim and ungraceful; its extreme shortness disclosed a pair
of shoes not worse shaped than the foot would inevitably
make them, but a size too large for the wearer. Old Adam
Smith had—after due measurement of ankle and instep—
triumphantly turned them off his last and pronounced " a
proper, 'cute, likely pair o' ties." In Northfield they looked
well enough, but in New York they wore upon their wrinkled
surface the indescribable " not-at-home" air, which is the appendage of all ill-at-ease strangers. Bonnet several stages
larger than the modern " scoop;" the crown ambitious of
size; the front enormously perpendicular, of green silk, spot-
ted with the assiduous wear of several winters, and frayed
around the edges—where the rigid wire inexorably ap-

peared on the surface. My case was not an exceptional one. "Altering" was unknown in Northfield.

A striped woollen shawl was pinned closely around the throat of this lay figure—the clasp, a huge darning-needle; its point repeatedly dipped in hot, red sealing-wax, until a respectable head had accumulated. In her hand she carried a gray cassimere satchel—essentially a home-made production —its strings bright-green "quality." What a target she offered for ridicule! What a dish!—infinitely varied to suit the most fastidious joker. But you could not have guessed from Madame's manner that she did not consider her fellow-passenger a princess. Not one stray side-glance indicated her perception of my incongruity with my elegant surroundings. I laughed in my sleeve at the "attractive" answer to her advertisement, and vainly wondered what she thought of it, while her limber tongue kept up its continual melody.

Aunt Hannah and Milly contrived to make me feel every moment in their presence my unfashionable attire, my extreme poverty. This New York dame, in her silks and satins, with admirable tact, contrived to make me forget it. Ignoring a consciousness of it herself, and by some species of magnetism drawing my thoughts from their centre on self, I soon lost sight of all else but her talk and graceful manner; by the time the carriage stopped I felt entirely at ease. The brilliant gas-light showed me a corner house, of rather imposing dimensions. The shutters were tightly closed; no stray gleam shone from its many windows. It looked solitary; deserted amid its more cheerful neighbors. From these, on every side, flickered out from the half-closed blinds many a tender radiance. As Madame descended the steps, let down by the obsequious footman, she paused, and half turning to me, remarked: "I forgot to tell you that I have several

friends staying with me for the present, also my two sisters
live with me, but you will not mind."

"Of course not," said I, "as my place is in the school-
room with the children." I said this rather hastily. I did
not want her to show me my place; I knew it already. I
mentally added, as I stepped to the broad stone-flags, "You
don't expect to be treated as an invited guest, Ruby Brooks?
You are a servant, regularly ordained; waiting only for the
work to be given you." Conscience patted my head, approvingly saying: "Do your labor, then, honestly, faithfully,
with no expectation of other reward than your pecuniary
one—save the recompense of your pupils' affection and progress."

At our ring, the door immediately opened. "Oh, Angie,
it's you!" said Madame, entering. She introduced her to
me as her sister, with some remark about placing her under
my tuition.

Angelica sighed, and tossed her auburn curls. "I am too
old for that now. How old is my rejected preceptress?" I
told her. "And I am near thirty," she said, with a glance at
her sister, which I could not translate.

"Impossible!" I said, in surprise. "I should not have
guessed it." I was then ignorant of the concealing arts of
the toilet, and the friendly hiding of defects by gas-light.
She laughed, and looked pleased. The door opposite opened. It was dimly lighted; but I saw that it was tenanted.
Figures clustered in twos and threes on sofas; and lounged
singly, on low, square, tasselled ottomans. Angie pushed
me forward, and announced my name, when there was a
gradual rising; and the throng, either from curiosity or merriment, surrounded me. One turned up the gas, laughing
at my start, as the vivid flame danced suddenly before my

eyes. Angie commanded silence for the ceremony of pre-sentation, but was indignantly put down.

"We prefer to introduce ourselves," cried one, stepping forward. "Theresa Joy, at your service, marm." She dropped me a low courtesy.

Others followed, imitating likewise the obeisance.

"Hush, you giddy prates! You should be silent before your seniors," exclaimed one, drawing up her tall form with a praiseworthy attempt at dignity.

"I am known and honored under the lovely designation of Sally Jones, marm; not so charming, quite, as my person; but answers tolerably." Sally wheeled around, and executed the Spanish for my edification. One and all looked wroth with me, *why* I could not divine. We were utter strangers; they were guests, I a servant.

What more they would have said and done remains un-chronicled, for the hostess now entered, real anger glowing in her large black eyes, and addressing Angie hotly, the rest shrunk back to silence. Ere I could wonder at this sharp language, Miss Theresa cut in defiantly:

"Well, she won't be a stranger long, will she, comrades?" A chorus of voices responded, in spite of Mrs. Selwyn's threatening aspect. Then the dinner-bell providentially sounded, and all discussion ceased. Mrs. Selwyn took me under her wing, and established me near her at table. Dinner proceeded quietly. A well-trained servant waited. Conversation was carried on in under-tones—almost in whispers. Madame grew confidential with the advent of dessert, and apologized freely for their previous rudeness. I ventured to ask if her friends would remain long. "An indefinite period," she replied, evasively.

Then I asked if I could see the children after dinner. She

17*

gave a little start. "Oh, I quite omitted to tell you, on our way home, that the darlings are yet in the country, surfeiting themselves with fresh air and cream." I was astonished, and I dare say looked so, for Mrs. Selwyn hastily added : "You think it strange I did not write you this news. Well, so I undoubtedly should, but I expected them home ere you came. I don't worry in the least. I have great confidence in Lucy, their nurse. Perhaps she did not receive my letter recalling them. I shall write again Monday. A day or two will make no difference. Ah! Miss Brooks, we city mothers sadly neglect such little matters as punctuality and promptness. You shall reform me. Oh, don't begin to refuse now! I assure you I will be a docile pupil, and do my best."

I tried to say something in reply; but stopped foolishly, my face glowing with confusion. All this was so strange to me—Mrs. Selwyn's easy, off-hand ways, and short, disconnected sentences. Then she besprinkled these latter with the oddest, rather bewildering gestures—intended, doubtless, to give emphasis to her talk, but which puzzled and confused me. Indeed, she gesticulated constantly. When her hands were not in motion, her head was; and her feet, also, kept time in soft pitpats on the thick carpet.

Her young guests' riotous manners and loud talking, when away from the restraint of her presence, puzzled me also. Instinct murmured in my unconventional ears that it was not the most perfect breeding. I looked up from considering these things to find Sally's sharp eyes fastened on mine. "A penny, Miss, for your thoughts!" holding out her hand. "Oh! girls, she is actually blushing. Now it's absolutely refreshing to see a blush that isn't produced by rouge; it reminds one of all sorts of verdant things from that magic paradise—the country. Cool rushing waters, green fields, and rustling foliage appear instantaneously to my recollection at witnessing that blush. None of *you* can do it, girls!"

"Don't be extravagant of them, Mademoiselle," spoke up another. "You will use them up presently; and there's no more forthcoming, when once they're gone. Better save them for gentlemen's admiring glances." One asked something of Madame now, answered by a stealthy look, which she appeared to comprehend, for she adroitly dropped the subject.

I was glad to get to my room. A bright fire in the tiny grate welcomed me. A mirror reflected the cheerful glow; a toilet amply furnished with—to me unknown—pomades and powders stood beneath, draped in snowy dimity. A pretty carpet; an easy-chair wheeled before the fire; a low bedstead, with snowy counterpane and plump ruffled pillows, in one corner; white holland shades at the windows—this was my peaceful-looking nest.

Ere I closed my eyelids late that night, I reflected long; I pondered well my prospects. They seemed to stare back at me with a hopeful glow. Common sense urged me to feel grateful for such a flattering reception, "so different from your expectations," she whispered. "The drudgery of a governess is a myth. Your lot is cast among pleasant places. Sleep, then, in happy oblivion of all distracting thoughts," she commanded. Yet, do what I would, a satisfied feeling would not enter into my heart. I explained this by saying, over and over again, that it was merely the chill reality always casts when different from expectation; such whimsical creatures are we; and I ended by rating myself as a fool, and trying to lose sight of my miserable imbecility in slumber. The city's roar sounded far, far in the distance.

I realized, in listening to the faint, yet distant, rumble of vehicles; to the policeman's frequent rattles, and the shouts and cries afar off, that I had indeed left the still, waveless pool of quiet, for the eddying circles of the whirlpool change.

The gray of morning faintly glimmered over the lofty roofs and spires. The street lamps were extinguished ere the revellers below sought their couches. I heard continuous arrivals for a long time after I had resigned myself to slumber. A piano, too, woke music throughout the midnight hours, and a sweet voice occasionally accompanied it. Then my strained ears caught a muffled sound as of dancers on the thick carpet, and frequent, merry laughs.

As may be imagined, I slept only at intervals; tired nature succumbing during a momentary hush in the festivities, only to rouse again with a start at being caught napping; only to rise in bed and stare around me bewildered, as a louder laugh or a gayer measure rattled out furiously, and floated up the staircase. Once I rose and peeped through the windows. As I expected, a flood of light oozed through the windows below, illumining the street. The houses opposite were dark and silent. I came fully to the conclusion that there was a party below stairs; a large one evidently, and a gay one certainly. I stole to my bed, and again slept.

The brief clang of opening and closing doors in the corridors again aroused me—then all was silent. I rose softly and dressed. Then I threw wide open the shutters and leaned out. Sweet to me looked that holy Sabbath morn. The sun was risen, but the thick clustering house-tops hid his disc from me; only glittering, radiating spears of light clambered resolutely over them, and told me that he was marching boldly towards mid-heaven. Bells floated soft vibrations on the cool air. The Angelus tolled its mystic trio for worshipping thousands; solemnly, slowly swung the prayerful melody. A peaceful quiet—born, alas! of sloth—brooded over the great artery of sound. It seemed as if the vanished night possessed some cleansing property, making purity usurp the place of poverty and filth in the almost vacant streets.

As I leaned out of the open window, indulging in a revery, half sad, half doubtful, a low tap sounded on my door, and a housemaid entered with my breakfast, and the information that "they all took it in their rooms." The day glided away; the eve was passed much as the preceding eve. All appeared to think that with twilight the sacred character of the day was ended, and light talk, interspersed with loud laughter, resounded through the house. I kept in my room, but was sent for from the parlor, much against my inclination. This was a large apartment, the walls covered with gilt paper, with crimson bordering. The same rich hue predominated everywhere. The carpet was crimson and white; the couches and divans crimson velvet. Oil paintings, in massive frames, hung from the lofty ceiling by large crimson cords with heavy tassels. Mirrors flashed back light from either end, and from the marble-carved mantle. Plenty of nicknacks strewed the oval centre-table. A pretty stand of beautiful shells lurked in one of the corners; but not a book or pamphlet was anywhere visible.

The ladies had retired to their rooms, but they presently re-entered, arrayed in full evening costume. Silks of the gayest hue rustled stiffly in, and cloud-like muslin floated airily around. On their bare necks and arms flashed diamonds and rubies. I found much amusement in watching them. Of the eight guests, one Lucia was by far the most beautiful. Her fair cheeks glowed like the pearly opal shells I was surveying; her ivory neck was encircled with gems; they glowed likewise like eyes of flame on her fair round arms. Pure white, of some fleecy material, swayed with each undulating movement of her graceful form. Her heavy braids of soft brown hair were looped low at the back to her shapely head. Large, dark-blue eyes completed the attractive physiognomy.

Sally Jones was present—a dark, would-be queen. Amber-hued satin set off her tall form well. A string of these beads twined around her massive throat, and wove themselves into bracelets or her muscular arms. Crimson flowers drooped from her black tresses. A girdle of the same color wound carelessly across her bosom and tied in a knot at her side. These two figures—a perfect contrast—I watched, to the exclusion of all others. I thought there seemed a sort of rivalry between them; at all events, Miss Jones bestowed upon Miss Lucia no very amiable glances.

"Are you a nun, Miss Brooks, that you affect such extreme simplicity of attire?" suddenly inquired a voice near me.

"I did not know your customs," I said, timidly; "and I have nothing wherewith to follow them. I feel strangely out of place here."

"Never mind; you will soon learn them," she said, carelessly.

"Is this a usual one?" I asked, absently, listening to the shouts of laughter from Jones.

"What? dressing for evening?" she asked, with a laugh. "Oh! yes. Is there any thing wrong about it?"

"Oh! I did not think of that," I returned. She continued, in a lower tone:

"We each have brothers and cousins in the city, and this is the only leisure they have; so Mrs. Selwyn invites them to pass it with her, and we just take a fancy to dress a little more than ordinary. We go out very little, Madame keeps us so close."

"At all events, when wearied of your hostess, you can return to your own homes," I said, consolingly. She was silent. "Mrs. Selwyn's sisters do not resemble her at all," I remarked presently.

"Which do you mean?" she asked, quickly. I pointed them out, at which she curled her cherry lip disdainfully.

"We are all her sisters upon occasion——" She stopped short on seeing my questioning glance.

The bell rang, and she turned away. I seized the favorable opportunity and darted up-stairs to my room, as I fondly hoped without being observed. There, I finished a long letter to Annah, and also a tale, commenced a year ago in Northfield. For a long time I sat turning its leaves, gazing dreamily at the familiar words, and pleasedly speculating as to its probable fate. Of faith I possessed an abundance. Not a doubt had I but that it would find ready, even eager, publishers, and I considered—when it reached the eyes of the great public—my fortune and fame as won. I resolved to sally forth with it, done up in a neat roll, and tied with a blue ribbon, early in the morning. Then I reflected, with serene content, that many hours of leisure might fall to my share, after other legitimate duties were disposed of, which I could fill with similar occupations. "Madame shall not wean me from such precious solitude," thought I. "It is certainly kind in her to invite me to the parlor, but it is done only in kindness; not because she wants me. 'It is not expected, either, that you will rush eagerly forward to comply; you do not desire it,' put in self-respect. 'They are uncongenial souls to yours, doubtless immeasurably su-

perlor: let them, then, keep to their height; you will con-
tentedly sink to your happy level.' "

The family conclave below stairs grew riotous; noisy
bursts of merriment greeted, from time to time, my peace-
loving ears. Sunday had hitherto been observed by all
around me as a period of scrupulous rest; as a day set
sacredly apart for reviving holy memories, for shaking off
from the heavenward-bound soul the sordid dust of clinging
worldliness. I could not help shuddering to think what those
thoughtless souls below stairs rendered it: a carnival season
of routs, and a mere mockery of observance. In the very
midst of the clamor I went to sleep—previously taking the
precaution to bolt my door. I had never been accustomed
to do this, and the previous night had forgotten it: now, I
reflected, all things are changed; it is well enough to be careful. I had occasion to congratulate my unusual care, for I
heard the knob softly tried late into the night—by whom, or
for what purpose, I was quite too startled to ask.

I went out on the morrow, after undergoing considerable
questioning from Mrs. Selwyn, and a good deal of raillery
from her guests at my ribbon-tied package. I do not propose
to relate a tithe of my experiences. One editor just glanced
at the title, after disdainfully untying the ribbon and shaking
out the leaves, as if infected:

" Won't take," he decided gruffly; " got scores of such unprofitable wares on hand. · Not worth powder enough to blow
them up." Glancing at where I stood, vainly trying to appear unconcerned, he added more softly, " Short, spicy tales
might do. A long story couldn't undertake." He took
particular pains to retie the package, and handed it to me
with an ironical smile. Another was just the reverse in manner, with similar judgment. Very blandly he discoursed

very elaborate his bows. I hardly knew at the time what he was saying; but, at the conclusion of a somewhat lengthy sentence, I took myself and bundle off the door-sill—literally bowed from the august premises.

"Well," I said, hopefully to my sinking heart, "this is not just what you expected; however, be brave and try again." I did try again and again without avail, and with each trial assurance grew apace: timidity, daunted, cowered for awhile in the nearest hiding-place. I rather liked the experience I was undergoing. Most refused briefly, without deigning a glance at my offering. Only one—a tall gentleman, with silvery locks and benevolent smile, frankly told me the cause of my defeat.

"True story; looks tolerable," he remarked, after hurriedly glancing over a few pages; "but you are not known. Beginners stand but a poor chance. We must follow the lead, madame," he pursued, smoothly. "There is nothing like appending to published articles a name that has achieved prestige; it sells your paper at once. The public is not always a discriminating judge, it is true. It often greedily swallows a washy draught from one of its favorites. Once gain a little renown, and you may offer it what you please. The 'Literary Reflector' will take your articles *then*, madame," he finished, smilingly.

"But the imperfect fruit must have *opportunity*, ere it can develop to maturity," I thought, half bitterly. Aloud, I merely said, "Then you refuse to read it?"

"*I* am willing," he said, quite patiently. "But *we* are not our own masters; we cater to our patrons' tastes, and often —sorely against our private judgment—serve up to them what to ourselves would be unpalatable fare. You may leave it, however; I will give it a trial.'

Arrived at home—home, indeed!—madame greeted me:
" Well," she cried, " her hands are empty ; our authoress
has disposed of the wonderful tale. Pray what magazine is to
be honored by its appearance ?" she asked, with a sweet,
though somewhat ironical, smile. I replied evasively, and
again inquired if my pupils had arrived. " No, indeed," she
declared; " I cannot imagine the reason of their delay. I
wrote on Monday, stipulating positively for their instant
arrival."

I looked at her steadily. She gazed back at me calm and
smiling. " I cannot fathom you," I thought. " You do not
seem anxious : you by no means show a maternal interest :
no solicitude appears for their unaccountable non-arrival." I
reflected on the singularity of her urging me to come immediately, and of her omitting to tell me of their absence. My
suspicions, once on the alert, were swift to discover other in-
congruities. I remembered glances interchanged with her
guests. Guests! Were *they* her guests? Theresa let fall,
the night previous, that she had spent a year with her—a
goodly time for a visit, and she never spoke of leaving. I
could, in reality, detect nothing wrong in this; yet my mind
refused to be quieted. A remark from Mrs. Selwyn, later in
the evening, balanced the scale; I decided to leave immediately. Bewildered and frightened, I felt certainly in a net,
surrounded by only one means of escape—instant flight.
But whither? That was the item to face. Forward, my
spirit resolutely urged. Forward! But the way was still
dark to my vision.

No. I must wait yet another night, I concluded ; and thus
resolved, my course shaped itself clearly before me. I went
out in the morning, after locking my trunk; stopped and
scrutinized playfully by Madame, who—apparently satisfied

that all was right—made no effort to detain me. I went first to the editor to inquire for my truant MSS. I saw its fate in his face as I came into his presence.

"I am sorry," he began, "but I'm afraid it is a little too flowery to take." He read a passage from the pages before him—poor heart, how it fluttered, as the ironical tone shivered many a bright delusion! "Oh, days of Arabian enchantment! Summer days of fair fruition, cloying with sweetness; satiating our poor human heart with the honey of Life's fairest side. A living reality while ye lasted, ye are become the saddest of memories—for never can those sunny paths again be trod. Gone is the dew from each tiny spray; the freshness from the flowers. Dry stalks rattle drearily; and are scattered by the wind—no longer a summer breeze—over the mossy turf, now shrivelled and brown. The birds are banished: Hope no longer makes nests amid the branches, It is not well to linger too long amid ruins. It is not well to waste precious moments of the swift-gliding Present in unavailing mourning for the Past." He paused, and pointed to another page: "Seal all remorseful questionings with the balm of wasted youth; stamp them legibly, as foolish dreams of unreflecting childhood. O'er their gray ashes chant no dirge; but rise rather to action. In the mould of the Has Been sleeps the purer strength of the To Be. Give it colossal life, and power, and beauty. Oh, let the whisperings of the 'still, small voice' drift downward into your soul, startling its dreary, selfish sloth, like a clarion call—to labor for humanity. Then, in after years—though the past landmarks can never be wholly obliterated, yet they shall be left so far behind in our memories, that we may view them as wayside graves; yet lurking far, far distant from our direct road of travel."

"I will take it, if you please," I interrupted. He silently . placed it in my hand, and I went out. When in the street, I tore it into a thousand fragments. I found a melancholy relief in sowing it broadcast, as I slowly wandered along; to me it was the burial—necessary, perhaps, but sad—of my grand dreams.

What was I to do? Where was I to go? I scarcely thought at first, as I battled bravely with this disappointment, and destroyed the labor of months. As my bitter feelings faded, the necessity of seeking an immediate shelter somewhere, recurred to me. I knew no one. I had no courage to seek for employment. The morning was spent, the noontide was long since passed, but I still strolled on, much too thoughtful to be weary. These past three days seemed like as many weeks; so full had they been crowded of reflections and cares both placid and bitter, of eager hopes and necessary changes. Then I surmised suddenly that I must be hungry—with renewed strength might enter clearer counsel. I bought some cakes, eating them as I strolled along, devising plans for the coming night. I believe all sorts of absurd spirits revelled in my brain for a few hours; but from each's method of compromising with propriety, I turned away with disgust. To add to my bodily discomfort— my mental could hardly have been worse—there began to descend, towards evening, a chill December rain. As I could not stand forever under awnings, or loiter in doorways of shops, without exciting serious suspicions, I left these friendly covers, and was soon drenched thoroughly. Still on, and on, and on. The streets were alive with people going home from their work. The lamps glowed one by one at the street corners. I began to quake inwardly at the disagreeable prospect before me of a gratuitous night lodging in the station-

house, and to pluck up courage enough to ask the inmates
of dwellings, "If they wished to hire a servant?" How
many I inquired at I know not; I kept no account; but at
each I got the same cool negative. I believe they did not
think me a servant, but some hardened character; probably
a night-walker, or an associate and accomplice of burglars.

"It is quite too late in the day to get a situation," observed one housemaid, ironically, as I turned from the door.
So it was. I felt its truth, and made up my mind to wander about until some policeman marched me off to my night
quarters. Desperate circumstances breed desperate measures
and natures. I do not remember feeling shame as I walked
along—unmolested as yet—only a feeling as if it was perfectly natural that I should be there, homeless, wet to the
skin, friendless, very nearly akin to a poor miserable outcast.

Does every one, while experiencing their most wretched
moments, recall, with vivid distinctness, their happiest hours?
I do. I did then. Miserable as I felt—disappointed—deceived—ready as I was for the most desperate steps, there
came before me the unbroken vista of the only happy years
of my life. I saw Demis, arch, blithe and happy, as I knew
her then. Mark thoughtlessly, boyishly gleeful. Mr. Hume
sedately reading, or fascinating us by his free, graceful talk
and magnetic manner. I experienced anew every pleasurable fancy. I renewed every merry chat—the incidents
of every walk. Every kindness, every affectionate look, every
caress, returned then to comfort me. I believe it is well
that it should be so; it shuts out for a brief space the present agony. The poignancy of misery lessens, and with its
ebb flows in again renewed hopefulness. I can never understand how one can commit suicide after such inner communing; yet I have heard of mortals sitting then calmly down

to ponder its utility—scanning the past bliss, the present despair, to weigh accurately the causes in favor of self-destruction, and then grasping madly at the thought of oblivion to earthly torments. I wonder at and pity them. It is so cowardly to sneak from the mastery of trouble! Yet who would be rash enough to sit at a tribunal of human judges to sentence such a soul? It is a terrible spectacle for the angels to witness—a terrible tale for their pens to record— how a human life, endowed abundantly with longings for happiness, can be goaded on by countless human influences to the verge of despair, and in one luckless moment plunged over it, unbidden, into the presence of his Maker and his Lord! It seems to me that the possessor of a happy past should live for the sake of that remembrance. Thus individualized, it is a solace, sufficient to weigh to the dust the mighty, absorbing, present evil.

Yet though I was in a measure comforted, it seemed to me I could feel a dim foreshadowing of the rash thoughts of those unfortunates who—the one false step taken—plunge thenceforth, with headlong velocity, into crime. Long-continued misery feeds recklessness. Then we are none of us planted so high upon the pinnacle of purity as to be beyond the reach of temptation. The happy are no judge of this fact; but let a great love turned to blasting sorrow, a great despair sweep over them, and see how soon the foundations begin to quake, the powers of perception grow obscured, and the power of resistance lessened. I felt that if I should be obliged to pass a week like this one day, I *might* follow their wayward courses; *might* break through the conventional laws fencing in the good from contact with evil. Happily, this fate was not in reserve for me. Whatever awaited me in the future, *this* night, at least, I was not to scour the dismal streets, or find a sleepless rest in the quarters for the vagrant and abandoned. A mere chance turned the scale, and saved me. As I turned a corner and gazed absently down a narrow street—uncertain whether to traverse it, or to keep on my direct course—I observed a woman, leading a little girl by the hand, emerge from a bookstore, and quietly gather up her gray dress ere moving on. She opened an umbrella, too, but after going a few paces, she seemed to regard the effort of carrying it extended more than it was worth; for, putting out her hand and feeling only a dim sprinkle of rain or mist, she shut it down again and used it for a staff. Something whispered me to follow them. I did so—keeping just far enough behind to hear their conversaion, and to watch their movements.

"Be thou quiet, Helen Mar," observed the dame, anxiously; for the child commenced to caper restlessly, and frequently attempted to break away from the maternal hand. "Thee is getting very unstable lately, I think," she continued, placidly. "I really think thy father and I had better move into the country once more."

"*Now*, what have I done?" asked the child, peevishly.

"Why, thou prancest along like a race-horse, Helen Mar; and thee always must stop to see the sights in all the shop-windows; and thee almost struck into a hipaty-hop just now, Helen Mar," she answered, with mild severity.

"I wish that I could learn to dance, like Lois Hill," remarked Miss Helen, mischievously. "She looks like a spirit when she's dancing."

"Hush thee, child!" admonished her mother. "What does *thee* know of spirits?"

"Well, at any rate, one can't go on a jog trot *all* the time, can one?" inquired the child, at once bringing her easy canter into strict conformity with the good dame's ideas of propriety exemplified in her own steady gait.

"So you're a Quakeress," I thought, as I followed the plump, short figure—hushing my own footfalls to catch the sound of her motherly exhortations. She had a pleasant voice—soft, flexible, and full of kindly intonations.

"Thee should begin to consider looks. Thee is getting old enough," she remarked. "I hope thee is not going to have an irritable temper, Helen Mar. I noticed thee didn't seem over pleased with thy present."

"I wanted 'The Twins in the Garden, and other Tales,'" pouted Miss. "But I never can have what I want. I heard Cousin Dolly tell theé to get me a book suitable for my age, and *that* one isn't, I'm sure. I'll ask Zaccheus now."

"Well, ask thy father, do. He will tell thee that there is no better book in the world than 'Silas Bridges' Life.' Thee is too young yet to know what is best for thee. I used my judgment in selecting one which will never wear out——"

"I wish it would, then!" cut in Helen Mar, pertly.

"When thou art an aged woman," proceeded her mother, smoothly, "then thou wilt love to peruse it, and for thy youth and middle age it will be a guide unto thy feet. One of these days thou wilt think differently on these things. Thee has a great deal to learn, my child."

"Mother, there's a woman following us—an awful-looking creature, too!" hastily interrupted the girl, sending a glance over her shoulder. "Ask her what she wants."

"Hush thee, daughter! Can she not walk the same pavement with us? She is doubtless some poor creature going home from her work," interposed the dame, in a lower tone. "Has she an umbrella, child?" I heard her ask further. Just then a policeman stepped to my side, and touched my shoulder. I looked around frightened.

" You have followed that lady long enough," was his rough accost. " Come, what do you want of her ?"

" I wished to speak to her ; I am only waiting for a chance. I want to ask her for a night's lodging," I replied, fearfully.

He laughed in my face coarsely, and chucked my chin. I drew back, gazing wistfully after the twain, receding slowly down the street.

" Oh !" said he, skeptically, " If that's the case, come along with me, and I'll accommodate you. You're a pretty-looking creature to speak to a *lady !*"

" I must speak to her first," I persisted, in a louder tone. " Then, if she won't give it to me, I will go with you."

The lady, it appears, overheard this colloquy, or my earnest closing remark, for she stopped, looked around, then turned and trotted briskly up to us.

" What does thee wish of me, poor woman ?" she kindly asked.

" Let me go with you, and I will tell you," I implored, shaking off the policeman's heavy hand. " I am not that which he takes me for," I continued, earnestly. " Don't be afraid, madam ; you need not feel obliged to keep me, after hearing my story, if you do not wish to," I urged ; at which bright idea the trusty guardian of the pave laughed.

" You'd better not keep her, madam. You'll be woefully sucked in," he declared, confidently. " I reckon I'd better save ye the trouble of hearing her story. It's allers the old one. There's hundreds of 'em now roaming round this very spot."

" I don't see any," declared the lady, looking innocently about her.

18

"Poh!" was his scornful rejoinder.

She looked searchingly in his face, as she asked: "What he intended to do with me, provided she refused to take me herself?"

"Oh, I'll lock her up safe enough for one night. It'll be a kindness to her, and to all the rest of 'em, if one could do it," he callously answered.

"I'm not one of those," I said, flushing indignantly. "For once you are mistaken."

"May be so," he returned, ironically. "I've no time to dispute it; but good people don't roam the streets in this fashion. I've watched you for three hours and over. This one come from the country," he added, to the lady.

"At any rate, thee shall go home with me," said she, quickly. "My door is not too good to open to anybody. Thee need waste no more words about so slight a matter;" and she signalled me to follow her.

"As you like, of course, ma'am," observed the watchman, moving away indifferently. As we walked along, I told my story. When it was ended, she brightened up considerably, and·said, heartily·:

"I'm glad I met thee. Thou didst not tell me thy name."

"Rubina Brooks."

"Well, Rubina, thee need worry no more—to-night, at least. Thou canst stay with me and mine; and this, not because thou hast proven thyself better than I expected—"

"I haven't proved myself at all," I ventured to observe.

"Well, I believe thee, Rubina, as much as if thou hadst; I know when anybody is lying. Thou art not a liar."

"I hope not," I said, fervently.

"But if thou art a poor unfortunate, thee can stay under my roof, likewise, and we will see what can be done for thee after to-morrow. Zaccheus will relish *that*," observed the dame, with sweet Christian charity. "Zaccheus is my husband," she continued; "and this is our daughter; and this is our home." She looked up at the row of cheerfully lighted windows. "Come right in," she added, with hospitable eagerness, while ascending the broad stone steps, and looking over her shoulder, to see if I was obeying literally the injunction. There was little fear of my running from the cheery prospect of such safe harborage, after a day of such despairing, drifting on cheerless uncertainty; with such miserable thoughts, such skeleton fears for company. She placed her umbrella in one corner compactly, then treated the mahogany bell-knob to a placid pull. After a moment of waiting, a slippered tread sounded in the entry; then some fumbling of the key in the lock ensued, and the unsliding of a bolt, with a sharp, sudden click; then the door swung slowly open, just enough to show us a man's face and form, peering out at us. It was a muscular form, though greatly bowed, either with grief or physical infirmity, for his years could not have exceeded fifty. The broad shoulders bent nearly double. They supported a pale, wrinkled face, but kindly looking; with a pair of dark gray eyes, humorous and pathetic by turns, one moment flashing with keen appreciation of some witty repartee, the next looming down their dark centres into your very soul, with a kind of sorrowful pity at the chance discovery of any troubled thought lurking there. The thin, red lips one might disown. The straight, stern, inflexible nose; the high, narrow forehead; the ungraceful form. But those eyes one could never watch a day without growing to love their shifting, intelligent expression, without cleaving to the sympathetic soul flashing fitfully through them. Of course I did not discern all this, did not draw these conclusions, while waiting out on those cold rain-splashed door-steps; they were after-thoughts in the acquaint-ance which followed this night's introduction. There, I only thought of getting to the light and heat within, to warm my aching, shivering bones at the glowing wood fire I heard crackling and roaring away in the parlor.

He stepped back hastily on seeing who it was that rang, and laughed.

"Oh! it's thee, is it, Judith? Thee's done thy shopping in right speedy fashion," was his quaint greeting, in a sweet silvery voice, as the lady entered. Helen Mar and myself filed in after her.

"Why, did thee think 'twas a Sabbath-day's journey to Klipstones and back, pray tell me?" was the good-humored retort, as she delivered into his hand a small-sized brown paper parcel, with the further inquiry: "Wilt thou take that, and tell me what thee thinks of it? Helen Mar wishes thy opinion on my purchase." She turned and looked at the girl, as if *now* was the time for her to present her former objections, that they might be done away with by the im-partial judge before her.

"*I'm* contented enough with it," rather sullenly observed Miss Helen, eying the parcel askance, as her prudent father patiently picked out the knot in the twine, rolled it up com-pactly, tucked it in his side-pocket, shook out the creased corners of the enveloping paper, then took a seat on the sofa, smoothed the paper over his knees, folded and handed it to his wife, who stood before him watching these proceedings with apparent interest, and glancing, from time to time, at her daughter. She looked as if it was the bitter thing that her past sorrow should be thus revived when it had nearly worn itself away.

"The Life and Religious Experience of the Rev. Silas Bridges," read her father, slowly, from the title-page. "Truly a good selection, Judith," he pronounced, approvingly, turning a long look at the marbled covers and cleanly cut leaves. "Thee had an eye to thy own profit, Judith, I conclude. Don't *thee* like it, Helen Mar? Was *that* thy mother's meaning?" he presently asked. She was silent, and began to chew her bonnet-strings into a round ball—occasionally pulling them from her mouth to note the progress she was making in this exemplary matter.

"Why, what is the matter with it?" asked her father, quaintly.

"Nothing," was Miss's perverse answer.

"Then thee'll take it, read it, and profit by it, and keep it on thy shelf for reference," remarked her smiling sire, making her a formal presentation. She flared directly. "I *don't* want it; I *won't* read it; I *shan't* have it on my shelf. I hate old Silas Bridges!" screamed Miss, passionately, abandoning the mastication of brown lutestring, and sinking a stormy heap on the entry floor.

"Look there, will thee, Zaccheus!" exclaimed her mother, despairingly. "Oh, hush thee, child!" she repeated, mildly, again and again. "Thee'll make thyself down sick"—surveying in meek astonishment the fast-dropping flood. Not so her father. He dropped the unconscious cause of them, stooped, lifted her tenderly, in spite of her kicks and screams, and planted her on his knee. He removed the little wet hands; he drew down the little drenched, crumpled apron from the tear-stained face, and surveyed it curiously. Then he pretended to seek all over the apron for a dry spot; having found a tiny corner, he wiped with it the streaming eyes, and sighed, ludicrously. This made Helen laugh hysteric-

ally, in which merriment her father good-naturedly joined—
prolonging the chuckle until Helen caught it up, and again
repeated it. "Never mind, Judith," he said, good-humor-
edly, as his wife picked up the little quilted bonnet, and surveyed its crushed proportions in mute dismay. "There."
He straightened her bent form with his kindly palms—she
evincing a marked desire to rest her comforted head on her
father's bosom. He gathered both tiny dimpled hands in
his own: his magnetism charmed away sorrow. "That's
father's little lady; now tell father all about it."

The "little lady" seemed to have now no grief to unbur-
den. She looked quite pacified, thoroughly delighted, and
supremely content. She turned on him a beaming smile,
whispering something confidentially. He replied with a like
confidence, and at its close she bounded from her perch,
picked up the despised volume, and ran off with it.

"That's just like Zaccheus," placidly remarked the dame,
turning towards me. "Oh! I forgot," she added, in a repentant tone; "and that's just like me. Zaccheus, this is
Rubina Brooks. I met her out here, and invited her to spend
the night with us. Only think, Zaccheus, she was out in all
this rain, and she must come immediately and get some dry
garments on." She seized my cold hand, and led me off to
her own room; brought out one of her own quaint dresses,
ripped out in deft fashion a broad tuck to enable me to wear
it more comfortably, and almost ere I knew it, I had undergone a nice warm bath, and stood forth a somewhat spectral-
looking Quakeress. Then my hostess appeared, to lead me
to the parlor, where—before me—she told her husband exactly what I had said to her in the street. He shook my
hand, cordially; drew a stuffed rocking-chair before the fire
—the same fire that sounded to me from the door with such

a sense of welcome in its leaping flames—inviting me to be
seated. Then he drew one opposite, for himself, and began
to talk in a gentle voice of various things—current topics of
the day—never once alluding to my vagrant condition, but
treating me precisely on the footing of an expected, welcome
guest.

Meanwhile his wife trotted nimbly from this room to an
inner one, preparing tea. I found pleasure in watching her.
" You keep no domestic," thought I, as I saw her lift the iron
kettle on the hob, replenish the fire, and perform various other
menial offices, occasionally assisted by her husband, who, in
the midst of his kindly talk, yet was ever on the watch to
serve her. She drew out a little round table, spread a snowy
cloth over it, placed thereon some delicate china, a roll of ba-
ker's bread, a plate of cakes, a glass dish of preserved fruit,
and called us to partake of it. The fare, though simple, was
excellent. The tea strengthened and refreshed me. As the
evening waned, I felt more and more at home. It seemed
the most natural thing in life to be there ; my weary spirit
had at last found a congenial rest. Zaccheus and Judith were
old friends. Even Helen Mar, pretty, arch, and wilful, rested very near to the groping tendrils of my affections, as she
came to my side and imprinted her crimson lips on mine for
a good-night kiss, ere being whisked away to her repose by
the mild, decided dame. I shortly after followed her to a
similar cot in a tiny whitewashed cell, with one little window looking out upon I knew not what prospect—a sanded
floor, a small, square stand with drawers, a stool covered
with carpeting, a chest covered with large flowered chintz,
and a low rocking-chair with an ample netted tidy. " I hope
thee will sleep well. Thee must remember thy dreams : they
will come to pass, thee knows. Good-night, Rubina," was

my kind hostess's farewell, as she looked in upon me, just as my eyelids were wearily closing in slumber.

I dreamed that night of innumerable things, all pleasant. Gay shapes and bright colors danced airy mazourkas across the border-land of unconscious thought. I smiled at them benignly, applauding their wildest fantasies, and floated off on a radiant sea of delight—fraught with a blissful sense that, in some way, I had reached home at last; that my troubled life had all been a dream; that I was yet in my father's house; the sweet gates of unthinking infancy not yet closed upon me. Only a child's cares of a day to shake off—the unfailing burden of the pilgrim waiting for me very, very far off, on the shores of my woman's life.

CHAPTER XXXIV.

THE Sabbath came round to this Quaker household full of peace. No aching sense of the duty, the absolute, unresting need of going to church. Only a calm, unprofessional worship of the serenely poised minds. Zaccheus and Judith, it is true, went off to their "meeting," in the afternoon. Helen Mar remained at home with me, for the most part becomingly quiet; only once or twice threatening to run riot over the sacred stillness of the day. As I rocked in the easy-chair, and read Helen's despised present, I could not help contrasting this day with the one of a week previous; the retrospection ending with a summoning of thankful verdicts in the present's favor, and a hope that this might be the precursor of many similar ones. I wondered what Mrs. Selwyn thought of my disappearance. I was pondering these things, when my host and hostess returned, and inquired kindly "How I had enjoyed myself." They seemed childishly pleased and gratified with my answer, and in the evening they fell to talking of what they could do for me.

"Mrs. Bates has been wanting a governess, but she left last week for Philadelphia," thoughtfully remarked Judith. She insisted on my calling them by their Christian names. Helen Mar frequently thus addressed them, and they never seemed to think it disrespectful or improper.

"Yes, and she won't be back this year," added Zaccheus. "Suppose we keep her ourselves, Judith. Helen Mar needs a teacher, sorely."

"Thee don't seem to consider the expense," mildly responded his wife.

"I will gladly teach her for a home until I can do better," I here observed.

"Thee knows that our will is good enough, Rubina; but we are not at all gifted with worldly favors," observed Judith, anxiously. "Zaccheus never thinks. I verily believe that he does not know we are poor," she added, with a smile. He laughed.

Thus it was quietly settled. I did not think a better situation likely to offer itself immediately. I had come down a decided step now in my mental calculations, and, instead of the extravagant promises of Hope, I began to pluck the sober premises of Reason. The green glimpses disappeared from my road, and showed me the white line of sun-baked dust beyond.

I liked my benefactors better and better with the close of every day; they were so thoroughly warm-hearted and genial; so fond of doing good, and so unostentatious in their

18*

mode of doing it. They were deeply imbued with the charitable, self-sacrificing spirit of true religion, and never, while I was an inmate of their home, did I hear either speak evil of one of their neighbors. Chastity glows—a bright star without profession; so also does true religion. They made no profession of piety. " We are fond of our meeting," was their frequent remark ; but they neither expected nor exacted my attendance, or passed strictures on the faith of other worshippers. I went with them a few times, but I did not like their "meeting." The stiff, silent rows of men and women, sitting opposite each other like statues; the long hour of dead silence, unbroken by a prayer or psalm, during which they listened to the whisperings of "The Spirit," and—inaudibly to other ears than their own—received and gathered to their hearts His preached revelations; the rebuking stare, if one moved from weariness, were to me inexpressibly irksome. When one of the brethren, or a pale, sweet-faced sister, was moved by the Holy Ghost, and constrained to expound these wondrous revelations, I could not but feel interested.

But these cases were rare, and the silent meetings many, so I gradually came to spend my Sundays at home with my pupil. She was quite too restless to be allowed often to accompany her parents. She flounced around on the benches in such unorthodox fashion as to seriously discompose the placidity of the Elders, and to disturb their feelings of devotion; paying no heed to the gentle shakes of the fawn-colored bonnets around her, or the frowns of the broad-brims. She was gentle and docile enough with me, and the Sundays which we spent together were the pleasantest of my life—delicious bits of dreaminess inserting themselves between weeks of thought and study, just as a day of joy ofttimes stands out a bright mosaic on the black enamel of other days of sorrowful gloom.

The Hoveys were not demonstrative people. Little by little you grew into their confidence. Then they made no fuss about their friendship. They told you a secret as quietly as they would have spoken of an ordinary domestic concern; never putting your fidelity to the doubt by exacting a promise of keeping it. If they honored you by their friendship, you were supposed worthy of it; and all contrary implication would by them have been deemed an insult. Theirs had been a love-match—an elopement; although their sober years laughed down in incredulity this primitive fact. Judith told me this one day. "He was poor then," she said, "and my parents were well off, and they were dreadfully opposed to it. *His* folks were Hicksites, and no less opposed to the match; so it run along for a long, long time, and finally we came to the conclusion that we would consult *our own* minds, and one night—it was dark as Egypt —I up and out of the window. Zaccheus Hovey was waiting for me there, thee may well believe, and we embraced and ran off together. Thee would have done the same, Rubina, if thee had loved him as well as I did. Well, I have never had reason to regret it, friend. That I can truly say."

"What did your parents say?" I asked.

"Oh! they never overlooked it in us. They turned us out of the meetings; but as we were away, we did not mind. Happiness is better than meetings, Rubina. Besides, it was a common thing; why, they turned my Aunt Rachel Hussy out because she went to hear the Hicksites preach. Her sister went too, but they did not deal with her, on account of her young family. Aunt Rachel had no children. That was a great while ago. They are all gone now. I did long to be reconciled to them first, but I have never been back there since we left that night. Zaccheus has, but they didn't know him. 'Twas after the rheumatism left him as he is now; and he is changed in other things besides that; but his heart is just the same as ever, and though I cannot with truth say, friend, that we are any richer in worldly goods than we were then, yet we have enough and to spare, and thee knows *enough* is as good as a feast."

" A contented mind *is* a perpetual feast, we are told," I said, smiling.

" Zaccheus has made me contented," she remarked, naively. " I used to fret some at the ways of Providence. He never frets—his disposition is so even. He accepts sorrows in the same thankful spirit as he does blessings; as part of the Lord's dispensations to us, and necessary for our spiritual growth. Our eldest -boy was stricken by lightning; they brought him in to me black and lifeless. I felt very rebellious for a season, but *he* never uttered a groan of discontent. I felt sore wroth for a long time after our next son died—our little Harvey—the merriest lad that ever blessed a mother's love. He was kicked by a horse, and died in the greatest agony. Zaccheus wept for his sufferings, but after they were over, and he lay still and cold in his little coffin, he raised up his voice and gave thanks. Rubina, *I* couldn't. I'm loath to say it; it was wicked; it was very unkind; but I turned and left the room while he was speaking. I went off by myself and tried to pray. I couldn't; I could only curse. Oh! it's terrible to think of now." She shivered at the recollection. " But I did. I actually cursed my Maker. Zaccheus found me after a time, raving away there in the garret. Well, Rubina, thee thinks he was displeased with me, and rebuked me loudly. Nay, child. He gathered

me in his arms, like as the heavenly Shepherd gathereth his
little lambs homeward, and wept with me till I grew soothed
and comforted. I told him, then, of my sin; how I had
cursed the Saviour. 'Thee can do him no harm, my poor
Judith,' he said, calmly. 'Thy cursing will not move him
one jot, or one tittle, till all his law be fulfilled. Let us
praise him, and let him do as seemeth him good. He knows
best what is good for us, and needful for our salvation.'
Well, friend, I was strengthened by his exhortations—Zaccheus has a great gift of counsel—and I ceased to mourn.
But not for long, for the Lord called me soon to give up my
sole remaining son—my Reuben; and again I rebelled. I
turned my heart against him, and locked it up in steely ire,
and I thirsted greedily for revenge. I wanted to smite him,
even as he had smitten me; I ceased to pray myself, and I
would not hear Zaccheus pray either. After a while he placed
before me two pictures. One was little Reuben lying dead
in his little cot; and another was a man, grim and hardened
looking, swinging from the gallows. ' It *might* have been
that. Which would thee have it be, Judith?' he said, kindly,
and I gave up the lad willingly from that very hour; for I
would rather bear children to become cherubs in the Lord's
mansions on high, than sinful culprits on earth. I see the
wisdom now," said she. " Worldly joys were fast deaden-
ing my moral sensibility. Any thing pleasant I drank with
eager relish. God sent these trials to rouse me and place
my erring steps straight. Was it his fault that I was stubborn and dull, and needed a repetition? All lessons, Rubina,
have their price; but thee knows, when rightly earned, they
are repaid by their own value." She paused and wiped her
eyes.

" You have seen trouble, indeed," I remarked, pityingly.

"'Twas a long time after this when Helen Mar was born," she resumed, placidly. " I besought the Lord to let me keep this one olive-branch ; for I began to think that our bereavements were a judgment upon us for the sin of disobedience to our parents' wishes. The Lord is merciful, and waiting to be gracious, Rubina. He graciously inclined his ear unto my request. But 'the heart is deceitful above all things, and desperately wicked :' I think *now* I am willing to submit to his will, whatever it may be, but I cannot be sure. I *might* be worse than ever, should she be removed far from me. I cannot bear to think of it; though Zaccheus would not be troubled. His hope and foundations are sure ; my feet slip continually in the mire of selfishness, and threaten to bury me forever. Then my husband's strength is my shield and deliverance : he intercedes for me, and saves me from my worst enemy—myself." She paused, her sweet face glowing with noble enthusiasm.

"You felt just as I should feel," I said, presently.

"Doubtless, friend," she answered. " Human nature is so very feeble. Our lives, at best, are but a dreary mixture of fraud to our *best* selves, and deceit to others. Our aims, perhaps, are high enough, and pure enough, but toward their attainment, through what deeps of selfish motives we wallow—in what treacherous quagmires of self-deception we stick fast ! Is such fruit the offering we should bring heavenward ? Is not the motive-power that which our Maker regards, rather than deeds or words ? These latter shrivel and fade away in the presence of Omniscience. They are mere worthless dust and ashes beclouding our deeper, purer, more spiritual natures."

"Is it wrong, then, to mourn our losses ?" I asked in surprise.

" No ; but to wrestle with, to resist the divine will, to refuse consolation when he sends it in abundance, is, and
ever must be, wrong, Rubina. Let us first purge our hearts
into purity, and divine succor will reach us, will draw us
up into a state of religious submission. It was long in coming to me, but it *has* come—unless I am again deceived;
and time only will decide that."

Zaccheus asked me one day for the street and number of
Mrs. Selwyn's residence. I gave it, and he returned shortly
after with my trunk. I was eager to know the exact nature
of his reception, but he would tell me nothing except that
he saw none of the inmates but Madame, and that she anath-
ematized me, warmly. " It will do no good to me to repeat
her words; or for thee to hear them. Let it all drop into
forgetfulness," he said, gravely. " She is a poor, sinful soul,
and merits pity rather than scorn." He broke short off, and
began to speak of Helen Mar's progress in study. " I think
she is bright enough," he began, " but she sadly needs discipline ; eh, Rubina ?"

" I anticipate no difficulty in that respect," I hastened to
say. " She is remarkably gentle, so far, and quite beyond
her years in her acquirements, or else my experience in teaching has been among children as much deficient in those studies where she excels. She seems eager to learn, in spite of
her restlessness. I observe that she cannot be coaxed to sit
long at any one study ; the monotony seems to irk her. So
I vary them ; give her a bit of one to learn, then a copy to
write, or a sentence to analyze, or a few words to spell. This
suits her ; she remarked at the close of yesterday, that it did
not seem long in the least."

In fact, we soon grew into warm friends. A more affectionate, merry, wilful child I never saw. She never was af-

fected into the least quiescence with her sober surroundings.
It was impossible to be lonely or sad when she was by ; she
soon kissed away the melancholy—never resting until smiles
or a hearty laugh crowned her efforts.   Her mother often declared that " her clatter was too abominable to be borne ;"
but her contradictory smile, as she said it, proved plainly
how quickly the sunshine would vanish from home should
" the clatter " prematurely cease.   She purloined my letters
from her father's overcoat pocket, immediately upon his entrance into the little hall, and standing seriously before me,
as I sat at work, would roguishly wonder if I had " not sewed enough ; I was pricking my fingers so dreadfully."   Then,
when I raised my eyes to see the origin of her anxious care,
the quick sparkle of her deep blue eyes was sufficient be-
trayal, and I would peremptorily order its delivery.   This she
always refused until I had made over my implements of labor into her custody, to be hidden beyond my reach for the
entire day.

My letters were all from Annah : though I heard once
from Mr. Hume.   It bore the Northfield postmark, where he
was again sojourning.   He expressed much surprise at my
absence ; wondered that I had not consulted his inclinations,
" so plainly expressed," and renewed his " hope that I was
now willing to listen to the guidance of a superior judgment ;
there was a limit to even his forbearance."   Stung at his unwarrantable tone, I replied bitterly.   To this I got no answer,
and I endeavored to reason down the pain I felt rising at
this sign of indifference or scorn, by the old, worn-out reflection of Northfield days : " It is much better so ; we are, on
some points, and must ever be, both in speaking and writing,
continually at variance."   It was yet potent, but would it
always prove thus salutary ?   Even now, at times, I blamed

myself severely, that I could not, or would not, advance one step, and stretch forth my hand to pluck—regret slyly whispered—the flowers of happiness. "And why should your will be paramount to peace?" added the same monitor; "why should ardent dreams of a progressive future mar the awaiting bliss of the present? You say that a union with him will be the death of your spirit's advancement; will dwarf every expanding faculty, and crown your whole nature with dishonor. Silly fool! his is a better creed. *He* says that woman has no need of progress. Believe him! *He* declares that woman's life is abundantly satisfied with daily crumbs doled out by its master's stronger hands. Accept the declaration, and bless the generous giver for this scanty fare! If, in this submission, you miss the excitement of the battle of life, the long struggle, the hand-to-hand combat, and the strength which flows from victory—will you not likewise escape its harassing cries, its torturing stings, sheltered and folded safe and close in the remote harbor of his love? If you lose the voice of the world's praise, will you not also escape its dangers?" And after listening thus to her soft persuasions—far oftener, reader, than I care to tell—will would rise up, scornfully; shake them off peremptorily: "If in combat and victory there is strength, then I, too, will battle in it. If in unrestrained knowledge there lurks sweetness, then I, too, will taste it. The dregs of no *master's* cup will I drain. I will have no crumbs from his table. Despite 'woman's destiny,' the fountain is open for me as well as you; and so, my would-be lord, farewell." Alas! that to some farewells there should attach the bitterness of death.

Annah's letters showed plainly that she was not happy, though she never stated thus broadly this fact. The record of her first week in school was full of plaintive misery. I

fully comprehended her sufferings, and wept over them.
Then I read it to Helen, whose eyes glowed with tremulous
pity. From Annah's letter I gathered that Millicent walked
with her to school, at her father's express desire—but vanished through the entry leading to the school-room, ere Annah could clearly see where she was going. Then she opened the green baize door, and timidly entered, only to meet
and shrink from the united stare of three hundred pairs of
eyes suddenly levelled at her. "I hardly knew any thing,"
wrote she; "I felt so ashamed, standing there all alone, and
I didn't see any vacant seats. Then I saw Milly, away at the
other end of the room, whispering to a big, ugly girl, who
looked at me and laughed. The girls near me began to giggle and hide their faces in their books, and to peep at me
from behind them.* Not one offered to move along and give
me a seat. It was a very large room, with wooden desks
around the sides, and rows of benches. A great stove stood
in the centre, red hot, and a square table, painted green, stood
not far from it, covered with books, at which sat a lady. I
don't know how long I stood there before she saw me; long
enough to see every thing in the room, even to the sums in
chalk on the long blackboard. At length one of the girls
laughed a little too loud; the teacher turned hastily and saw
me. She came forward, and asked me if I was a new scholar.
'Yes, ma'am,' I said, feeling ready to cry—at which answer,
the girls smiled again and looked at each other. 'Come this
way and I will give you a seat,' she said, kindly; and she
found me a vacant desk, and brought a book for the morning
lesson. 'Did you come alone?' she asked, in a low tone. I
told her just how it was, Ruby, and she nodded, and went
away; but after the recitation was over, she called Milly out
before the green table and publicly rebuked her. I felt sorry

for her then, but I got over it afterward, for she told her mother *such* a story about me. She won't walk to school with me now, nor hardly ever notices me when there. She came along just now, and asked me who I was writing to. I told her, and she wanted to read it. I wouldn't let her, and she was angry directly. ' I suppose you have been setting me out nicely to your sister,' said she ; ' ain't you ashamed of it ? You are nothing but a dependent; I tell the girls so too.' " There was much more in the same strain. The whole letter was a recital of petty yet stinging slights and insults, requiring ready, sympathetic care. I wrote an immediate answer which I hoped might prove an antidote.

This was the precursor of many such. During this year her letters were nearly all of this stamp—dotted with pleasant oases of warm affection for her few friends. She made frequent mention of Milly and Edward's sayings; their sarcastic attempts to entertain her; and then she dispatched the glad news that they seemed to repent of their unkindness, and relented their teasing.

" I am contented now," wrote this sweet, simple soul, " for I never knew how to answer them back. I don't think they will trouble me any more." I was glad too; but the next bulletin confounded the rumor. I quote her words : " They invited me to ride with them last week for the first time. I thought it a wonderful change ingrafting itself on their conduct, and I was full of delight. I sat on the back seat with Millicent. Edward sat with the driver. It was very pleasant for a while, though Millicent said nothing to me. She would lean forward at intervals to drop a remark to Edward, or to laugh at his jokes with the driver. Edward is a coarse fellow. I don't like him. When she did so, she would glance superciliously at me to see if I was watching her, and if I didn't smile at what he was saying she curled her lip in disdain. I didn't care. I didn't mind it at all. It was pleasure enough for me to watch the people in the streets; to feel the swift motion of the carriage and to know that I was having a ride—the first and last since I have been here. Aunt and Milly ride almost daily; but they never ask me to go. Presently the sky grew cloudy; then it grew darker and began to sprinkle, and the driver turned around for home. Then it rained violently. Edward sprang hurriedly over the seat. 'Do you mind changing places with me, Miss Hannah ?'—he always calls me Hannah, as well as Milly—he said, insolently; at the same time taking my hand to pull me up. I hesitated; for I liked neither the tone nor the request. I began to see why I had come—to be the subject of fresh sport for them. Then Millicent spoke up in her cool way, and said, smiling: 'Why don't you go, child ?'—I am as old as herself—'can't you see that he wants to sit by me, you fool ?' she whispered in my ear; and so—I was a downright fool to do it, Ruby—without saying a word, I clambered over the seat and took his place. Of course, I was soon wetted through ; although Miles—who looked sour and cross enough at them—did his best to keep the rain off me. He pulled up the boot high, and tucked his own over-coat around me; but for all that I was soaking wet when we reached home. I didn't care for that; but it was rather too mean to laugh at me, as they did. I heard them giggle and whisper behind me, and Miles did too. He whipped the horses all the harder for it. Once I heard him mutter something about 'that damned little whiffet of a puppy.' Aunt Lucas met us in the hall. She never looked at me. 'Oh ! Milly, I was afraid you would get wet,' she said, anxiously, feeling of her clothes to see if they were damp. 'Such rain

I never saw before! How lucky you were!' The rain ran from my garments in tiny drips; my bonnet was ruined; I was cold and miserable. But nobody noticed it. I was suffered to gather up my sodden skirts and pick my way up stairs to my own little room, where, but for your well-remembered words of love at our parting, I should have sunk to the floor disheartened, and prayed to die. Don't laugh, sister; I did a far wiser thing. I took off my streaming garments; I bound up my dripping hair, and went to bed, to sleep and dream of you, Ruby; of you and our little home, which looks so far—so dreadfully far away in the dim future. I can see it yet, however. It lures me to make every effort to reach it. I have both good news and bad with which to finish up this letter. I have been promoted in my classes; I am to play at the coming examination, and I shall take singing lessons next quarter. I think the teachers like me, for I never laugh at them, and some of the young ladies do. They say I make remarkable progress in music. Now for the bad: I caught a slight cold after my ride last week; but it is nothing dangerous, so you must not worry. It is only a slight huskiness, which will soon wear off. I should not have mentioned it, but for my promise to tell you every thing."

A year and a half of effort, and no nearer the goal—my brightly cherished, fast becoming impossible, goal—but none the less cherished for that gloomy vista. I was still at Mr. Hovey's—Helen Mar's teacher. Through these friends' exertions five more day pupils were added to my school, and Judith allowed me the use of their one front room as a school-room. My prospects thus began to brighten a little, until I found, at the close of this second year, that my fortune barely sufficed to clothe Annah and myself—leaving a shrunken purse and the renewal of exertion to begin the next round of hope upon.

"Never mind," I suggested, as disappointment tugged too heavily at my heartstrings. "I must try to find something else to do to eke out my slender income; and in the mean time I must assiduously cultivate patience." Annah's letters were my comfort. They told me that her old tormentor, Edward, was no more seen at the Lucas's; his place was usurped by a rival. "You can't guess who," wrote she; "so to ease your suspense I will come to the point at once. It's the schoolmaster; our old friend, Mr. Hume. It seems very curious that he should turn up here Milly's lover. She says he is. He is vastly improved in person and address since Northfield days, though, of course, I knew him directly. He made a miserable pretence of not recognizing me, expressing considerable surprise at the introduction. He certainly does not like to see me around; never speaks to me if he can avoid it. I don't know why; he used to notice me a great deal; we were excellent friends, as I well remember. At any rate, I don't trouble him much with my presence. Am I an eyesore, sister? Sometimes, when Aunt and Milly are not by, he treats me better. Sometimes he says such unaccountable things, I don't know what he means; I dare not tell Uncle John, and none of the others would believe me—but I never answer him. If he was not a minister, Ruby—but I am foolish to write you all this, and so I shall say no more. Milly joined his church last Sunday. He is settled here as a minister. One more year and I shall be through my studies. I confess I am all impatience for the time to vanish; but it moves, to my thinking, on crippled wings. I cannot yet sing; the huskiness does not leave my voice, and I cannot account for it. I cough none. I feel well. I *am* well—and I can play if I cannot sing—so I endeavor to be content. Milly had a Christmas present this year—a fine piano. I do so enjoy it. She is taking lessons on the harp, and Uncle John urged me to begin also; but I shall attempt no morn than I can bring to perfection—a piece of wisdom I owe to you, my Ruby. I think of you constantly in the intervals of study. I weep for you, too, in secret, and pray for you; would that it could lessen or lighten your toil. I do long to see you. Nearly two long years without even a glimpse. Come to me soon; do, do; come, if only for a day, or let me go to see you. Uncle John frequently speaks of you, and says, 'it is time she made us a long visit.' I think so too; so, please your ladyship, regard it as a doxology duty, and not to be shirked any longer."

I considered this plea for a whole day; but decided that as I was in the middle of a term, the visit must wait longer. I wrote this much to Annah—adding, that if she liked to venture on a trip to see me, instead, I should be delighted to see her.

It was full six weeks ere I got an answer. This was a brief kind note from Uncle John: "Annah was very sick. They thought it a slight illness at first—not necessary to rouse my fears; but she was growing worse, and called for me constantly. Would I start immediately? and not be frightened, as there was every reason to hope for her ultimate recovery."

"Would I start?" I repeated, bitterly. Of course I would. I got ready without the delay of a moment. I put my things together as in a dream; making unnecessary journeys from garret to cellar after I knew not what, until waylaid by Judith, who followed me very motherly, and asked what I wanted. She watched me anxiously at first; then took pity on my distracted state of mind, and helped me to collect my wits when they went staggering, by dropping kind, placid observations. I heard her gratefully and assented, but came directly to the old topic.

Dear reader, have you ever noticed, when laboring in the mire of a heavy sorrow, or pressed down by an overwhelming care, how the mind shrinks suddenly from its former expansion, and keeps on narrowing, contracting, shutting in its walls upon itself, until the one grievous thought stands isolated there from all contact with sympathy? There it reigns supreme—not the less a burden that it is a kingly one—and looks out upon the gay, happy world around its sphere in wonder. Consolation! Who speaks of consolation? "Go away—away! leave me alone; do not speak to me!" it says, in its secret cell. "Your words sound strangely; so widely short of the mark; so unfeeling. What do *you* know of that which *I* feel? Leave me to myself."

So sounded Judith's efforts to console me, as she folded my dresses, gathered my books together, and zealously prepared jellies and cordials in a neat little box, for me to take. "It may not be as bad as thee thinks, dearest friend," she said, with genuine pity softening her voice. "Don't thee go to borrowing of trouble. He is a hard paymaster, and will dun thee sorely." I smiled absently, "Now thee shall keep thy pupils. I will speak to their parents this very night. Thee will find every thing all right and ready for thy hand when thee comes back to us."

'I groaned inwardly. "What did I then care for pupils? What if she should die? He said she was very sick," I whispered, in terror; then shrank quivering from the boldly expressed fear.

"She will not die, Rubina, unless the Lord wills it," said Judith, gently. "He holds thee in the hollow of his hand. Rely on him and be comforted."

Her simple faith was a torture. "Die and leave me," I apathetically repeated, going away from my sweet, would-be comforter. Oh! she cannot. She never would of her own accord, and heaven will not be thus cruel. Just now, when a thread of light begins to streak my labors; when the long separation seems about to draw to a close. No; it cannot be. Yet, what should tempt me to dream otherwise? What have I ever done to merit forbearance? What have I loved that He has not ruthlessly taken? Friends wither from my grasp, like new-mown hay under the sun's fierce glare. Must idols always be broken? I asked again and again, with bitter tears. I am stricken; render me not utterly desolate. "My life is a famine in the midst of abundance; feed and succor it, or cut it off entirely," I prayed, "for, as it is, it but cumbereth the soil with weeds."

Zaccheus took me to the dépôt. I saw the cars steam like a roaring lion up to the station. I went in; took mechanically the first seat which offered itself, and meekly suffered Zaccheus to place me in a better, at his gentle suggestion. I felt his kind parting hand-clasp, and heard, as though it was an echo afar off, his low, musical "Good-by, friend! God guide and speed thee safely!" and was vaguely conscious of being borne onward by a mighty force, which yet lagged remorselessly—leagues behind my onward speeding thoughts and fears. It was foolish and useless, of course, to try to quicken our pace by repeating, mentally, all the exclamations of impatient teamsters, to goad on their tired steeds; but over and over I sounded them, until I found one of the passengers curiously regarding me. I had no fancy

19

to be thought insane. I considered that I might really
become so, if I allowed my fears so to influence me. I endeavored for the rest of the way to zealously keep my eyes
on outside objects. Fields, fences, trees, brief lovely glimpses
of the river, and cool suburban residences met my stare and
vanished. Precipitous rocky ledges, sandy banks shelving
down to the track, down which children, freckled, bonnet-
less and hatless, put their bare, brown feet, and recklessly
slid. I hoped, heartlessly, that we might run over a few by
way of excitement; but they were too used to the sport to
be capable of fear, and they sent after us merry shouts of
defiance. Then the city began to send along its highways
straggling indications of its nearness; tall, narrow dwellings,
and the absence of court-yards. And finally, we rumbled,
and whistled, and steamed in at the long covered dépôt.

Annah was too ill to know me when I reached the house.
Uncle John took me up to her room at once. Aunt Hannah
sat by the bedside, fanning her. She greeted me quite
warmly, and seemed relieved to abandon her post. I paid
no heed to her lengthy explanation of the manner of her
attack, or to her dreary recital of symptoms. It was sufficient to know and feel that she lay helpless before me. I
only cared to know the nature of the medicines on the table,
and the hours in which to administer them. I felt cool and
calm as I summoned my energies to their work. " No abandonment to weakening emotions now," I said, desperately,
as I lifted the emaciated form into a more comfortable posture ; throwing out the heated pillows and substituting cool
fresh ones. She was delirious, and raved constantly of her
school, her studies. Then she vented her vexation that she
could not master the piece of music before her, in terms of
heart-rending impatience. Anon she moaned wearily, and

called plaintively for "Ruby; Sister Ruby; my sister. Why don't you bring her to me? You keep her shut up in that dark hole all day, and no light creeps in to her, as she sews, sews, sews, and works, works, works, and I want her. I want her, I tell you, and I *will* have her too. She is mine, I say. What do the dragons want of her, that they creep and crawl around her so? I wish I could kill them; but I cannot. Oh! dear, dear." The weak arm fell powerless on the quilt. I watched with her alone. In the morning Milly came in, rather constrainedly offering to remain in the sick-room while I went down to breakfast. Accordingly I left her. How gloomy the great rooms looked below, as I softly journeyed through them on my way to the basement! A death-like hush seemed to settle on every chair, table, and cornice. The gorgeous curtains draped the windows like solemn palls prematurely falling before a too vivid glory. I held my breath as I glided through, and felt for the slippery banisters leading to the dining-room. Here all was cheerful.

"We live here since she was *taken down*," observed Aunt Lucas, pouring out my coffee, which I drank in silence. "How did she rest?" she presently asked.

"She talked constantly," I returned.

"Yes, she has been out of her head now for over a week," she said, sedately; "but Doctor Mansfield says that is to be expected."

"What does he say ails her?" I asked.

"Brain fever, brought on by too much study. Her throat is affected some, too," she replied, with an air of indifference that I did not relish. The doctor came while she was speaking. I went immediately up-stairs. He was feeling her pulse as I entered. He was a tall, thin, grave man, and he bowed, without speaking, as Milly introduced me.

" I am glad you have come; she needs constant care," he said, as he prepared a new prescription, and took his leave.

" Is there any hope, doctor ?" I managed to inquire, as he crossed the threshhold with a careful stride.

" Of course, my dear woman, great hope; but the danger is not yet past," he said, in a low tone. " I shall come to-night and stay awhile with her. If she sleeps, do not waken her on any account." He bowed low and trod softly down the long staircase.

She did not sleep. All day she prattled ceaselessly, sinking at intervals into a kind of murmur, totally unintelligible. The domestics came frequently to inquire if I needed any assistance, and Susan, the chambermaid, watched with her while I took my meals. Milly went off in the afternoon for a fortnight's visit, declaring that it was too dull and dreary to be longer borne.

A week passed, ere she knew me. The doctor declared all immediate danger over, but stipulated expressly for the greatest caution against a relapse. I was only too thankful for this; thankful that she knew my voice, and loved the caresses I bestowed upon her, for she had not yet seen me. Her eyes were badly inflamed and swollen, and were kept scrupulously bandaged. Neither could she utter a word. The ravings of delirium seemed to have utterly exhausted her strength; her greatest efforts only producing a whisper. She complained more and more of her throat; of the pressure encircling it—trying to remove it by tearing at it with her feeble fingers.

Altogether we had more cause for fear than for hope, as days, and weeks even, wore tediously away, and brought no very formidable steps toward that land of promise to an invalid—entered through the golden gates of convalescence.

CHAPTER XXXV.

During all this time I had not once met Mr. Hume, who was a frequent visitor at the house. Three months had swept away since my arrival. I passed them for the most part in anxious, solitary nursing. I sought and obtained slop-work from the shops with which to employ my leisure hours, and when Annah slept or dozed, I sewed diligently; then, while my fingers fought the coarse garments with their tiny weapons, my thoughts battled none the less resolutely their monopoly of bitter discontent. I often wondered that he never asked for me; but after the usual daily pondering of the matter, I one day reflected that very likely he was unaware of my presence in the house—it is so galling to pride to admit the idea of forgetfulness. "Milly or her mother are not likely to speak of me to any one, especially if they thought it would gratify me, and they know that we were once friends," thought I, apologetically. "And though he knows, probably, that Annah has been dangerously ill, and is even yet too feeble to be visible below, he might suppose her to be in the tender charge of a hired nurse; a natural supposition, as Aunt Hannah and Milly are never in the sick-room, or, as she is out of sight, most probably she is out of mind also. A lover in the presence of his mistress is not apt to think of aught else. *Her* lover! But he was once mine." I stung my shrinking heart again and again with this useless accusation: it gave me back only humble silence. Then my pride rose. "If he *did* know of my proximity, and did not choose to see me—did not choose to be civil for the sake of the old friendship, it was well enough," I reasoned. "What did I care for him? what, indeed ! He was so unsubstantial (I cast about vainly for a better word, and said this, after all, with a smile), so deceitful, so selfishly tyrannical." "Oh! but you don't think so *now*, whatever you may once have thought," ironically interrupted Reason, with her cold, galling smile. "When others bear · away the favors you scorned, you start up eager to accept them." She was ready, and pluming herself for an argumentative battle. I felt it, and skilfully avoided her. I bit my lip in disdain, and put down into its former dark corner in my heart the lingering tenderness which had so long lived there half smothered, but which was always persistently struggling upward to the daylight—sending tiny, clasping shoots to plead for it; for a sunnier warmth, a richer mould, heavier dews. "Lie there until the resurrection," I said, half angrily. "I will not care for you ; I will not think of you, even ; go in peace."

After all, I could and did foster the shoots with delighted willingness. At first I felt ire at his marked neglect, then sadness, then forgiveness. I caught myself very often framing excuses for him, and overwhelming my own conduct with bitter reproaches. Oftener than I care to tell, I made him like unto a god, and was more than content to sink worshipping at his feet. No Roman fanatic ever kissed a shrine with more insensate devotion, than I, in my loving imagination, wore away, with like caresses, the sharp edges of his character. I filed them with many, many reveries, in which each one took off something rough, ragged, and formerly hateful to me, until the surface stood forth, rounded into lines of faultless beauty. Yes; absence from him, and neglect on his part; the dull, absorbing images of daily cares and toils, and my own indignant denials of the unwelcome fact, were insufficient to uproot this love, which grew with a rapidity that appalled me. And the bitterness of the cup was my full consciousness of his utter unworthiness. I knew all the while that with renewed communion with him, perhaps with even a look, my old stubbornness would revive; my-hero sink again a serf. But that did not abate one whit the passionate ardor of the present longing for his presence. Do you care to ask the reason for this love? the processes by which the tiny archer sunk his shaft there unbidden, unwished for—keener than steel in the fleshly tabernacle? I know not. My former affection for him—half smothered in passionate resentment—was but dying embers to this fierce flame now raging: it had never been worthy of the name. It was not that Evil, in my nature, was supreme. It was only that Good lay dormant, and Evil, roused by its torpor, throve the more vigorously. Little by little, it grew a delight to think of him constantly by day, and to dream of him by night. Then, if waked by a random noise, my thought, waking likewise, still kept its guiding-star in vigilant view, and magnetically plunged after it.

A woman loves best when the object is withdrawn from her. Pity for an injury, a repulse, a slight, a misapprehension, real or fancied, leads the chase. It is but a step from cold disdain, from absolute indifference, from scorn even, and a desire to ridicule, to a passion so pure and glowing, so forgetful of visibly repellant points, so full of the generosity of self-sacrifice, that to swamp his faults and vices in a veil of marvellous virtues, is but the work of an instant; that to live for him, to suffer for him, to die for him, becomes to her thought the only bliss for earth—the only martyrdom fit for heaven.

Oh! if such love be a delirium, it is none the less priceless, as it gilds the inner life with sunny reflections, and wakes it to more vivid perceptions of outward beauty. The eye, turn it where you will—upon the printed page, the glazed case-ment, bare white walls, or cold, gray ashes—sees, but discerns none of these things, for the sunlight, the mellow starlight, the glimpses of distant, dreamy Edens that make the dreari-est surroundings seem lovely. Then the harsh sounds of ev-ery-day life grow musical. The mind hears continual vespers, and wild, sweet songs of praise float with every unconscious heart-beat to the Author and Source of this strange emotion. Every thing divine is love. , Then why should not this spark of divinity in us acknowledge its originator? Love to love; the grosser subject to the purer, the human to the heavenly, but still the same essential essence, pursuing the same immor-tal destiny.

When the street-door bell rang I often opened my door to catch, perchance, the tones of his voice in the hall below. I was surprised to find how I thrived on this scanty aliment; on the brief echo of a common-place greeting as he entered, or the faint ripple of a laugh. These I gathered to myself and exulted over for hours, if not roused from my selfish mood by a whispered request from Annah, or at her gently expressed wonder at my long silence. She could not note the changes in my face, for, dear sufferer, she could yet see nothing. Her recovery to her former perfect health began to assume a doubtful hue. A swelling appeared on her round, white throat, which grew steadily in size, and was very op-pressive. She would gasp for breath, and clutch at it with her feeble fingers, as if to rend it from her. When she spoke, it was with a huskiness inexpressibly painful. She made vigorous attempts to sit up, to walk; she seemed to look hopefully forward; she spoke cheerfully when she alluded to herself, but that was seldom. I was not deceived by her as-

sumed cheerfulness. I knew, by one little incident, that she
considered her case hopeless. This was when one day, coming suddenly upon her, I found her praying. She did not
hear the door open, and I stood still one moment to listen.
It was barely a whisper, but yet quite audible: "Help, oh
help her to bear it!" was the burden of the cry—then, after
a pause, "Take me now, dear Saviour; leave me not to be
a terrible burden; it is easier to die than to linger on through
years of helplessness." I shut the door, and stole softly
away, unable to hear any more of the soft, agonized pleading.
This secret, unspoken conclusion of hers haunted me. It
banished all regretful love-dreams, and stirred within me remorseful thrills for their indulgence. She *must* recover. I
dreaded to allude to it openly; yet inwardly it fretted and
goaded me to all sorts of desperate shifts to learn its truth
or falsity. I descended to employ petty meannesses as scouts.
I blush to think of numberless times in which I played the
eaves-dropper. Many a time I stole to my aunt's room—
where in the morning she was quartered with Milly—and
placing my ear to the keyhole, listened. A word here and
there I caught, but of these I could not string enough together to make any sensible meaning. The doctor was grave
and silent, and pitiful. His few phrases were of a hopeful
strain always. He doubtless disliked to confirm or implant
fears, as long as a strand remained on which to weave a
healthful coil. I dogged his steps down stairs sometimes
to the family room, where he usually made a brief, friendly
call, on coming from the sick-chamber. My care procured
me nothing; he never spoke of her. I spied in the servants'
quarters, and as their voices were generally pitched several
octaves above the kitchen din and bustle, I found no difficulty
in hearing them. Very amusing things my inquisitiveness

19*

gained for repayment; odd remarks about sweethearts and
wakes, with frequent reference to Miss Milly and the minister. I did not comprehend these latter allusions. They spoke
of something being wrong; what? I cared not, now—no
word of what I longed to know.

It was Susan, a kind-hearted girl in the main, who finally
told me. She came up one day to inquire if she could be
of service. I thought of nothing, and thus told her, but she
lingered.

"How be her eyes, Miss?" she asked, in a whisper.

"Very painful to-day," was all I could utter.

"Dr. Mansfield says she'll be stone-blind for life," next observed she, timidly. "None will tell you, but I tell 'em *you*
ought to know, and so I did," was her somewhat confused
apology. "I feel for you, Miss; I do, indeed," and the kind-
hearted girl broke fairly down with a sob. "Miss," said she,
presently, wiping her eyes with the back of her plump hand,
"you'd better take the air a little; it'll do you good, and I'll
stay here with her. You look as thin as a rail; do let me
stay, and go."

I finally yielded, and went noiselessly down stairs. As I
passed the drawing-room door I heard Mr. Hume's voice, and
the temptation was strong to stop and listen. "Why do you
not frame an errand in there, and so gain a greeting, or at
least observe how your unexpected presence affects him?" a
momentary inclination suggested. Pride indignantly repelled
it, and with a sneer told me not to stand dallying there like
a fool. I softly opened the massive door, stepped out, and
as quietly closed it. It was a warm evening for autumn.
Twilight blent its soothing radiance with the streaming gas-
light at each corner. There were sudden flushes in the atmosphere, which made the heat at times almost oppressive.

Then as sudden a current of fresh air cooled it. Happy families clustered in cheerful parlors with wide open blinds and windows, enjoying the evening reunion. Merry couples chatted laughingly on pleasant balconies, or leaned over their iron railings to exchange gay badinage with acquaintances in the street below. These sauntered up and down the pavement, decked in light summer habiliments. Gay birds of Paradise they looked—apparently strangers to any thing that smacks of care or sorrow. It was a night in which to live out of doors. The essence of summer, condensed into the more pungent airs of autumn. Only a moon was needed, to swing her golden ball among clustering stars in the cloudless blue arch, and thereby add a finishing glory.

I walked along; but, charming as the night was, I did not enjoy it. Gay and mirthful as the scene was on either side, I was not amused thereby. I turned and went homeward— quite too sad at heart for an aimless evening stroll. Mr. Hume, it seems, had departed; at least, I heard no voices as I entered the hall, and mounted the dim staircase. In the upper entry I met Susan returning to her charge by the back stairs leading to the kitchen. In much surprise I questioned her; she interrupted me by explaining that Miss Milly had sent her for a glass of water.

"Miss Milly! where is she?" I asked briefly.

"In there." She pointed to the door of the sick-chamber. "She came in while Miss Annah was asleep——"

I left her speaking, and opened the door; but I stood paralyzed on the threshold; for, like a fiend glowering over its mortal prey, stood Milly by the bedside, her eyes dilated with horrible triumph, flaring a candle slowly to and fro before Annah's inflamed, sightless orbs. She held in the other hand the bandage that had covered them when I left the house.

I was so shocked, that for a moment I could not command my voice; then I must have made some strange noise foreign to human ears, for she started in affright, looked around, and dropped the candle. I was quivering with rage by this time. I advanced towards her.

"Stop," she almost shouted. "Don't come near me looking like that. Don't you touch me. You dare not."

"See if I dare not," I retorted savagely, as I clutched her by the throat, and shook her heartily. She tried to speak, to scream, but could only gasp as I held her in that vice-like clasp, while Susan looked on in dismay, and Annah vainly whispered me to "let her go—let her be"—not rightly comprehending the scene, but vaguely feeling that something was wrong.

"My God, I believe I could kill you," I said exultingly.

Susan screamed, and ran away—for assistance, I suppose. Aunt Hannah quickly appeared, very white, very much frightened, but desperately angry, as the strong gleam of her eye told plainly. Behind her was my uncle, whose ring, following mine, had but just sounded. I kept my hold.

"What does all this mean?" stormed Aunt Hannah, advancing and striking down my arm. Milly dropped helplessly at my feet. "You wicked woman, you've killed her; you've murdered her," screamed her mother, flinging up her hands and sending forth a piercing yell.

"I hope I have," I said, recklessly. "But there's no such good fortune. The devil is not so easily killed."

"John! Susan! call the officers. Don't let her escape," she screamed frantically. "Oh! I always knew 'twould come to this," she moaned. "She has such an awful disposition!"

"Very true," I observed, still quivering with excitement.

"You own it, then. What a brazen face!" she declared.

"If you refer to my cousin's disposition, it is very evident," I retorted. I stooped to feel of her. "Oh! she will live to make more mischief yet," I added, as Milly here kicked out at me, and struggled up on her feet. I don't know what they would have done to me—my aunt and cousin together—if, for almost the first time in his henpecked life, Uncle John had not interfered. Even now I cannot comprehend by what means he wrought his courage to such a pitch of resistance. They raved and shrieked like mad women. Of that sick-chamber, for a space—whether long or brief, I cannot tell—they made a hell. Then the domestics swarmed on the scene; astonished, frightened, they stood aloof and whispered together.

"You turn against your own child," at length exclaimed Aunt Hannah, sobbing hysterically — thereby becoming somewhat calmer. Milly gave him a sullen glance, and fell back behind her mother.

"No I don't, Hannah," he said, sinking at once into his old character. "But I didn't want you to abuse her like that, right before my face and eyes, if I could stop it; and there's no knowing what you might have done. You lost your reason."

"'Twant nothing before, I suppose," she answered shortly. "What if she had strangled Milly? would you have interfered, I wonder?" with a sceptical sneer.

"I wasn't afraid of it," said he, calmly. "I don't say that she was altogether right, but she must have had some provocation to act as she did."

"Oh yes, Mr. Lucas. Of course *she* had. No one else *ought* to have provocation," she said spitefully.

He looked distressed. "Tell us how it was, Susan," he

implored; "and all of you listen. You are a truthful girl, I believe, and whatever you say we will believe."

"No indeed we won't. I won't for one," interrupted my aunt, with a vengeful twitch of her chair.

Susan flared at this, and there ensued a long altercation between mistress and maid, during which I picked up and replaced the bandage, and whispered her "not to mind it." She felt for my hand, and kissed it. "Don't get angry for me, Ruby; it is not worth while."

"Isn't it?" I muttered, not quite calmly; "we shall see!"

Susan, for once, was victorious over her mistress, and finally commenced her story, amid the indignant glances and open mouths of the wondering servants. It was plain that they considered her a sort of heroine, and that this affair, if it did not spread beyond the kitchen fireside, would there afford food for endless repetition in the years to come.

"You see, Mr. Lucas," she began eagerly, "I told Miss Ruby, there, that I would stay with her sister while she took an airing. She ain't skursly stirred from the door sence she come here, and I thought 'twould do her good. She hadn't been gone but a trifle, when Miss Millicent she tripped up, and, says she, 'Susan, run down and get me a drink. I'll stay here till you come back, if you'll light me a candle,' says she. 'It isn't dark,' I says, for I knowed Miss Ruby allers set without a light, and I wanted to do what was right, if I could. 'Get me one, girl,' she snapped out."

"Snapped out! You'd better be careful how you put things," interposed my aunt. "It may be better for you in the end."

"Well, she *did* snap out, and she called me *girl*, too," doggedly asserted Susan—covertly smiling at the cook, who nodded her head in token of her stanch support.

"You talk of being careful," again diverged the narrator, turning to her mistress. "You are the ones to be careful. I hain't lived here so long without knowing some things as Miss Millicent would rather not have come out."

"What do you mean, you low-lived thing?" demanded Milly, angrily.

"I mean what I mean," responded Susan, stoically, "and if put to it, I'll tell—let what will come of it. Well, to proceed. I went for the water, and when I come back, she was drawing the light—so—right afore the bed. It's a mercy it didn't scorch 'em. She'll be blind now, if she wasn't before." She finished with a pitiful inspection of the sufferer.

"I meant she should be," spitefully said Milly. "She won't get any more praises. She can't play any more, either, and I'm glad, and I just as soon as not that you all should know it." Nobody replied. The servants gave one last look at us, and filed silently down stairs—Susan at their head. Uncle John looked horror-stricken.

"How much longer do you intend to be quartered on us?" My aunt turned on the threshold to hurl this malicious query.

"As soon as my sister can accompany me, I shall bid you farewell forever," I responded.

"I thought she would live with us. I hoped so. We will all forgive and forget this dreadful night," said Uncle John, timidly.

"I thank you, Uncle. You will always have my warmest gratitude; but as for the others—I knew they disliked me; but I never dreamed of this."

They both flounced scornfully down the stairway. Uncle John dropped a few more kind words on the wound, and reiterated his former request for their forgiveness, which my tongue granted, but my heart refused to sanction; and then we were left alone.

"Alone," I said; and yet not so, if hard, bitter thoughts are to be considered company. I felt an added twinge of defiance in my nature as I reviewed the scene, and looked out from this new stand-point on the still darker future. It was indeed a bright day to me, when we finally got away. This was not until winter snows had fallen, melted, and given place to renewed airs of spring. My sister was to be blind forever; the decree had formally gone forth. The swelling left her throat: she regained her voice in a measure, but she could never again sing. She bore her afflictions patiently: I constantly repined and wept over them.

I had written frequently to the Hoveys through the year. They knew of these events as they transpired, and answered with the balm of sympathy. "Come, as soon as thee can," they wrote; "both thee and thy sister. Some way will assuredly open, and thee can be sure of a home with us." And at last we came. Helen Mar was delighted. She skipped like a kid around Annah, kissing her rapturously. Her father smiled, and hoped "thee has found an object on which to work off thy superabundance of caresses."

I had a plan in my head, waiting only for these kind friends' approval: to move to a little room, wait and advertise for scholars. I was ready to meet and answer their objections, and Zaccheus soon procured me a room only a few blocks removed from themselves. I worked all day to make it cheerful; though as I scrubbed the floor to a snowy whiteness, and polished our little stove, I reflected sadly that I was taking all this pains for one who could never see the result. She heard the pleasant bustle, however, and said "she could imagine how things were looking."

"I have just thought," said Judith, "that when thee was away thee had a call from a young man, who said he was Andrew Jackson. Helen Mar thought him a queer specimen," laughed she softly—then, recollecting herself, she stopped. "He seemed by his attire to be a clerk."

"I shall be glad to see him," I said simply.

"Annah, child, what is it?" She was feeling along the wall—slowly and cautiously.

"Nothing *now*, Ruby," she answered, with a brighter smile than I had yet seen her wear. "I perceive that this space will hold a piano, and I was hoping that you would get pupils enough to warrant hiring one, and then I can give lessons, you know. It's all that I can do."

"My darling, can you read the notes?" I said, in a low tone.

"Oh, that is nothing. I know the instruction-book by heart. I can teach beginners, and as to sheet music—if some one will read it to me once correctly, I can remember and give it to them," she eagerly said.

"But I cannot do that, Annah."

"Never mind, we will wait and see first what success you have," and she smiled hopefully.

My little home grew very dear to me. Mr. Hovey supplied us liberally with comforts, and as for luxuries, those we could do very well without. I kept the floor spotless; the tiny stove shining. On the high mantel I piled my few books. A low bench ran around one side; over it I drove pegs for bonnets and shawls. I had a small pine table, too—painted red; this served us in a double sense—for our meals, or as a desk for reading and writing. I got an easy-chair for Annah, and a low rocking-chair for my own use. In one corner stood our little bed—a gift from Judith. A small mirror hung above the table, which Helen Mar adorned with wreaths and festoons of colored tissue-paper. A sad litter her artistic freak cost me: for days she haunted the room, a matronly pair of shears depending by a steel chain from her slender waist, and clipped and strung to her heart's content. A balloon-like article of the same gay hues hung from the ceiling.

I remember well the delight of our little band, when a timid knock announced my first pupil—save Helen; the next day I gained another, and at the end of the month I counted twenty bonnets on the pegs; the low bench was full.

Don't think, reader, that you are to be wearied with a prosaic account of my school; its petty area of irritations; its simple pleasures. I have no desire myself to review the experiences lurking there. Suffice it to say, that in a moderate measure I prospered; slowly but surely I gained the love of the children and the confidence of the parents. My numbers increased. I added another bench to the room; rented a piano for Annah, and—oh joyful day for her!—she commenced giving lessons. This was a full year from the day we took possession, but not once had she repined at the delay.

During this year we saw Andrew Jackson frequently. I looked for the raw, gaunt youth of Northfield; in that stead came a tall, finely formed young man—almost a stranger. Like scores of others, he had come to the city to seek his fortune, convinced—as he remarked, with a dash of the old egotism—"that in the country a man of talent can do nothing worthy of himself." At every visit I noticed how the rustic armor was fast dropping from his speech and manner. He told me sad news of the old farm-house. Uncle Joel had left the church, and been "labored with" by the deacons and elders for this unchristian conduct, but vainly. "He never goes to church now," quoth Andrew. "Where he keeps himself is a mystery. The farm was sold at sheriff's sale; there's talk of redeeming it, I believe; but people generally think it's a pretty doubtful case. I tell you, Miss Brooks, that sermon did the business for Squire Martin. He lost all of his ambition, and it broke up the revival completely."

Andrew's leave-takings were but signals for a longer tarry; for protracted questions about Annah's music, and petitions so confidentially made, that it seems a sin to tell them here. He caught my smile one day; perhaps it enlightened his own perceptions, for he colored, stammered some excuse for leaving, and, snatching up his hat, vanished hastily.. Poor lad! I had no thought of being so ironical. He saw that I divined his secret, and it galled him sorely. Oh! why can we not hide our sweetest secrets from other prying eyes? Though of the fairest texture, they become gross, commonplace, when the world sifts its hot, curious breath over them. I was sorry for him. As for Annah, she innocently wondered what made our friend start off in such a hurry; and unwilling to implant a conscious expression on her sweet face, I framed some evasive answer.

CHAPTER XXXVI.

"It is nine years since we left Northfield, Ruby," observed Annah, one day, thoughtfully counting them over on her thin white fingers.

"Yes, darling," I assented, lifting my eyes to note her

meaning. She seemed lost in thought, so I resumed my sewing. Silence lasted an hour by the clock; broken only by the ring of my scissors as they slipped from my lap to the smooth, bare floor—during which I, too, went wandering in that distant Northfield life, so far behind my present that it seemed a weary travel. "Nine years, indeed!" I echoed, and a sigh followed.

"And all this time, Ruby, you've been teaching, without bringing your fortune any nearer. How you used to talk of it! Where are all our grand dreams, our wonderfully fine visions, Ruby? We get no glimpses of them now."

"They are merged in reality; we have no time for dreaming," I answered.

She smiled. "You don't mean to say that our dream ever became real, do you? Why, we dreamed of fame, and wealth, and power, besides scores of minor things!"

"I'm afraid they are indeed gone, Annah; lost on the receding shores of youth, where they first took life and shape. I have got past that now. We are in a sense independent: we earn our support. I trust you are content with that, my darling," I said, a little anxiously.

"Oh yes," she hastened to say, laying down her knitting —she could knit beautifully—then, a little earnestly, "Shall you ever return there, do you think, Ruby?"

"I don't know. Should you like it? we can go at any time," I replied. "It is not so long a journey. We can spend the coming vacation there, if you choose—that is, if you feel strong enough for it."

"Is it a long vacation?" she asked, vacantly.

"Surely you know, love," I said, astonished at the question. "It begins in August, and lasts until November."

"How lonely you will be, sister! I forgot—" was all she said in reply.

I put down my work and looked at her. Where had my eyes been the past year, that I had not discovered how much thinner and paler she was getting; how hollow her cheeks were, under the poor, sightless eyes? It was no unfamiliar vision, yet it smote me like a new revelation : the precursor of dreads unexpressed, yet keener than a two-edged blade. I rose and crossed over to her. "You are not well to-day, my darling?" I questioned anxiously.

"Oh yes, indeed." She never complained.

"No, you are not," I persisted.

"I feel a little tired, that is all. I think it is this June sun; it is so oppressive." I scanned her in silence : she felt it : " You are looking at me earnestly, Ruby. What do you see in my face that is unusual?" She reached for my hand, and softly stroked it with her own pale fingers.

"God only knows, my child," I quivered out, taking her up in my arms, and putting her slight form on the bed. "Lie there and rest; for you shall knit no more this summer, nor give another lesson."

"Oh yes—" she began ; but I cut her short. "Oh no ; you are just to mind me, you know. You have worked too much already. I am a brute not to have perceived it."

"You are wrong. It is not that. I should like to work —it is but little at best—as long as I can; for soon the night cometh in which no one can work," she murmured, dreamily. "How shall I feel hereafter, if I let you toil for me, while I lie idle here able to help you?"

"Oh ! Annah——"

"Sister Ruby! *my* sister," she began, and paused—— "Should you feel it to be wrong if the good Father should call me away from you for a season—not to stay from you forever, you know—only to go before you and find the way? You have had such a hard life—it's *all* been hard from the beginning, hasn't it, dear?" And I have done nothing to lighten it. *He* knows it as well as I, sister, and He is going to let me do something for you at last—you who have done every thing for me, my mother, sister, and friend. He wants me to go and find a home for you: then when you come, all you will have to do. is to enjoy it. I can feel how pitiful He is, dear; how sorry for our troubles. And it is joy for me to go. I shall love my task, and Demis will help me. Dear Demis! I think of her more and more: I can almost see her sometimes; I know she is with us. I should like to be buried beside her; but not in Northfield."

"Annah," I sobbed, "you must not talk so. I cannot bear it."

"I won't, then," she answered, sweetly. "Forgive me; I supposed you knew."

An intense hush followed, during which twilight silvered every object in the room, then slowly shifted to vague shimmering rays of moonlight. It was a young moon, and vanished almost ere the tardy sunset cradled it. The glimpse I got ere it set looked ghostly. But so did every thing. What was there that did not appear for a little time and then vanish? Yea; the very table on which I rested my head, the very chair on which I sat, the clothes I wore, were stamped with the destiny of decay. I was enjoying, beholding their prime: the meridian must soon be passed. And so of human lives. Our straining eyes discern no footprints on the other side, but not the less are they moving there; not the less are we too changing.

Oh, bitter, bitter thought! It is no comfort to the

mourner to be told consolingly that we shall some time follow our departed. They are rent from our warm, sympathetic present. The past may afford us sweet food for gleaning memory after the years have been long garnered; but in the first anguish of bereavement, the future's promise seems only empty, tasteless husks of mockery.

"Bereavement," I say? Yes! For the *real* parting is not when death sets his final seal on matter, and the enfranchised spirit soars free. The icy deliverer is often welcomed as a benefactor, for it shortens unavailing pain. The parting pang is when the first thought that your loss is swift and certain crowds clearly into view; that the battle has been fought 'twixt life and death, between health and disease, and the latter have prevailed. No two words in our language strike the senses with such a jar as these, " No hope." Then the dreary looking forward, with the keen present grief, and the sacred hush which fills the rooms, and awes our very breath into silence, and envelops our stiffening faculties in mute affright and sobbing.

The door opened. I half looked to see a spirit; but it was a man's form groping through the darkness, a man's voice, cheerful and loud, which spoke. "Oh, it's Andrew," said Annah, rising, while I struck a light. " And we haven't been to tea," she added, with a smile.

Andrew looked astonished. "I think I will take it with you, then," he laughed, " if your sister will permit."

I tried to answer cheerfully, while preparing it, but it was a poor attempt. When I had seen them seated at table, I put on my bonnet and shawl. "I must go out into the street a few moments," I said to Annah's inquiry, "it is such a good time now, dear; I never like to leave you alone." I almost ran to the Hoveys. As I burst open the door where they sat, they rose startled. My wild, frightened manner must have brought the conclusion of some dreadful catastrophe. "Is Annah dying?" was all I could bring my lips to utter.

"Good heavens! Thee don't mean it." And Judith hurriedly patted away for her bonnet.

"I mean is she ill enough for that?" I explained. "I never thought so before to-night, but she has been talking strangely—something very unusual with her." I saw Judith glance at her husband. Helen Mar—now a tall, stately young lady—rose and left us.

"Thee had better be told now, friend Rubina, that thy sister will never be any better. But don't thee be troubled, she may live with thee years yet; only think how long thou hast had her, and she is not much worse."

"Much worse," I echoed bitterly. "I hoped she might be getting better all this time; and to think that I have done nothing for her."

"Thee can do nothing, Rubina. I consulted our physician long ago about the case. He saw her here one day, and frankly told me that he could do her no good. If she should recover her sight by an operation, she would go the sooner. And he is a man well skilled in medicine, as thee well knows, Rubina. Thee must not rebel; God will temper the wind to the shorn lamb," said Zaccheus, in his deep melodious voice—the tones quivering with pity.

"We must all give up our friends when the summons comes," added Judith, placidly tying her drab bonnet. "I will walk back with thee, my friend."

I closed my school the next day. Andrew was invaluable to me now. He came daily; he brought all sorts of delicacies, and spent hours in efforts to amuse her. She could not see the sadness which overspread his face, when she lay back on the pillow quite spent with her brief exertion of talking; nor the deep wistful gaze in which his soul called unto hers. If she guessed the truth from the tones of his voice, and his constant, tender care, she never spoke of it, or seemed conscious. And how changed indeed were their relations! Her merry girlhood had cheered him, and encouraged ambition towards a higher life. "It was for *her* sake I came to New York," said he sorrowfully. "I wanted to make myself worthy before I dared ask for her, and now it has all come to this. Of what use has it been?" he finished, despondingly.

"Don't ask that, Andrew. You little know how your mere presence comforts. Of use it has been, though, as yet, hidden from you."

I could have wept daily at the sight of this affectionate devotion of the tall, strong man to the weak, blind girl, during those sultry summer days, had I not felt the need of husbanding sorrow for him for a far darker day of grief.

And at last it came. I pass over the first shock of sorrow. I cannot speak of the full cup of torture pressed close to the shrinking lips; for its poignancy will never lessen in memory. Here was a transition, silent and peaceful. Some flowers wither prematurely from their stems; pinched by sharp winds, nipped by unkindly frosts, they shrivel in a reluctant heap and leave a black, barren stalk behind. But the most fragrant of roses fall noiselessly earthward, and then—their full, perfect life accomplished—their departing odors leave on our stricken hearts a faint shadow of what in due time will strengthen to a healing balm. Let us patiently await the sovereign cure.

A broken shaft rises to mark the spot where Annah sleeps,

20

far from the city's noise ; and only one line roughens the pure marble : " I am going to find you a home." They were her dying whispers, as I bent, in an agony too deep for tears, over her departing spirit.

CHAPTER XXXVII.

HERE, something whispers me to pause. It says, " Suppress the further record of a longing, disappointed life." The succeeding years, which are only repetitions of the previous ones of baffled effort. The weary struggles for subsistence, as my pupils gradually dropped away into men and matrons' places in the world, and none came to take their places. And the reluctant disbanding of the vast army of hopes and fears, which people annually with dismal graves every earnest heart. Perhaps I might discover the hidden blessing lurking amid the thorns piercing me, did I seek for it dispassionately. I confess I cannot do this. Age and toil have furrowed my frame, have taken ample toll for each passing year; but my heart—poor foolish member!—keeps its fair round lines untarnished; its legacy of immortal youth. It glows with as eager hopes as ever. I still detect it looking forward with a trusting confidence, never destined to be levelled by any barbed arrow of disappointment. How can I check it? Is the tide-wind that sucks the marrow from our bones, the strength from our erect stature, the roundness from our muscles, also to sap the foundations of our mental nature— the greenness and vigor of our souls? I trust and believe not. That which we lose shall we not some time find again! That which is taken, shall it not be restored? Time is but an unfinished volume ; or, rather, a scrap-book of disconnected fragments of one great story. Death steps in ere the interest in it ceases, and says sternly, "To be continued;" and where our volume abruptly closes, there our next opens. Eternity takes up the unfinished threads of our dusty hopes, fears, loves, and griefs, and weaves them firmly into one massive woof; it brightens, it refines, it polishes. And the conclusion of the theme waxes and wanes far onward in the infinite years. Or, shall it *ever* end? In the atmosphere of immortality shall aught of decay exist? Shall not the dews of divinity baptize it with never-fading splendor?

What finite mind can grasp these mysteries? dare criticise an Infinite Author? dare pronounce with heedless confidence upon the proper point for the interesting tale to culminate; when God shall write "Finis" below the close of the last tragic chapter?

What the grave shall shut upon here and open to me beyond, I know not. I have signs: I see visions. But I place no faith in things so terrestrial assuming a celestial garb: nevertheless, they serve to comfort me a little, and to keep Hope bright and active. Then, when the rosary of Time is numbered, on the last receding pearl I trust to slip quietly and with perfect faith to the Great Father's bosom.

CHAPTER XXXVIII.

Ere I close I must speak a word for a few characters in these pages. Andrew Jackson lives—an honored, useful, happy man. Yes, "happy." Time, the great consoler, brought healing on its wings for him. His sorrow deepened, expanded his whole nature, and in the genial warmth of what thus became a blessing his spirit grew afresh; grew kindly sympathetic with all mankind, and thus took on added lustre—for, every doubt removed from a poor pilgrim's heart, every sorrow lightened, blesses abundantly the doer, and gives him added strength. Goodness multiplies ere it returns to the heart that gave it birth: if no trumpet sound of Fame greets his life here, a higher, holier applause lives in hundreds of human hearts—made bold and strong through him.

And why should I not be thankful that happiness tinges his remaining years; even though I still linger amid the shadows? For *her*—out of the darkness into the light; yea, eternity's light. For *him*—out of the gloom of earthly hopeless mourning for her sweet human presence, into the open sunlight of peace. And in due time another love crowns his life; if less fervent than his first sad dream, not less tenderly constant. A few years after Annah's death, there was a sober wedding at the Hoveys': two lives married in the presence of three witnesses, after the beautiful Quaker ritual—silent and impressive. Their home is but a stone's throw from my lodgings, and it is my favorite resort. Helen Mar still dubs him playfully "a queer specimen," as occasion brings to light some long-hidden noble deed; but it is to be observed that each revelation of this nature increases the admiring love in which she holds her "bonnie husband."

Zaccheus and Judith quoted their son-in-law, his sayings and doings, on all occasions of mild disputations between them and their Quaker brethren. "Thee must be aware, friends, that Andrew knows," was considered—by themselves— equal to a judge's verdict.

Andrew was indeed to these good souls an honored son. Tenderly and with filial reverence he smoothed their pathway to the tomb; and now his every act blesses their holy memory. His is a stately home; for wealth has crowned his efforts. He hoards it in no miserly coffers, but literally fulfils the most impressive of all the Divine commands—Charity; confident that in sowing the good seed broadcast, as but an humble almoner of the Lord, he will finally gather to himself a whole harvest of abundant sheaves.

I never hear now from Aunt Hannah. I have never looked upon her face since our separation; her cold farewell was the last word I ever heard her utter. Uncle John came to see me soon after Annah's death.

Poor man! He was much changed; he wept as he went away. He long ago descended to the dark vale; his life, I firmly believe, shortened by family bickerings and disgrace, for a sad story reached me soon after. Milly's conduct, her sad career, her shameful flight, is too shocking a history to be written here. Where she is now, I know not. And the companion of her crime—*her* minister, *my* schoolmaster —of him I cannot speak. I loathe his vices; I abhor his crimes. And his sojourn in —— brought not a few to light. He shamefully degraded his holy office: his name, plucked from the church records, hurled from the shining heights of favor, lies forever buried in ignominy, enwreathed with contempt when—as it seldom is now—spoken.

I hang a veil before this picture when I wish to lose myself in memory. Then I cherish tender reflections of the days that are gone: they hang like a purple mist over distant mountains. Again the awakening aspiration, the eager hopes of ignorant fancies, burn within me. I live over again the petty jealousy; the fierce hate; the sense of vacant depths answering to my yearning; the chill of feeling it all in the power, to be summoned at the will of an indifferent experimenter; of feeling the warmth of his professions, but simu-

lated to hide ignoble purposes—Oh, Demis! surely yours was
a preferable fate, for you lived not to let it torture you.

And Northfield.   Can the years touch thee with changeful fingers and not leave the impress?   Dear secluded ham-
let among imprisoning hills!   My thoughts haunt thee steadily; I can settle to nothing for the winter until I go and see
thee. This I said to myself, reader, one night after pondering
the matter well.

No lumbering "stage" awaited me at Chispa.   This was the
first wheel of the chariot, change.   I looked eagerly from the
car window as we drew near Northfield.   The mountains still
towered their wooded slopes heavenward.   The meadows
and hill-sides were as fresh and green as ever.   But a serpent-
like trail of iron wound around the hills, plunged down the
shallow gorges, and stretched away, away over the broad
commons.   Our locomotive wheezed "down the grade," and
brought up most respectably at the side of a low-roofed,
brown-painted station.

"Here's the dep-o!" sang out a strong nasal voice behind
me, with unmistakable satisfaction.   A feminine voice responded.   It was a conjugal duet.   "Yes, and for my part
I'm glad on't.   Here, you take Natty and I'll see after the
duds.   There's them crackers; if you've a mind to tuck 'em
int' your overcut pocket, you may: bub's whet his bill on 'em
all the way, nearabout.   Young'uns at his age are so craving."

"Well, that's the talk," chuckled the nasal tones, as he
picked up the 'craving' youngster, and was marching off to
the tune of "Wall, woman, you gather up the fragments, that
nothing be lost:" she recalled him.

"Hold on a second.   Here's them handbills that the little
boy was so perlite as to give us: them's the names of
taverns down to the city.   You may as well put 'em in your

pocket too, for may be we'll take a notion to go there, some day, and then they'll come handy; and here's one I want to look over at my leisure, and if it's what it professes to be, I shall give it a trial: my hair's gittin' desp'rate streaked latterly." The matron sighed audibly.

I smiled, as I left them still huddling various articles into a small faded satchel; but it set me thinking how inexorably age treats our poor smouldering vanity, and strips us of our bonny graces. I almost echoed the matron's sigh; then I smiled disdainfully at my weakness, as I plodded up the street past Lawyer Prince's cottage, now grown into a stately dwelling.

I did not know the streets. By some unaccountable perversity they had widened and taken unto themselves sidewalks. Rows of maples bordered them; not yet attained to any remarkable altitude. White trellised boxes surrounded and protected their shaky trunks.

But the old houses themselves had taken on airs, too, and patched themselves up with bay windows, and verandas; and the great chimneys had toppled down to make room for their slender successors; and the old brass knockers had given place to bells. The grounds enveloping them looked pleasant. Gravelled walks swept downward to the street. Shrubs dotted the turf; and flowers bloomed in gay profusion. Painted shingles at the corners told me the names of the streets—formerly known by universal consent as " Pork Lane," " Piping Alley," and "Thunder;" very unaccountably they had flowered into "Myrtle," " Summer," and " Elm Streets." The stores had trebled in number, and risen to three-storied importance. Over their front stood forth the symbolical letters for secret gatherings. But the farmhouse was unchanged. The same old stone kept its office at the gate. The same shrubs bloomed in the same spots in the yard. The same—or others exactly like—green paper curtains were unrolled before the tiny paned windows. No door-plate, no ivory bell-knob here: the same brass knocker—as bright as gold—on the green, double-leaved door. I lifted; let it fall three times, with a sonorous clang, starting an echo from the neighboring hills. Footsteps hastily scudded along the entry: the door opened one of its leaves, and revealed the face of my neighbor in the cars. With one hand on the door-latch, the other vigorously restrained the frantic plunges of a two-years-old boy, to rush from the maternal restraint.

"Aint you 'shamed now, sonny?" she said reprovingly. "Natty dont see the lady, does he! He mustn't act naughty, but be mother's little man." The little man might be Natty, but he was not *my* Natty of long ago. I had some difficulty in making the good woman understand my errand. Then I found that she was Darwin's wife—"Martha Butterfield that was," she said with a laugh; and finally she removed my things, and to my eager inquiries for Debby and my aunt, said, "Yes, I guess we'll make a raise on 'em," and opened the door to the kitchen. It looked much as of old, save that the listing-seated chairs had vanished—replaced by more modern ones of cane. An old woman drooped by the open door over a pan of dried apples, which she was industriously coring. She did not hear my entrance. "They aint wormy none, as I can see," she muttered to herself; 'mazin likely apples for this time o'year, I think. I was a tellin' Miss Martin this very day that—"

"Debby, how do you do?"

She lifted her eyes. So wrinkled a face I never before beheld; red eyelided, toothless; the form thinner far than of yore, and bent nearly double. I never should have known her if we had met elsewhere. She tried to raise her old shoulders, but the weight of nearly a hundred years would not give way. She sank back again, peering up at me through her glasses with evident curiosity.

"Whose that, for massy's sake?" she managed to cackle, after a moment's silent survey.

"Don't you know me, Deborah! dear Deborah." I took and pressed her dry, withered hand. "Think back a good many years. It's an old friend."

"Why it's—no, it *can't* be nuther. Wall, massy to us; do tell me now if '*tis* ra'ly Ruby Brooks, or her shadder. Your voice sounds like her'n; but you don't look like her, else I've forgot. I spect she's dead long 'fore this. We ain't hurd from her, none on us."

Still I kept her hand. With the other she removed her glasses, rubbed her eyes, and resumed gazing at my face. "Nary a look o' *her*," she muttered. "T'other one wan't never han'some, as you may say; but she looked kinder cum'ly, too, after all; and I allers told her that han'some is as han'som does; but this one aint one nor t'other. Who be you?"

"You must remember that Ruby is older," I said simply. "Are you glad to see her?"

A gleam of recognition smote her withered face. "The Lord's sake alive!" she gasped, letting fall her pan of apples, as she started up and seized me by both hands. "I guess I am. I'd gin up ever 'spectin' to see ye ag'in. Wall, wall, and here ye be!" she crooned delightedly. "But ye're longer favored than ye used to be, Ruby."

"Have you got a kiss for me, Debby?" I stooped forword.

20*

"Bless her. She wants to kiss the old woman, does she? Yes, I guess I have. Got forty, got a hundred, got a million;" and the poor old soul fairly broke down. I had hard work to soothe her. She declared that she was not crying; all the while her sobs and gasps were painful to hear. Then she seized me by the neck, and—vigorously for her—implanted kisses on my cheek, until I managed to extricate myself. Mrs. Martha looked on and laughed, while drawing out the table; but said not a word until Aunt Rhoda entered. She looked almost as old as Debby, and far thinner. As Mrs. Martha introduced me, she shaded her eyes with her hand, scanned me narrowly, and replied in a querulous tone to my greeting. Then she declared her disbelief in my identity. I attempted to convince her, but she interrupted me with, "I dont want to hear no sech gammon." I may as well add here, that during my whole stay she would not be brought to recognize me; but treated me exactly like a stranger. She alluded—in my hearing— to "Martha's company." After a day she ceased to notice me. It was clear that she still hated me cordially.

From Dwight, in the days which followed, I gained a history of all the changes in Northfield. Of his father's being "cut off from the church on earth, and the congregation of the saints, root and branch," by Elder Fuller; of the farm being sold for debt, and his own efforts to redeem it. How Ira had never "lifted a finger to help them;" and how proud Amanda had grown, "as homely as sin, and as selfish as the devil, if she is my sister," he indignantly ejaculated: "she's got seven young ones just like her, only twice as hateful, and she don't step foot in here only at Thanksgiving and Christmas, and so on. Mother went to live with her after we broke up, but she didn't stay long; they're too near alike about

some things. Amanda as good as turned her out. I told
the old woman I could keep her if no one else could."

Then he spoke of the Pierces; of Olive's devotion to
her sister, who would never in this life be any better. "You
can't shet her up so close but what she'll git loose," said he.
"She'll smash winders, and bark like a dog, and mew like a
cat, and she hates children like pison. She's been complained of time and time agin, and once she was sent to an
asylum; but didn't do her no good. She wore Mrs. Pierce
out: she died three years ago, and Eleil, he got married,
and went off to Californy. Olive and her father stays there:
nobody goes nigh 'em once in a dog's age. I don't know
what'll become of 'em. The farm's goin' to rack an' ruin as
fast as it can; it wants a manager. Ira ought to work it,
but he won't. Amanda might help Olive too; great strappin' crittur—weighs a hundred and eighty clean; but catch
her a doin' it! No, indeed." It was a short, sad biogra-
phy. I wept bitter tears at its recital.

My stay lengthened to a week. I made Olive a brief
visit. It was sad to see the wreck of her former buoyant
self, moving so drearily around the deserted rooms; yet it
was noble—this faithful, serene fulfilment of a life-long
duty. She wore her old cheerful smile, however. Solitude, neglect, and trial, had not chilled or embittered her
feelings, or clouded her joyous faith in the Future's reserve
for her.

"I *know* he will come back *some*time Ruby," she said, as
I spoke of Mark and his long absence. "I can wait: what
are a few years?"

Alas! that this single hope should be reft from her. Not
then did we know that the clarion tones of war had pierced
his ear afar off; that his soul leaped responsive; and that his

wandering feet returned to join in the impending conflict.

Oh! eager hearts, which swelled on that fearful day with hopeful pride, and thirst for the laurels of victory. Alas! that your confident dreams should so soon crumble to dust. *Some* forms must fall, we know. The pant of the rising lion must be appeased. Our country's soil is stained with sacrificial offerings of her bravest and best. The life-blood of Freedom flows over the fiendish heart of Treason; a sure, though costly regenerator. Brave souls: silent, yet speaking. For thee rests in the future years, on thy country's bosom, immortal gratitude and praise. No brave young life has gone out obscurely in her defence; it shall be relit at the splendid torch of history.

I did not go up to Uncle Jesse's. All things there were changed, and become new. The dear old faces had vanished. One by one, as their life's work waned toward completion, they dropped placidly off into their long, dreamless rest. Strangers kindle home fires there, on the old familiar hearthstones. Unknown faces flit to and fro in the great rooms—haunted, to me, by the forms of the dear departed. "The places that knew them shall know them no more" on earth; but let us hope and believe that they are not therefore homeless. Earth for heaven is no paltry exchange of tenement. Crumbling imperfection for fadeless immortality. The willow for the golden crown. Sackcloth and ashes, for the sinless robes of " Life Everlasting."

THE END.

www.ingramcontent.com/pod-product-compliance
Lightning Source LLC
Chambersburg PA
CBHW022027120726
47901CB00006BA/1483